Old McDonald Had a Funny Farm

Old McDonald Had a Funny Farm

Mary McDowell

VANTAGE PRESS
New York

Cover design by Polly McQuillen

FIRST EDITION

Published by Vantage Press, Inc.
419 Park Avenue South, New York, NY 10016

Manufactured in the United States of America
ISBN: 978-0-533-16124-9

Library of Congress Catalog Card No.: 2008907581
0 9 8 7 6 5 4 3 2 1

To Grammy and Grandpa Johns, Grandma Mary and
Grandpa Mack, without whom none of this could be

Contents

Prologue   1

1. Easter, 1960   3
2. The Science Project   21
3. Chas   40
4. Fish Fry Time   61
5. The Science Fair and the Open House   81
6. Crazy Days   98
7. Lazy Days   119
8. Proud to Be American   144
9. The Orange County Fair   164
10. Sleeping under the Stars   185
11. The Force of Nature   205

Epilogue   231

Prologue

"Oh, hi there. I didn't see you coming up the walk. No, no, you're not interrupting anything important. I was just sitting here watching the clouds drift by, and it reminded me of when we were all children passing the afternoons trying to distinguish shapes in the moving clouds. And from that, I just slipped into daydreaming and reminiscing about when we ran around like wild Indians. Some of us really were, although we didn't know that little tidbit at the time, and it wouldn't have changed things, anyway. There in our neighborhood, everyone was the same as everyone else. We didn't even have a real leader—we just decided, and everyone just agreed, to do the same thing. The Ortolanis and the McDonalds were the first children in the neighborhood, and then, after a while, came the Chateaus. The first were the most numerous, in the beginning, and the Ortolani children—a little older than the McDonalds—were always ready to lend a hand, especially fourteen-year-old Tony. Nobody cared that Tony and his family were Italians. In fact, Melody, the oldest of the McDonald tribe, was absolutely heartbroken when the Ortolanis moved up to central California because Mr. Ortolani bought a vineyard near Fresno. Their house remained empty for quite a while. Melody and her siblings played among themselves until Karen and Colette Chateau moved in next door. They didn't care that old Mr. Chateau was a French refugee (whatever that might have been) from the war. They *were* fascinated by the fact that he was a hairdresser; he had closed the backyard patio and transformed it into a beauty salon. Mrs. Chateau worked as a warden in the Orange County jail. We didn't have much to do with Mr. and Mrs. Chateau because they were always so busy with work and all, and Mrs. Chateau didn't really care much for the other kids in the neighborhood."

"What?"

"No, she didn't really walk with her nose in the air; Mr. Chateau was really nice to all of us, but his wife just didn't want us disturbing her in her free time. She was a little tough, I guess, probably because of her

1

work, which couldn't have been too easy. It's just, I don't know . . . a feeling that we had. Anyway, Karen had ballet lessons every day after school, but when she came home we all played together.

"As I was saying, Honey and Ross McDonald loved kids. Most of us called Honey—and most of the other mothers (and even some fathers)—by her first name, instead of Mrs. This or Mrs. That. It wasn't lack of respect on our part, because we did respect them, but they, in their respect and love for *us*, told us we could use their names. Most of us kids felt loved by most of the adults in the neighborhood, at least during the Sixties, when we were growing up.

"You know, a lot of history and progress was made during the Sixties; most of it was good, though not all of it, just like the kids in our neighborhood. By the time Melody started school, the tract had filled up with families full of children to play with: the Smiths, the Stormers, the Kings, and others. Most of us were pretty good, although we all had our moments, of course; there were a few bad apples, but even they weren't always bad—just *almost* always. To tell the truth, we were, on the whole, just normal, though very lucky, everyday kids of our time. There was magic in the air surrounding us, which made life sweet—the magic of being alive and knowing that we were loved.

"Anyway, as I was saying when you came up, I was thinking of a spring day much like today . . ."

1

Easter, 1960

"Wow! Look at that big one there on the left," Melody said.

"You mean the one that looks like a fat old dragon with five legs?" her sister Jan asked.

"Yeah, that one, but it's not a dragon, dummy. Put your glasses on and look at it better; it's the Easter Bunny scratching his ears."

"Well, yeah, I guess it could be, but rabbits only have *four* legs."

"I know, but the other thing is an Easter basket full of chocolate eggs. Gosh, I wish it would roll over and we could catch all the Easter eggs as they fall from the sky."

"Yummy! That sounds good," said Jan, "Whoever finds the most eggs shares, okay? Hope it's milk chocolate—that's my very favorite."

"Okay. You take the milk and I'll take the dark chocolate. Promise?"

Giggles from seven-and-*a-half*-year-old (as she quite often pointed out) Melody McDonald and from Janice—two years, two months, and two days younger—pealed through the cool, early-morning air. Usually, the girls were in the house at 5:30 A.M., with Jan in bed and Melody next to the heater reading a book or doing problems from her second-grade arithmetic book (usually way ahead of the rest of the class), but yesterday was Good Friday, the last day of school before the Easter holidays, so Mommy and Daddy had let them sleep in the big tent out in the backyard. It would be a typical early spring day in good old Sunny Southern Cal, but it had sprinkled the night before, leaving the long, lush green grass slightly damp. The rainstorm had been a surprise: the weatherman had predicted a clear, starry night, followed by a bright, sunny Saturday. Fleecy white clouds, the remnant of the light shower, and the object of the girls' discussion scudded across the awakening sky. Melody and Jan had actually been outside for at least a good half hour, searching for the cricket that had awakened Melody with its chirping. It was when all their endeavors had proven to be in vain that the two girls had stretched out on their backs, looking up at the fluffy clouds.

The girls' giggles turned to shrieks as the neighborhood mocking-birds, in a not-so-whimsical attempt to enliven the morning, engaged in a mock battle, divebombing the girls and swerving at the last minute.

"I hate those dumb birds. I wish Missy would wake up and catch them. They think they're really funny when they do that," declared Melody. The little Sheltie, hearing her name, lifted her ears, sniffed the air, glared at the annoying birds, and fell back to sleep. "A big help you are, hm! Or else—" she turned back toward Janice—"*you* could tell 'em to get lost, ya know. You're so bossy, ev'ryone minds you."

"Yeah, or you could shake your hand at 'em. *No one* wants to get in the way of your fist."

"Well, they don't seem too worried about Missy's frown, your orders, or my punches. Maybe if Peter the Bomber came and let one go, they'd take off. If the smell doesn't kill them, the noise will."

"Prob'ly. But we'd be goners, too. He's a killer."

"Uh-huh. Oh, well . . . ," sighed Melody. "Let's hope Daddy doesn't mow the lawn today. If he does, the Easter Bunny won't have anywhere to hide the Easter eggs tonight, and looking for them is even better than waitin' for 'em to fall outta that Easter basket up there in the clouds."

The almost-four-year-old Mark stuck his head out of the six-man (or eight-kid) tent near the girls and grumbled, "What're you doin' out there? It's too early to get up an' you're makin' too much noise. Come back in an' sleep or I'll go an' tell Mommy."

"Go ahead. She'll just yell at *you* fer wakin' her up. Anyway, we're just talkin' about the chocolate eggs the Easter Bunny's bringin' us tomorrow. What kind do you wanna get?"

Mark blinked his bleary eyes and pulled his drowsy head back into his sleeping bag like a hibernating turtle. The early morning cricket that had awakened them had long disappeared and, as the morning sun slowly rose in the sky, the two little girls rolled over in the grass and drifted off to sleep.

Melody was so excited, she could hardly wait for tomorrow to come. Last week, Mommy and Daddy had bought her and Jan brand-new matching dresses to wear in church tomorrow. They were so pretty with all those bright purple and pink flowers and those cute, lacy, white

4

Easter bonnets. She loved going to the church services and singing in the children's choir. This morning they'd have the last choir practice before Easter. They were going to sing a really neat piece—Mrs. Jarvis said it was a spiritual—called "Go Down Moses." Then, Mrs. Jarvis took them to try on their black choir robes with the white tunics over them. And since it was Easter Sunday, they'd be singing in two services instead of one.

There were always a lot more people at Easter service for some reason. Maybe because the Balboa Peninsula and Balboa Island were *the place* to be during Easter week, and it was wall-to-wall people. Everyone wanted to go to the beaches, get their first tan of the year, and swim or fish off the piers. And in the evening, you could go and ride on the gigantic Ferris wheel at the Balboa Pavilion and eat bright pink cotton candy. You could also take the ferry from there to Balboa Island. A lot of famous people live there, and Mommy said that the man who was Tarzan in the movies used to say hello to her every morning when she walked to school.

Anyway, Sunday school would last only for an hour tomorrow, so there would be time for the extra service. And even before going to church, Mommy and Daddy would lead them all into the kitchen to see the pretty colored baskets that the Easter Bunny brought, with the colored eggs, the jelly beans, the tiny hummingbird egg candy, and the big chocolate bunny or chicken (or hopefully both). Then, in the afternoon, after lunch, the Easter egg hunt would take place.

After choir practice, Gramps had come to pick Melody up at the long white church with his black and white station wagon and take her to eat lunch with him and Grammy. That was always fun, because Grammy always had that yummy sourdough bread with tiny tot sardines. After lunch she would take a walk with Gramps along the water line, where she gathered seashells until Mommy came to pick her up and take her home.

When she got home, she found their old babysitter, Jesse, waiting there with the other kids. Jesse said that Mommy and Daddy had something important to attend to, so she was taking care of them. That was okay, because even if Jesse really was "older than the hills and twice as ornery" (as she always said), she played with them and brought them presents.

But *now* she had to suffer pure torture. No ponytails or braids on Sunday. Uh-uh. No way. So Melody and Jan had to sit perfectly still for a whole hour while Mommy put their long cornsilk hair in *pin curls* and then dried their hair with a hand-held hair dryer. Too bad they couldn't use Mr. Chateau's. That would dry their hair in five minutes. It would have been okay if Melody could have curled up in the easy chair and read *The Black Stallion*, the book that Daddy had brought her from the library yesterday, together with *The Happy Hollisters*, but Mommy said that she couldn't get to her hair if Melody did that, so she had to sit still in a straight-back chair. At least Daddy's scary movie was about a cat—a panther, in fact—that turned into a pretty lady. Or, was it a pretty lady that turned into a panther?

"Mickey, sit up straight and stop squirming," said Honey, calling Melody by her nickname. "When you slide down in the chair like that, I can't reach the ends of your hair, because you're sitting on them."

"Ah, Mommy, it's too boring just sitting here. This old movie is so dumb. The pretty lady *kisses* those guys, and then when she's a panther she scratches 'em all up. What's so scary about that? All cats scratch people when they're mad. And I can see why she'd be mad if a guy kissed her. I'd throw up if a guy kissed me."

"Just *sit up straight!* It takes longer if you slide down, and even longer still if you argue. You didn't see Jan sliding down, now, did you?"

Deciding not to answer this last question or to look directly at Jan's smirking face, Melody slipped back into her own thoughts. She was too uncomfortable just sitting here without even a book in her hands. And the movie really was too boring and not scary at all. It was probably just as well, because just as much as she loved scary movies, with other people getting in trouble with monsters, she most definitely did not like scary nightmares with the monsters running after *her* as fast as they could while she couldn't even move her feet to get away from them. She even woke up her mommy with her screams, but the monsters kept coming until her mother was able to shake her awake. Sometimes they were only a step away before she woke up. When this happened, she couldn't get back to sleep until Mommy hugged her and rocked her in her arms. This usually happened when *all* the monsters from *all* the movies ran after her, even Frankenstein, who had a hard time even walking in the movie. And Dracula turned into a bat, just like the lady in *this* movie turned into a panther, and divebombed her just like those dumb mockingbirds. *I bet it would be fun to turn into some kind of animal, though,* she thought. *I'd like to turn into a horse and run as fast as the wind and jump over fences. It would almost be like flying. Or . . . maybe I could turn into an eagle and soar in the middle of the clouds. And then I could beat up those pesky mockingbirds and make them leave the neighborhood. Then, I could turn back into me and they could write about me in the newspapers and I could be like Superman, even if I am a girl. Wow! That would really be neat. Or maybe . . .*

"Melody, wake up! You're done."

After eating two big sardine pizzas made by their mother, Melody, Jan, and Mark lined up behind their father, and they all tramped out from the kitchen into the living room. "Daddy, can we watch *Bonanza* with you before going to bed tonight? PLEASE!" A resounding chorus of "Please, please" rose in the air as the three of them danced around Ross like Indians around a totem pole. "It's still early, and we promise we'll go straight to bed as soon as it's over. We won't even ask to play hide-'n'-seek. *Please.*" Little Kenny, at two and a half, was already snug in his bed, sound asleep. Ross and Honey looked resignedly at each other over the kids' heads. They'd been hoping to convince the kids that an early evening would be just the trick, because they had so much to do before they could go to bed, but obviously the group was not to be put off quite so easily. While Honey stifled a giggle behind her hands, Ross shrugged and started peeling the kids from his arms. After grabbing a cushion from the couch and placing it behind his head, he stretched out on the wooden floor; the kids raced to position themselves on his outstretched arms and got ready to enjoy another exciting adventure with Ben, Hoss, Little Joe, and Adam Cartwright, not to mention all their wonderful horses. Little Joe had a particularly beautiful pinto. As usual, Little Joe got into trouble after rebelling against one of Ben's too-right decisions (Joe had left some red berries in his pocket and they stained Hop Sing's wash load), and Hoss had to shoot the mountain lion that had decided to eat Joe for dinner. After Ben and Little Joe made up and the last strains of the *Bonanza* theme song drifted into a very long word from the sponsor, Honey turned off the TV, and Ross rolled over on his knees, scattering the nodding group, hoping to make a fast getaway. The kids were faster, and immediately retaliated by jumping on their "bucking-bronco" daddy's back. After they had all been "bucked" off onto Gramma Mary's hand-braided rug, Honey gathered them all together,

7

and they sang the traditional song "Here Comes Peter Cottontail," before being herded off to bed:

Here comes Peter Cottontail
Hoppin' down the bunny trail,
Hippity, hoppity, hippity, hoppity,
Easter's on its way.

As the last shrill notes faded away, three small forms shuffled silently down the hallway, stopping off at the bathroom to wash their faces and teeth before heading off to bed.

"Mommy, Daddy, can we get up now? The sun's up and it's shining through our bedroom window and I can't sleep." Honey tapped on Ross's shoulder and whispered, "Ross, what time is it? Melody's right outside our door claiming it's time to get up, but I'm sure it can't be that late; I'm still exhausted and I can't even open up my eyes. They seem to be glued shut."

Rolling over on his left side, Ross squinted at the bedside alarm clock, "Good grief, Mickey! It's only four o'clock in the morning. It's too early, even for you. There's a full moon, and *it* is shining through your window. Just close the shutter, and *please* go back to bed—don't call us, we'll call you, in about three hours."

"Okay, Daddy. I'll try; maybe I'll read a book."

"That's fine, Mickey." Listening to the pitter-patter of Melody's footsteps as she reluctantly headed down the bare wood floor toward her bedroom, Ross turned to his wife and asked her, "Honey, doesn't that child *ever* sleep? What ever have we *done*, and *why?*" Without really expecting an answer, Ross settled back down onto his pillow and soon his shallow breathing joined Honey's in rhythmic unison.

The early morning sunshine filtered through the curtains on the wall over Ross and Honey's bed, but that wasn't what finally woke them. No, it was the creak of the bedroom door across the hall from theirs. "Mommy, go potty."

"Okay, Kenny, Mommy's coming. Hold on there, big boy," Honey assured him. She rolled over and grabbed her blue chenille robe; it almost covered her bulging form. "Ross, wake up. Mickey'll be here in a minute and it's probably better to be ready for her this time. She'll probably have Jan with her this time, and I'm sure Mark's awake, too. I'll go help Kenny, and come right back."

True to Honey's prediction, Melody and Jan slipped under her arm as she opened the door and flung themselves onto the bed, just as Ross burrowed under the covers in an attempt at self-preservation. Of course, it didn't work; the two of them, undeterred by blankets and sheets, were more than a match for him: they, too, tunneled under the covers in close pursuit. Their giggles, resulting from Ross's tickling them in retaliation of their attempts at pulling him out from under the covers, reached the farthest (and most hidden) corners of the house. In a matter of seconds they were joined by another small form—that of Mark, who had never had problems in joining in a family free-for-all. The ruckus, having evolved into a gigantic pillow fight, continued until Honey returned with her youngest. Kenny tried to break from his mother's grasp and join the fray, but Honey's next words stopped everyone in midaction, as though they had been magically transformed into statues.

"Everybody, line up behind Daddy and me, and let's go." A feeling of expectancy charged the air as the four kids jostled for first place in the line.

"Biggest first, smallest last."

"Aw, Daddy, Mickey's always first. It's not fair."

"If we go smallest first, biggest last, you're still not first, so . . ."

"Yeah, but at least the others can see. Melody's taller'n we are, and we can't see the goodies the Easter Bunny bringed us."

"Brought us," corrected Ross. "Okay, this time we'll let you go by twos. First, Jan and Kenny; then, Melody and Mark. No, Melody, don't ruin the morning with discussions and whining. They won't work, anyway. Now, everyone, hold your partner's hand. And *we're off!*"

Six pairs of feet started down the hall, with four pairs of said feet carrying little people barely able to contain their excitement as they walked as sedately as possible (in other words, not very) behind their parents. The family rule was that all people under the age of ten had to close their eyes at the end of the hall, until the kitchen door was opened and Ross had slipped in to make sure the Easter Bunny had finished his work. To their surprise, the door that had been opened was not the kitchen door, but the living-room door. Their eyes widened to the size of large saucers as they gazed in awe at the living room, which had been transformed into an Easter paradise; the awed children let slip oohs and ahs at the wonders before them. Easter egg streamers, in pastel shades of green, yellow, pink, and blue, were strung across the ceiling, with dozens of Easter Bunny balloons in the same colors dangling from them, dancing or bouncing enticingly in the draft caused by the open door. But these wonders were not the most amazing things in the area: on the far side of the room, under the large picture window, were two real Easter Bunnies—a pure black one with warm brown eyes, wearing a yellow ribbon around its neck; and a pure white one with pink eyes and ears and a bright red ribbon. They were hopping around behind a small white picket fence, on top of pink and green Easter basket grass. Next to the fence stood a large blue metal rabbit; its back was elongated and open, with a seat just right for a four-year-old boy. Its long ears framed a steering wheel, and four wheels were hidden by legs that seemed ready to take off and hop at any moment. When Mark climbed into it, he just *knew* that it was his; getting ready to take off, he squeezed the right ear and delightedly discovered that it beeped just like a real horn!

"Don't you dare start driving that in here right now! The Easter Bunny didn't leave enough space. Wait until after breakfast," Ross said. Mark climbed reluctantly out of the rabbit car. He gazed at it longingly as Kenny grabbed the soft, fuzzy, stuffed rabbit that leaned over the fence while it held out a real carrot for the real bunnies. As he hugged the cuddly toy, he stuck the carrot in his mouth and started to chew it.

"Oh, Kenny, the bunnies have already chewed on that carrot. Give it back to them," Honey said.

"Carrot good. I eat."

Jan looked hopefully toward the live bunnies and asked, "Is the one with the yellow ribbon mine?"

"I don't know. There's a tag on the ribbon; why don't we read what it says?" Honey took hold of the little black bunny and, reading the name "Jan," handed the bunny into her daughter's waiting arms. "Be careful; he wiggles, so put your hand under his hind legs so he won't fall, okay?"

Melody had already rolled up the long sleeves on her flannel nightgown so that she could better enjoy the soft sensation of the little white bunny. As she reached out to open the tag on the red ribbon, Honey, in a teasing tone, informed her, "Well, I really like this little bunny. Ross, what do you think? Shall I keep this little baby for Junior when he or she gets here?"

"No, it's mine. Don't you see the red ribbon? Red's my favorite color just like yellow is Jan's. See, just read the tag—it says, "To Melody, from the Easter Bunny." And, on a more plaintive note, "And maybe Junior won't even like rabbits. He'll be too little. It's mine, Mommy. Daddy, *please!*" With the last quavering note, she threw herself into Ross's arms.

"Oh, sweetheart, I'm sorry. I was only teasing; you seemed so sure of yourself. Of course, she's yours. Here, hold her like I told Jan."

"She's so soft, Mommy. Look how pretty her ears are—all white with pink inside. Can I call her Pink Ears?"

"You can call her whatever you want to. Jan, what is your bunny's name?"

"Blackie, 'cause he's all black."

"Okay, kids. Leave everything in its place, including that carrot, Kenny; give it back to the bunnies—and let's go eat breakfast. We need to get on the ball; we have to eat and get ready for church. After church, Grammy and Grampa Jenkins and Grandma Mary are coming for lunch. Then you all know what comes next."

"The Easter egg hunt. Hooray!" they all said at once.

Four little people very reluctantly left four new prizes; indeed, Melody attempted to take Pink Ears into the kitchen with her. By the time Ross and Honey convinced her to leave it in the little pen, Blackie had already finished off what was left of Kenny's carrot.

"Okay, kids, line up and close your eyes before we go into the kitchen," Ross said.

"Why? We already had our surprise from the Easter Bunny."

"Just do it, okay? It's time for breakfast. Is everybody ready?" Ross opened the kitchen door and the children opened their eyes. Another awed silence followed as the four siblings entered the room with their mouths agape.

"Wow! How and when did the Easter Bunny do all this?" Melody asked. Again, pastel Easter streamers hung from the ceiling. Unlike those in the living room, which hung from one side to the opposite side, these hung from the lamp over the table and ended at each child's place around the table, each strand being attached to a gigantic Easter basket filled with all sorts of wonderful goodies. The wonderful surprise of the bunnies—living and not—in the other room had driven all thoughts of

11

Easter eggs, jelly beans, pom-pom chicks, and chocolate bunnies and chickens from their minds. But now, everything came back into focus.

"Look, he brought us doughnuts for breakfast. Can I have a chocolate all-the-way-through-one?" Despite the fact that Melody was as skinny as a toothpick, she ate like a horse and anything with chocolate in it, especially bittersweet, was her favorite. In fact, there was a huge bittersweet chocolate hen in her basket that she could hardly wait to put her teeth into, but if there were chocolate doughnuts, well, then the chicken would last longer.

After a quick breakfast of doughnuts (there were several chocolate all-the-way-throughs) and milk, everyone scurried to their rooms to begin preparing themselves for church. "And I want everyone's bed made before we leave or there will be no Easter egg hunt this afternoon," Mommy said. Jan and Melody banged on their parents' door: "Mommy, we've put on our shoes and socks and slips, but we can't put on our dresses because we can't get them over our heads with these stupid pin curls, Kenny just put his shirt on upside down and Mark put his shoes on the wrong foot and won't let Mickey help him put them on right, and he's also back in the living room driving his car all over, even if you said he can't. Can you come take our curlers out so we can get our dresses on?"

"Oh dear. Just a minute, I'm putting on my shoes. *Mark!* Get out of that car right this minute. Do you hear me?!"

"What car, Mommy. I'm not in the car, see? You said I could drive it after breakfast, but I'm not. Mickey won't help me with my shoes; I can't tie them."

"Of course not; they're on the wrong feet."

"But, Mommy, they're my shoes, and these are the only feet I have." Complete silence followed this statement. The logic was absolutely irrefutable.

"You need to put the longest part in the middle, just like your feet. See, this is your big toe, but the shoe that you put on has the pinky there. Understand? Good." Whistled strains of "Here Comes Peter Cottontail" reached her ears. "Ross, do you think you can help the boys while you're whistling? It's getting late and I have to fix the girls' hair."

"Yeah, I can do it, even if I'm not whistling."

"You're not? Then who is? Melody and Jan don't know how, and

Mark's here with me. It can't be Kenny, can it? He's too small. Kenny, come here, so Daddy can help you get ready."

The little boy stuck his butch-cut head through the door. "Kenny, whistle like Daddy. Hear?"

"Very good, but let Daddy help you get your shirt on right. Come here, big boy."

Fifteen minutes later, Ross and Honey packed the kids into the car and headed off to Newport Beach for the church services. All four children walked demurely near their parents as they entered the church, which was beautifully decorated with pots of snow-white Easter lilies and bright yellow daffodils, just like the ones growing beside the McDonald's driveway. After the Sunday school lessons, Honey accompanied Melody to the choir room, and then joined the others in the front row of the chapel. Groups of people, in brightly colored clothing that vied with the beautiful sun-brightened stained-glass windows illuminating the chapel walls, streamed through the doors toward the welcoming pews. Waves of joyous organ music accompanied the festive throngs. Feelings of hope and thanksgiving hung in the air with comforting warmth. It was a day for celebrating the resurrection of the Lord Jesus Christ. The adult choir stood, divided, in the external aisles of the chapel, and began to sing the triumphal Easter hymn:

Christ the Lord is ris'n today,
Alleluia.
Sons of men and angels say,
Alleluia.
Raise your joys and triumphs high,
Alleluia.
Sing, ye heav'ns, thou earth reply,
Alleluia.

It was so beautiful sitting between the two choirs as the voices echoed back and forth, and the triumph of the Lord rang in the congregation's hearts. After the pastor's sermon, the children's choir, seated behind the pastor, rose to sing, clutching battery-lit candles in their hands. Melody was both excited and nervous at the same time and she fought to stand up straight as her knees wobbled and threatened to collapse from the emotion. She was singing in the choir for the first time, and it was wonderful, but what if she sang a wrong note there in front of everyone—she would die. But no, there was her family, sitting in the front row, and so she knew that everything would be all right. Mrs. Jarvis lifted her arms and began to lead the very young singers:

When Israel was in Egypt's land,
Let my people go.
Oppressed so bad they could not stand,
Let my people go.
Go down, Moses, way down in Egypt's land,
Tell old Pharaoh, Let my people go.

Melody's heart began to slow down. She had done it; she had sung the right words in the right rhythm on the right notes. It was wonderful singing in a choir and the congregation's reaction made her feel like she could fly like an angel. At the end of the last service, as she and the other fifteen boys and girls of the junior choir walked in double file down the center aisle of the chapel with their candles shining brightly, the pastor let loose a cloud of snow-white doves. Just as the young choir members were leaving the chapel to take off their choir robes, one of the doves left its circling companions and settled on Melody's shoulder. She wasn't surprised—lots of birds landed on her shoulder (though not those pesky mockingbirds)—but this bird just heightened her feeling of peace and joy. Wanting to share this feeling, she turned around to search for her family in the midst of the festive crowd. Suddenly, she felt a hand clasp her other shoulder. Turning around, she came face-to-face with Grammy Jenkins. "I see you've found a new friend, Mickey." The dove flew off to join his fellows as Melody and her grandmother hugged each other.

"Grammy, you came to hear me sing. What a neat song, huh? Where's Grampa? Is he here? Are you coming to our house for lunch?"

"Oh, slow down; one question at a time. Yes, dear, the song was wonderful. Grampa is at work. You know the police have to work sometimes on holidays—unfortunately, even on Easter. There are much more people here at Eastertime, you know. He'll try to come later on, when he finishes his shift. Yes, I am coming to lunch and also to the Easter egg hunt. Then, if Grampa doesn't make it in time, your Grandmother Mary will take me home."

"Are you coming home with us in our car? Oh, please, Grammy. You can sit in back with me."

"Yes, sweetheart, I'm coming in the car with you, but I think I'll sit in the front seat next to your mommy and daddy. Shall we go find the others, now? I'll bet that your Grandmother Mary is already waiting for us at the house. Take my hand and come along now, there's a good girl."

"Ooh! Looky there, Jan. Now I know how the Easter Bunny could get everything done so quickly. He had help. See all those toadstools all over the backyard? They're signs that fairies were here," Melody said in an awed tone, "because fairies always make them grow, so they have somewhere to sit. I bet they were here to help the Easter Bunny hang up all them streamers and stuff in the living room and kitchen."

"You're prob'ly right. If not, how did the Easter Bunny get everything on the ceiling? He can jump, but not so high, and he can't stay high for long—he would fall down and make noise. He didn't want to wake us up."

"Yeah. You're prob'ly right."

A quick look out of their bedroom window had presented Jan and Melody with a suggestive panorama worthy of the Baba Yaga. Snow-white, umbrella-shaped mushrooms sprang up at odd intervals in the emerald green grass. They appeared to have been made from spun sugar and looked good enough to eat, but even these two girls knew that looks can be deceiving. The light rainfall two nights earlier, followed by the two warm, sunny days, had produced the engaging, but highly poisonous toadstools, the favorite seats of fairies and elves. The poison was, naturally, a protection from predators and little children, and that's why the magic people chose them. So intent were the two girls in observing the fairyland outside the window (which they were not supposed to be doing) that they completely forgot that they had wanted to spy out the land for a head start on the Easter eggs.

The ride home from church was as uneventful as the lunch that Grammy, Mommy, and Gramma Mary had prepared was delectable. Gramma Mary's baked beans and barbecued chicken wings were always a welcome addition to every family get-together, while Honey's baked ham—decorated with pineapple slices and maraschino cherries in the center, and with cloves studding the entire surface—together with the green and potato salads, was a mouthwatering Easter tradition. To top off the culinary wonders, Grammy had baked one of her famous apple pies, which they had eaten hot with a topping of vanilla ice cream.

After lunch, the kids had been sent to their rooms to change into clothes that were more suitable for running around in the tall grass. They had also been told to do just that and *not* to look out their bedroom windows. This was the catalyst: they wouldn't have thought of looking, strangely enough, if someone hadn't suggested it. So entranced were they at the sight of the toadstools that Melody and Jan hadn't changed out of their dresses yet, and so, when the call came to go out back to begin the hunt, they weren't ready. Moving quickly, the girls unbuttoned each other's dresses. After Jan took hers off, she hung it neatly on a hanger and carefully hung it up in her closet, while Melody, pulling hers off over her head in a hurry, tossed it in a heap on the bed. "Melody, pick it up and put it on a hanger; it'll get all wrinkled if you throw it like that. It's not a baseball, you know," Jan said.

"I'll do it later, after the Easter egg hunt. C'mon, we're already late. Mark and Kenny will get all the eggs if we don't hurry."

"Naw, Mommy and Daddy won't let 'em start without us. Don't argue; just c'mon. Don't you hear 'em calling us?"

"Hey, first we gotta get dressed." Slipping on a pair of pedal pushers and a long-sleeved T-shirt, the sisters ran out of the house and got in line with their brothers as the time came for the beginning of the Easter egg hunt.

"Okay, on the count of three, you can take off. One, two, and three . . ." Soon, the youngsters (plus Grammy, who was helping out Kenny) were all fanned out over the backyard, running here and there as they caught sight of an egg under a tree, or in the branches of the orange tree, or under the rose bushes, or hidden in the tall grass that Jan and Melody had discussed just the day before. Soon, their squeals of joy, whenever one of them found an egg, could be heard all over the neighborhood. Fourteen-year-old Charlene Krankopf looked longingly over the fence as the four McDonald kids started counting their eggs to see who won the prize for finding the most eggs. Melody edged over near Honey. "Mommy, why don't we give some of our things to Charlene, like we do at Halloween. Just Charlene, though, not to her creepy brother."

"It's fine with me, but you'd best ask your brothers and sister if they want to do it, too. We can't force them, you know."

When Charlene noticed that Honey and Melody were looking at

her, and then talking, she jumped down from the wall that separated the two backyards and ran into her house. She was terribly shy, because she wasn't quite as cute as most of the girls her age and because her brother was one of the biggest bullies in the neighborhood. Mr. Krankopf was a truck driver and was very rarely at home. Mrs. Krankopf was very nice, but she didn't believe in parties of any kind, and so the McDonald children often shared their booty with Charlene and even with Frederick at times. After the eggs were counted and the prizes given (Mark found the most), Melody and Jan collected the offerings for Charlene, and took them over in a decorated basket. "Is Charlene here, Mrs. Krankopf? We brought this basket of candies over for her. We hope she likes them."

"She can't come to the door right now, but I'm sure she'll appreciate the offer. Thank you very much."

The two girls skipped on the way home. It had been a wonderful day, but it wasn't over yet. Grammy and Grandma Mary would be going home soon, but it was Sunday, and Easter Sunday at that. First, they'd get to watch *Lassie*, and then, as an Easter special, they got to see *The Wizard of Oz*.

"Mommy, can I have another ham sandwich? They're yummy with all that mustard. Can I have a piece of pineapple and a cherry, too?" Jan asked.

"That's 'May I', not 'Can I,' Jan. And yes, you may, but drink your milk first. I know you don't like it, but it's good for you, so drink up."

"Okay, but it's so yucky. Can I—oops, I mean, may I—have some chocolate Quick in it? It tastes better that way."

"Hey, I've got an even better idea; let's put some Coke in it," Ross said.

"Oh, Ross, where do you get these weird culinary ideas from, anyway? I mean really—Coke in their milk?"

"Yeah, Daddy, that sounds yummy. I want some, too. Daddy always has neat ideas," Jan said. "Me, too," Melody said.

"Okay, you win. Go ahead, Ross, put a little Coke in everyone's milk. But, you all, when you get a tummy ache, don't come running to me. Call your daddy; he's the one with the clever ideas. Right, Ross?"

Ross ignored her cynical smile and started dramatically as he looked at his watch. "Hey, kids, let's hurry. *Lassie* starts in exactly five minutes and you all know that Mommy doesn't allow food or drinks (except popcorn, which we are *not* eating tonight) in the living room. So, eat all sandwiches and empty all glasses quick as a bunny hop, and let's go see what new adventure Lassie is facing tonight. And then, Dorothy, Toto, and all their friends in Oz."

"Mommy, can—oops! May I have another Easter egg?"

"Melody Jane McDonald, where do you put everything? You've already eaten three eggs, four ham sandwiches, and drunk three glasses of milk. I think that's enough. Otherwise, you really will be sick tonight."

"No, Mommy, I won't. You know I hardly ever get sick." This last was true. For some reason, Melody never caught a cold or the flu or anything else, for that matter, until all the others were catching whatever bug was floating around for at least the second time. And even when it did catch up with her, it was a much lighter version than the one the others caught.

"Three minutes, kids." Seeing that his progeny were finding it difficult to get a move on, Ross went and turned on the TV. The last syllables of the "word from our sponsor" were being pronounced. After a slight pause, the whistled notes of the *Lassie* theme song came on the air. Immediately after, four chairs screeched as four little people hurriedly pushed them away from the table. The house shook to its very foundations; it seemed as though a small herd of elephants had entered the house, instead of four anxious children rushing to arrange themselves on Ross's outstretched arms. Resignedly, Honey collected several half-eaten sandwiches from the table and put them outside in Missy's bowl. She then padded into the living room and sat heavily in the easy chair, rubbing her aching lower back.

"Mommy," Melody asked, rolling over and leaning on her elbows, "why do the swallows come back to the same place every year? And always at the same time? Why is Timmy worried just because they didn't get back at the usual time? Do our swallows always come back the same day? Huh? Why do they use mud instead of grass, like the other birds do?"

"Uh . . . Mickey, be quiet. If you talk so much, the others can't hear the TV. Turn around and listen to what Paul and Ruth are explaining to Timmy. Shh."

Melody turned quickly back toward the television set so as not to miss a single word of their explanation. Lassie and Timmy found the missing messenger bird, which had been caught in a trap. Timmy let it loose, and it flew back to join its flock. The next day, the entire flock flew into the valley, to everyone's joy. Now they knew that spring had really come. As Ruth and Paul hugged Timmy, and Timmy hugged Lassie, the whistled theme signaled the end of the episode.

Mark twisted toward Honey. "Mommy, can we have popcorn with the movie? We always have popcorn with movies," he said.

"Aren't you guys full, yet? You've been eating all day: candies, eggs, sandwiches. If you don't stop eating so much, you are all going to get as fat as me," she responded.

"But Mommy, we're too little to have a baby, and that's why you're fat, isn't it? Do you mean babies grow in your tummy when you eat too much?" Jan asked.

"No, Jan, lots of people get fat when they eat too much, but that doesn't mean they're going to have a baby. For example, Daddy could get fat"—Honey waited to go on until the series of giggles that followed the suggestion of Daddy's getting fat ended—"but he could never have a baby, because he's a man."

"You mean that men can't have babies? How come?"

"Oh, look, Mickey, *The Wizard of Oz* is starting. I'll go make that popcorn now."

Melody, Jan, Mark, and Kenny focused their attention on the projected film. They'd seen it before, because it was a traditional Easter transmission for the pleasure of the younger TV viewers. The fantastical world of Oz never failed to fascinate the younger McDonalds. Each year, Melody seemed coerced to ask questions such as: "Why are the Munchkins so small?" "Why does Dorothy want to fly over the rainbow?" "Why did the wicked witch of the East dissolve when the water fell on her?" and "Why are the flying monkeys mean first and then nice?" This year, however, she seemed completely absorbed by the movie, and didn't ask a single question. Honey and Ross both gave a small sigh of relief, because her questions weren't exactly of the type that were easy to answer, and they were afraid she might infect her brothers and sister with the same kind of inquisitiveness. As Dorothy opened her eyes and hugged all of her friends, the McDonald parents thought they'd gotten off scot-free this time. Of course, tomorrow would be another day, and with four kids, you never knew what was going to happen next. In fact, it was a pretty good idea to be always on the alert with this group. Thank goodness, Kenny had already fallen asleep and Mark was almost there. Now, Honey only had to listen to Melody's and Jan's prayers, and then she could go to bed, too. It had been a *very* long day.

After she finished tucking in Mark's and Kenny's blankets, and had given them their good-night kiss, she crossed the hall so that she could hear the girls' prayers and tuck them in for the night. Jan had already joined her brothers in dreamland, but the ever-ready Melody was waiting impatiently for her mother, although her head, too, nodded precariously as she said, "Now I lay me down to sleep, I pray the Lord my soul to keep. If I should die before I wake, I pray the Lord my soul to take. God bless Mommy and Daddy, Jan, Mark, Kenny, Junior, Missy, Grammy and Grampa Jenkins, Beau Maurice, Gramma Mary and Grampa Mack, Pink Ears and Blackie, Dorothy, Toto, Glenda, the Munchkins, the bluebirds that fly over the rainbow, the Tin Man, the Cowardly Lion, the Scarecrow, Auntie Em, Lassie, Timmy, Aunt Ruth, Uncle Paul, the swallows, Charlene, all my friends at school, Mrs. Short, Mr. Barley. Please help me to be a good girl, so I don't make Mommy and Daddy go crazy. Please bless all your angels and Jesus and the white doves in church. Amen."

"Nighty-night, Mickey. Sleep tight, don't let the beddy bugs bite." She hugged her daughter and edged toward the door.

"Nighty-night, Mommy." As Honey's hand reached for the light switch, a very sleepy voice murmured, "Mommy, how do they make rainbows? Isn't it easier to just walk under them than to fly over them?"

"G'night, Mickey," said Honey as she turned out the light.

2

The Science Project

"Mickey, come eat breakfast. It's almost time for school. What are you doing? You've been up since five o'clock; are you dressed at least? Hurry!"

"I'm coming, Mommy. Wow, I can hardly wait to get back to school; it's so much fun and I get to see all my friends and Mrs. Short again."

"Go sit down at your place. What cereal do you want this morning—Rice Krispies, Cheerios, or shredded wheat?"

"Rice Krispies, please."

"Okay, is everybody ready? Are you all smiling? Let's begin." Three sleepy voices mumbled and one chirped out:

> Good morning to you, good morning to you.
> We're all in our places with sunshiny faces
> And this is the way we start our new day.

None of the voices that accompanied the mumbles were very sunshiny. Some eyes were not open yet; some were still glued shut even. Instead of smiles, their mouths were wide open in ear-splitting yawns. The chirpy voice belonged to Melody, who was wide awake and rarin' to go.

After the weeklong Easter vacation, she was ready for her school and social action again. Of course, the vacation had been fun, too; they had slept in the tent every night and Karen Chateau had slept over one night, too. Last Monday afternoon, when Daddy came home from work, he built a big rabbit pen for Pink Ears and Blackie in the backyard. He used chicken wire and wooden poles, with a big wood door on one of the sides so that the rabbit owners could get in to feed and cuddle their pets. The next day, he built a little house, or "hutch," for them that had a big entryway that opened into the pen, so the bunnies would have protection from the rain and cold weather. Melody and Jan helped out, and even Mark tried to help by hammering nails into the poles, though not always in the right place. One of the most important things that Ross and Honey had tried to instill in their children was a sense of responsibility, and taking care of animals was one of the systems they used. The days had flowed by—not quickly, but not slowly either. It was too early still for the turtle days that precede summer, but this vacation was too short for flyaway days. But finally, school was about to begin again, and the days would be full to the brim.

"Mickey, are you done eating yet? You have to brush your teeth and I have to do your braids. Have you made your bed yet?"

"Yes, Mommy, I'm all ready to go, except for my teeth and my hair. See, my books are on top of the TV. Can I just have a ponytail today? That way we'll get done sooner."

After all was said and done, Melody gave her mother a kiss as she walked out the front door. "Don't forget to pet Pink Ears for me; she likes to be scratched behind her ears. Be careful, though; she kicks hard sometimes." She skipped down the stairs of the front porch, books in hand.

"Melody, did you leave out your library books for Daddy? He's coming home later to get them."

"Yeah, they're on my bed. Can he get more for me this time?"

"I don't know, but I'll tell him you asked. Have a nice day and say hi to Mrs. Short for me."

"Okay, Mommy. Bye-bye, see ya later."

It was a beautiful day; the sun was shining brightly, transforming the dewdrops on the emerald green grass into flashing diamonds. The sky was a brilliant turquoise, without a cloud to be seen. As she reached the corner house, three houses down the block from hers, one of her best friends came out the front door. "Hey, Andrea, wait. Let's go together, okay?"

"Okay. Hurry, though, or else there won't be time to play before they raise the flag."

The two friends presented an enchanting picture as they skipped off down the road to school together: Andrea, with her waist-length black braid and creamy skin; and Melody, with her waist-length cornsilk ponytail and her very fair complexion. Both girls had freckled noses, but Andrea's freckles were concentrated in a few chocolate chips, while Melody's seemed as though someone had sprinkled sand on her nose. Together with their friend Marsey Delta, they were the fastest runners in their school, boys or girls, and their favorite pastime was playing a game of horses together. The boys in the neighborhood always played cowboys and Indians and tried to catch them with their lassoes; it was actually quite useless to even try—the three of them were just too fast. There was another hindrance in trying to catch these three wild "horses": when they came to the picket fence that separated Andrea's house from the house next door, the boys had to run around it into the street, while the girls simply jumped over it and continued on their way.

However, this morning the two of them were not running or jumping. They had much more important things on their mind: how each of them had passed the Easter holidays. Andrea had gone to visit her aunt near Bakersfield, so she didn't yet know about the new additions to Melody's menagerie.

"The Easter Bunny brought you a *what*? A real, live bunny? Wow, if my mommy says yes, can I come and see it after school? What's it like? What color is it? Is it a boy or a girl?"

"Sure, you can come. It's a girl and she's all white with pink eyes and pink on the inside of her ears. That's why I called her Pink Ears. Jan got a black one with brown eyes, a boy. She named it Blackie. They're really cute and soft, but when you hold them, you have to put a hand under their back legs, or they get scared and kick you. They have long toenails and it really hurts when they scratch you."

"Oh, look, there's Kate. Hey, Kate, c'mon, let's all go to school together, okay? Wait 'til you hear what the Easter Bunny brought Mickey."

"Good morning, children. Welcome back to school. Did you all have a nice vacation?" Mrs. Short, Melody's second-grade teacher, was really neat. She was young and pretty, with almost shoulder-length, reddish blonde hair that she always wore curled under. She was one of the most popular teachers in the whole school, and her students, including Melody, loved her to pieces. In fact, Melody considered herself one of the luckiest kids in the school, because Mrs. Short had been her first-grade teacher, too. There were two teachers for every grade, and when one of the second-grade teachers left the school, Mrs. Short had moved up to the next grade, together with Melody. She was a good teacher, because she taught her students by involving them in projects and taking them on field trips, and then having them write essays on what they had done. "Students, this year, our principal, Mr. Barley, has decided that the school will host a science fair. The students from the third grade on will be allowed to participate individually with their own projects, but first and second graders will participate together in their classes. Now, I have an idea for something that we can do together as a class. I think it would be a lot of fun to work on it together. If someone else has another idea, we can vote on that, too, all right?" Murmurs of agreement crossed the classroom as all the students nodded their heads.

"Good. Now, here's my idea. One of my husband's friends raises chickens, and he has offered to give us an egg for each one of you; plus, he has promised to loan us one of his brooding hens, who will keep the eggs warm by sitting on them. We will need to take care of the hen for twenty-two days before the eggs hatch, so we can take turns feeding her and changing her water. When the chicks are born, we can watch the hen's behavior and observe how she takes care of them. Our best drawers can draw pictures of them as they grow, and then we will write essays on what has happened from the first day that we bring the eggs until just before the science fair. So, what do you think? Are there any more ideas?" No one answered. "No? all right then, all in favor, raise your hands." Twenty-seven hands shot up into the air. "If you don't agree, raise your hands." One hand shot into the air.

"Peter, you already voted once." Several class members snickered. "Are you for it or against it?" Embarrassed, Peter mumbled, "It's okay, I guess."

"Okay, children, that's settled; this evening I'll talk to our friend and in the next few days we can begin our project." There was an explosion of noise as the children began to clap their hands and raise their voices in cheers.

"I'm very glad that you all like the idea, but now, let's all calm down. Please pull out your arithmetic books, and let's do the problems on page two hundred thirteen. Now, who can tell me what we need to do to add up these three columns? What is the difference between adding up two numbers and adding up three numbers? Nicky Ruff, what do you think?"

"Well, uh, well, you add up the numbers on the right, and then you do the ones next to them, and then you add the ones on the left. If a column adds up to more than nine, you add the first number on the left to the next column, I think."

"Very good, Nicky. You may sit down. Veronica, please come to the blackboard and show us how to do problem number one. Helen, you come and do problem number two, and Melody, you come do number three." The three girls walked self-consciously to the blackboard as their classmates watched them, and someone sniggered behind their backs. Not daring to look back, they each picked up a piece of chalk and began to calculate the sums of each column.

"Veronica, don't use your fingers—try to do it in your mind. Melody, you can't have finished yet—you just started. Check it and make sure you have it correct." She paused a moment to give the girls a chance to finish, and then said, "All right, girls, have you all finished your problems? Show us how you worked them out, so that the others can see how it's done. Veronica, you go first."

"Eight plus seven is fifteen, so we write five and add one to the next column. One plus seven, plus one, equals nine, so we write that next to the five. Two plus three, plus four, is nine, so the answer is nine hundred and ninety-five."

"That's right, Veronica; you may return to your desk. Helen, please explain your problem to your classmates."

"Well, three plus three is six, plus four is ten, so we write zero and carry over one. We add one to seven and get eight, plus one is nine, plus two is eleven. We write one and carry one. One plus one is two, plus two is four, plus four is eight. So the answer is eight hundred and ten."

"Very good, Helen. You may sit down. Melody, it's your turn, now."

"Zero plus nine is nine, plus three is twelve, plus four is sixteen. We write six and carry one over. One plus six is seven, plus seven is fourteen, plus three is seventeen, plus five is twenty-two. We write two and carry over two. Two plus two is four, plus three is seven, plus two is nine. The answer is nine hundred and twenty-six."

"Very, very well done, girls. Are there any questions on how these problems are done? If not, please start doing problems four through ten. You have half an hour, and then we'll go outside for a ten-minute recess. Jeff and Doug, please stop talking and do your problems."

Half an hour later, the children were in line, ready to go out and play. The playground was a child's dream because it had games and facilities of all types: slides, a jungle gym, bars, several tetherball poles, hopscotch, four-square, two-square, volleyball and basketball courts, baseball diamonds, two sets of swings, and huge fields for running in. The Costa Mesa School District had the idea that an active body creates an active mind. Melody was quite happy, because she liked to play almost everything. One of her favorites was tetherball. The older students who didn't know her very well thought she would be easy to beat, because she was so small, but she usually surprised them with the strength of her built-in left fist. She could usually get the ball wound around the pole at least three or four times before the big kids knew what had happened, and by then it was usually too late to catch up. Of course, the challenge her left hand offered had proved to be both a trial and a help. The trial was basically because she was born left-handed; and not having regular-size fingers somewhat limited her, or so some thought. Legible writing proved to be somewhat problematic—she couldn't control the pencil as well as some people, including herself, would have liked, and sometimes she skipped words while she was writing because her hand didn't move as quickly as her thoughts. But, she learned to do a lot of things just because people said that she couldn't. She was always ready to meet a challenge. In the meantime, it was also a protection—not just for herself, but also for the others. If she got really angry, she would stick it in her mouth and thus avoid hitting the other person. Her right hand wasn't as strong as her left hook. She was feisty and had a quick temper, but she wasn't belligerent; she was, however, always ready to defend the weaker victims of the neighborhood bullies.

"Hey, Melody, whaddaya want to do now? We have ten whole minutes. After those problems, we need some fun. Let's play on the swings."

"Oh, hi, Veronica. Sure; bet I can fly higher 'n' you." The two girls raced to the swing sets before the other kids could reach them and take all the swings. There were the two sets—one set had five swings with special seats that had straps across the back of the seat so that the smaller children wouldn't fall out backward, while the other set had six swings without the straps, for the bigger children. Vickie and Melody headed straight for the smaller ones; there were still three left, two right next to each other. The girls headed for the latter and, positioning themselves in the seats, prepared for the takeoff.

"On the count of three we take off. One, two, three and go!" The two of them pushed off and started pumping back and forth—legs ahead, pull with arms; legs back, arms push. As she soared higher and higher, the wind blowing her hair in her face, Melody felt as though she could fly as high as an eagle; maybe, if she jumped as she flew ahead, she *could* fly like a real bird.

"Hey, Melody! Be careful; in a minute you'll fly over the top backward."

The warning bell rang and the two competitors stopped pumping, pushing, and pulling and started slowing down until their feet dragged on the ground. They ran back to the classroom and Veronica said, "You win. Wow, I couldn't believe how high you were going. You were really flying. How do you do it?"

The tardy bell rang as Melody answered, "Oh, I just thought how it would be like to fly like an eagle, and I guess I did, sorta. We'd better hurry; everybody else is already in class and Mrs. Short'll get mad at us if we're late. C'mon, let's go."

The girls sidled silently into the room, hoping to get in unobserved. Fortunately for them, the others were just starting to sit down in their places. Unfortunately, Mrs. Short was not fooled by their nonchalant look of innocence.

"Melody, Veronica, recess wasn't long enough for the two of you this morning, maybe?" Several of the other children snickered behind their hands. "I think maybe you can make up for it by staying in after school for another ten minutes. You both live fairly close to the school, don't you?" The two of them looked glumly at each other and nodded. The takeoff and flight had been exhilarating, but the landing had not been quite up to par.

"And if any of you find the situation funny, you can join them, all right, Peter?" After this, a look of panic crossed the girls' faces. All giggling stopped in the classroom.

"All right, girls, sit down in your places. Now, class, as you can see, I've placed sheets of paper on your desk tops. Please take out your pencils and write about your Easter vacations and what you did during the week. When you've finished writing, please draw a picture of what you thought was the best part. The crayons are on the counter. You have time to write your stories until the bell for the lunch break rings."

Melody's biggest problem was trying to decide what she would and wouldn't write. So much had happened and Melody didn't write very fast, because if she did, no one could read what she wrote, and they only had an hour until lunch. She decided to write about the rabbits; the Wednesday after Easter had been Mark's birthday, and he had specifically asked for a bunny, too, because he was as he said, "four years old and big enough to take care of a rabbit—look just how good I take care of

Missy." This last phrase had left everyone laughing until tears came to their eyes, because *everyone* knew that Mommy fed Missy and that Daddy cleaned up the backyard. And besides, it was usually Missy that took care of the kids, not the other way around. Anyway, on Wednesday morning, when they all traipsed into the kitchen for breakfast, there was a pile of birthday presents at Mark's place at the table. After he had opened some of the presents, which contained Tinkertoys, construction blocks, and a new ball, Daddy brought in another cute little bunny, a kind of orangey-brown color, which Mark promptly called "Brownie." In Melody's opinion, her brothers and sister had a distinct lack of imagination when they were thinking up names for their pets. You didn't see her calling her rabbit "Whitey," now, did you? Of course, they were little and didn't read very much. Even Jan, who was really smart, couldn't quite get the hang of reading yet. Maybe she would next year when she started school. Anyhow, she guessed their lack of imagination wasn't really their fault.

The lunch bell rang just as Melody was putting in the final touches on her drawing of the three little bunnies. She couldn't find the right shade for the kind-of-orange spots around Brownie's eyes, in between his toes, and inside his ears, so she decided to use just regular, everyday orange. It would just have to do. She tried to be precise in everything she did, and she was usually successful, except for keeping her part of the bedroom clean; there, she was a complete failure. She wished she had her crayons from home; she had sixty-four different colors, and she knew that the right one was there somewhere.

"Melody, you can wake up now. You've been sitting there with that crayon in the same place for five minutes. It's time for lunch." Mrs. Short stood looking over Melody's shoulder. "Is there some problem?"

"Oh, no, Mrs. Short, I was just trying to decide what color would be best to substitute for the real one that isn't here," explained Melody. "I have one at home, though. I *could* bring it with me after lunch," she wheedled.

"No, dear, because then all of your classmates would want to do the same thing and it wouldn't be fair, because not all of the other children have colors at home. It looks fine just the way it is, so don't worry."

Melody handed Mrs. Short her story, and walked out the door, where Missy was waiting to escort her home. The two of them ran happily together, Missy leaping with joy at being with her beloved friend, and Melody cavorting like a wild horse, all cares and thoughts of detention slipping through her mind like the wind blowing through the wheat plants in front of the school.

Detention wasn't really too bad that afternoon. Mrs. Short had said that they needed to stay for only ten minutes. Melody and Veronica spent the time erasing the blackboard, picking up the papers that their classmates had left on the floor, cleaning the blackboard erasers, and dumping out the trashcan. They knew their time was up when they went outside with the trash basket and Missy was sitting, waiting calmly for Melody to finish working. At the sight of her, Missy set her tail to thumping and gave a slight whine of greeting.

Veronica asked, "Does your dog wear a wristwatch or something? She's always here waiting for you just when it's time to go. She wasn't here a few minutes ago when we banged the erasers on the wall, so she doesn't come way ahead of time, just when it's time to go."

"Naw, it's just a feeling, I think. She always knows, and Mommy doesn't tell her to go; she just does it. It's neat, huh?"

After being dismissed, the two girls and the dog walked toward home, each absorbed in their own thoughts. At the end of the street, Veronica turned toward Melody and said, "Oops! I forgot my mother didn't know I would be late; I didn't tell her when I went home for lunch and there she is waiting for me at the door. I'm in big-time trouble, now. See ya tomorrow at school, if I'm still alive."

"Yeah, I gotta go, too. Andrea and Kate are supposed to come to my house to see the bunnies. Of course, they know I'll be late, or at least Kate does, 'cause she's in our class. Andrea lives down the street from me, so she'll have seen that I didn't come home yet. Man, I'll see ya later. Bye!" And with that she ran down the street just in time to meet Kate, who was just coming out the front door, on her way to Melody's house to play. At the end of the block, the two of them met up with Andrea, and the three little "fillies" hightailed it all the way to Melody's house.

Three days later, the promised science project began to take place when Mrs. Short brought a big reddish-brown, broody hen in a cage and thirty large white eggs. The hen glared at the twenty-seven children from inside the spacious chicken wire and wood cage that would be her home for the next couple of months, until the newly hatched chicks would be big enough to stay on their own. The baleful, orange eyes glinted with disdain as the eager children of the class gathered excitedly around the cage, hoping to get a closer view of their new, temporary classmate. She began to click her beak and to bristle her feathers menacingly, rustling the straw in her large warm nest, as several of the students began poking their fingers through the holes in the chicken wire in the hopes of touching her soft, glistening feathers. A large brown whicker basket—of the type used for a hefty picnic lunch—was set next to the enclosure on the long counter that ran from the door to the far wall. A number of the students edged toward it curiously; when one of them lifted a hand to open it, Mrs. Short spoke.

"Mr. George Cooper has sent us one of his favorite hens and thirty eggs; that's enough for one egg for each of you, plus three extras, in case some of them don't hatch. Now, here is an assignment list of who will be required to feed Rebecca on which day. She already has food as well as water for today; as you see, the water goes into this tube here on the outside of the cage and the feed goes into this little trough right in front of the nest. Can any of you tell me why the food and water are so close to Rebecca? Yes, Raúl?"

"That's because if the hen gets off of her eggs during the incubation period, they will get too cold and then they won't hatch anymore, because the little chicks inside the eggs need to stay very hot. ¿Es la verdad, Señora Short?"

"Thank you, Raúl, that's quite correct. Now, every day, at the end of the class and just before you go home, I will read the names of the two of you who will be taking care of Rebecca the next day, so that you will know to come straight here before lining up for the flag-raising ceremony. Next on the list," she continued, indicating the large basket: "the eggs are in here. Everybody line up and we'll choose our eggs. I'll write your names on them, because they are very delicate."

There was a great rush to be first in line, accompanied by shoves, scuffles, and giggles. "The next person to shove another will be sent to the end of the line and will be the last one to choose an egg. Let's *try* to be a little more *civilized*." The shoves and scuffles transformed quickly into a series of stifled coughs. The giggling intensified. The children then quietly assembled themselves into an almost straight line that slowly advanced toward the eggs.

"Hey, Melody, it's Thursday; how come you aren't wearing your

Brownie uniform?" whispered Katie, who was standing right behind Melody in the line. "Andrea said that her mother said we're going to start a new project, today."

Melody looked glumly at Katie. "Yeah, well, Mommy said I can't go anywhere for now, except to school. She was real mad at me 'cause I didn't go straight home after school. I clean forgot to tell her I was staying after school for ten minutes, and she doesn't understand Missy when she talks, so now I can't go to Brownies or play outside or anything. After she sent you and Andrea home, she made me stand in the corner for ten minutes before dinner. She said it was only ten minutes, but it seemed more like an hour. It was kind of funny, 'cause there was a teensy little spider that kept trying to lower its thread, but I blew on him every time he got near my mouth, and he ran back up it. It's hard not to giggle when you have a spider going up and down its thread in front of your face, but Mommy would really have been mad if I'd of laughed. The other brats were watching *The Lone Ranger*, but I couldn't even see Silver. Man! I had to keep my hands straight at my sides, too; what if that stupid spider had decided to climb into my mouth. Yucko! It would have been all her fault. And worst of all, Jan sat there snickering the whole time. Brat!" At this, Melody lifted up her eyes in time to see several other pairs of eyes staring at her.

Katie lowered her voice and asked quite softly, "Well, if you can't go out and play or come to something important like Brownies, what do you do?"

"I have to stay on my bed. I can't even play with my toys, and Mommy says Missy can't come into the room, either. That's awful, but at least I have my books. Yesterday, I read a real neat one about some dinosaurs. There were a triceratops and a stegosaurus that were good friends with some kids our age. It takes place in Arizona. Today, I'm going to read another one about the happy Hollisters. It's called *The Happy Hollisters and the Mystery of the Little Mermaid*. It just came out."

"Who are the happy Hollisters?"

"Oh, they're a family almost like mine, except they have one more kid than us. Well, so will we, pretty soon, I guess. Anyway, they're luckier, because their mother and father never keep them from doing whatever they want. They get to go all over the place and have lots of adventures and solve all kinds of mysteries. And *I* have to stay on my bed and just read about them. It's not fair!"

"Melody, would you like to stay after school again today?" With Melody not having paid much attention to what was going on around her, Mrs. Short's question caused her to blush a bright tomato red right up to the roots of her hair.

"No, Mrs. Short, my mommy says I have to go straight home after school. I can't even go to Brownies today, so I can't stay after school."

After the class' laughter died down and Melody's blush had receded from her hairline (leaving her scalp a more normal color), Mrs. Short said, "Then, would you please come and choose the egg you would like, so that the line can move ahead? Thank you, dear."

The rest of the week had seemed to just drag by, even though there had only been two more days left to go. On Saturday, Daddy had taken the other kids to the airplane park with a big picnic lunch and everything, but Melody and Mommy had to stay home. It was *so* boring; the only thing she got to do on Saturday was help Mommy pull out the weeds mixed in with her tomato plants. Normally, it wouldn't have been her first choice for an exciting weekend, but this was far better than doing nothing at all. When she had arrived home Thursday afternoon after school, ready to plunge into her *Happy Hollisters* book, she had discovered that it—and all her other books—had been taken from her room and placed in her parents' out-of-bounds bookcase, in their bedroom. Her mother's answer, "Go do your homework," to her own simple question "What am I supposed to do?" was quite unsatisfactory: she had already done her homework in the first fifteen minutes after she had gotten home, when she usually had her after-school snack. "Do it better" was just as unsatisfactory—it was already perfect (that is, if Mrs. Short would be able to read it; her handwriting was *not*, however, going to get any better overnight).

Yesterday hadn't been much better. When Mrs. Short had read the names of the two students who would be taking care of Rebecca on Monday, she had almost fainted because of the embarrassment—she and Peter would be working together. If she absolutely had to work with a boy, it would have been much better to be together with Nicky Marcuzzi. He was a big crybaby, but he was nice and he most certainly did not have a gas problem. Not only were Peter's bombs smelly, but you could hear them a mile away; it was like those new supersonic airplanes that flew over now and then, making the whole neighborhood shake and tremble as though a real bomb had been dropped on their heads.

As she had lain on her bed looking up at the ceiling, she had a sudden inspiration—a little spider was spinning its web right in the corner between the wall and her closet, and she thought if maybe she could see how it was done, she could make one (a web, that is) for Halloween. It couldn't be that difficult to do, if a little spider could do it. It looked really easy from far off, but as she got closer, she couldn't figure out where the thread was coming from. She had seen her mother make socks for Daddy, but Mommy had little balls of yarn hanging from her knitting needles. Here, there were no little balls of thread, without stopping to mention knitting needles. How was it done? She returned to her bed and thought about it for a while. She then decided that it would be better to ask her daddy about it, because she could come to no definite conclusion.

Unfortunately, Daddy was no more communicative with her than Mommy was. Usually, when she asked questions of a certain technical nature, Daddy would try to explain it to her or else he would change the subject. When he replied, "Be quiet and eat your dinner," to her query as to how spiders made their webs, she knew beyond a shadow of a doubt that she was definitely in disgrace. The worst of it was that she couldn't even look in her *Giant Golden Book of Nature* for the answer, because that too had been sequestered. She was so unhappy that she almost forgot to be curious.

Anyway, today was Saturday, and Melody found herself kneeling down in the dirt pulling out those stupid weeds. She'd have rather pulled out the tomato plants, but *that* would have definitely put her mother in a bad temper; those tomatoes were her pride and joy. It was kind of dumb, though, because she was allergic to them, just like Melody was, and Daddy didn't like them, and who cared what anybody else thought about them? As she lowered her hand to grab another bunch of weeds, she saw a flash of emerald green and white stripes. She reached out her hand and was surprised to find a weird caterpillar slinking across her arm. Weird, not that it was hairy or anything, but because it seemed to have two pairs of eyes—one on each end—and a long, curved, and pointed horn on what she assumed was the head.

"Hey, Mommy, look at this neat caterpillar. It's really pretty, all green and white stripes and a bunch of red circles all along the sides. What kind is it?"

"What? You found a *caterpillar* in my tomato plants? Kill it right this instant. They're worse than the weeds because they eat everything."

"But, Mommy, it's so pretty, can't I put it in a jar? What kind is it, anyway?"

"It's a tomato worm, and it digs holes in the tomatoes with that horn. You're right, though, it is pretty. Why don't we go get a jar to put it in, if you want, so we can keep it far away from my tomatoes." Honey pulled herself up from the chaise lounge and went with Melody into the kitchen.

After procuring the jar, they put a few holes in the lid so that it could breathe, and added a few blades of grass so that it would have something other than Honey's precious tomato plants to munch on. Melody took it to her room and placed it on the window sill so that she would be able to look at it while she was stretched out on her bed.

"Hey, Mickey, I think you've worked enough today. Go wash your hands and let's make some chocolate chip cookies before the others get home." With this invitation, Melody's restriction period was finished, so she hurried to wash her hands before her mother could change her mind. As she walked back into the kitchen, Honey was just pulling out the long tube of Pillsbury refrigerator cookie dough. Together they pulled out the cookie sheets; while Honey cut the dough first in slices and then in fourths, Melody placed each little piece carefully on the flat pans. "How long do they have to cook, Mommy?"

"About twelve minutes. Then we have to wait a few minutes before we can eat them, because they fall to pieces if you try to take them off the pan before they're ready. When they're done, we'll sit down with a nice big glass of milk and two cookies each, okay?"

"Mmmm. I love chocolate chip cookies. But, Mommy, if they're triangles when we put them on the pan, how come they come out shaped like circles?" At that moment, the timer on the oven rang, and the two of them turned to look at the cookies in the oven, to make sure they were fully cooked. You could tell they were done by the slight browning around the edges. As she bent to pull them out, Honey murmured to herself, "Saved by the bell."

The rest of the day passed in relative peace; just as Honey and Melody were finishing up their cookies and milk, Ross and the rest of the crew walked through the front door and began claiming their portions of the goods. Of course, a good game of chasing all around the park was a good way of working up a more-than-healthy appetite, and that is exactly what happened.

"Hey, Mickey, whachha lookin' for?" Jan asked.

"Do you remember that neat-lookin' caterpillar I found the other day when I was helping Mommy clean out the weeds in her tomato plants—that green, striped one? It's not in the jar anymore, and I don't know how it got out; the lid's still screwed on tight, and the holes aren't big enough for it to squeeze through. It was here last night when we went to bed, and I wanted to take it to Show and Tell at school today."

"Oh, brother, Mickey, you're always losing your stupid bugs all over the place. Can't you keep the darn containers closed?"

"It was closed, but I have to open it sometimes, so I can put more grass and leaves in for it to eat."

"Let me see the jar. Oh, look, it's right here underneath the lid. I think you need glasses. It's weird, huh? I've never seen one like that one before. Usually we've got those woolly black ones. You've caught tons of them before and they're really cute."

"Oh, well, I've gotta hurry, or I'll be late for school and Mrs. Short won't let me show my caterpillar in Show and Tell."

She ran out of the room and down the hall. Honey caught her before she ran out the door and she gave her a big hug. "You know, I've been thinking about that tomato worm you've got there. I've never seen one this early in the year—they usually start showing up when there are already little green tomatoes on the plants. Maybe Mrs. Short can talk about them in one of your science classes or else you can do a story about them. Have a nice day and try to be good, okay?"

She ran off to school, meeting up with Andrea and Katie, who were both quite happy to have her with them. They were less happy to see her "bug."

"Ugh, Melody! Where do you get these strange things? How can you stand to even touch them? They're horrible!"

"No, they're not. Look at these neat stripes and these circles that look like big red eyes. I think it's neat."

"Yeah, well you would, I guess. Anyway, try not to make Mrs. Short mad this week; we're making presents for our mommies for Mother's

Day in Brownie Scouts this week. It's going to be real neat, Mommy said. Vicky's mommy is going to show us how to make 'em."

"What are we making?"

"We don't know, but my Mommy says it's something real neat, so you'll just have to be there and find out."

"Oh, man, I just remembered something. C'mon, I've gotta hurry; I have to feed Rebecca with that weird-o Peter today. It's a big responsibility and I don't want to blow it, or I really will miss Brownies again. Maybe Mrs. Short would even make me stay after school with Peter. Augh! Quick!"

Unlike the week before, which had seemed to be at least a year, this week flew by; Melody was free again, and freedom had never seemed so precious. The hours seemed like minutes and there never seemed to be enough time to do everything she wanted to do. It turned out that Mrs. Short actually knew quite a bit about tomato worms; she, too, had a vegetable garden, where she had a small supply of tomato plants for herself and her husband, and it seemed that this particular caterpillar usually had a heyday in her garden, too. Fascinated by their odd coloring and shape, she had read up on them and discovered that they came out in late summer, whereas the moths, grayish brown and known as hawk moths, that were born from their cocoons (or pupas) usually came out in this period. She said that there may have been some eggs that, for some reason, hadn't hatched last year, and one had hatched now with the warmer weather. She told Melody to tell her mother to look out for others, because they could really kill off all the plants if there was a bunch of them.

Today was Sunday, Mother's Day, and Melody was really excited. The last two schooldays had been really fun, because in Brownie Scouts they had made a really neat present for their mothers. Mrs. Frost had provided every girl in the troop with an oval bar of soap (Melody's was pale green), sequins, straight stick pins, some string, beads, a thin cord, and cheesecloth. Of course, no one could figure out what you could make with all those different things, especially because there wasn't even glue. "We're going to make a fish," said Mrs. Frost. "All right, gather up your materials, and I'll show you how to do it."

They had been fun to make, and easy, too. All they had to do was fold their piece of cheesecloth in half, put the bar of soap in the middle and tie it up tight with a piece of string, thereby forming the body and the tail. Then, they had stuck the sequins and beads onto the sides with the pins, making the eyes and scales. To finish up, Mrs. Frost showed them how to wind the cord in and out of the tiny holes in the cheese-cloth and then make a knot so that the fish could be hung in the closet, or else left as a decoration in the bathroom. It smelled really good, too, and if Mommy liked it, she thought that she would make one for Grammy and one for Gramma Mary, too (that is, if Mommy would buy her the things she needed to make them with).

Then, Friday, in art class, they made Mother's Day cards. They colored them, but Mrs. Short had also brought some fancy things for them to put on the cards. She had finished hers in time, so Mrs. Short had let her make one for each of her grandmothers, too. All things considered, she felt she had made up for all the time she had lost the week before.

Now, she and Daddy and all the little kids were working on making breakfast in bed for Mommy. She and Jan were making buttered toast, Mark was coloring the napkin, Daddy was making scrambled eggs with peanut butter, and Kenny was getting underfoot. Those three had drawn pictures on the paper that Gramma Mary had brought them from work and then this morning they had picked some clover flowers and wild on-ion flowers that were growing in the backyard. Kenny had wanted to add a toadstool that was out there, too, but Daddy had convinced him that it might be better to leave it where it was; otherwise, where would the fair-ies sit when they came to visit them? The point had been well taken.

"Come on, kids, everything is ready to take in to Mommy, now. Have you practiced your song yet? No, Mark, I really don't think your mother would like root beer in her milk. She has already pronounced herself on the subject, remember? Now, let's go. We have church this morning, so we need to let Mommy have time enough to eat and then get dressed."

All the gifts were on the tray, ready to be opened. Honey thanked each of the givers for everything with an ecstatic hug. She was especially pleased with the soap fish from Melody and concurred that it would be a lovely and much appreciated gift for both of her grandmothers. They de-cided that they would buy the materials and make them tomorrow.

"Mommy, I wanted to give you a big toadstool, but the fairies said no, 'cause they needed it. It was purty and white. So, here are some flow-ers, instead."

"Thank you, Kenny, and thank you, too, fairies. Make good use of it."

The days passed, and the time for new things got closer and closer. Two weeks had already passed since the class had chosen their eggs for the science project, and only eight more days were left until they should hatch. Rebecca was becoming more and more surly every time someone got close to her cage to put her feed in the little trough. She would click her beak at them, but nothing else. Tomorrow would be Melody's second time around. This time she would be working together with Nicky. That was much better, because Peter had started pulling Rebecca's feathers the last time, and Mrs. Short said he couldn't help feed her anymore. She had then asked the class to find out all they could about the care of little chicks. Melody remembered that the Krankopfs raised their own chickens, so she had gone to ask Mrs. Krankopf questions about what they needed to do to take good care of their science project after they had hatched from the eggs. She had just finished writing her report on the piece of paper that Mrs. Short had given each of them, when Mommy had called everyone into the kitchen for dinner.

After dinner, since the sun was still shining, Daddy had gone outside with the whole group of them and started swinging them around, holding them by the arms. When everyone got back into line for a third time around, Ross took off, running down the street to the end of the block, and the first game gave way to a new game of tag, also known as "Who can catch Daddy?" As the game got into full swing, even Karen and Colette Chateau, their next-door neighbors, started running with them. Finally, after a good fifteen-minute race, Ross collapsed on the front lawn under the yellow acacia tree in flower; seconds later, he was completely hidden from sight by a mass of squirming children.

Now, it was dark outside and most of the kids were in the living room playing with each other. Melody had finished her homework and was now reading, while she waited for the beginning of the television program for the evening. She was totally engrossed in her book when she heard her name being called.

"Mickey," Honey called from the living room, "Have you finished your homework, yet? *Leave It to Beaver* is beginning, and then it's time for bed. Tomorrow's a school day."

"Yeah, I finished it a long time ago; my homework is on the kitchen table. I was just reading my new *Happy Hollisters* book that Daddy brought me from the library today. I'm coming now." She closed her book, made sure that her homework was ready for the next day, and ran to join Mark and Jan on their father's outstretched arms in front of the television. As she moved through the door, one of her father's famous paper airplanes (which she had tried to copy once without much success; they looked similar, but hers refused to fly farther than an inch without doing a nosedive) whizzed past her ear and landed on the kitchen table. Mark went to pick it up before settling down with the others to watch their last television program of the evening. He didn't notice the other sheet of paper that floated gracefully toward the floor, landing in Missy's food dish near the outside kitchen door.

3

Chas

Once, Grammy cited a little poem that seemed to perfectly sum up the character of her little Melody. The poem, written by Henry Wadsworth Longfellow, is titled "There Was a Little Girl." It goes like this:

> There was a little girl who had a little curl
> Right in the middle of her forehead.
> When she was good, she was very good indeed.
> But when she was bad, she was horrid.

An infuriated Melody was the epitome of the poem's last words as she stamped out of the house that morning, screaming bloody murder, and revenge on all of her siblings, and slammed the door so hard that the house shook to its very foundations. Swirling dust danced in the rays of the sun that filtered through the transparent white curtain that hung in front of the picture window in the McDonald's front room. Outside the house, the sun shone brightly while early bird sparrows and red-winged blackbirds sunbathed in its warming rays and pulled unwilling earthworms from the dew-softened soil. The rising external temperature contrasted greatly with the house's internal temperature of approximately forty degrees below zero. Frost glistened on all the metal fixtures in the house and you could feel the blood in your veins turning to ice. The other three siblings stared around at each other in unmasked terror and panic. They waited until the glass panes in the window stopped rattling before they had the courage to discuss the event between them.

"Boy, is she ever mad? I sure don't know what happened to her homework; do *you* guys know where it went to?" Jan shivered as she thought about how Melody's fist would fly if one of them was found guilty.

"No way," shivered Mark as he tossed the little paper airplane in the air toward Kenny. It floated silently through the air and "landed" at Kenny's feet. As Kenny bent to pick it up and launch it back toward Mark, Jan asked them suspiciously, "That airplane you're playing with isn't, maybe, Melody's *homework*, is it?"

"Nah! It's that airplane Daddy made for us last night, and he wouldn't use Melody's homework for that, would he? I mean, I know an airplane is purty important, but Melody's homework is, too, I guess. She sure thinks it is, anyway."

"Hand it over to me and I'll take a look at it. It probably isn't, but he could have made a mistake, couldn't he?"

"I guess. Here, catch." Kenny sent the airplane wobbling toward Jan, but his aim was slightly off and the plane veered off course toward the goldfish bowl.

"Oh, no," cried Jan. "Catch it before it goes swimming with the fish." The words ended in a shriek as the plane nosedived into the water. "We'd better try and pull it out before Mommy comes out of the kitchen. You know how much she likes those fish. Mark, go get a chair and hold it for me while I climb up and pull the plane out of the water."

"Yeah, ya better get it out before it gets too wet to dry out. If it's wet, it won't fly too good."

Jan was more worried about its being Melody's homework and being too wet to dry. She looked around uneasily before climbing up on the chair; Honey was talking on the phone, but she didn't sound very happy. If she managed to get the airplane out before her mother discovered it had gone into the fishbowl, everything would be okay, but if Honey even saw her up on the chair like that, oh, dear! . . . she didn't even want to think about it. Honey was the best Mommy in the world, but lately she was so nervous; everything they did seemed to make her yell. She looked toward the fishbowl: the plane was still floating, but the point seemed poised to make a nosedive toward the bottom. It was time to take action. Just as she was raising her hand to pick out the plane, a sudden gasp made her turn quickly around. The room temperature dropped another ten degrees; the sight of Honey standing frozen in the doorway caused Mark and Kenny to let go of the chair. Jan flew through the air, taking the airplane and the fishbowl with her. The scene that ensued was, if taken out of context, hilarious. However, the participants in the scene found it horrifyingly in context. Four fish were flopping on the floor, amid the gravel, the braided rug, and children. The airplane, unfortunately, was completely soaked and impossibly beyond repair. The kids seemed to have been pulled out of the Back Bay, and the permeating odor in the room seemed to sustain this last theory. Nothing in the room had been left intact; there wasn't one square inch of dry floor.

"You three! Pick up those fish right now; we have to put them back into the water before they die. Jan, you go and get a bowl of water to put them in. After that, everyone into the bathroom, at once! Hop to it!" After catching all four fish, they were herded into the bathroom without further ado, like a flock of bedraggled sheep, where they found themselves plopped unceremoniously into the bathtub full of bubble bath water.

"Man, this stuff stinks. All perfumy and all. I liked the fish water better."

"Yeah, well, you'd better not complain. We're lucky she didn't spank us before dumping us in here like this. Why didn't you guys tell me she was there?"

"Well, she just kind of turned up all of a sudden; first she wasn't there, and then she was. We tried to tell ya, but before we could say anything, you were on top of us. You'd think someone that big would make more noise. We're little, but we make tons of noise."

"Yeah, well, we'd better try and be a little quieter and not get into so much trouble. Mommy's always upset these days; maybe she's tired of being kicked by Junior. That baby moves around too much. We gotta try and help out a little more."

"Are you kids clean yet? Hurry up in there." Honey stuck her nose into the bathroom, and after noting that the Back Bay air had left the premises, she rinsed the three of them off and sent them off to their bedrooms to get dressed. Making sure that Jan was putting on clean clothes, she then ducked into the boys' room and helped them get dressed. After getting Kenny into his jeans and his T-shirt, she turned to face Mark and saw that he was completely upside down.

"Mommy, my clothes don't fit me anymore; I think I need some new ones."

She had to repress a giggle before she answered him. "Oh, Mark, you're more trouble than Kenny when you get dressed. Just look at you. Of course you can't get your T-shirt on right: you're trying to get your body through the neck. And, there are two pant legs—one for each leg, of which you have two. Someday, maybe your daddy can teach you the difference between left and right, so you can get your shoes on in the correct order. Come on, let's get you straightened out, so you can go outside and play while I go clean up the living room."

When the changes had been made, she collected the two boys and went to see how Jan was faring. Shiny clean, and smelling like flowers, the three children were ushered out into the backyard to play. It was a fun backyard with plenty of things for active little children to do. But, these three had a mission—no playing around for them until they had done something that would help out their mother. But what could they do to help? As they puzzled over the dilemma, Mark was inspired with a wonderful idea: "Let's feed the rabbits! That's not too hard; even we can do it. It's fun, too." They responded to this suggestion with a chorus indicating their general agreement. They had actually fed the rabbits several times by themselves, albeit under the surveillance of their parents.

"Mark, you go with Kenny and bring the bowls, and we can fill them up with the little pellets and then we'll fill up their water bottle," Jan said.

Unfortunately, things didn't work out exactly the way they had planned. As Mark attempted to carry the bag closer to the hutch so that they wouldn't need to open and close the door and make several trips back and forth, he stepped into a gopher hole hidden in the grass, dropping the heavy bag of grass pellets, which served as food for the bunnies. He tried to gather up the pellets that had fallen out, but it was a losing battle; there were too many of them and the grass into which they had fallen was too long and thick. "Hey, Jan and Kenny, come and help me pick this junk up. It's all over the place."

"Oh, Mark, what a klutz you are. Why didn't you just take the bowls like I told ya to? It would have been easier," Jan said.

"Yeah, I know, but I wanted to save time so afterward we could play a little bit before Mommy calls us for lunch," Mark responded.

"Well, you sure saved a ton of time this way. I don't know if we'll even get to eat lunch at this rate. I guess we'd better get out the bunnies and they can pick it all up for us. Maybe they'll even mow the lawn a little, too."

"Yeah. The grass is a little long. Maybe Daddy will thank us for our 'hard' work, 'cause then *he* won't have to do it. We'd better hurry, though, 'cause I'm not sure Mommy'll understand the idea, and she won't be real happy seeing the rabbits out of the pen."

The three little helpers ran quickly to the rabbits' pen so that they could put their plan into action. They had put the rabbits near the pellets and were just on their way to the swing set to play for a few minutes, while waiting for the rabbits to finish eating breakfast, when they heard an ear-splitting shriek coming from the direction of the outside kitchen door. Mark said, "Uh-oh. We're in for it now. Mommy saw the rabbits. Let's hide, so maybe she'll think that the bunnies got out all by themselves." The three of them ran as fast as their little legs could carry them, quivering with fear behind the rabbit hutch, hoping beyond all hope that their mother wouldn't notice their presence when she finally caught up with her prey. Surely the rabbits would have taken off when they heard Mommy's screech. Unfortunately for them, the rabbits were too intent on eating the bounty under their paws to take note of the fury that came rushing upon them; it was too late for them to escape, so she grabbed them by the scruff of their necks and put them back into the pen.

"Okay, you guys. If you don't want to join the rabbits in the cage, it would be a real good idea if you were to come here *now!* I'm not blind and I can see you perfectly well there hiding behind the hutch. Now, *march!*"

"Boy, she's not just not blind, she's got X-ray vision, just like Superman. Wow."

"I heard that, Mark. You're right, I do have X-ray vision, and when I'm mad, I have super hearing and give super-hard spankings. So, if you know what's good for you, you'll come here *right now!*"

Thoroughly convinced of their mother's supernatural powers, the three siblings left the temporary safety of the wooden hutch and edged carefully past Honey toward the house. They weren't real keen on having all the neighbors watch the scene of their destruction. They walked as slowly as they could because they were convinced that the longer they took to get to the house, the longer they could put off the inevitable. When the disconsolate group finally arrived at the house, their waxen faces were streaked with tears. "We just wanted to help, Mommy. We just goofed in doing it," Mark said.

"Well, you can all go to your bedrooms and think about how you can help without goofing up. Being careful is a good way of going about it."

"Can we eat lunch? My tummy's growling."

"We'll see after a while, Mark. Now, all three of you, go sit on your beds and *think*."

An hour later, Honey called her children to lunch. It was a meager meal, consisting of one peanut-butter-and-grape-jelly sandwich and a tall glass of milk, which was eaten in a complete, strained silence. No one complained because they all felt that the punishment was, more or less, deserved. Even Jan drank her milk without commenting; she was still thinking. When they had all finished, they were redirected to their rooms to take their afternoon nap.

After assuring herself that they were all safely on their way to dreamland, Honey slipped silently into the living room; after lowering the volume of the Doris Day record on the hi-fi, she began to fold the laundry that had accumulated during the day while she had tried to remedy her young assistants' efforts. Totally absorbed in the soothing tones of "Once I Had a Secret Love" and the rhythm of the work, an innocent Honey was completely oblivious to other sounds in and around the house. She did not hear a thing as Jan slid off her bed as she began to put into action the plan she had thought up to help out her mother. It was a no-fail plan; Mommy would be really happy, this time.

They were sitting up on the bed, ready to turn out the light. It had been a long day, but private time for the parents of four children was hard to come by and they always took the few minutes before Ross fell asleep to discuss the day's goings-on.

"Ross, I swear that one of these days, if those kids don't kill me, I will kill them. They've been driving me crazy all day. Oh, dear me! Why didn't I flush them all down the toilet when they would still fit and no one knew they were around?"

"Yeah, I can just see the headline in the *Daily Pilot:*"

Suburban Housewife, Mother of Four,
Arrested for Mass Drowning

"If you think that's good, just think about the story:"

Harassed mother of four, with number five on the way, pushed beyond all limits of normal self-control, flushed her four harassers down the toilet early this morning. A jury of twelve housewives and mothers declared the defendant not guilty of any criminal charges, declaring that her actions were justifiable as simple self-defense. Judge Blakely released Mrs. McDonald after hearing the jury's verdict, declaring himself pleased by the young woman's forbearance at having resisted so long. The jury applauded the judge's decision with a five-minute standing ovation. One of the jurors was heard confiding, in admiring tones to a fellow juror, that she wished she had thought of it years before.

The two of them started laughing so hard at the idea that tears started rolling down their cheeks. Their hilarity was touched with hysteria; Honey clutched her swollen abdomen as she attempted to catch her breath. Ross managed to wheeze out his question, "What did they do this time?"

"Well, to be really fair, I don't think it was intentional on their part. It all started out this morning just before Melody left for school. She couldn't find her homework and started blaming everyone else for having taken it. Of course, they all denied it categorically. She left the house in a huff, screaming bloody murder at everyone. I found it later on; at this point I was beginning to wonder if it was too late to flush Missy down the toilet, too. I have no idea how she got hold of it, but she was on the side of the house chewing on it. When I called the school to let Mrs. Short know that Melody had done her homework, Mr. Barley started laughing because everyone knows that this is the oldest and most worn-out excuse that children come up with to explain why they haven't brought their homework to school. I guess I became a little cool when I said that I would send it with Melody tomorrow if he really insisted. He stammered out an apology and said it wouldn't be necessary, that he would take my word for it. I'll send it anyway, slobber and teeth marks included."

"Do you think you might be just a little oversensitive, Honey? You have to admit it sounds like a pretty overworked excuse. I know I used it when I was a kid, and we didn't even have a dog."

"Probably. I did, too, but we had Tar Baby, and he really was guilty of the crime at least once. It does work, though. Anyway, when I got off the phone and went to vacuum the living room, I found another surprise waiting to happen at my appearance. Kenny and Mark had been playing with that paper airplane that you made them last night, but Kenny's aim isn't all that good, so it ended up in the goldfish bowl. Jan wanted to 'save me time' because I was on the phone and she didn't want to 'disturb' me; she had Mark hold on to a chair while she climbed up on it so that she could pull the plane out of the fishbowl. Well, I startled Mark when I walked into the living room and he suddenly let go of the chair, pushing it over as he tripped. Jan had her hand in the fish bowl and it fell on top of her as she fell to the floor, spilling water and goldfish all over the place. Thank goodness, the bowl fell on her stomach, so it didn't break. I refilled it, but it took us a while to capture all the fish and put them back into the bowl, because every time we got our hands on them, they slipped out. To make matters worse, every time I bent over, the baby kicked me really hard; I guess he or she doesn't like being folded in half. Anyway, we finally got them all collected and put them back into the water just in the nick of time. At this point, all three kids were crying for who knows what reason, probably in anticipation of what I would soon be doing to them. I hadn't spanked anyone; I didn't even have the strength to yell at them. Of course, Jan was all wet from the water that had been in the fishbowl. The boys smelled as though they had been on one of your fishing trips, I guess because in a way, they had been on a fishing trip. Of course, it was necessary to change all three of them. The odor was skin deep, so they all needed a bath and quick.

"After I had them smelling like people again and not the Back Bay, I showed Mark and Jan what clothes to put on and then went to dress Kenny. Did you know that *your* son Mark has a definite problem in distinguishing left from right and back from front? Jan got dressed just fine, but Mark had his shoes on the wrong feet again—I'm sure that if he could get them on backwards, he would—and his shirt was on with the pocket in the back and the neck where the tummy ought to be. He also had both legs in the same pant leg. I'm convinced that he has this problem because you switch everyone's clothes around." She stopped to catch her breath again as the baby gave a particularly violent kick and Ross snorted.

"Anyway, after I got him straightened out, I sent the three of them out back to play while I tried to clean up the living room floor in peace. I had no idea that such a small bowl of water and four goldfish could smell up a room so badly when out of their element. Phew! Well, while I was washing the breakfast dishes, I noticed a distinct lack of the racket that usually accompanies our group of children at play, so I decided to step out the side door to see what was going on. I shudder when I just think of the sight that met my eyes: Mark had decided he wanted to feed the bunnies. Well, the sack was obviously much too heavy for him, so it slipped out of his arms and fed the back lawn instead of the rabbits. They tried to gather everything up, but it was almost all covered up by the grass, so . . ."

"So, they let the rabbits out so that *they* could gather it up," Ross said. Honey nodded glumly. "See, I know our kids just as well as you do. Let me guess what happened next: you went out back to yell at the kids to put the rabbits back in the hutch, and the rabbits, startled by your voice, took off, running all over the backyard, causing a general free-for-all when the kids went running after them, right?"

"Partly. The *kids* took off and hid behind the hutch. The bunnies were too intent on eating the rabbit pellets and grass, so they didn't even hear me coming. I just scooped them up and put them away before they even knew what hit them. They're guiltless. The guilty parties were herded into the house and shut in their bedrooms, so they could think about what they'd done up to then."

"Did they think about it?"

"*I* think they thought about what they were going to do next. After lunch, I sent them to take their nap and I went to fold the laundry in the living room. When Melody came home, she went to change her clothes, so she could go outside and play for a while. I had told her to be quiet, because I thought Jan was still sleeping. Seconds later, a scream of rage that would have frightened a fire-breathing dragon issued forth from the bedroom. I raced into the room to see what had happened; Jan had decided to use her time cleaning the bedroom. Her side of the room was immaculate, but every single one of Melody's possessions was on her bed. She was furious because, of course, there was no way she could go out and play. She couldn't even sit on her bed and pout, because there wasn't room. Jan's taunting comment 'That's what you get for not keeping your side of the room clean,' didn't help matters, either. There was nothing to do but put everything away, or at least, that's what I thought. I left the room with Melody complaining and Jan giggling snottily.

"Fifteen minutes later, which I thought was much too soon, Melody called me to come and see what she had found. It was a big spider. Its legs were at least four inches long. Repressing my loathing of the creature, I explained to her that it was a daddy longlegs spider. When I told her it was poisonous, but that its legs were too long for it to bite people, she asked me if she could keep it in a jar. I told her it was better to keep it outside, so she took it out, and didn't come back until just before dinner.

She said she got distracted watching it make a web. She went straight to her bedroom, and finished cleaning it in record time. I hate to think where she put everything. I'll probably find out at the most inopportune moment."

"I think I can hazard a guess; where was the spider?"

"In the closet. . . . Ah, I'll probably find out tomorrow when I help her choose her dress for school. Anyway, then you came home and they decided they were more afraid of your spankings than my hairbrush. They didn't get into any more trouble. Whew, what a day!"

"Well, yes, I thought they seemed a little subdued at dinner. Would you like me to go have a little chat with them?"

"No, I think we ironed things out pretty well. But there's one thing I'll tell you now: if this baby doesn't stop kicking me so hard, I'll flush *him* down the toilet as soon as Dr. Timberlake leaves me alone in the room with him. He's getting a little too violent for my taste."

"How do you know it's a 'he'?"

"Because no girl would ever treat her mother like this. Trust me, it's a boy."

Ross put his arm over Honey's shoulder and pulled her closer to him. "If I kiss it, will it make it better?" Honey giggled and snuggled up closer under Ross's arm.

"I know they're just kids, but sometimes I wish they would act every day just like they did last Sunday. Right, it was Mother's Day, but I'm a mother every day of my life, aren't I? Oh well, I guess it could have been worse; at least they were in it together. They really are obedient children for the most part if they are told precisely what to do and what not to do. They aren't malicious, even if they do sometimes pull out spiders. Mickey loves them and thinks that everyone else should, too." She sighed as a slight buzz from Ross's side of the bed answered her last comments. Looking over into Ross's face, she discovered that he had fallen asleep during her musings. Shrugging, she nestled down closer to his protective warmth and drifted off to dreams of an unknown assailant that kicked her mercilessly in the stomach.

When Melody returned home from school for lunch the next day, she was surprised to find Grammy there, preparing lunch for her. The other kids were already seated around the table, immersed in an unusual (for them) silence. The others stared at her as she shouted, "Hi,

Grammy! What're you doing here? Where's Mommy? Did Grampa come, too?"

Reaching down to give her granddaughter a big hug, Grammy said, "Well, Grampa took your mother to the hospital. It looks as though your new brother or sister is on the way. Your Grandmother Mary and I will be taking turns being here with you during the day until your mother comes home with the new baby. Your father will be here in the evenings and at night. Now, go sit down and I'll serve up lunch."

"Wow! I hope we get a new sister. There are already too many little brothers. Boys are so dumb—you always have to help them get dressed and stuff like that because they *always* get their things on wrong," she said, looking pointedly at Mark.

"Well, Mickey, we'll just have to wait and see. I'm sure you'll love the new baby, even if it could be a new little brother." Mickey sat down in her place at the table and Grammy gave her a bowl of vegetable soup and a peanut-butter-and-strawberry-jam sandwich.

At that moment, the front door crashed open as Ross ran through it and into the kitchen. "Daddy, Daddy, guess what? Mommy's at the hospital and she went to get us a new brother."

"Oh, Mark, be quiet," said Jan. "We don't know it's gonna be a brother for sure. I think it's gonna be a girl. I don' want another brother. Two are more than enough. I'll tell Mommy to send it back if it's a boy!"

"Oh! You two are so dumb!" Mickey snickered, as she rolled her eyes skyward. "You can't choose what you want and get rid of what you don't." Before a war could break out, Ross intervened. "Kids, shut up, sit down, and eat! *Now!*" In a calmer voice he added, "Edith, I take it there hasn't been any news yet from the hospital? I stopped in at the plant to load up the truck for my afternoon deliveries and they told me that you had called. They gave me the afternoon off, so I came straight home in hopes of news and so that I could change my clothes before taking off for the hospital."

"No, Bill hasn't called in yet, and he promised he would as soon as there was news. Would you like some lunch before you go?"

"Thanks, Edith, but if you just fix me a quick sandwich while I'm changing my clothes, I'll eat it on the way to the hospital."

Five minutes later, he grabbed the sandwich from Edith's hand, pecked each child on the cheek, ran out the door, and jumped behind the steering wheel of the still idling car. The group he left behind could hear the squealing of the tires as he sped around the corner at the end of the block.

"Boy, he sure is in a hurry," commented Melody.

"He sure is, and you should hurry along, also, dear. It's getting late, and you must be on your way to school."

"Ah, Grammy, can't I stay home? C'mon, I wanna hear when my new sister is born. Can we go and see her at the hospital?"

"No, you can't. You are all too young. You have to be twelve years old before they will let you into the hospital."

"But they let me in when they took out my tonsils, and I was only four, then. I even got to stay there for a week and I ate a lot of ice cream."

"I want my tonsils out, so I can eat ice cream, too. I'm four."

"Nah, you don't want to take your tonsils out; your throat hurts real bad and you can't go outside and play, and there's lots of blood all over the place and you know you're scared of blood."

"Melody, they let you into the hospital because you were a patient. Now, please hurry or your father won't let me come and help out. Your mother and father need for you all to be very obedient, especially when they bring the baby home."

"All right, Grammy, I'm ready to go now. See you later." As Melody skipped out the door on her way to school, her Grandmother promised, "As soon as we have news, I'll call the school and have them send you home. Don't worry, Mickey."

"Okay, Grammy, bye-bye. Bye, guys. See ya later."

"Push, Honoria. I can see its head, so we're almost there. Now, hold your breath and *push!*"

Honey pushed. This fifth time in the birthing room was neither the easiest nor the most difficult; the most difficult and most exciting time had been with Melody. When Honey had gone to the hospital, it was because she *knew* she was having an appendicitis attack. She'd been having bouts of excruciating pain since midnight and her mother had told her what, according to Edith, was going on; she herself had given birth to five daughters, and had recognized the symptoms quite easily, but Honey was not to be convinced. After all, she was only six months along, and everyone knew a pregnancy took nine months to complete. You couldn't even tell yet that she was pregnant; she couldn't zip up the skirt she was wearing, but that was the only sign. But, when they got to Camp

Pendleton, where the military hospital was located, and Edith had told the guard their reason for being there, Honey was suddenly surrounded by a military escort, with blaring horns admonishing all and sundry to move out of the way because a new baby was ready to enter the world. When the doctor told her that Edith had been quite right in her diagnosis, she'd had no choice but to accept the truth, especially when they raced her off to the operating room. After two hours of soul-rending back pain, her "appendix" was "extracted" as she wailed out a high C that would have made the great soprano Renata Tebaldi turn green with envy. The nineteen-and-a-half-inch-long, four-pound-two-ounce, gray-blue form, with pointed ears that were more than slightly reminiscent of an elf, caused a stir of panic as the doctor pronounced a clipped order: "incubator—run!" (The easiest had been Kenny, who had slipped out like greased lightning.)

"Honoria," Dr. Timberlake's calming voice, followed by a furious roar, broke through her reminiscing, "you have another fine son. Another towhead, just like all the others—and look at all those curls. Now, Nurse Brandley will take you up to your room and Nurse Kelley will take this fine young man up to the nursery, while I will go and inform Ross and your father of the new arrival. After all that work, I think I have the right to go and do the fun stuff. I love to see new fathers' looks when they hear the news. Of course, it's not Ross's first time around, but I'm sure he'll be in the room before you."

Honey interrupted the doctor's monologue with a sigh. "Whose hard work? I knew it could only be a boy; who else would put a mother through the trials I've gone through lately?"

"Well, I'm sure he'll prove himself worthy of all the trouble he's put you through. Oh, look at what he's doing now."

Honey looked over at her new son just as he flopped himself over onto his right side. "Now there is something you don't see every day. That is one strong young man you have there—a weightlifter if I don't miss my guess. Well, well, on your way upstairs, now. We'll see you there shortly. Nurse Brandley, please accompany Mrs. McDonald up to her room."

Edith answered the phone on the second ring. There was a certain urgency in the sound; it may just have been her own anxiousness, but she was certain that it was quite important, judging by the vibrations in the air. She had just finished putting the kids down for their nap, which had prohibited her from answering the phone on the first ring. "Ross? Oh, good, it's you. Is there any news yet? She just came out? What did Dr. Timberlake say? Another boy? Well, I know two little boys who will be thrilled, and two little girls who won't be all that excited at first, but I'm sure that they will get over it quickly. You really do have very affectionate children, you know. Oh, I just saw Missy take off down the street. I wonder where she's headed for. Now, how is Honey? Have you seen her yet? And the baby; how is he? The doctor says he's going to be a *what*? A *weightlifter*? Well yes, dear, your father was a weightlifter, now that I think about it. It could run in the family, I imagine. Oh, I'd better hang up; I promised Melody that I would call the school and let her know about her new brother. What? Melody already knows? How? Did you call the school first? Ah, Missy. You're right, they're running up the driveway right now. Well, give Honey a big hug for me and a kiss for my new grandson. I'll talk to you later, dear. Oh, wait! You forgot to tell me his name. You know Mickey will ask that right away. Charles John? That's a lovely name. Send Bill home when he's finished cooing at his new grandson. All right, good-bye. Love to all three of you."

Just as Edith hung the receiver on the hook, Melody burst through the front door. "Grammy, Grammy, Missy just told me I have a new brother. I don't even care that it's a boy; Mark and Kenny aren't really all that bad. When're they coming home?" As Melody stopped to catch her breath, an idea came to mind for a new tactic at being able to see the baby before they brought him home from the hospital. "Maybe Daddy could take us to the hospital and we could stand outside and Mommy could wave to us from her bedroom window and show us our new brother from there, too. Neat idea, huh? What's his name, Grammy?"

Edith decided she'd better answer before Melody came up with a new string of questions; goodness gracious, but that girl had more questions inside her than all five of *her* daughters put together. Besides, she too had a few questions to put to Melody. "His name is Charles John and he was born an hour after you went back to school. Yes, the idea is feasible, but you will need to talk to your father about it. I'm sure he will agree, though. Now, you told me that Missy told you that you have a new brother, but did the two of you bother to let Mrs. Short know you were coming home? You don't have your books with you, so I imagine you were at recess and just took off. Shall we call the school and let them know where you are?"

Melody's lower lip quivered as she gave her beloved Grammy a hurt look. "Natcherly, I told her—she's the one who told me that Missy was looking for me. When I got back to school I told her that Mommy was in the hospital and that my new brother or sister was on the way. I was sitting by the nurse's office playing jacks with Jenny and Sandra, and when Missy told me about my brother, I had already gotten up to my nines. Mrs. Short told me I could go home and not to worry about my books; she said I didn't have to do any homework because today is a special day. She was real happy and told me to say 'Congratulations' to Mommy and Daddy. I bet Jan's mad, huh? She really wanted a little sister. A sister would have been nice, but a brother's okay, too, I guess."

As Melody headed off toward her bedroom to change her clothes, Grammy put her finger to her lips and told her not to wake up Jan, because she had just lain down when Ross had called with the good news, so she didn't know about her new brother yet.

When Melody opened the bedroom door, Jan—who had been standing behind it with her ear at the keyhole, trying to hear exactly what was going on, ever since the phone rang—pounced on her. "What's going on? Do we have a new sister now? When are they bringing her home?"

"Nah, we have a new brother. His name's Charles John. Weird, huh?"

"Yeah. Can we send him back? I don't wanta brother; a sister's better."

"Thanks, but no, ya gotta keep what ya get in these cases. Anyway, I'll bet that he's real cute."

"Remember how cute Kenny was when they brought him home from the hospital? He's still cute when he doesn't have to wear that stupid patch on his eye."

"Yeah, but even then he's fun, because he looks almost like a pirate. Too bad it's not black. Okay, I guess we can keep him even if he is a boy."

"Guess what? Grammy said maybe Daddy would take us to see Mommy at the hospital; we can't go in, but she can wave to us from the window, and we can see Charles John from there, too. Neat idea, huh? *I* thought of it, ya know."

"Yeah! Let's hope Daddy says okay."

The boys received the news of Charles John's birth with exultation, but when Daddy told them they could go with him to the hospital the next day to visit Mommy from the window, it was almost impossible to contain their excitement. Only after Ross thought aloud that perhaps it might not be such a great idea for all of them to go to the hospital, where they would probably disturb the other patients (not to mention their little brother), were they able to calm down a little. His consideration was greeted at first with unbelieving silence, which was almost immediately followed by a series of howled protests that threatened to become even more thunderous than their shouts of joy.

Ross reconsidered. He had to; he had a bad headache after all the excitement of the birth of his third son and the reaction of the other four had only increased his discomfort, but he hadn't really intended to hurt their feelings. "Okay, kids we'll go; just calm down a bit. And remember, tomorrow you really do need to be very quiet. Even if you will be outside, the noise can enter in through the open windows, okay? Now, everyone give Grammy a big hug and a kiss good-bye, and then all of you file into the kitchen. I brought home two pizzas; one with pepperoni and olives, and the other one with anchovies."

As the children filed quickly into the kitchen, Ross took Edith and Bill aside and thanked them for their help. "Honey will be very glad to see you tomorrow. She's in room three sixteen. Dr. Timberlake said that if Charles keeps going on like he has been, they can come home the day after tomorrow. Now, go on home and get some rest. Edith, I'm sure you're tired; staying with those four is enough to wear anyone out, even someone much younger than you. I'll talk to you tomorrow. Now, good night, and thanks again."

After seeing Edith and Bill to the door, and making sure there were no toys, blocking the way to the car, that Bill could stumble over with his wooden leg, he hurried into the kitchen to oversee the dividing of the pizzas. He had a sneaky suspicion that the night ahead of him would be very long without Honey's assistance, and it would be better if any and all discussions could be cut short from the very beginning. They really didn't quarrel very often, but pizza was a very serious subject in this family; maybe he would have done better buying two of each kind. By the time he got into the kitchen, the kids had already opened up the first carton, and the rich, spicy aroma of hot pepperoni and a melted mixture of mozzarella and cheddar cheeses reached his nostrils. He hadn't realized, until that moment, just how hungry he was, but the enticing scent tantalized his taste buds. He wondered if Shakey's had home delivery; it was probable that he would be able to eat an entire pizza by himself. Taking the phone off the hook, he dialed the pizza parlor's phone number; after receiving the confirmation that they did indeed have home delivery, he ordered another two pizzas and went to join his offspring at the table.

"Daddy, I don't think that these two pizzas are going to be enough for all of us tonight. I helped Grammy fix a salad before you got home, but we're really hungry, and these pizzas smell too good. I could eat one all by myself—you know how much I *love* pepperoni and olives. Mmmm!"

"Well, Melody, I guess we'll just have to do with what we've got . . . for the moment. I ordered two more pizzas, but it'll take a while before they get here. Okay, Mark, would you like to say the blessing on the food tonight? And remember to thank God for your new brother, too."

"Okay, Daddy. *God is great, God is good, let us thank him for this food. And God, thank you for giving us a new brother and not another sister. Amen.*"

As four sets of hands reached toward the appetizing triangles of pizza, Ross commented in passing, "Girls, I don't think I heard you say 'Amen'? Am I losing my hearing?"

"No, we just don't agree about the sister part, right, Jan?"

Jan nodded her head in agreement with her sister.

Oh, dear, thought Ross, *I think I have a long two days ahead of me before Honey gets home. Dear God, please give me the strength and patience to get through this time without putting Honey's wishful thinking into action.* "Mark, they're right, there. The remark was uncalled for. Mark, say you're sorry, and girls, please say 'Amen' so that we can get these pizzas eaten. One, two, three, go."

Mark's mumbled "Sorry" was followed by the girls' chorus of "Amen," and Ross proceeded with doling out the various pieces of pizza. Just as they finished devouring the succulent treat and were cleaning up all the stray crumbs, the doorbell rang and the second round began.

Yesterday's trip to the hospital with the kids had gone much better than Ross had thought it would. There were a few times in the car when

Ross had considered turning around and taking them all back home and leaving them there to contemplate the configuration of a living-room corner while he went to visit his new son; they had been saved by the fact that there just wasn't a babysitter to be found at that time of day, not to mention the fact that it was Saturday. The high-school-age sisters Cookie and Linda Bejune, were out shopping together, and Jessie was preparing lunch for her husband. Of course, it was also a last-minute request, so he couldn't really expect too much. Anyway, his last-minute admonishments, before letting them out of the car, seemed to have taken effect, and the four of them had behaved exceptionally well, all things considered. Their squeals of delight and shrill greetings to their mother and brother had not been terribly disturbing, and, in fact, the other new mothers had also expressed a desire for similar visits from their older children. Naturally, they—the children—had made several attempts to convince Ross to let them actually enter the hospital, and had even tried to beguile Dr. Timberlake with their most winning smiles and toothiest grins, but he, too, was adamant in insisting that it was against the rules. A warning look from Ross had kept the doctor from giving permission to Melody; he also realized that it wouldn't be fair to the other three, who were just as ardent in their desire to give a worthy welcome to the newest member of the family as Melody was, so he said nothing.

After Honey had caught all of the kisses that had blown to her and exchanged them with kisses of her own, Ross herded the kids back into the car and headed for home. It was a beautiful day, and he didn't really feel like going straight home, so they stopped off at their favorite sandwich store and bought barbecue beef and ham sandwiches, which they decided to eat at the "Airplane" (Costa Mesa) Park before heading off toward the house. Just as they were driving out of the parking lot, the sign on a new specialty store caught Ross's eye, and he swiftly turned the car around, swerving to miss a car that was leaving just behind him, and came to a screeching halt right in front of the store. While he explained his idea to the kids, all five McDonalds climbed out of the car and walked double file into the store. The contents of the store were enough to keep the attention of the kids, and the containers were sufficient to keep them out of trouble, even if they would have been able to safely carry the goods out in their pockets. Of course, with the new surprise for Honey having been bought and carefully stashed in the trunk of the car and placed on the laps of the kids, there was absolutely no question in their minds as to whether they were going to the park or not. The kids didn't care; Ross had let them help choose the different components of Honey's welcome-home present, and when they got home, they got to help him put the whole thing together. It had taken the entire afternoon and well into the evening before they had set up the surprise to the satisfaction of all concerned. The sandwiches had been consumed as soon as they had arrived home, and Ross had prepared peanut-butter scrambled eggs and chocolate milk with Coke for dinner, all of which had been consumed in the twinkling of an eye. Ross had put the last finishing touches on the surprise after the kids went to bed.

Now, he wasn't quite sure he had done the right thing; the kids had assured him that the idea was perfect, and that was really the reason that he was beginning to wonder about the choice. He reached over and patted Honey's hand as they drove toward home. The baby sleeping calmly in her arms yawned as she looked up and smiled at Ross. "Yesterday, the kids and I bought you a little surprise on the way home. They're really excited, because they helped choose it and we worked all afternoon and evening on it before going to bed. Just think, they didn't even look for excuses not to go to bed. Can you believe that?"

"Wow, that really is strange. You're sure they're not sick or anything? What surprise? Whose idea was it—yours or theirs? They gave me plenty of surprises the day before I came into the hospital."

"They're fine. Originally it was my idea, but they cottoned right to it. And they worked hard, I'll tell you."

"Okay. I'm not completely reassured, but I'll take your word for it." The rest of the short trip toward home passed in silence, interrupted only by the baby's low gurgling and Honey's cooing response.

As they drove up the driveway, the welcoming committee raced out the front door waving a huge banner that had been painstakingly colored by the kids and written by Ross and Melody. WELCOME HOME MOMMY AND CHAS!!!!!!!!! it said in a blazing fire-truck red that contrasted strongly with the emerald green grass and the deep azure of the sky. Honey choked on the name "Chas" and turned as red as the written words.

"Mommy, I'm the biggest; can I hold Chas first?"

"Mommy, can we look at him?"

"Wow, look at how cute he is, even cuter 'an Kenny was."

"His eyes are real blue, Mommy, almost as blue as yours are."

"Tiny fingers."

At this, Chas started waving his arms and hands in the air.

Honey turned toward Ross as their older children admired their younger brother. "Is this the surprise you had waiting for me? I was worried that they had done another one of their attempts at 'helping' me, but this is very nice."

"We-ell, it's *part* of the surprise. We kind of thought Chas was a little less formal and it might make him feel a bit more as part of the family. Here, give Chas to me and close your eyes. Don't worry, I'll lead you into the house. Careful, there's the step. And the next one, too. No, Kenny get out of the way, or you'll make Mommy trip and fall down. Then how would that be? Hi, Edith, we're home. All right, Honey, we're going through the door. Okay, turn right here and close your eyes real tight—don't peek now. Are you ready? Okay, open your eyes and look straight ahead."

At first the contrast between the dark caused by her closed eyes and the light emanating from the object at the far side of the living room made it difficult for Honey to distinguish just what the object was. "Do you like it, Mommy?" Melody said. "Daddy chose the a-qua-ri-um. And the rest of us got to choose the fish. Do you like 'em? See that big white one with the three black spots on its side? It's called a 'kissing grammy,' but Daddy said we can call it the 'Mickey' fish if we want, 'cause I chose it. It's cute, huh? The store guy chose that weird, long, skinny one that swims along the glass because he says it'll keep the aquarium clean, sort of. He sure looks funny, doesn't he?"

"Oh, yeah, Mommy, I chose those dinky ones with the red, green, and blue stripes on the side. Daddy said we could have more than one 'cause they're so small; that's why there are so many. Kenny chose those big black-and-white-striped ones with the strings hanging from their fins." Jan paused, then added knowledgeably, "Angel fish, the store guy said. What're mine called, Daddy?"

"Neon tetras." In a low voice that only Honey could hear, he added, "The 'Mickey' fish is called 'kissing gourami.' "

"D'ya like *my* fish, Mommy?" Mark asked. "It's that bright blue and turquoise one with the long, wavy tail. It looks like it's wearing a skirt, but the guy said it's a boy. Weird, huh? He said you can only have one in a tank, 'cause if there's more 'an one, they start fighting. It must be neat to see, but Daddy said one was enough."

"It's beautiful, Mark. The whole surprise is just wonderful, the best ever. I love everything about it, especially that you put it right here on the coffee table, where it can't fall off and get broken."

"Yeah, Mommy," chimed in Kenny. "Didja see we put the goldfish in, too? Now they got lots of room to swim in, just like us when we go to the beach an' the Iddla tiger shark tries to catch us."

Edith walked into the living room just as the whole group started laughing their heads off at Kenny's last remark. "What's going on in here, anyway? I can't believe you're making all this racket while my youngest grandson is trying to sleep. Ross McDonald, give me that child and then all of you line up and march into the kitchen—lunch is on the table waiting for you. Shoo!"

The tiny infant blinked his eyes at the shimmering lights in front of him, and cooed happily as his admiring Grammy took him into her arms. Charles John—Chas—McDonald had come home.

4

Fish Fry Time

Four days had passed since Chas McDonald had come home to 20281 S.W. Pine Street, and Melody was once again at school. It was an ordinary, everyday Thursday in Mrs. Short's second-grade classroom at Bay View Elementary School. Most of the girls in the class had on their light-brown Brownie dresses, dark-brown felt beanies, with the tan "dancing brownie" on the front, and their dark-brown, ankle-length Brownie socks with the Brownie Scout emblem on the side. Almost all the boys had on their dark-blue and yellow Cub Scout shirts and neckerchiefs and blue jeans. Thursday was the pack and troop meeting day. It was after lunch, and the children were completely immersed in a surprise arithmetic quiz. Outside, the sun shone brightly, and the little kids in kindergarten were just getting out of school for the day. Suddenly, a small, almost imperceptible sound sent a palpable electrical charge crackling throughout the room: "peep." Galvanized into action, all heads turned as one toward the cage on the counter near the door, and, as though prodded by an electrical wire, the entire class stood up without a moment's hesitation. As they began to head toward the counter, Mrs. Short called them to attention. "Yes, children, it seems that our chicks have begun to hatch, and right on time. However, it is a very critical time, and if you excite Rebecca too much, she will leave the chicks, and they won't have the heat they need to dry off after they have finished hatching. The process will take quite some time, so you will have more than ample time to finish your quizzes. I will call you one by one as your eggs begin to open, so you will be able to watch your own eggs hatch. Now please sit down and finish studying."

At her words, the children reluctantly sat down and began solving the arithmetical problems before them. At the end of the quiz, Mrs. Short set them to drawing pictures of what they thought their chicks would look like, and she called them, one by one, to go watch as their eggs began to hatch. When Melody's turn came, just before recess—which she was quite content to forego, this time, in the light of previous factors—she was fascinated by the happenings: first, a single small crack transformed into a series of cracks, forming a web that covered the entire surface of the egg. Then, with each new crack, Melody became more and more anxious, dancing back and forth and hopping from one foot to the other. "Wow! It looks just like when my mommy cracks open a hard-boiled egg," she exclaimed enthusiastically. Her eyes opened wide as the chick's beak broke through the web on the shell and began to stick its head out; the shell then broke completely open and the ungainly little chick flopped out onto the warm area near Rebecca.

The sight was not exactly what Melody was expecting. Disappointed, she remarked, "Ugh! What happened to it? How come he's all wet? It's ugly. And what's all that stringy stuff all over it? It sure doesn't look like the chicks you see in the pictures in books. Is it sick?"

Mrs. Short chuckled at Melody's reaction at the unexpected appearance of the newborn chick. "Well, your chick looks just like the rest of them, you know. Of course, you can't see the rest of them now, because they're under Rebecca, starting to dry out. But, no, there's nothing wrong with your chick—I assure you that it's perfectly normal. Later, during the science lesson, I'll explain everything. And, by the way, that's 'Why,' not 'How come.' "

Unconvinced of the final outcome, Melody continued, "They're *under Rebecca*? But won't they get squashed? I mean, she's so big, and they're so small, and plus there are all the other eggs, too, and they're hard. Or, maybe not? Do all the shells crack up like that?"

"Yes, they do. But, there aren't really that many left now, maybe only three or four, and most of them are just about ready to open. Now, go outside and play for a few minutes. It's been an exciting day, and you need to blow off a little steam. Don't worry—we'll mix recess and PE, so nobody will be late." And with that, Melody shot out of the classroom like greased lightning.

In the days that followed—as the workload grew heavier—the newness and excitement about the chicks began to wear off. For the first few days the children would look surreptitiously toward the cage full of chicks and the hen when they thought Mrs. Short wasn't looking their way. Every once in a while, a little, round, fuzzy head would pop out from under Rebecca's protective wing; the day after the hatchings, the chicks had already completely dried off and the wet, bedraggled vulturelike monsters had transformed into the soft, fuzzy cotton-ball chicks that the class had been expecting. At first, they had begun imitating Rebecca as she marched about the long cage, but when the children came close to them, "oohing" and "awing," they became very shy. When Rebecca clucked at them and began to open her wings like a large protective umbrella, the chicks hurried and hid under her ample spread. Unfortunately, they were too many—even for her—and so there was always at least one of the smaller ones that got pushed out of the way in the frenzy of the moment. They were getting bigger, now, and some of them already had their first real feathers on the tips of their wings and tails.

There had, unfortunately, been two casualties: they had either fallen, or been pushed, into the water trough, and since chicks are not well known for their great swimming abilities, they had met a premature death. Now, there was exactly one chick for each member of the class and the children worked diligently to make sure that no others died. The one black chick had been delegated to Peter; in the absence of a black lamb, they all considered this a reasonable substitute.

Of course, as in every seemingly happy situation, something was just bound to go wrong, and it did. Only twenty-nine of the thirty eggs hatched; it was necessary, therefore, to get rid of the remaining egg, which was a ticking time bomb. After Mr. Watson, the school's janitor, had carefully disposed of the egg in the big Dewey's Dumpster across the street from the school grounds, near the "waving" green field of succulent, not quite mature wheat, the entire class breathed a sigh of relief.

That afternoon, as the children headed toward home, some of the boys started kicking a ball back and forth between them. Suddenly, one of the groups of boys gave a great shout of triumph as one of the team members kicked the ball into the trash can along the way. Boys being boys, Geoffrey jumped into the can so that he could retrieve the ball. Unfortunately, he jumped square on top of the unhatched egg.

It happens from time to time that an unwary skunk will attempt to cross Palisades Road, near the Orange County Airport, or else Mesa Drive, at the same time a rushing car is passing by. The acrid odor that results from these encounters is a subtle and suave perfume when compared to that emanating from the exploding rotten egg. Poor Geoff! The explosion had covered his hair and face with a noxious, greenish-yellow substance. All the children in the vicinity pinched their noses and scattered in all directions. Their catcall, "Skunkhead," continued to reach him long after the callers could no longer be seen.

Melody's first impulse also was to run away like the others—it really wasn't a very pleasant odor at all—but she was torn between her instinct of self-preservation and her desire to help the poor hapless victim of someone else's carelessness. Of course, no one could have foreseen that the ball would end up in the dumpster or that someone would jump in after it—it was not an everyday experience. And, poor Geoff had known nothing about the rotten egg; he was only in the first grade and so he had nothing to do with the project. Mrs. Short's class wasn't even on the same side of the building as the first-grade classrooms.

In the end, Melody's kind heart won out and she went over to help the poor, gagging boy climb out of the trash bin. "Boy, you sure did a good job of it, didn't you?" she asked as she struggled to keep from gagging herself. "It's too bad you didn't know that egg was there, but then your class is on the other side, huh?"

Geoff nodded his head as tears ran down his face, mixing in with the horrible muck that was already there, helping to keep it liquid and gooey. "Yeah, my mommy's going to kill me when she smells me, because these are brand-new clothes, and she said to be careful with them because they have to last me for a while."

"Well," said Melody wisely, "you shouldn't have jumped into the trash can like that with your new clothes on. Trash cans *always* smell bad. And you just happened to jump in right after Mr. Watson put the egg there. That was real bad luck."

"Yeah, well, the ball is mine and the other kids would of left it in there, so I had to go get it out myself."

"Okay, I'll go home with you and maybe together we can convince your mother not to kill you. Then, when I go home, maybe I can convince *my* mommy not to kill *me* 'cause I was just helping you. So, where do you live?"

A week had passed now since that eventful day which had taken place four days after the hatching of the chicks. Geoff's mother, though not particularly excited about the boy's presence, had to concede, after Melody's explanation of the facts, that he was more or less innocent, and he had gotten off with a simple remonstration. Honey, too, had forgiven

Melody for being late; thanks to the unpleasant aura that had permeated Melody's person, she had had more than sufficient evidence to uphold her version of the facts. She had been sent straight to the bathroom to clean herself up. However, even after a thorough cleansing, she still continued to exude a certain distinct odor that was not her usual scent. The fact that no one wanted to stay around her left her slightly subdued. By the following Monday, though, the smell had disappeared and Melody was once again her usual vivacious self and people were a little more secure in getting near her. Geoff still had a slight odor problem, but his, too, was finally beginning to fade.

Just before leaving school that day, Mrs. Short had given all the children in the class a mimeographed copy of a letter from Mr. Barley to take home to their parents. Melody could hardly wait to give it to her mother because it announced the upcoming Science Fair/Open House that would be held on June 8, just a week before the regular school sessions would close for the summer. Of course, there would be a special summer session for all the dumbbells, but Melody didn't have to go unless she wanted to; at this point, however, she was more than ready for the beginning of the summer holidays, and wasn't at all interested in passing her days in a hot classroom.

Anyway, almost all the kids in the school were excited about the Science Fair, because they were all convinced that their projects were going to win. Melody felt sorry for all of the other participants, but she knew that their class project was the best in the whole school—just look at the big success they'd had, and the pictures they'd drawn were really neat, too. Veronica and Kate got to write up the story; she had to admit her own handwriting was dreadful, so she wasn't upset about that. Anyway, some of the pictures that she drew were going to be in the exhibit, so that was okay. The only sad part was that after the exhibit they would have to give Rebecca and her chicks back to Mr. Cooper. Her own chick, Blondie, was just like almost all the others. Almost all the pale yellow fluff had given way to reddish-brown pin feathers, with a touch of black on the tips of the wing feathers. It was much bigger than the little fluffy ball of eleven days ago, but it was also much more interesting now.

Important announcements in the McDonald home were made at the dinner table when all members of the family were present. Dinner with the McDonalds was never a quiet affair in any case, but when there were announcements to make, especially like the ones that were to be made that evening, the noise level usually rose to a loud roar. The loud buzzing around the table provoked by Melody's announcement of the school's Science Fair/Open House was faintly reminiscent of that produced by a whole swarm of bumblebees; everyone loved an Open House because there were so many fun things to see, plus the refreshment tables seemed to never become emptied of the luscious goods provided by the members of the PTA. Jan and Mark were always jealous of the schoolgirl Melody, because she got to do so many neat things while they had to stay at home and be bored all day.

The announcement that really got everyone going, though, was Ross's: "Okay, kids, listen up. Who can tell me what's going on next weekend? I'll give you a hint: when it's alive, it lives in the sea, and when it's dead, it's good to eat."

"Yuck, something in the sea can also be good to eat?" Melody, who had never been a great fan of seafood, was completely at a loss.

"I know, I know!" shouted Jan and Mark together. "Fish!"

"And how is fish best cooked?" inquired their father innocently. Melody answered, "Fish sticks."

"Fried!" responded the younger chorus. "The Fish Fry! Yippee!" At this, all four of the older McDonald kids got up and started dancing around the table. Even the seafood-hating Melody was quite content to eat the deep-fried Icelandic cod that had been served every year since 1945 at the Costa Mesa Park.

The annual Costa Mesa Fish Fry is a fund-raising activity offered by the Lion's Club of Costa Mesa, California. It not only offered excellent fried cod, but there was also a great number of other attractions that made it popular for all age groups. These attractions included a large Ferris wheel, bumper cars, a roller coaster, and different booths. There were games and contests, including the Miss Costa Mesa beauty pageant and the cutest-baby contest. Of course, there were also a number of speeches offered by the Lion's Club president and the city mayor. The aura of excitement that permeated the entire zone was palpable and no one, child or adult, was entirely immune to its pull. This year, the proceeds would go toward repairs for the bleachers surrounding the baseball field in back of the park itself. The baseball park was a result of the funds gathered at the first Fish Fry (way back in 1945).

The next three days seemed to move with snail-like sluggishness for the McDonald children, but finally Friday, June 3, rolled around.

Melody wasn't sure if she would survive the hours between five A.M. and six P.M. Going to school would help a little, but then the question would be if Mrs. Short would survive five hours with twenty-seven very anxious children with only one thing on their minds: the Fish Fry. They didn't even pay the attention due to Rebecca and the twenty-seven chicks that morning.

"Children, may I please have your attention? We have only three more school days until the Science Fair/Open House, and we really need to start getting things in order, if we wish to win the prize." Mr. Barley has said that there will be a free ice cream party for all winners, if it's a class that wins; and a free subscription to the *Weekly Reader*, the newspaper for elementary-school students, if the winner is in one of the older classes. Speaking of which, if any of you wish to subscribe to the *Weekly Reader*, you must let me know by the end of next week. That way, you can begin receiving it as soon as possible. I will give you all the subscription form at the end of school today. Are there any questions?"

Melody raised her hand.

"Yes Melody?"

"But, Mrs. Short, aren't there four school days, counting today?"

"There are, but on the fourth day, everything has to already be in the cafeteria because the judging will begin just after school begins. Then, after lunch, all of the classes will be allowed to look at all of the entries. The winners will be announced that evening at the beginning of the PTA meeting, before we go into the different rooms for the Open House. Of course, we also need to decorate our room so that your families will have an idea of what we have been doing during the second half of the school year."

As the class digested this last bit of information, Mrs. Short added, "I would truly appreciate your cooperation for these last few days. Now, I have here three tickets for any ride at the Fish Fry tonight, tomorrow or Sunday. I'll give one to the three who get the best grades on their arithmetic assignment. Please turn to page two hundred twenty-five and do the exercises that are listed on the board." And with that promise, all twenty-seven heads bowed down over their desks, and the only sounds that could be heard—apart from an occasional giggle—were the scratching of their pencils on the paper covering their wooden desks, and Mrs. Short, who gave an almost inaudible sigh of relief.

"Now look, you guys, before we leave, we need to get a few things clear. First, don't go wandering off on your own. Your mother and I seem to have a lifetime membership with the Lost and Found booth. It would be really nice if for once we could all stay together and not have to go pick someone up. You all agree with me, don't you?" At this, four little heads nodded vigorously, while a skeptical Honey met Ross's eyes over said heads with a sardonic grin. Her eyes conveyed the message, "Sure thing, bud." Ross shrugged and continued.

"Second, Kenny, what is your last name?" "McDonald." "Mark?" "McDonald." "Jan?" "McDonald." "Melody?" "McDonald." "Very good, all of you. Now, just in case you forget your promise and end up for the nth time at the Lost and Found booth, please remember to tell them your last name along with your first, okay?" Again, the same nodding heads and the same sardonic grin.

"Now, for the third item on the list, have you all gone to the bathroom? As you know, there are bathrooms there at the park, but I truly doubt that they will be very clean for now with all the people at the Fish Fry. So, if any of you need to go to the bathroom, do so now or forever hold your peace." They all nodded again and Mark asked, "What peas, Daddy? You haven't given us any peas. What do we need peas for?" Melody tried to explain what Daddy was trying to tell them. "Not the kind you eat, the other kind. It means, you dummy, that you have to wait to go potty. You can't do it there." Honey ran to get a little sweater for Chas for later on, wiping her eyes and holding her sides as she left the room. Ross rolled his eyes toward the ceiling, and corrected his son and daughter, "Thank you for your 'help,' Melody, but that's 'peace,' not 'peas.' Hold your peace means to not complain." Again, all heads nodded, but the grin was missing. Honey had decided to wait until the end of the interview before rejoining the group.

"Last, we're only going to stay for a little while, just to see what's going on and maybe go on a ride or two, so when Mommy and I say it's time to come home, I don't want any complaining, or we won't be coming back tomorrow. Is everything clear enough for you?" Once again, the heads all nodded.

"Okay then, I think we're ready to go. Honey, have you gotten whatever you went to get yet? We're all ready to go, here." Honey reentered the room, put Chas into the baby carriage, and they all piled into the car.

The trip had taken only ten minutes, but the children's enthusiasm had made it seem more like ten hours. As they drove into the parking lot, Mark had already started to open the door so that he could jump out as soon as the car stopped. Ross made a mental note to the list of requirements that would be repeated tomorrow afternoon before returning to the festival: do not open the car door until the car has stopped. It seemed useless to comment on it now, as they were all out of the car by that time, anyway.

After rounding up the scattered group in one place, Ross admonished them, "Okay kids, please don't forget your promise." The nods were once again repeated. "Now, what do you think—shall we start off with something calm first, like maybe the hammerheads?" He was not referring to the bell-ringing hammers. Ross was the bravest man the McDonald kids had ever met, and it was probably this bravery that pushed him to certain extremes, but Melody and Mark were all for it.

They tried convincing Jan, but she wasn't about to go with them. "Uh-uh. No way, you guys go; I'll stay here and keep Mommy and Chas company." Kenny was rarin' to go, but he was too little, so he stayed behind with Honey, Jan, and Chas while Ross and the other two quickly got in line for the hair-raising ride.

At long last, their turn rolled around. The kids started clambering onto the seats aboard the two-man compartment. Just as Mark was being pulled up by Melody, he felt an unfamiliar hand on his shoulder. Then an unfamiliar voice said, "Excuse me, young man, but you're not tall enough for this ride. Sir, your son will have to stay here. The young lady can go aboard, accompanied by an adult."

"All right. Mark, do you see Mommy over there? Go stand with her and the others, and Mickey and I will be back as quick as a bunny hop." After making sure that Mark was headed in the right direction, Ross jumped on board the ride and fastened his and Melody's seat belts, slamming the door closed. As Ross and Melody's compartment swung rapidly to the highest point of the device, Mark turned around to wave to them, but they were too busy trying to keep their heads upright to see him; they didn't see the gleam that came to his eyes as his gaze fell upon the Ferris wheel. After that they only had time to grab the bar in front of them and hold on for dear life. The hammer went up and down, the compartment swirling around with breathtaking speed, for five long (and to Melody, interminable) minutes. When the beating and swirling ended at last, a very disheveled and wide-eyed pair of McDonalds got down from the car. Melody, giggling and slightly hysterical, turned to Ross and inquired, "Can we do it again?"

Chuckling, Ross answered, "Well, seeing as how your face is green and I can hardly stand up, I think we'll pass on it tonight and go for it tomorrow afternoon. What do you think—shall we go join the others and take a turn on the merry-go-round? Do you see them anywhere?"

"Oh, look; there they are, over there waiting for us at the edge of the crowd behind the barrier. But I don't see Mark there with them. I wonder where he went."

They quickly went and joined Honey and the other kids enthusiastically, and Ross asked Honey, "Hey, where's Mark?"

"Isn't he with you? I haven't seen him since the three of you went to stand in line."

"Oh, dear, it looks like somebody forgot rule number one. Well, let's go and see if we can find him at the usual spot." Just as they were taking off, they heard the loud crackle of static as the loudspeaker came on. Honey and Ross looked at each other and shrugged their shoulders resignedly: it wasn't the first time, nor, they imagined, would it be the last. They headed automatically toward the Lost and Found booth.

The voice on the loudspeaker said: "We have found a young boy of approximately four years old at the base of the Ferris wheel. He's blond, is wearing a red and white striped T-shirt and jeans, and says his name is 'Mark.' He's not sure of his age and can't seem to remember his last name. Will Mark's parents please come and claim him? Thank you."

Ross and Honey felt as though a thousand eyes were fixed upon them, burning holes through the backs of their heads. "At the base of the Ferris wheel? My gosh, how in the world did he get there and whatever was he planning on doing?" she whispered.

"I haven't got a clue. I can't even begin to imagine what he was doing there, but what do you think of just leaving him where he is?—then, nobody has to know who he belongs to."

Before Honey could respond to this audacious suggestion, she felt someone tugging on her skirt. "Mommy, Kenny go get Mark?"

Ross answered, "Yes, Kenny, but I think we'll *all* go and get the young rapscallion. Come on, you all, let's go." As they neared the booth, Ross continued, "Now, you guys, don't say a word, okay? I'll handle this." The usual head-nodding followed this statement. *Yeah, sure,* he thought, *and my name is 'Donald Duck.'* The children held back as they reached the booth; Ross looked over the counter and discovered Mark sitting calmly on a stool and eating a piece of fish. Looking up, the truant boy smiled, stood up, and walked around the counter to join the rest of the family.

Calling to the man behind the counter, Ross announced himself. "Excuse me, sir. My name is Ross McDonald, and I, unfortunately at the moment, am the father of this 'lost and found' item. I just wanted to introduce you to the whole family, because I'm sure you'll be seeing quite a lot of them in the next few days. They all have a very strange tendency to disappear at the most inopportune moments. Now, this young lady here is Melody, followed by the charming Jan. You have met Mark. He is closely followed by Kenny. It's odd that you found Mark by the base of the Ferris wheel, because it's actually Kenny who is most interested in mechanics. I guess it was just a question of opportunity and timing. This is my wife, Honey, with our youngest, Chas. I'm not really expecting any problems with the last two; it's just a matter of form."

The Chamber of Commerce volunteer, bewildered by this rather unexpected speech, held out his hand. "Doug Morton, here. It's a real pleasure, Mr. McDonald. We really do enjoy getting to know the participants in the Fish Fry. Your son has all the makings of a fine future mechanic; when we found him, he had already begun unscrewing the bolts at the base of the motor. Thank goodness, we found him before he had done any real damage; he isn't strong enough to loosen them very much. All we had to do was tighten them back up again. No real harm done."

Flabbergasted, Honey managed to squeak out, "Loosened bolts? How did he do that? They must have already been a little loose. I mean, he's only four years old, and I don't think even Ross would be able to unscrew a bolt without a wrench."

Embarrassed, Mr. Morton continued, "Well, as to that, actually, he did have a wrench. Didn't he bring it with him?" He paused before continuing. "I suppose that look means no. I guess one of the machinists must have inadvertently forgotten it and left it lying there at the base of the ride. That's probably what attracted young Mark's attention in the first place. As I said, though, there's no real harm done. Of course, we'll talk to the machinist about this tomorrow morning when he shows up for work, as he has already gone home for the evening. Don't worry about it; it wasn't the boy's fault. Now, if you will please excuse me, I need to speak to that man over there. It's been a real pleasure to have met you.

Enjoy the rest of your evening here." With that he turned and began talking to a distinguished elderly man, who turned out to be one of the promoters of the event.

"I can't believe what just happened," Honey sputtered. "Whatever possessed them to leave a *wrench* at the base of one of those rides, where *anyone* could get to it? Mark, whatever were you doing there at the base of that ride? You could have been hurt! Don't you ever do that again! Ross why don't you say something to him?!"

"Well, I might, if you'd stop yelling at him long enough to let me get a word in edgewise, but actually, I think you're doing a good enough job of it by yourself. Mark, your mother is right; just what do you think you were going to do there? I am pretty sure I had told you to go stand with your mother and the other kids. In fact, unless my eyes had deceived me, I am pretty sure that I had seen you head in that direction. So, why were you there in the first place?"

A strange silence fell over the entire family. It was rare that a member of the family became speechless, but at that moment Mark seemed incapable of articulating a single word. Odd, strangled sounds issued forth, but there was no clear meaning to them. "Would you mind repeating that, Mark? It wasn't very clear, so you'll have to speak up a bit so that all of us can hear. So, let's give it another try, okay? Why were you at the base of the Ferris wheel with a wrench in your hand?"

With a terrified look at his mother's white face and his father's big, strong, and *very* heavy hands, Mark tried again. "Uh," he managed to get out. "Uh, 'cause it was there?"—he said it as a question.

"And how did you know that it was there?" his father continued. "Uh, 'cause I saw it shine in the lights when I turned around to wave at you guys. You didn't see me, though," he added glumly.

"He waved to us. Why didn't you just go to your mother and *then* wave to us? No, don't bother to answer; I'm sure there's a logical excuse hidden there somewhere—sooner or later it'll come to the surface. Okay, let's pack up and leave; I have a headache, and it has nothing at all to do with the hammer ride."

"But Daddy, you said we could go on the merry-go-round!" "We just got here!" "It's not fair! Just 'cause Mark tried to undo the Ferris wheel, how come *we* can't stay and go on rides?" "Cotton candy, please." The outraged children raised their voices in a chorus of disapproval at this latest act of injustice, caused by the mishaps of the newly elected social outcast. Ross remained steadfast in his decision until he over-heard Jan's caustic comments to her brother, which were followed by Mark's response.

"Good goin', Mark. Couldn't you have waited a little while before getting into trouble? What a dumbbell," said Jan.

"I'm sorry, I didn' mean' ta get in trouble. I couldn' help it, it was just shinin' there like that an' I just *had* to see what it was. When I saw it, I forgetted where I was—it looked just like that one I got for my birthday, only bigger." Gone was the memory of that luscious fish he had been given; tears streamed down his face for the first time that evening, and Ross relented.

"Okay, we can go on the merry-go-round. Everyone hold on to someone else's hand, and please don't someone else get lost. The next one of you that gets lost, gets left behind. No ifs, ands, or buts. I might be persuaded to buy some cotton candy, but that's it. Let's go." With that, he took hold of Mark's hand and the seven of them took off in search of fun, but not adventure; there had already been way too much of that for one evening, even for the McDonalds.

Saturday morning dawned bright and early, but Melody was up and around even earlier than the sun. Stretched out, she was avidly reading her *Giant Golden Book of Nature*. It was so interesting because it didn't talk about just different kinds of animals, but also about plants and the earth itself and about how it was put together. It also talked about how the sea and the ocean got salty and all about tides and the pull of the moon. And it talked about the universe and all the planets, and the composition of the atmosphere, and why we can breathe the air around us. But, the best part of all was when they described the different species of animals. It explained about the different groups and what their various characteristics were: for example, it talked about how mammals all had at least one hair (how weird that was; she couldn't figure out where the dolphin's hairs were—she'd have to ask Mommy about that when she got up, she guessed. What was even weirder was that she had always thought that dolphins were *fish*—they sure *looked* like fish, anyway. And look at that neat spider, the giant golden garden spider; she'd never seen one like it yet, but it sure looked interesting, with those big black legs, and the round black body with all those neat yellow stripes all over. It was really cool. Lost in her thoughts and fantasizing about how neat it would be to have one in their front yard (with its giant, impenetrable web, of course) on Halloween night, Melody hadn't noticed that she was no longer alone. Mark's voice hit her like the Santa Ana winds, causing her face to burn bright red as she jumped three feet in the air; a remarkable feat—worthy of a circus performer—considering the fact that she was lying on her back at the moment of impact.

"Hey, Mickey, what're ya lookin' at there? C'n I see it, too?"

"Mark, don't you know you shouldn't sneak up on people like that? I could have had a heart attack, you know."

"Oh, sorry; I did make noise, ya know. Hey!" he exclaimed, looking down at the open page in her lap, "What a neat spider. I saw one like it the other day in the backyard, near the rabbits. It was really neat, even better'n the picture in your book."

"You did? Okay, let's go right now and see if it's still there. Hurry, before it goes away!" Excited by the thought, Melody slid off the couch and headed quickly toward the kitchen door.

"Hey, Mickey wait, we can't go out there now. We still got our pj's on, and the grass is all wet outside. Mommy'll get real mad if we get all wet."

"Oh, Mark, what a dummy you are. We always sleep outside in the tent and it's too hot outside for the grass to be wet. What difference will it make if we just go out there now?"

"What are you two doing out here at this hour of the morning?" Jan's sleepy voice inquired, interrupting their very important discussion. "The sun's not even shining yet."

"Yeah, it is, but you can't see it 'cause your eyes are still shut. Anyway, Mark found a neat spider and we're going to see if it's still there."

Jan's eyes suddenly popped open, announcing that she was now wide awake. "Don't you dare bring that thing in the house, 'cause I'll tell Mommy if you do, and then they won't let us go to the Fish Fry this afternoon. We didn't get to do much last night 'cause of you, Mark, so don't go gettin' all of us in trouble again, you hear?"

"And if they hear you yellin' like that they won't let us go, either. So, if they won't let us go if you tell 'em, it's not too smart to go tell 'em, huh?" Melody retorted logically. "And anyway, I didn't say I was bringing it in, I just wanted to see if it's as purty as it looks in the book. Just 'cause you and Mommy don't like spiders, it doesn't mean they aren't neat or anything. And don't be so bossy all the time. Maybe you'll be a teacher when you grow up."

Just as Jan was puffing up, ready to pronounce her rebuttal, Honey walked into the room, making her decide that perhaps it was better to just forget the whole thing. In any case, she'd stopped Melody from bringing the spider into the house, and that was the most important thing.

"So, what are the three of you discussing so early this morning? I think we need to go get something into our tummies, and then go out and do some yard work out in the backyard. Daddy wants to mow the lawn this afternoon, but we have a pretty good idea that there are a number of toys hidden in the middle of the grass that need to be picked up before he can mow. We have to get that done fast, because then all the cut grass has to be raked up and thrown into the trash can. So, what are we waiting for?"

The grumbly, growly attitudes of the three kids changed quickly into whoops as they ran into the kitchen, waiting for Mommy to come and put their cereal bowls at their places. You never knew what long-lost treasures were to be found hidden among the long blades of grass, and afterward, it was always fun to go jump into the clumps of raked up grass. Of course, it got kind of itchy if the cut grass got up inside your shirt, but no one worried about that, because they'd go take a bath after they had finished with everything. Mark and Melody winked at each other over their bowls of Cheerios as they thought about another "treasure" that they could look for while they were looking for toys, without any interference from Jan. They smirked at Jan as she mouthed at them, "You better not let Mommy see it."

The rest of the morning rushed past them without notable incidents. Mark and Melody searched carefully through the grass for any hidden treasures, all the while heading carefully toward the rabbit pen in an unobtrusive manner. Of course, they also had to be careful of eagle-eyed Jan, who was trying to observe every step they made. They took their chance when Kenny yelled out that he had found something of Jan's—her favorite doll, in fact—that had been missing for quite some time. They ran quickly toward their goal while Jan jumped up and down with her baby pressed to her chest. The giant yellow and black spider was still there, waiting patiently in the center of his web for some unsuspecting insect to come up against the sticky threads. As they observed its movements in complete silence, awed by its beauty, they also noticed the strong, short legs near the mouth that served, they imagined, for shoveling the unsuspecting insects, which got trapped in the invisible web, into its mouth; the only reason they could see the web was because they knew it was there, and because they weren't looking toward the sun. "Wow," Melody whispered reverently, "you're right; it is even neater than it looks in that book. Maybe if it gets enough bugs to eat, it'll stay here until Halloween; it would be just perfect for the decorations for my birthday party, huh?" At that moment she looked up and noticed Honey eyeing them suspiciously. "We'd better get back to work before she gets Daddy to kill it. C'mon."

A number of other missing treasures were found that morning, and even a few that were completely new had been discovered. The best one had been a little green toad—one of the kind with little red cheeks and the big grin. All but Jan, who resolutely looked the other way, gathered around the lucky finder—Mark, this time—trying to get a good look at it. They also glimpsed a mean old alligator lizard, but it slithered out of everyone's way before anyone could get their hands on it. It was just as well, because alligator lizards are not well known for their mild temper, and they had already seen what could happen if the stupid lizard got mad at them. One time, Missy had confronted one, and it bit her on the leg and didn't let go until Ross had decapitated it. They were *not* something to tangle with, unless you were ready to pay the consequences. It wasn't really worth it; Missy had had to wear a bandage for a week until the wound healed, and then she kept on limping for at least another week. They were kind of pretty, though, with their yellowish head and dark-brown-and-tan bodies with the black-and-brown checkerboard stripes, that made them look a lot like those Indian bead bracelets. Oh, well. . . . All the McDonald kids had more or less learned to leave them alone.

After all perishable and breakable items had been found and removed from the knee-deep grass, Ross had gotten to work pushing the lawn mower in even rows. As he forced the mower ahead, the kids worked behind him: one wielding a rake, one pushing and another pulling the wheelbarrow, and one gathering up armfuls of the cut grass and placing it in the barrow. When Melody finished raking up, she helped Jan pile it onto the ever-growing mound. Honey sat comfortably on the chaise lounge, watching the others work as she rocked little Chas to sleep.

They had all decided to skip the grass-jumping contest, because they were all too anxious to go to the Fish Fry. Ross had promised them that, if they behaved themselves, he would let them stay until dark. He nurtured some doubts as to their ability to keep their promise, and he was willing to be a little lenient in his decisions, but . . . he got a headache just thinking about what had happened the preceding evening, and he was not at all sure of being able to face another, similar experience two days in a row. He was particularly adamant in his instructions that afternoon before they left, repeating them several times, and insisted that each child repeat them after him. He added a new rule, too: "You will turn your head the other way if you see something shine, and you will take Mommy's hand for strength in resisting the temptation to see what it is." He hoped fervently that his forbearance would pay off.

Of course, now they were here, and rule number one had already been forgotten by everyone but Chas, who, of course, was not an independent entity and definitely not ambulatory. Ross rolled his eyes, shrugged his shoulders and took off after his scattering offspring, leaving Honey to pull out the baby stroller and position their youngest, and most obedient, child comfortably into its waiting protection. The only problem was that this usually entailed the use of at least three hands. Just as she was shaking her head and wondering how she was going to accomplish this feat, a familiar voice greeted her nervously.

"Ah, Mrs. McDonald, we meet again. Do you need some help there with that stroller? Let me pull it out and set it up for you. Well now, where is young Mark? I'm sure he isn't out there wielding a wrench today; all the workers checked and double-checked to make sure that there were no tools left lying around this morning. Oh, by the way, they're just beginning the cutest-baby contest. Why don't you enter your little boy, Chas, isn't he? The prize is a full-size layette with a gift certificate for fifty dollars for baby clothes at The Watermelon Seed and a month's free diaper service. Good luck!" And with that, the hapless Mr. Morton ran off to his waiting Lost and Found booth, hoping fervently that he would *not* be seeing the McDonalds there today.

Just as Mr. Morton was entering the haven of his booth, a breathless Ross arrived at the car, followed by four eager children. "Well, dear, I found them—they were at all four corners of the park. Mickey was just getting ready to slide under the rope surrounding the pony rides. Mark was at the top of the tail of the airplane, getting ready to jump. Jan was staring greedily at the goldfish bowl, trying to judge how easy it would be to throw the Ping-Pong ball into it so she could win one. On the other hand, Kenny here was already in line, waiting to get his plate of fried fish. How he thought he was going to buy it without money, I have no idea. I do have an idea now as to what our four eldest children would like to do today. I know what I'd like to do, but we did promise, and they worked hard all morning. I'd have thought they wouldn't have enough energy left to get into trouble. Oh, well, shall we get going? Oh, sorry I didn't help you get the stroller out. How did you do it by yourself?"

As Ross stopped to catch his breath, Honey answered his question. "Well, an acquaintance of ours passed by just after you took off. You remember Mr. Morton of the Lost and Found booth, I'm sure. He was very nice, actually, although he took off in a great hurry. Perhaps he saw you coming with 'young Mark.' He did mention a contest coming up soon, and invited us to participate with Chas. The prizes aren't at all bad. We could at least try."

The words had barely been uttered when the loudspeaker crackled with static and Ross, wincing, looked around to make sure that all of his dear children were gathered around. They were. His sigh of relief was accompanied by the announcement that the cutest-baby contest would be starting in five minutes and that all of those who hadn't signed up, but still wished to participate, could do so now.

"Well, let's do it. Chas hasn't broken any rules, so he deserves to have his chance."

Seated at the long picnic table, the McDonalds were enthusiastically discussing the afternoon's activities as they indulged themselves with the enticingly flaky Icelandic cod and the French fried potatoes. Although Chas hadn't won first prize, he had been one of the runners-up and been awarded a month's diaper service from the Busy Stork diaper company. All things considered, Honey was quite pleased, because with five young children, life was, to say the least, hectic, and the elimination of the very necessary task of diaper washing was a big relief, even if it would only be for a month.

After the loud applause for all the winners, the McDonalds headed off as a group toward the various rides. Naturally, Melody insisted that, since she was the biggest and should have first choice, they should all head toward the pony rides. But instead, they went on the merry-go-round, the idea presented by Kenny. Afterward, Mark thought it would be neat to go on the Ferris wheel. All heads shifted in that direction and, after inspecting Mark's pocket, they all thought the suggested ride was highly feasible and would be quite enjoyable. The wheel wasn't high enough to cause nausea, but it was lofty enough that they could observe the whole park and see what they wanted to do next. After a family vote, it was decided that Melody's ponies couldn't wait any longer, especially because they had noticed that the line wasn't getting any shorter, the sun wasn't quite as high in the sky as it had been before, and that Melody had a very sour look on her face; they all agreed that if they put it off again, it was probable that they wouldn't make it in time and Melody would definitely not be pleased and would possibly ruin the rest of the day.

The four plastic bags, each containing a goldfish, attested to the fact that someone in the family had good aim and judgment of the amount of force essential to sending four Ping-Pong balls into the small goldfish bowls. Jan had wanted to go there as soon as they got off the ponies, but Ross—knowing that even goldfish, inhabitants of a watery home, could suffer from seasickness if subjected to certain conditions—had decided that it would probably be better if they were to go to the concession just before going to eat. Instead, they went on Ross's favorite ride: the bumper cars. After that, letting Honey have her fun without having to worry about Chas, they all jumped aboard the merry-go-round one more time, letting Honey, Ross, and Chas sit in the swan seat. Jan grabbed a rabbit; Mark, a lion; Kenny, a zebra; and Melody. . . . Did you guess it: a frog? Melody, as always, was unpredictable; with ten horses there, she chose the only frog. As the ride started to gyrate, people pointed fingers and stared at the unusual sight of the petite, very feminine-looking little girl seated astride such a strange mount. There was nothing to do about it—some things never change.

Later, after all the excitement died down and the McDonalds finished eating, Ross proposed a last-minute suggestion. "What do you all think about one more round on the Ferris wheel?" Even Melody, the most adventurous of the group, greeted this suggestion with a stony glare.

"But Daddy! We just ate and our tummies are full. Yuck!" A resounding chorus of "Yuck!" rose up around him.

"Okay, then, what do you all say to a nice sno-cone and then we can be on our way home. It's late and we've had a very long day. Tomorrow's Sunday, so we want to get an early start after church. They're having the finals in the Harbor Baseball League—the Newport Dolphins against the Costa Mesa Bulls. It should be pretty good. We don't want to miss that now, do we?"

"Yea!" "Can we play baseball with them?" "I'm rooting for the Bulls" "Tutti-frutti sno-cone, please." The chorus rose up again in complete joy and Ross turned toward Honey, "See, I can be as diplomatic as the next guy. I've got them ready to go without even having to get mad. I finally figured it out: you've got to suggest something you know they don't want, together with something they do. That's perfect child psychology at work."

The rest was easy; they traipsed wearily to the car as Melody and Ross ate their root beer sno-cone; Jan, her cherry; Mark, his lime; Kenny, his tutti-frutti; and Honey, her raspberry sno-cone. There were no discussions as the four kids crawled into the backseat. They were already sound asleep by the time the car drove up into the driveway. Honey hurried into the house and put Chas into the crib and ran back out to help Ross carry the other kids back into their bedrooms.

"I'm okay, Mommy," Melody mumbled sleepily. "I can walk into the house by myself. It sure was fun today." As she stumbled into the house, she placed the goldfish, which she still clutched tightly in her hand, onto the coffee table, near the aquarium. It rolled uncomfortably in its sack, next to the other three sacks that would soon be placed into the aquarium with the other fish.

Somehow, Honey managed to get the two girls into their pajamas and into bed without waking them up. She didn't notice that Melody was clenching a leg of the little green toad with the red cheeks, but there was no longer a wide grin.

5

The Science Fair and the Open House

"Mommy, hurry up; it's getting late and I want to play tetherball before school starts. Ouch!" An anxious Melody hopped from foot to foot as Honey struggled to braid her eldest daughter's hair.

"I could hurry faster if you would stop moving around so much. I wouldn't pull your hair, either, if you could just stop dancing for a couple of minutes. I don't know where you get all this energy; I would have thought that after all the moving around we did this last weekend, you'd have calmed down a bit." She twisted the rubber band around Melody's braid and said, "Okay, you're off!"

Melody grabbed her books from the buffet and raced toward the door. "Bye, Mommy, see ya later. Today at school we're getting the classroom ready for the Open House on Wednesday. Maybe I'll be a little late this afternoon."

Honey looked over at her daughter and noted that the girl was forgetting something important. "Hey, don't forget your lunch." Honey handed the Caspar-the-Friendly-Ghost lunchbox over to Melody as she rushed back in and gave her mother a peck on the cheek.

Honey gave a sigh of relief as she watched Hurricane Mickey barrel down the street. The other kids were still in bed; this last weekend really had been hectic. Of course, after Friday evening's escapade and Saturday's hard work and running around the Fish Fry, Sunday had actually seemed quite calm. Yesterday, after arriving home after church, they changed their clothes and leisurely took off for the last afternoon of the Fish Fry. It was almost over, but there were still two more big events that would be taking place during the afternoon. One of these was the Miss Costa Mesa contest. No one in the family was particularly interested in who won, but Ross just wanted to show off his beautiful wife, who, regardless of the fact that she was the mother of five children, he felt was much prettier than any of the girls who participated in the contest.

Heck, she was only twenty-seven years old, and looked about twenty-one—the same age as many of the girls that had entered the contest. Just before the final judging, the twenty hopefuls paraded across the stage before the judges and the crowd in their uniform dark-blue, one-piece bathing suits. Mark's unsolicited, loudly pronounced comment, "Why do their legs jiggle like orange jell-o?," was greeted with gurgles of suppressed laughter by the judges and the crowd alike while another spectator expressed his approval, "Well said, boy; go join the judges on their stand." Jan and Melody guffawed loudly and bent over in totally unladylike hilarity, completely belying their parents' nonchalant glances in all directions as they attempted to feign ignorance of the identity of the "new judge." The moment passed as the spokesman for the official judges stood up and reached for the microphone. After announcing the first and second runners-up, he cleared his voice and announced, "And the new Miss Costa Mesa for nineteen sixty is . . . number fifteen, April Tennyson." The girl was a tall, willowy, flaxen-haired blond—the complete opposite of petite, dark-haired Honey.

As the loudspeaker once again emitted static before announcing the imminent closure of the Fried Fish stand, Ross and Honey stared down guiltily at the four smiling faces before them. Of course, no one was missing and they all returned their stares innocently. With that, they all took off and, after buying bright pink cotton candy for everyone but the sleeping Chas, headed toward the tall picket fence that separated the regular Costa Mesa Park from the Harbor Area Baseball Park. The league finals weren't actually a bona fide part of the annual Fish Fry, but they took place so close together on the final day that almost everyone attended the game as a general rule. Of course, it was a little difficult to obtain tickets for a family as big as the McDonald family, so they usually went and watched it over the part of the fence nearest to the bleachers. It had been an outstanding game, with the Costa Mesa Bulls now barely beating the Newport Dolphins, six to five, in the bottom of the tenth inning. Honey ended up having to pay Ross and Mickey twenty-five cents each, because she had been sure (being a Newport Beach girl herself) that the Dolphins would have won.

They were filing out of the park when Melody suddenly remembered that she still had the ticket that she had won at school on Friday. Naturally. She always remembered things inconveniently at the last minute so that they could prolong their fun. Some things never changed, and Melody was easily included in those things. After discovering that the ponies had already been packed and taken away, she looked around with a downcast look and noticed that the hammerhead ride was still up. "Daddy," she wheedled, "you said we could go on the hammerheads again. C'mon, let's go!" No one was waiting in line, so they scrambled immediately into place, and the ride took off once again, scrambling their poor heads and stomachs. At the end, they jumped queasily to the ground, Melody disdaining the hand proffered her by Ross. "Naw," she declared, "I'm a big girl now."

Passing by the Ferris wheel, they noticed Mr. Morton as he supervised the dismantling of the big ride. "Hi, Mark," he shouted, grinning. "Wanna come help out?" Honey had immediately squelched the idea, although both Mark and Kenny had demonstrated a definite gleam of hope in their eyes. "I think we'll pass on it this year, if you don't mind. Maybe in another ten or fifteen years you might ask again." All of them had waved good-bye to the others. Honey was quite relieved to be leaving and Mr. Morton was definitely glad that he had survived the last two days without another close encounter with "young Mark."

And now, sitting alone on the living room couch, she discovered that she was exhausted. It was understandable, but she really didn't have time to be exhausted. She had a house to clean, animals to feed, kids to wake up (she would put this off as long as possible, for obvious reasons), clothes to fold, lunch to cook . . .

A loud wail from the back bedroom reminded her of other more urgent tasks at hand—diapers to change (thank goodness, the diaper service would begin tomorrow), bottles to wash and fill. She felt her hair turn gray and her skin wrinkle at the mere thought. *I'm really much too old for this. I need a vacation.* She got up and wearily headed toward the bedroom to change Chas's diaper.

That afternoon when Melody returned home from school Honey called her excitedly into the backyard. "Hey, Mickey, come out here. I have something neat to show you. Hurry!"

Melody raced out the back door, knowing that if her mother said something was neat, it most likely was. She tried to think of what it could possibly be as she dropped her books onto the porch and ran to the back chain-link fence, where Honey was waiting for her. There was someone else on the other side of the fence. She recognized him as she reached her mother's side. "Oh hi, Ian. What's wrong with Pansy?" The big white sheep with the black face was lying on her side, bleating mournfully.

Sixteen-year-old Ian Mackenzie gave a soft chuckle. "Oh, there's nothing wrong with her, she's just getting ready to lamb. I'm hoping to be able to show the lamb at the fair in July. It's the first time for her, though, and she's sort of feeling the pain. Do you want to watch?" It was a more-or-less rhetorical question; Ian knew perfectly well that a team of wild elephants wouldn't have been able to pull Melody away from the scene, and that even had they been able to do that task, they would have had to tie her up with a ten-inch-thick rope afterward. Melody knew she didn't have to answer, so she just crept up as close as she could to the fence. She could have easily climbed over it, but she really thought that Honey might draw the line at that, and besides, she didn't want to upset the already nervous Pansy. Pansy was just a little over a year old; last year she had been Ian's 4-H-club project. She had won him a blue ribbon at the county fair last year and a lot of people had made offers to buy her from him, but he had become too fond of her; he decided to keep her and raise other lambs to sell at the fair.

As she crouched down so she could watch more closely, Pansy gave an exceptionally loud bleat and stretched out abruptly while her body was racked by a particularly strong contraction. At the end of the movement, Melody saw a pair of tiny hoofs pop out, followed by a rumpled head, and at last the rest of a tiny lamb fell to the ground, struggling to get out of the wet membrane in which it had passed the last five months as it grew in preparation for the birthing cycle. Pansy turned her head toward the newborn lamb and nuzzled it tenderly with her nose. However, she wasn't able to accomplish more than this, because her swollen body was suddenly racked with pain as she gave out another bleat filled with fear. "Ian, what's happening? Is there really something wrong, this time?"

Ian smiled kindly at Melody's worried face and turned toward Pansy with a curious look on his face. "Do you know, I think Pansy has an extra-special surprise prepared for us. Don't worry, but just keep on watching for a few more minutes." In the meantime, the young man helped the little lamb rid itself of the bloody, wet membrane, so that it would be able to breathe.

Ten minutes passed as poor Pansy's bleats grew more and more agitated and her abdomen became tenser. In between contractions, the pain-racked ewe licked the fuzzy wool of the newborn lamb, helping it to dry more quickly. "Just a couple more minutes and you'll see her surprise." Then, one more loud bleat, and Melody's worried gray-blue eyes opened wide in delighted surprise as a second lamb plopped to the ground. "Wow, there were two of them. That's why poor Pansy was so fat." Pansy's bleating had transformed into much softer baa-baas as she tiredly nuzzled both of her newborn lambs. The day was warm and the first lamb had already begun to dry out and was already trying to get up onto his feet. As he stood up, he wobbled uncertainly toward his mother and began sucking hungrily on one of her teats. After only a few more minutes, the other lamb joined the first as Melody oohed and ahed with delight. By this time, Jan and Mark had awakened from their nap and were heading out to see the miracle of new life in the form of two fuzzy new lambs.

That night, at dinner, the main topic under discussion was the birth of the two lambs. Mark and Jan were particularly excited; it was the first time that they had seen such small lambs so close up. Of course, they had seen lambs at the fair, but they were usually older and larger than these two. After the lambs had finished drying and had eaten to their satisfaction, Ian had taken one in each hand and permitted the children to touch them. The short wool was coarse, but soft, and it had been fun when the lambs had begun to sniff at them and then to try to suck on their fingers, making the children giggle. They had been very reluctant to go when Ian had told them that it was time for the lambs to sleep, because it had been a very tiring day for the two of them; being born was not an easy process, and they needed to build up their strength.

Melody had been strangely quiet that evening during the discussion, and Honey began to worry; this type of silence was usually an indication that Melody was trying to figure out an appropriate (or, more likely, an inappropriate) question about the lambs. Trying vainly to forestall the inevitable, Honey tried to ask questions about the upcoming activities at school. Unfortunately, Melody was not to be put off. "Mommy, how do lambs get into their mothers' tummies?"

This time, all the children's eyes were riveted on their mother, and it was Ross's turn to grin at Honey as she attempted to come up with a sensible answer. She couldn't, so she did the only intelligent thing possible: she passed the buck. "Well, I guess you should probably ask your father; you know he's the expert in these things." That wiped the grin off of Ross's face. All heads turned in their father's direction as he mouthed, "Thanks a lot."

"Well, uh, yeah. Have you seen how sometimes, uh, Blackie bumps up against Pink Ears and Brownie? Well, sheep do the same thing, and sometimes, when the boy sheep bumps too hard against a girl sheep, it, uh, makes a lamb start growing inside the girl sheep's tummy. And when he bumps *really* hard, it can make two lambs grow." Hoping his bluff would be accepted, he stood up and offered to get seconds of mashed potatoes and steak for whoever wanted them.

Again, Melody was not to be put off. She seemed to think about Ross's answer. It seemed plausible, but something bothered her. "But Daddy, Pansy was all alone in her pen, so how could a boy sheep bump into her too hard?"

"Oh, that's easy; it doesn't happen right away. Do you remember when, around Christmastime Ian had that big white sheep that you liked so much and said it reminded you of a pony because it was so big? Well, Snowflake was a boy, or ram, as a boy sheep is called. He was always bumping into Pansy with those big horns that he had, remember?"

Melody seemed to accept this answer, and Ross and Honey both gave a sigh of relief. It was a simplified version of the truth, but that didn't mean it would have automatically been accepted by Miss Inquisitive. Sometimes she was worse than the Spanish inquisitors of old.

"Well, Melody, how was school today? How far are the preparations for the Open House going? You haven't mentioned anything about the Science Fair, either."

"Oh, I forgot. Pansy's new lambs made me forget to give you this form. Look here. Mrs. Short gave us this form and asked if you could bring cookies or Kool-Aid or something for refreshments. They're asking all the Moms, 'cause we get to go visit all the different classrooms, so we can see what all the other kids have done this year in school. Then, I can see what I get to do next year in the third grade, too. And Jan can see what kindergarten is like."

"So, what do we get to see Wednesday in your class?"

"Oh, I can't tell you that, you know. It would ruin the surprise. But it's neat, and so is the Science Fair. I bet we're the winners. The chicks are so cute, their feathers are growing, and they're all different colors.

They'll announce the winners at the end of the Open House, just before we go home." With that, Melody closed her mouth (something that rarely happened) and refused to say anything else about the Science Fair, or the Open House.

The excitement crackled in the air on Wednesday morning, June 8, 1960, at Bay View Elementary School. The children filed anxiously into their classrooms after the raising of the flag to the orchestral arrangement of the Star Spangled Banner. Yesterday, they had taken all the science projects into the cafeteria—where they would be exhibited, and where the judging would take place this afternoon. Today, after the Pledge of Allegiance to the flag, the classes would be led into the cafeteria/auditorium where the classes of children would all have the possibility of looking at the other classes' projects. Mr. Barley was in his element; he truly loved all the children in his school, and believed that they should all have an equal possibility to show their talents. He realized, of course, that not all students had the same talents, but it was the moral obligation of all scholastic employees to find the talents they did have, and hone them to a fine point, in such a way that the students would have a better chance of inserting themselves in the adult world. They were able to do this through educational activities, such as this Science Fair, and regular teaching methods. He was convinced that this school employed the best teachers available in the Costa Mesa School District and maybe even in the state of California.

There were two practices that Mr. Barley absolutely prohibited at his school: corporal punishment and skipping grades. If any teacher felt that the former was necessary for disciplining certain students, they would have to either change their minds or search for employment elsewhere. Because of this, Mr. Barley was considered fair by both students and parents. And, there were lots of activities at the school: sports events, academic events—science fairs, field trips, spelling bees—and programs for fun. There was even a special education class for children with learning difficulties or physical impairments. Of course, he thought ruefully as he carefully grabbed two of his rather more difficult students as they tried to sneak out of the school, some "talents" were less useful than others and perhaps should not be overly cultivated; this, naturally, depended on your point of view, and you never knew what use they could be put to.

After accompanying the two boys to their classroom (he would have to see about putting the O'Hara twins in separate classes next year, although this could add other complications), he headed off to his office, asking the secretary to call the different classes, starting with K-1 and K-2, into the auditorium so that they could begin to enjoy the projects that had been prepared by the other children. The smaller children probably wouldn't understand a lot of the things, but they would undoubtedly be fascinated by a lot of them. He was sure that Mrs. Short's second-grade class project would catch the interest of all the children. It might be a good idea to place a sort of guard to avoid problems like missing chicks. He was pretty sure it wouldn't happen, but he wanted to make sure that no child would be tempted beyond his or her strength to resist. At the end of the visiting period, the children would be allowed a small snack, and then would go back to their classes to finish preparing for the Open House that would take place that evening and would include the families' visit to the Science Fair and to the various classrooms. During this period, the parents could also vote for their favorite exhibit and then they could speak with the teachers about their respective children's progress during the scholastic year. At eight thirty, the final votes among parents and judges would take place, the winners would be announced and awarded their prizes. Refreshments would, of course, be served at the end of the evening, and all of the children—the winners or just participants—could be congratulated for their fine efforts. He was glad he wasn't one of the judges, because all of the projects were great and he would have been hard put to decide whose was better than some one else's. That gave him an idea. He took the phone off the hook and began to dial a certain friend of his, hoping it wasn't too late.

Mrs. Short was having a difficult time keeping her charges in line as they tried to "march silently and in an orderly fashion" toward the auditorium. There were two entryways; the one closest to their classroom had been blocked off, and so they had to walk a little farther than usual. The open doorway to the cafeteria faced toward the principal's office, so they really did do their best not to call his attention to them. He was nice, but his little discussions made most of them feel slightly uncomfortable, especially when they knew they were completely in the wrong, or even just a little. They were giddy with relief when they finally entered the big room and were faced with all of the completed projects. Of course, they all knew perfectly well that theirs was the best of all, but still, it was awe-inspiring to see the projects of the other kids, and some of them were really interesting. There was one that showed the different stages in the growth of silk moths, and Melody liked that one the best after theirs. That was the project offered by Mrs. Livingston's third-grade class, the class she hoped she would be in next year. Of course, if Mrs. Short taught the third grade next year, that would be even better, but one really shouldn't try to push one's luck.

Another project that Melody liked was the one where some kids in the sixth grade had tried to build a volcano. It looked like one, all right, but they were having a few problems trying to get the thing to erupt. There was a button to push, but nothing happened. Maybe when she was a little bigger and knew how to do that sort of thing she would be able to make one that worked. One of the first-grade classes had drawn a bunch of pictures of dinosaurs; at least, that's what was written on the board where they were pinned up, but Melody didn't remember ever having seen dinosaurs anywhere—in any book, that is; there weren't too many dinosaurs walking around these days, thank goodness—that looked even remotely like these. Oh, well, she had to remember that they were "little" and that little kids sometimes had a strange concept of what things *really* looked like. Now that she thought of it, though, Mark was even smaller than those guys, and his dinosaurs actually *looked* like dinosaurs. Anyway, they did okay for first graders; you can't expect miracles.

A loud yell from the other side of the room woke her from her reverie on first-grade dinosaurs—it seemed that someone had finally been able to get the volcano to erupt. Unfortunately, now they couldn't get it to stop, and the red-colored foam was starting to fall onto the floor in a large, steaming puddle that, had the room been on a decline, would have headed in her general direction. The sixth graders in charge of the volcano giggled nervously as they attempted to stop the flow that they had previously tried so hard to get into movement. One of the teachers ran to get the janitor so that he could mop up the mess on the floor. Fortunately, the eruption had stopped by the time Mr. Watson showed up, and the students' interest had started to focus on other projects.

By the time Melody and the rest of her class had seen all of the other projects, they were convinced that they would win first prize. Rebecca and the chicks had performed beautifully in front of the other students. The chicks were brave enough now that they didn't always hide under their mother's wings whenever someone looked at them or came too close to the cage. It was a good thing, too, because they were much too big for that sort of thing and Rebecca clucked at them when they tried. The class had put a little bowl of chicken feed beside the cage so that the other children could have the thrill of feeding the chicks; that way, they were saved the trouble of feeding the chicks themselves, and the others could enjoy the flurry as the chicks (and their mother) rushed toward the food and started pecking at it. The idea had been Raúl's, but everyone had approved. As they all filed out of the auditorium/cafeteria, they congratulated themselves on what seemed to be a sure win. Mrs. Short had taken pictures of the chicks when they first hatched, and then after they had all dried out, so that the others could see the contrast; it would have been difficult to convince others of that difference: it was something you had to see to believe, and drawings just couldn't have rendered the idea. Everybody liked Veronica and Andrea's drawings of the chicks as they grew up; and the history of the chicks, written by Raúl, had also been a big hit, even if he had put a few Spanish words in with the English. All in all, it really had been a fun morning, and the children could hardly wait for the evening to come, when they would be able to show off their project, and everything else they had done during the school year, to their families. Just as they got to their classroom, they heard a loud boom!—and all heads turned automatically toward a bewildered-looking Peter, who, shrugging his shoulders, looked up at the sky. At that moment, a silver sliver of an airplane shot through the sky, leaving a long white trail behind it. The whole room reverberated, but fortunately, nothing fell except for one of the newspaper articles—which the children had brought for current events, and which talked, quite appropriately, about sonic booms. The boom had frightened some of the children, and most of the rest were much too excited to pay attention to anything that might be taught. Considering that, plus the fact that there were only five minutes of class left before lunch hour, Mrs. Short decided to let them go early.

"Don't forget to bring your parents and brothers and sisters with you. Okay, class, we'll be seeing each other this evening; try to rest a little this afternoon so that you can be in your best form."

The children ran out the door just as the bell rang. There was a little skirmish as Peter and Raúl, neither of whom was particularly thin, tried to run out at the same time. All of their classmates, in rare high spirits, laughed at the two of them, and then with them, as the two culprits realized how funny they must have looked and joined in the laughter.

It had been a *very* trying afternoon in the McDonald household. Melody had come home bursting with the same excitement that had taken hold of the children at school and it had lasted throughout the day. It was also quite contagious, and shortly after Melody arrived home, she had infected all the other McDonald children, too. She tried to explain to her siblings about the different science projects, and by the time she had finished, the older three were running around the house, driving poor Honey out of her mind. As a last resort for saving her sanity, she sent them out to the backyard to feed the rabbits and to see how Pansy and her lambs were doing. Ian was a very patient young man, and he surely knew more answers than she did about sheep and lambs. That didn't mean, of course, that he would be able to answer all of Melody's questions; they really needed a nice encyclopedia that they could send Melody to every time she came up with her unanswerable questions that usually put them into a funk.

She had been pulling out the last sheet of cookies when the three of them came galloping into the kitchen. She had been able to fend off requests for cookies from the two younger children, reminding them that they would surely be eating those and several other types, too, that evening at the open house. It was much more difficult to rid herself of Melody's stony, accusing glare: "You didn't call me; we *always* make cookies together." She had tried to smooth out the frown on her eldest daughter's face: "I really needed your help to keep the little kids out of trouble. I couldn't have made the cookies for tonight if they had been in and out of the house, and the cookies are for *your* open house." The reminder had helped a little, but she could tell that Melody was still a little hurt.

And now, after all the rush of preparing dinner, getting all the kids and Ross dressed and ready to go, she was here at the open house. Of course, she had had to redo Jan's hair—four ponytails were at least two too many—and put pants on Kenny in place of Melody's skirt. She sometimes wondered if Ross's help was worth the trouble. Now, she and Ross were waiting to talk with Mrs. Short; she had beckoned to them as they walked through the classroom door, but at the moment she was talking with Regina Snow, Veronica's mother. While they waited, she and Ross were looking at the current events billboard, with the sonic boom article still hanging on only one tack. Remembering the big boom that had sent her youngest children into hysterics and had Missy trying to fit under the couch (how the dog had gotten into the house in the first place was a mystery), she thought it quite apropos that that particular article was hanging loose. Her mind wandered, and she wondered what Mickey had done this time; not that Mickey usually got into trouble for anything at school, but no teacher with good news would have such a glum look on his or her face when asking to speak to a child's parents.

"Honey, have you seen this article here?" Ross's voice interrupted her reveries. "It talks about the Fish Fry and the cutest baby contest. Hey! look here, there are a few words about Chas's third place. Do you remember them taking this picture of the three winners?"

"Heck, no. Let me see it," she answered curtly. "That's what I thought—the *Daily Pilot*. Do you remember that hole we found in the newspaper Monday evening? Now we know what was in it before Mickey cut it out for current events. Well, he did come out pretty cute, didn't he? They have a good photographer."

As Ross and Honey continued their walk around the room they noticed that there were several papers with Melody's name on them, the lowest grade being ninety-nine; several even had bright gold stars on them. Honey was becoming more and more confused, as she wondered just what it was that Mrs. Short wanted to talk to them about. Her bewilderment didn't last long, though, because just as they were looking at Melody's artistic rendition of the class' field trip to the dairy farm in March, Mrs. Short came and tapped them on the shoulder.

"Hello, sorry it took so long, but I had a small problem that I needed to iron out with Mrs. Snow. Now, we have another problem with Melody. I'm really at a loss as to what to do about this. I'm afraid that Melody's report card is not going to reflect exactly what her homework and school-work grades would like to express." At this remark, Honey and Ross's confusion returned full force.

"What I mean to say is that, even though I had to put A's on all of her assignments, they weren't exactly what she deserves. I've noticed that she puts forth a minimum of effort, just what she needs to get an A, but *I* know perfectly well, as I'm sure that the both of you do, too, that she is perfectly capable of doing much more. So, for her report card, I've decided that I will judge her against herself, and not in comparison with the other children. I've spoken to Mr. Barley about this, and he agrees with me that this is the only solution. As you know, there is a 'no-skipping' policy here at the Bay View School, which is as it should be. The problem is that Melody needs to be stimulated in such a way that she *will* achieve what she *is capable* of achieving. Do you have any idea what the problem can be?"

Ross and Honey had remained completely silent, with their mouths slightly agape, during Mrs. Short's exposition of her problem with their daughter. "Uh," began Ross, "uh, no. Of course, we have noticed that she asks a million questions a day that we don't always know the answers to, but we've never seen her *not* do anything. I still remember that famous day when the dog ate her homework and she wasn't very pleased about it."

Honey thought to herself, *Oh boy, is that ever an understatement, if I ever heard one.* She continued, out loud, "Just what is the problem?"

"Have you looked closely at the assignments that are here on the board? Her arithmetic work is right, but I have to look really close, because sometimes she makes some really incredible mistakes that seem to have been done deliberately, and aren't at all easy to catch. I know perfectly well that she knows how to read, but she stumbles over Dick and Jane, probably because if a tongue could run, hers would. She skips words when she writes and, as you may have noticed, her handwriting is really terrible."

"Well, that's understandable, if you consider the fact that she was born left-handed, and had to learn to do everything right-handed; did you know that she even ties her shoes backwards?"

"As a matter of fact, I do. Well, that explains a few things. I have an idea that her brain probably moves faster than her hands, and her tongue. She needs to concentrate a little more. She just doesn't take as much time as she should. For example, have you noticed this story she wrote about when your family went to the dairy farm in March?"

"Of course we noticed. It's there on the board with that big gold star on it; but, excuse me, wasn't it a field trip that the school all went on? She talked about it for days. She even told us about how it took two whole buses to take everyone." She paused to think a moment, and then continued, "I did think it a bit odd that she hadn't made me sign a permission slip, but then, I was pregnant and thought it had either slipped my mind or else Ross had signed the slip. Oh, my goodness. Where did she learn all this stuff about dairy farms, if she didn't go on a field trip with the school?"

"Uh, I think I may be the 'guilty' party here," Ross replied. "Honey, do you remember when I went to the dairy in March, to see about whether or not they could start delivering to us every day? Melody went with me, along with Jan and Mark; she must have taken off on her own without anyone noticing, but heck, I was there only ten minutes. I realize we're talking about Melody, but how the dickens did she learn all that stuff in only ten minutes?"

At that precise moment the young "lady" in question skipped into the room. When she saw the perplexed look on her parents' faces, she almost skipped out again: that look usually foreboded an upcoming explosion. However, Mrs. Short called her back just as she reached the door.

"Melody, please come here a moment; we need for you to clarify a situation for us." Melody reluctantly turned around and returned to the room. She looked innocently into everyone's eyes as Ross began by stating, "Melody, we were just discussing this delightful story about when you went to the dairy farm. Would you mind explaining to us how you found out all this information on dairy farming?"

Melody sighed with relief as she answered, "Oh, don't you remember when we all went to the dairy to ask about everyday delivery and you left me behind? I went and talked to the man who was milking the cows and he showed me how they do it; he let me try, but I almost broke my arm pulling, without getting even a drop of milk. It was fun, though. The cows told me I should have squeezed, not pulled, but the udders were too big—I couldn't even fit my whole hand around them. I did get a couple of drops out that way, though, and the milker said I was good. The cows told me that there are lots of different kinds of grass in the fields, but they really like alfalfa the best, although they like clover okay, too. I told Mommy we went on a field trip because I didn't want her to get mad at you for leaving me behind. Mommy, I know what clover tastes like, 'cause we've got it here at school, but what does alfalfa taste like?" Not waiting for an answer, she took off after her brothers and her sister as they passed by the classroom door. The three adults looked at each other in bewildered silence. Mrs. Short spoke first.

"Well, I guess she told us, didn't she? According to scientific studies, her information was absolutely correct, but, talking to cows?" she spluttered.

"Yes, well, if a cow doesn't know what it likes, who does? I ask you. Now do you see what we go through at home all the time?"

At that moment, Honey looked up at the wall clock; noting that it was already eight thirty, she opted to interrupt the upcoming discussion on the odd quirks in Melody's character before it got into high swing: the subject was vast and, considering the relative lateness of the hour, the discussion could last until midnight. "Excuse me, Mrs. Short, but when are they supposed to announce the Science Fair winners?"

She had barely finished asking when the bell rang, and Mrs. Short, taking hold of herself, announced, "Now."

They hadn't noticed that all of the other parents had left the room, so they were all alone. As the three of them left the room, and Mrs. Short locked up, she said to the McDonalds, "Do you know, it has been a real pleasure having Melody in my class the last two years. I've learned a lot from her, and I must say that it will be odd not having her next year. I've only been teaching three years now, and I don't even remember what the first year was like. I'm sure it will be quite boring next year without Melody asking inopportune questions."

Walking down the corridor toward the auditorium, Ross grinned and mentioned lightly, "Oh, don't worry. There are more of them where she came from. Jan starts school next year and Mark, the year after."

Mrs. Short stalwartly straightened her shoulders, looked at the two of them and responded, "Well, after Melody, I believe I'll be ready for just about anything." And with that, as the McDonalds looked around for their lively horde, she walked through the open door of the auditorium and went to sit with the other teachers up on the stage.

"Wow, what a neat time!" Jan said. "Didja see how neat the kinnergarden room was? They had all sorts of neat drawings and paintings and Mrs. Smith said that the kids did 'em. They even had little tables for ev'rybody and they even showed us where they hang up our towels and smocks. Why do we need towels? We don't take baths there, do we? Maybe after playing in that neat sandbox I saw there?" That evening, before falling asleep, Jan chattered incessantly about the Open House. Without waiting for an answer, she continued by commenting on her own question, the worried look slipping off her face, "I don't think we do, 'cause Mrs. Smith showed us the bathrooms, too, and there weren't any bathtubs or showers there. Mrs. Smith is really neat and I'm glad she's gonna be my teacher next year. Did ya know that kids in kinnergarden only go to school in the morning?" This time, taking a pause to catch her breath, she turned expectantly toward Melody, giving her time to answer.

"Of course I know that you go to school until lunchtime; I went to kindergarten, too, you know. The towels," Melody added snidely, "are for sleeping on. You always have to take a nap after playing outside when you're in kindergarten." Changing the subject, she asked, "Did ya like the Science Fair?"

"Yeah, it was pretty neat. Mr. Barley let us pet one of the chicks, but they weren't as soft as Blackie and Pink Ears and Brownie. They were cute, though. Do you get to bring yours home, now the Science Fair is over? It was fun making that volcano erupt, too. Mark pushed the button to make it go, but when Kenny pushed the button to make it stop, it wouldn't. Where were you, anyway?"

"I was running after Mark and Kenny, who were running all over the school. I finally caught them way out on the baseball diamond, way out there by the back fence. Mark was almost over the fence, but Kenny kept slipping and his foot kept going through the holes in the wire. That's why his legs were all scratched up when we were getting ready for bed. Then, I had to explain to Mommy and Daddy and Mrs. Short how I found out all that stuff about cows. I don't think Mrs. Short, who is the neatest teacher at school, believed me. Mommy and Daddy did, though." Her comments were met with a slight grinding sound; Jan had finally slipped off to sleep and was now gritting her teeth.

Long after Jan had drifted off to dreamland, Melody was still having a hard time getting to sleep. She was sad, because Jan had reminded her that now that the Science Fair was over, they would have to return Rebecca and her chicks to their rightful owner. Mr. Cooper had been really nice about sharing them with her and her classmates but Blondie was really cute now and she would miss feeding them—even though that meant spending early mornings before school with Peter. Oh, well, she still had Pink Ears to take care of, with the advantage of not having Peter around. She was excited, because she and her class had come in second, and Mr. Barley had given all of them a bright red ribbon with SECOND PLACE written on it in gold. Second Place was pretty good, she supposed, but she was also a bit disappointed because the winning project was one she had been sure didn't have a chance. Well, okay, it was interesting and everything, because it showed the planets as they re-volved around the sun in their own orbits. The only problem, and sixth graders should have known better, was that the planet closest to the sun was Mercury, *not* Mars. The judges should have known, too, for that matter. Oh, well, it had been fun, even if she didn't get a free subscription to the *Weekly Reader*. Mommy said she would get her a subscription, anyway. It was so much fun, because it helped you learn a lot of stuff even during the summer, and there were games and puzzles to do. She remembered that last summer there had even been an article on the planets and their movements around the sun. She giggled to herself. Maybe *that* was the reason the judges had decided to give those kids first place with the blue ribbons; maybe they hadn't gotten the newspaper last year. Anyway, the study on silkworms got Third Place with white ribbons. Mr. Barley had given all of the participants a nice green ribbon just for trying, and said that he would give ice cream to the whole school tomorrow during recess. He really was a neat principal. And with that happy thought, Melody fell asleep.

6

Crazy Days

"Mommy, I'm bored," she whined. "There's nothing to do around here. Can I go swimming?" Even though summer vacation had already begun, Melody was finding it difficult getting used to having so much time on her hands; she had gotten up at five o'clock, just like on every other weekday morning of the year (excepting Christmas, when she woke up at four o'clock).

"Melody," responded a rather exasperated Honey (who was foreseeing an endless summer before her), "do you happen to see a swimming pool full of water somewhere nearby here? It's only seven o'clock and summer vacation just started this morning; go read a book."

"I already did. I finished all of the books that Daddy brought home from the library for me."

"Well, go read them again; you might have missed something."

"I've read them three times already; I've almost memorized them. When's Daddy going to the library again?"

"He just went on Monday; you can't have already finished them. He's not going again until next week. Look, why don't you go out and feed the rabbits? I'm sure they'll be happy to see you—they're always hungry, and you know how you like to hold them. *I* know, why don't we go out together? I like to hold and pet them, too. Your brothers and sister are still asleep, so it'll just be us two and the bunnies. Hurry now, and take off your slippers or they'll get all wet from the dew." Immediately putting her words into action, she and Melody shed their slippers, and the two of them snuck out the side door.

It was still fairly early and the sky was still wearing the pastel colors that would certainly be discarded as the sun rose higher and higher. It was also relatively cool, but the fact that the grass was already dry suggested that the day would be typical of mid-June; in other words, a scorcher. Their ears were met by the incredible chorus of bird song, each bird singing its own distinct melody, each melody different from the others—except for those pesky mockingbirds, who imitated everyone else in turn—but all coming together to form a heavenly harmony, a hymn of joy and thanksgiving to their maker. Only one voice marred the beauty and peace of the morning: a large black crow flew by, his raucous caw causing even the most intrepid of the mockingbirds to hush their voices until it had completely passed by. Fortunately, it was just passing through, and the moment was over in a flash. Even that moment had been magical, in its own way—the sun beating on the bird's shiny black feathers caused iridescent colors of green and blue to glow like jewels in the midst of his normally drab suit.

The rabbits were already awake, immersed in their morning ablutions. Their ears quivered and their noses wriggled in anticipation as Melody and Honey drew closer to the hutch. Almost two weeks had passed since Ross had last mowed the lawn, and the bright emerald green grass was once more long and luxuriant, a perfect snack to offer three famished rabbits. The two of them grabbed a big handful of the tantalizing treat and fed it to the bunnies through the holes in the chicken wire, giggling as the three fuzz balls nibbled avidly at the offering.

Completely immersed in the joy of sharing this time alone together, they were utterly astonished when the morning peace was once again rent by a long, piercing wail.

"Oh, my gosh, I forgot all about Chas. The poor kid; he's probably hungrier than these rabbits. Sorry, Mickey, I guess I'll have to go feed him and change his diaper. Want to come with me?" With that, she got up and headed toward the house.

"No, I think I'll just stay here a few more minutes, until the bunnies have finished eating." She lay back and inhaled the sweet scent of the torn grass and the fresh air. She let out a sigh of satisfaction and wished she could just lay there and absorb the warming rays of the sun. She sneezed as a bright red ladybug landed on her nose, the black spots on its wings merging into one as she squinted to get a closer look at it. She put her finger up to her nose in front of the friendly little beetle; when it climbed to Melody's fingertip, she began to solemnly chant, "Ladybug, ladybug, fly away home; your house is on fire and your children are alone." As she pronounced the last word, the little insect obliged and, lifting its wings flew off, Melody imagined, toward her home to save her children. It was like a magical enchantment; Melody was fairly sure that bugs couldn't understand people talk, but the chant never failed: the ladybugs *always* took off on the word "alone." They *never* took off until it was pronounced, so it had to be magical. Still considering the matter, she lay back down in the waving grass and watched a pair of white cabbage butterflies flutter by in an exotic, weaving dance that quickly took them out of her range of vision. The hypnotizing drone of a bee buzzing nearby in its search for sweet clover honey set her to thinking about the last week of school.

True to his word, Mr. Barley had made sure that all of the Bay View Elementary School students had gotten a cup of ice cream during recess on the afternoon following the Science Fair. The first-, second-, and third-place winners all got vanilla and chocolate marble, while all the others got plain vanilla. Still, it was pretty nice of him, because word had gotten around that he had paid for the extra ice cream out of his own pocket. There weren't many school principals around who were so understanding. On Friday, her whole class had tearfully said good-bye to Rebecca and her chicks. They'd had the fun of having her with them for almost two months, and they had all become quite fond of her, and of course, they had seen the chicks hatch. Even Peter shed a tear or two when he saw his little black chick go out the door. Monday, they had taken end-of-year tests in arithmetic and spelling, and Tuesday, Mrs. Short had made them read from their *Dick and Jane* book. She had never read such a boring book as those two *Dick and Jane* books, with their dog Spot. Whoever wrote those books sure didn't know dogs very well.

Anyway, they didn't do very much yesterday (Wednesday). Mrs. Short let them do a lot of PE and they drew pictures and finished reading about Dick and Jane and Spot. Thank goodness, next year they would have different, more difficult books to read. After lunch, Mrs. Short gave them back their tests and they went over the answers together as a class. Everyone glared at Melody, because she had gotten all the answers right; she just shrugged—there was nothing she could do about it. Finally, it was time to go home and Mrs. Short handed out their report cards. Thank goodness, Mommy didn't get mad at her. That C in handwriting kind of messed things up a bit. She got A's in reading, science, art, arithmetic, English, spelling, and PE, and a B in geography and history and conduct. Phooey. Of course, she didn't really understand what was so great about getting all A's—it didn't mean you were better than someone else, just different.

That bee just kept coming closer and closer, and his low buzz was making her eyelids droop, just like Dorothy in *The Wizard of Oz* when she and her new friends were falling asleep in the poppy fields just outside of Oz. And just like Dorothy's group, which was awakened by the dog Toto, so she was awakened by a barking Missy. Of course, Missy was not alone, but was accompanied by a group of brothers and a sister.

"Hey, Mickey! Whachha doin', hidin' out here all by yerself in your pajamas? It's late and we ate breakfast and you didn't get any and Daddy just got home. He said he brought us a surprise and for you to come and see, too." Having brought their news, the three of them turned around and retreated back into the house for Daddy's mysterious surprise.

Looking back up at the sun, she discovered that it had done quite a bit of moving westward: it was now almost straight up in the sky. She stood up and, dusting the grass off her jammies, headed toward the house.

"Oh, it was about time you got in here," Jan's bossy voice greeted her. "Look what Daddy brought for us. It's called 'slip 'n' slide.' You hook it up to the sprinkler and turn on the water. Then you sit on it and slide all the way to the end of it. And," she added with a smirk, "it's yellow. Neat, huh?"

"Yeah, it's really neat. Can we try it out right now?" The once "bored out-of-her-shoes" Mickey was suddenly alight with the idea of something to do. And this would really be fun!

"Okay, kids, go get in your bathing suits and Mommy'll hook the sprinkler up and we'll see how everything goes. And Mickey, before you change, bring me all your library books. Mommy says you've finished, so I'll just take them back before I come home from work."

"Okay, Daddy." She ran off to her bedroom and was back in a flash with her stack of books.

"I'll get you some more, okay? Do you want some more of those *Happy Hollister* books? There's a whole bunch of them."

Already halfway to her bedroom, she turned and called back, "Sure. Can you get me some of those *Pollyanna* books, too?" Not waiting for an answer, she ducked into her bedroom, slipped quickly into her bathing suit, and raced out the front door to join her brothers and sisters as they began their slips and slides in the front yard.

Ross had already left, leaving Honey alone on the job, surveying the situation, but she was already in over her head. "Ross Jenkins McDonald! Don't you dare jump on the slide with that wrench in your hand—it will tear the plastic! It's not yours in the first place—it's Mark's—so what are you doing with it in your hand, anyway? *Put it down now!*" This last came out as a shriek as the wrench flew straight at her; he had thrown it haphazardly right *after* tossing himself onto the slippery strip.

He was, of course, not the only offender. Honey continued, "Mark Allen McDonald, take those flippers off your feet! This is *not* a swimming pool and you do not need them." It was too late—he was already on his slippy-slidey way—but he did, luckily, have the presence of mind to lift his feet up into the air. This resulted in an unexpected tailspin that caused immediate hilarity on everybody's parts, including Honey's. At this point, the situation developed into an acrobatic free-for-all as all the children tried to outdo each other in new acrobatic tricks. Their squeals of laughter, naturally, attracted all the other kids in the block and soon all of the other mothers were thanking Honey in their hearts for saving them from the first-day-of-summer insanity.

Honey gave up trying to control all the neighborhood children to make sure that there were no prohibited objects on them; it was a lost cause: there were too many of them. Earlier that morning she had pondered an endless summer; at this point she wondered if they might be able to just skip July and August this year. Better yet, if she was to maintain *her* sanity, maybe it would be a good idea to just play right along with the crowd. She went into the house, changed into a pair of shorts, got Chas ready, and returned to the front yard. Well, if you can't beat 'em, join 'em, was her motto. Soon everyone was taking turns at pulling Chas along the slide and laughing as Honey took her turn at slipping along in the cool water.

One by one, the neighborhood children reluctantly left the game as their mothers called them home for lunch. Finally the last hanger-on left and the McDonalds were alone. "Okay, you guys, let's go eat. You can play on the slip-and-slide this afternoon, after your nap. We'll do it in the backyard, though, so that we can water the grass there, too. It doesn't really need it, but . . ." A strangled sound that issued from Melody's throat stopped Honey at midsentence. "What's that? Yes, I know you're a 'big' girl now, but you are going to take a nap because you'll be staying up later at night; school's out, and it stays light until later. Now, does soup and sandwiches sound good? Since it's Melody's first day home, she can choose which soup. We'll also eat peanut-butter-and-jelly sandwiches. It's such a nice day; let's go eat on the picnic table out back." Melody chose vegetable soup because "those pieces of corn and the lima beans are really yummy." She was still disgruntled, but the idea of staying up later in the evening helped to still her tongue. Maybe Mommy and Daddy had something special planned.

Naptime passed really quickly; in fact, Melody couldn't believe she had actually been so tired. Maybe it was because she had spent so much time running and jumping around. She now felt so refreshed and rarin' to go. Mommy had been right: a good nap was just what she had needed. She stood up and stretched, slipped her bathing suit on as quietly as she could, and then walked on tiptoe to the door; it wouldn't do to wake up Jan or the others, so she slid quietly out the door, closing it silently behind her. She couldn't believe the house could be so calm during the day. Not wanting to disturb anyone, she decided it would be okay to slip out the side door and go sit out in the sun for a while (it seemed as though even Mommy was sleeping—well, she had done an awful lot of jumping and sliding around; old ladies like Mommy shouldn't go do all that kind of exercise, it was bad for them). Wrong! She had just opened the door a crack, when another sound made her jump two feet into the air.

"Melody, what are you doing out of bed, and where do you think you're going?"

"I took my nap, and I'm not tired anymore, so I wanted to go lie down by the clothesline. Don't worry, I didn't wake up Jan," she whispered.

Honey's voice took on an exasperated tone. "Melody, you couldn't have already slept and rested—you've only been in your room five minutes. It's impossible. Please, go back to your room and lie down for at least half an hour." Her tone was more urgent now.

"Can't I just go lie down on the cement by the clothesline?" she wheedled. "I promise I won't make any noise. I'm not tired anymore, and I really did sleep. Please."

Honey reluctantly gave in; it was useless, really, to insist. She could tell that her first-born was truly wide awake. She wished she had *half* of Melody's energy. "All right, go on out, but first promise me you won't make any noise until the other kids wake up. Then, we'll hook up the sprinkler, and you can all make all the noise you want." She almost sighed aloud with relief as Melody nodded in agreement.

The little girl just about let out a whoop of joy, when she suddenly remembered her promise to be quiet. She knew perfectly well that, had she let out that whoop, she would now be heading back toward her bedroom, where she would be staying the rest of the day with a very sore bottom. Of course, she might have had to sit and wait for the very-sore-bottom part. Mommy rarely gave them spankings, but Daddy had very big hands, and his spankings were a hundred times worse than Mommy's, except for that one time just before she'd started kindergarten. . . . She shuddered just thinking about it. And so, instead of whooping, she murmured, "Yippee!"

The sun was very high in the sky, but it already leaned more toward the western horizon than the eastern one. Melody plopped down on the overheated sidewalk, facedown, and stretched out as far as she could. Of course, she wasn't wet, so she couldn't leave her imprint on the ground, but she could later, after they all got wet again. She just wanted to absorb as much heat as she could. It was nearly as quiet outside as it was inside (it seemed that the very air was trying to remind her of her promise), but now and then you could hear a mother bird chirp to her little ones in a sort of lullaby as she tried to get them to sleep. It was too hot even for the bugs to be flying around. There was, however, a long line of very intrepid ants that filed along a crack in the cement. As she looked more closely at them, she noticed that they were marching in double file, or rather, that some were coming and some were going. She noted, too, that sometimes two of them, moving in opposite directions, would stop and shake antennas with each other. Melody, of course, was very interested in knowing how many there were of them, where they were going, and why they were going there in the first place. Thinking that it might not be a good idea to get up, she decided to slither toward Mommy's vegetable garden to see what they were all looking for, because it looked like the ones that were going away from that area all had little morsels on their backs. Little morsels of what, she couldn't figure out, so she slithered still closer to the edge of the little garden.

Yuck! She wished she hadn't been born with such a curious nature—there before her was a snail shell covered with black ants crawling all over it, inside and out. There didn't seem to be anything left in it, but there were millions of ants. Suddenly, it didn't matter how many there were—she couldn't have counted that far, anyway, because there were trillions of them, and they just kept coming. Poor snail. Whatever was it doing out in this sun, anyway? It was way too hot for snails, and they always dried up in the sun, if they weren't careful. Oh, well, there was nothing she could do about it now. What was done, was done, she thought philosophically.

She rolled a couple of times and found herself back where she had started from. It sure was hard trying to stay still. She wanted to get up and run around, but she had said she would lie down on the cement and be quiet. Maybe later she could go and look at Pansy and her little lambs. They were getting lots bigger, and Ian was really proud of them. He was more than sure he could get a blue ribbon for them; they were really woolly and they always nuzzled her hand when she went to see them. She wished that *she* could have a lamb, but that was really silly—she had more than enough animals, as it was, or so they said. If you asked her, you could never have enough animals. She supposed it was all a matter of opinion.

Then, when she was done talking to Ian and petting the lambs, she knew another neat place that she wanted to go look at—a place she had found the other day—a place full of blue-belly lizards just waiting to be caught. She rolled over on her back, put her hands under her head, and looked up toward the sky. She hoped everyone's naps would hurry up and finish, so they could start playing on the slip-and-slide. If it got too late, she wouldn't be able to catch any of those lizards, because they didn't stay out when there was only shade—no cold-blooded animals did. She knew where they hid, but it was hard getting them out of their holes. Oh, well, she was sure that she could find the time: Mommy wouldn't insist upon her playing on the slip-and-slide if she didn't want to. The only problem was that she did want to. So, maybe she could go lizard hunting before she petted Pansy and her lambs. She was distracted by a bird that flew by; it looked like a blackbird, but it seemed to be bleeding under its wings. *That's silly*, she thought, *how can it fly, if it's bleeding under its wings? And yet, there's that big splash of red there, in plain sight. Under both wings, too.* She puzzled over the dilemma for a while, long after the bird had already winged its way to wherever it was going. She heard a cricket chirruping away somewhere in the grass, and turned her head every which way, trying to find it. Of course, she was quite unsuccessful in her endeavor, and wondered if it was the same one that had awakened

105

her and Jan on that long-ago day before Easter. An airplane—taking off from, or landing at, the Orange County Airport—zoomed by overhead. It was low enough that she could see the windows, and some undefined forms near them, so she waved at them, hoping that someone could see her and wave back. She couldn't see them, though, even if they did, because the plane was much higher now, heading toward the ocean; there was now no doubt that it had just taken off. Only small planes took off from there, so maybe it was heading out to Catalina Island. She didn't think so, because it didn't look like a seaplane, but it could be, she guessed.

The plane set her off to thinking about the time she, Mommy and Daddy, and Jan and Mark had gone to Catalina Island in the seaplane. It had been really neat. When they had landed in the harbor, the water had splashed their windows. That had been really funny. Then, when they got off the plane, they had to walk over a sort of ramp that bounced, and Jan had almost fallen into the water just before they got to the wharf. Of course, Mark was still little and Mommy carried him off. Then, they went into the airport and got their suitcases. Their hotel had been pretty close to the airport, but to get there from where they were, they had had to take a taxi. It was almost dinnertime when they got there, so Daddy took them out to a seafood restaurant. It was a good thing they had hamburgers there, too, because she had been starving, and no way was she going to eat fish.

After dinner they took a walk along the shore and looked at all the boats. Some of them were great big fishing boats, and some were just little rowboats. There were a few sailboats, like the ones near Grammy and Grampa's house, but the very best one was the glass-bottom boat. In fact, Daddy walked right up to the ticket booth next to the boat and reserved seats for the five of them on one of tomorrow's morning outings. Melody and Jan were really excited, even though they weren't quite sure what a glass-bottom boat was good for. She had thought it might be kind of dangerous, because what if they hit a big rock or something and the boat bottom broke? They would capsize and everybody who didn't know how to swim would drown. She hadn't been worried about her family, except for Mark (because he was too little to know how to swim); the people she was worried about were the ones who didn't live near the beach or have a swimming pool and so had never learned how to swim. Daddy had laughed at her and said that there was nothing to worry about. There were lots of things to see on the island, so they had walked around until Jan started stumbling over her own feet. Mark had already fallen asleep an hour before in his stroller, so Daddy declared it was time to go back to the hotel.

The next morning, the sun had seemed a little hazy, and so Daddy had tried to make fun of them by saying that maybe the boat wouldn't leave the pier. They knew it couldn't be true but still, sometimes Daddy could be really convincing. After a light breakfast in the hotel (you never knew; none of them had ever been on a big boat before—except Melody, when she was born, and that didn't count—and they could get seasick, of course), they all took off for their big adventure on the sea. Daddy still hadn't told them what to expect—he could be pretty annoying at times—but he said it was just so he wouldn't ruin the surprise, so no one had known exactly what was going to happen.

When the family finally got onto the boat, they had walked down a short ramp that led into an enclosed area that was furnished with a series of cushioned seats situated along the entire inner wall of the boat. You couldn't cross directly from one side of the boat to the other, because there was a long wooden rail that separated the seats from the main attraction of the boat: a thick glass bottom. The most astounding thing about the bottom was that you could *see the water* underneath the boat. Once they were in their places, and their seat belts were buckled, Melody took it upon herself to investigate a little more closely, and discovered that not only could you see the water, but that there were also lots of small fish swimming around and nibbling on the barnacles and mussels clustered on the pier's supporting pillars. She had been so absorbed in watching tiny, jewel-like fish that she had been taken completely by surprise when the engine, after a few splutters and spits, roared into life and the large boat began to chug out of the harbor. The boat's captain stood before all the visitors on the ride and informed them that the trip would last approximately forty-five minutes, and that in that time they would see a great deal of the island's underwater marine life, much of which were found only in the waters surrounding the island. The lights in the cabin lowered and the captain had advised everyone to start looking directly at the glass, because at any moment they would be able to see one of the fish that was typical of the area: the bright orange Garibaldi fish. All spectators watched attentively at the forest of bronze-colored and olive green seaweed. At first, all they could see was the waving tendrils of seaweed and water in varying shades of blue and green, but as they watched more avidly, they could see two bright orange splotches, as the Garibaldi fish began to materialize before their very eyes. "Wow! Giant goldfish! Look how neat they are."

"The fish that you see before you," the captain explained, "are examples of the adult Garibaldi fish, which gets its name from the bright orange-red color of the shirts that the one thousand followers of Giuseppe Garibaldi, the famous Italian patriot and hero of two continents, wore during their campaign to unite a severely divided nation. There, coming out of the weeds, is a younger example of the same fish, distinguishable by the bright blue polka dots, which the adults do not have. If any of you are planning on going scuba diving later on, be careful: these fish are afraid of nothing and can actually be quite aggressive."

As the boat proceeded along its way, the captain continued to point out a number of other fish, including a very shy moray eel and a gigantic black sea bass. However, the fish that had interested Melody the most was a very strange "fish" called the California horn shark. "That is a shark? It sure doesn't look like one. Where are all its teeth and its horns?" she asked. In fact, this brownish, polka-dotted shark hadn't seemed very long, and instead of gliding effortlessly through the water, like most sharks do, it had seemed to be trying to walk clumsily along the sand at the bottom of the ocean. And, unlike most sharks with their long thin noses and sharp, protruding teeth, this peculiar shark had a short, round mouth. All in all, it didn't look anything like the sharks that you could sometimes see around the Newport Pier trying to eat fish off the hooks of unsuspecting fishermen.

"The California horn shark is a nocturnal creature, so we are very lucky to be seeing one at this time of day," the captain had announced. "This shark is fairly sociable, but some caution is required when approaching the spines found along his back."

Just as they were entering the harbor at the end of the trip, Melody had gasped as she saw the shadow of what seemed to her to be . . .

At that moment, a sudden movement to her right caught her attention, pulling her abruptly from her musings on the Catalina trip. She shifted herself back onto her stomach and continued rolling until she reached the object that had attracted her attention. It looked like a little bird, but if it were, why hadn't it taken off while she was trying to get close to it? She had certainly made enough noise although, she hoped, not enough to wake up her brothers and her sister get herself in trouble. Cautiously, she edged closer to whatever it was, and silently popped her hand over it. There was no struggle, or attempts to get away from her clutch, so she slowly opened up her fist, hoping that she hadn't killed it.

What she held in her hand was a small ball of grayish-black feathers that sort of resembled a big, black thistle, especially weightwise. She was mystified by the object: she had no idea what was holding the feathers together, because there were no bones, no meat or glue, no thread, nothing. And yet, the feathers weren't loose—they were all connected in some mysterious way. Of course, this would require some very serious investigating, but she would have to be very careful, because it was probable that her brothers and her sister would want it too, because it really was neat. The problem was, Where could she hide it for now? She definitely couldn't take it into the house, because then she would probably get in trouble for not keeping her promise, even though her siblings would probably be out in the yard pretty soon.

Just as she was pondering the problem, the thundering horde came rushing out the patio door, followed by a rather flustered Honey. "Hey, you guys, wait. You can't do anything yet—I haven't set the slip-and-slide up yet. Just hold on to your britches. Kenny, go get your bathing suit on; you can't go on in your undies. Melody, you've been out here 'til now, so would you please go help Kenny get his suit on? It's still hanging up in the bathroom near the shower curtain. While you're helping him, I'll get this thing hooked up. Oh, Mark and Jan, please go into the front yard and get the sprinkler." An exasperated Honey ran her fingers through her hair as her offspring took off in their appointed directions.

As Kenny and Melody (who had decided to take advantage of the diversion and hide her newfound object under her pillow) entered the house and Mark and Jan went to get the sprinkler, Missy came out from behind the kitchen door and began to sniff the plastic strip with some apprehension. Her worry lightened some when Honey turned on the sprinkler and the water started spraying over the backyard. She immediately began jumping back and forth through the spraying water as it weaved back and forth. Her excited barks soon turned to disappointed whines as the spurts of water died down and the water game filled up. Her eyes lighted up again as she saw the kids jumping and sliding on the strip, and thought that perhaps this new game might be just as fun as the old one. Just as she was preparing to join Kenny on his next slide, Mark grabbed her by the tail and Melody announced, "No, Missy, you can't go on there; your toenails are too long and you might rip the plastic. I don't think the other kids would like you very much if that were to happen. Just sit here, and when we're done, Mommy'll turn on the sprinkler and you can play there." With a forlorn sigh the frustrated dog plopped down on the grass beside the sprinkler and watched while the McDonald kids continued to have fun, fun she couldn't join them in.

After watching the fourth car that passed theirs with all passenger eyes glued to the McDonald's car, Honey turned toward her husband and asked, whispering, "Ross, why do you suppose all those people are staring at our car, this time?" It wasn't unusual for people in cars passing theirs to stare; sometimes they sped up or slowed down, just to get a better look at whatever they were looking at.

"I don't know. I didn't fix up the girls' hair, so it can't be that. Maybe we have a flat tire, although it doesn't feel like it. I'll take a look at it when we get to Russ's. It's here, just after the next stoplight."

As Honey looked into the rearview mirror to see how her hair was, she noticed that the people in the car behind them were staring, too, driver included. She also saw why. "Ross," she whispered, "do you think we can leave Melody at Russ's when we leave? Or maybe, all four of the older kids? Melody's sticking her hand in her mouth again, but I'm sure it's not her idea, unless they've been quarreling, and I don't think they have been; we'd have heard them and they're all giggling back there."

Ross raised his eyes toward the ceiling of the car. "Well, Melody's easy; she's always being left behind. The others are a bit more difficult; they always follow the food. Hey, you guys—knock it off, or I'll go straight home without stopping at Russ's and you will all go to bed without eating dinner!" At this very precise invitation, all four children sat straight in the backseat, and Melody sat on her hand.

As the Scottish poet Robert Burns mentioned in one of his poems, "The best laid plans of mice and men often go astray," so had it happened to Melody's plans for the rest of the afternoon. She did not go and pet Pansy and her two lambs, nor did she go lizard catching. Of course, she hadn't really been too out of sorts about it, because what happened to change them was actually much better: when Daddy came home, he made everyone wait until he got *his* bathing suit on and then they all

110

piled into the car and took off for the beach. Of course, it was only Thursday afternoon, so they didn't go to Little Corona or Big Corona beach, because they always spent the whole day there at the tide pools or body surfing. No, they went to the Tenth Street Bay, which was good, too, because it was really close to Grammy and Grampa's house. They always went there to take a shower in the little shower in back of the house, and then Grammy always let them choose one of her candies from her crystal candy dish. The beach itself was a lot of fun—even though they usually didn't stay there long on weekdays—because there were a number of things to do; there was a neat float out in the middle of the bay; it served as a diving board, or you could stretch out on top and get a suntan or, better yet, you could go underneath and collect mussel shells. This was fun, but what happened next was what made it really fun. There were some thin, silver-colored fish that their daddy said were called smelt and that swam all around the float; they were very greedy for the mussel's hearts. Now, extracting the heart was not a job for the queasy-stomach type, but the McDonald children had no such problems. Our childish heroes were not in this, you must understand, for questions of generosity; no, they held high hopes that by using these mussel hearts and string, they would be able to catch a few smelt and take them home for dinner. Melody wasn't particularly interested in this aspect of the question, but she really would have enjoyed catching at least one, and then, probably, throw it back into the water. Up until this moment, none of them had had any success, but it was something they just couldn't resist—it was a part of them.

Another thing they particularly liked to do was build dribbled sand castles. The place was ideal, because there were no waves to destroy them immediately after they built them. Sometimes they even found some pretty shells that they could put on them for decoration. They always dug a moat around it and then filled it with water poured from their little pail.

Another fun thing to do was bury Daddy under a ton of sand. Of course, they didn't cover his face, because then he wouldn't be able to breathe, and who would drive them home then? Mommy knew how to drive, but she had to hold Chas with both arms so she couldn't drive. The kids all knew how to drive—Daddy always let them hold on to the steering wheel—but none of them, not even Melody, could reach the gas pedal. Therefore, they never covered Daddy's face with sand. This usually happened at the end of the afternoon, just before it was time to go home; if they wanted to prolong their stay just a little bit longer, they all scattered in different directions after finishing their "work of sand art," because Daddy would shake off all the sand and come running after them. It was, of course, a game with precise rules: you could run and swim as far and as long as you wanted to, but as soon as Daddy caught you, you had to rinse off and go sit on a towel until everyone got caught.

Now, all informalities having been taken care of, they were on their way home and would soon be stopping off at Russ's hamburger stand to get dinner. There were benches that could be used, but sometimes they were all filled up, and you either had to go home and eat or else eat in the car. That was okay, too, but it was always more fun eating at the stand. Melody hoped, as they drove into the stand's parking lot, that she could have a cheeseburger and fries and a giant root beer with lots of ice. She was absolutely famished, and she knew that if she didn't eat something soon, and a lot of it, she was going to die of hunger. Russ was a really nice guy, even if he was old—he had gone to school with Daddy, and *everyone* knew Daddy was almost as old as the hills—and he always let you choose exactly what you wanted on your hamburger. Melody always liked a double portion of dill pickle chips and mustard on her hamburger; Mark, Jan, and Kenny always had ketchup and tomato slices on their hamburgers, too, but Melody and anything to do with tomatoes didn't get along too well together, except maybe ketchup on meat loaf, and tomato sauce on pizza and spaghetti, but those were cooked and didn't count. Daddy always had raw onions on his hamburger, but no tomatoes. Mommy ate hers just like Melody did.

"Daddy, can I have triple pickles? And a giant root beer, too?"

"That's 'may,' not 'can,' and if Mr. Russ says you may, then he will give them to you. And Melody, I really don't like you doing that little trick of yours with your hand. Someday, someone will have a heart attack while they're watching you, and there will be a terrible accident. It's bad enough when you do it at the beach or the park, but it's dangerous on the road. And Jan, you may wipe that grin off your face, because I know perfectly well that the idea was yours in the first place." Jan straightened up and gave her father a very serious nod of her head, but the minute he turned around to order their dinner, the grin returned to her face.

While Ross waited in line to order and then pick up their dinners, Honey and the kids all headed for the benches in back of the building.

112

For the moment no one else was there, but the situation could change quickly; they hurried and filled up one whole table-and-bench set. Soon, Ross joined them and began doling out hamburgers, French fries, and drinks, which were consumed in short order by his anxious family members. Chas, of course, guzzled down a bottle of milk and then drifted off to sleep as his brothers and sisters all headed off to the toilet before piling into the backseat of the car.

Of course, with all the excitement and clamor, it was understood that the inevitable would happen. About three miles ahead, just before the turnoff, Honey, who up until that time had been carefully rocking Chas in her arms, noticed that a certain, particularly shrill voice was missing from the general uproar. "Kids, is Melody in back there with you?"

A rousing chorus answered her, "No," with Jan adding, "We think she got left in the bathroom there at Russ's."

An exasperated Honey asked them, "Well, why didn't you tell us she wasn't here before we left Russ's? It would have certainly been helpful on your part, had you let us know, don't you think?"

The three children looked at each other before shrugging their shoulders. Again, Jan blandly responded, "You didn't ask us."

Ross and Honey looked at each other helplessly—you just couldn't deny their logic. "Okay, let's go back and get her." Honey looked hopefully at him and asked, "You don't suppose . . . we could just, uh, leave her there?"

"No, she'd just run us up a huge bill for all the hamburgers and fries that she'd eat, and then she'd come on home. We'd better go get her while we're still ahead." And with that, he abruptly changed lanes and did a quick u-turn back toward the direction they had just come from.

Two minutes later showed that Ross's dire prediction had already started to come true; Melody was seated on the picnic bench, calmly munching on a double cheeseburger, without the onion and ketchup, but with double the dill pickle chips. Pressed securely against her thin chest was a giant root beer with crushed ice.

Ross stared at her through the open window, trying to catch his temper before asking her, "What are you doing here?" Of course, he should have known that his rhetorical question would have an equally obvious answer.

"You left me here, so I got a hamburger while I waited for you to

113

come back and get me. I knew you would, sooner or later." At this re-mark, Honey rolled her eyes and looked guiltily in the other direction.

"Well, get into the car so we can go home." This being accom-plished, Ross continued, "May we know exactly *how* we left you behind?"

"I don't know. I was last in line for the bathroom, and when I got out, you weren't here anymore."

At this point, an exasperated Honey exclaimed, "Why were you the last one in line? You were the first to finish and get up from the table; you should also have been the first one in line, or at least before your broth-ers and sister."

"Well, I was, but then a really pretty butterfly flew past, and I tried to catch it. By the time it was gone, everybody else was either back in the car or still in line. I got back in line, but when I got out, you were gone. I'm sorry, but it was really pretty, bright yellow with black stripes and bright blue spots in the bottom corners. I wanted to show it to you, but it got away. Don't be mad. I promise, I won't do it again." A tear trickled down her cheek, and she looked so forlorn and penitent that her parents, knowing full well that the promise would be forgotten in half an hour, didn't press charges, although they did mention that the price of the hamburger would be deducted from her weekly allowance. She cringed at the thought, but figured she'd probably be able to earn something in the next few days with a good old Kool-Aid stand in the front yard. At five cents a glass, she was sure to make up for the loss of the hamburger money in a hurry.

Five minutes later, as she walked through the front door, she found a nice stack of books waiting for her on the living room hutch (not the one the rabbits lived in—this one held her mommy's best dishes. She had no idea why they both were called "hutches," since they didn't look anything alike and they had completely different uses. Oh well, there was no understanding adults.) that Daddy had brought home after work and that she hadn't had the chance to look at yet, since they had gone straight to the beach as soon as Daddy got home. "Wow! Two new *Happy Hollister* books; neat! And who is Doctor Dolittle? Hmm; it looks like he likes animals. Maybe I'll read this one first. And Pippi Longstocking: I've heard of her before. Boy, I can hardly wait until to-morrow, so I can start reading."

In fact, there was no time to read that evening. After everyone had changed into their pajamas, everyone except Chas filed into the living room and dropped onto Ross's outstretched arms, ready to watch *Perry Mason* before going to bed. Just when Paul Drake had found the most important clue, Jan's gritting teeth, Mark and Kenny's low rumbles (and Ross's not-so-low rumbles), and Melody's ear-splitting yawns informed Honey that perhaps she would have to wait for the reruns to see who was the real guilty party. She didn't really care; she, too, was having a hard time keeping her head from nodding. She was definitely not used to all that exercise, and after all those falls on the slip-and-slide, she was pretty sure there were a few bruises in a place that only one person could see. So, one by one, she lifted several heads from her slumbering husband's arms and led each one of them as she would a sleepwalker. Despite her obvious drowsiness, Melody protested having to go to bed when the sun was still shining; there was, however, nothing she could say about it when she fell asleep while brushing her teeth. After somehow getting Melody into her bed, Honey went into her own bedroom and pulled down the sheets.

Rousing Ross was another story. He was six feet two in his socks, and she was a whole foot shorter, so there was no question of her carrying or dragging him off to their bedroom. She tried pushing him, but he just rolled over onto his side. Tickling him wasn't a very good idea, because he grabbed her and pulled her down with him. She managed to wriggle, regretfully, from his grasp. Ready to give up, she stood up and turned off the TV, planning to lie back down and wait things out; at that moment, the complete silence did what no other action had been capable of doing: Ross woke up, headed down the hallway, and plopped down on the bed. Sighing with relief, Honey followed him, limping stiffly down the hall. She was already asleep before her head ever hit the pillow.

It was a week later; the days had passed more or less the same way as the first had, slipping noisily from one day to the next. It was early Saturday morning, although not as early as one might think, when thinking about Melody. She had become accustomed to getting up a little later, although not quite as late as the other members of the family could have hoped for. It was six A.M. and Melody had only been up for about half an hour. It took time to get dressed, of course, and she first had gone out back to pet the rabbits. They were getting nice and fat now, with all the grass and rabbit pellets that they ate. Melody had thought that they needed to get out and run now and then, but Mommy had advised her that that would not be an excellent idea—they were much faster now, and maybe Missy was the only one who could catch them if they decided to go for a walk on their own. Now, after giving each one a handful of grass, she was heading out to the front yard, looking at the ground and thinking that maybe she might be able to find some little frogs or some kind of lizard to add to her menagerie. Maybe later on they could go catch butterflies at that house that had the poinsettia trees and the bright purple flowers that looked like they were made from paper. And then, she looked up.

No, it couldn't be true; either she was still asleep and dreaming, or else her eyes were deceiving her. Melody pinched herself on the arm and looked again. She was awake and the horses were still there, so she blinked her eyes. They were all still there at the curve of the cul-de-sac at the end of the road—there were already five of them and they were bringing out two more. Oh, how beautiful, and that brown and white pinto was *sooo* cute! That black one looked so much like a miniature Fury. Wow, she hoped Daddy would give her the fifty cents that it usually cost to take a ride on the ponies; last week she didn't get her allowance and they hadn't set up the Kool-Aid stand yet. Today was allowance day, but she only got a dime anyway, and that was a long way from fifty cents.

She had already gone pony-back riding before, not too long ago actually, at the Fish Fry. They had even brought the ponies here last summer and she had ridden them then, too. But, it was impossible to ride too much, in her opinion. Of course, it was too early to ride for now: the ponies had just gotten here and everybody else in the neighborhood was still in bed, even Mommy and Daddy, and the best way *not* to get to go riding was to wake them up early on Saturday morning. *Maybe,* she thought, *the ponies' owners would let me help feed them while they were waiting for everyone to get up.*

Of course, no one at the pony rides would be expecting a seven-year-old at that time of the morning. They had hoped to have everything in place before their prospective clients were out and about. They should have known, having been there other times, but with all of their traveling around, they had forgotten. Because of this, Melody's reedy voice came as quite a shock, causing them to jump three feet into the air when she asked them, "Hi, can I help you feed the ponies?

They're really neat." Once they got over their shock at not being the only ones up so early, they graciously let the little girl feed each of the hungry ponies a handful of hay. As she stood patiently in front of the chomping animals, she began to formulate a perfect—in her eyes—plan. "Mister, if I help you brush the ponies, can I have a ride on the cute pinto? I promise I'll do an extra good job. Please! I *love* horses." As far as plans go, it really wasn't too bad, but there was a slight drawback—she was still a minor, and in California there were certain child-labor laws that prohibited such things. The two men struggled to keep a straight face as they pondered the best way to turn the girl down without hurting her feelings. It was not an easy process.

"Look, little girl, we'd love to let you help us out, but just think about it for a minute. If we let you help us for a ride, we'd have to let all the other kids in the neighborhood help out, too, and so we wouldn't be able to earn a dime. And, if we don't earn any money, how can we buy food for the ponies?" This way of looking at it was pretty convincing, but Melody wasn't ready to give in yet.

"But," she whimpered, her lower lip trembling, "they always say that the early bird gets the worm. I was the earliest kid in the neighborhood, so you could just say that I got here first and you don't need anyone else." The trembling lip usually worked in most discussions, but in this case she could see that it was going to get her nowhere. She blinked back the tear that burned her eye.

When she opened her eyes, she saw that the sun was just beginning to filter through the bedroom curtain. She rolled over and saw that it was only five-thirty A.M., time to get up. That dream sure had seemed real; she almost wished it had been, because it would have been fun to ride a pony. Oh, well, some other time. She got up and got dressed, taking care not to wake up Jan. She snuck out the kitchen door and went out to pet the rabbits and feed them a little grass. She figured they would probably have to mow the lawn before they did anything else that morning. After giving each of the bunnies a handful of the long grass, she headed out to the front yard, thinking that she might find a little frog out by the big oak tree in the Krankopfs' front yard. It was still early enough that the California sun hadn't yet dried up the morning dew, and that was usually the best time to find those tiny, bright green tree frogs. She hadn't found a lot of them, but every once in a while you could find one on that tree. Maybe they didn't come to their house because of the pink oleanders growing by the porch, or maybe because they didn't have a tree, or at least, not in the front yard. There was that orange tree in the backyard, but maybe they didn't like oranges. A slight movement over to her right made her turn around, thinking that maybe there was a lizard climbing up the mailbox pole. And then she saw them.

She was sure that she wasn't dreaming this time, because her feet were all wet from the grass, but she pinched herself on the arm just to make sure. There they were, all seven ponies, munching on hay, while their owners spread straw on the ground, so that when they carried the children on their backs, they wouldn't hurt their hooves on the pavement. They were surprised to see Melody at that hour of the morning; it was, of course, only six o'clock, and most normal people were still in bed. They permitted her to pet the ponies when she asked, but she knew better than to ask if she could help brush them so that she could have a free ride. She didn't think her dignity could survive being refused in real life. In fact, she had another plan that she was sure would work without any problems.

7

Lazy Days

Melody, through personal experience, discovered the truth that day of the saying that you should be careful about what you want, because if you really want it, you'll get it. The only problem is that what you think you want might not turn out to be exactly what you thought it was. All the other kids were in the front yard playing on the slip-and-slide; she, on the other hand, was in the backyard with Ross, gathering up the grass that was left behind by the lawn mower that was being pushed by her father. When she had made the suggestion to Ross, who was a firm believer in the child-labor laws of the state (except when referring to his brood and gardening; this was, after all, a family business), he had accepted the offer without a qualm. The sun shone bright and hot in the sky, making the work hard, sweaty, and not nearly as much fun when done alone as it was when her brothers and sister were there to help her out. A few tendrils of long blond hair had escaped from the tight braids that had held them, and were presently stuck to Melody's face, itchier than mosquito bites; rivulets of perspiration slid down her spine and between her shoulder blades, but riding those ponies would make it all worthwhile, even if they only went around in circles and they had to use saddles. She hoped that when her turn came, that pure black one would be free, so she could pretend she was riding Fury; if not, the brown and white pinto would be okay, too, because then she could pretend she was Tonto, riding along with the Lone Ranger. She knew, though, that if she didn't hustle her bustle—whatever that was—she wouldn't be riding any of the ponies, because they would be gone by the time she got out there. It was a good thing that her daddy had said that she only had to rake everything up—later, they would give the mowed grass to the rabbits, which would be very grateful for the tasty snack. Melody knew that there was a lot of clover mixed up in the grass, and that it was really sweet. She had a sneaking suspicion, though, that her siblings would also get to ride the ponies, but maybe she would get to ride two times; it was only fair, of course.

It took another half hour of deep concentration before she finally finished; she didn't even stop when there were lizards that tempted her, wriggling their tails while they tried to catch insects that had been disturbed by the lawn mower or by butterflies that fluttered softly in her face. She did stop once, though, when one of those blackbirds that looked like they were bleeding under their wings flew overhead. Ross had told her that there was absolutely nothing wrong with the bird, but that it was called a red-wing blackbird because of the red markings under its wings. Thus assured, Melody returned to her raking, continuing until it was all gathered in two huge mounds. When the work was finally done, she fell to the ground weakly, wishing that she could automatically transport herself onto the slip-and-slide; her arms felt as though they would fall off her shoulders, and she wondered if she would even have the strength to hold onto the reins. Her reveries were interrupted by Honey's voice calling her from the back door.

"Hey, Mickey, hurry up and take your pony rides. When you finish, you have to hurry and pack your suitcase; Grammy just called to let me know that she and Grampa want to come and get you after lunch, so you can stay with them until next Saturday."

Nothing could have worked better in helping her to regain her strength and good will. Wow!—a whole week at Grammy and Grampa's house. She jumped to her feet, grabbed an armful of grass, holding it against her with her left arm, and ran out to the front yard, her other hand extended toward her father so that she could get her money to go on the pony rides. When the other kids saw her heading toward the ponies, they all stopped slipping and sliding and started off behind their elder sister. They had only taken a few steps when they were stopped firmly by Ross.

"No, you don't. Melody has worked all morning so that she can ride the ponies, so we'll just let her go first. Do you all think it's fair that she should have to work and that you guys can all go without having to do anything except have fun?" The question was, of course, rhetorical, but three heads all bobbed up and down, approving the idea that they should, indeed, have this privilege. Melody would not, of course, have agreed and neither did Ross. He did, however, come up with another idea that was approved by all.

"What do you think about letting Melody go for one ride, and then all of you, Melody included, going for another round?" This suggestion was greeted with a round of applause. "So, go get dried off quick as a bunny hop and then we'll all go get in line and wait our turn."

As the McDonalds waited in line, Honey, holding Chas in her arms, leaned back against the wooden bars surrounding the ponies' track. The sun was hot and her back was killing her, but she really wanted to watch as the kids rode happily on the ponies. The line moved slowly and so it was quite easy to just drift off drowsily into a sort of daydream. Ross had the other kids under his watchful eye and Chas was sleeping with his head on her shoulder. Of course, the children had their eyes on the ponies and so everyone was taken quite unawares when Chas let out a loud wail. Honey quickly turned her head in time to see one of the ponies, a feisty, dappled gray who had been nibbling on poor Chas's ear, jerk back, startled by the loud noise.

"Hey, lady, you should never lean back on a fence when there are ponies around. They're unpredictable and love to chew on whatever they find at hand. It doesn't matter if it's grass or an apple or somebody's hand; it's enough that it's there and available. What's worse, the baby has made him nervous and I don't know if we can make him walk calmly. Just get away from the fence or he's liable to do it again." Properly chastised and thoroughly embarrassed, not to mention being worried about her poor six-week-old baby's ear, Honey quickly distanced herself from the ponies, and watched as the other four climbed onto their stamping steeds. Naturally enough, Melody, having seen the character of the gray pony, immediately chose that one. Honey groaned to herself. *What a daredevil that child is and a traitor, to boot!* She looked up in time to see Melody wave as she and the pony took off a little faster than normal, bumping into the pony in front of them. She looked back down at Chas and bounced him up and down until his happy gurgling told her that he had fallen back asleep.

"Hey, Mommy! Did you see me on the pony? He was really fun—even better than the black one." Melody and the others danced around their mother, risking waking up their brother again.

"Okay, guys, let's go eat. Campbell's soup and peanut-butter-and-jelly sandwiches." And with that, she led the whole group, Ross included, into the house for lunch.

Two hours later, Melody, with her suitcase, bicycle, roller skates, and bathing suit (perhaps the most important article after the pile of books), was once again seated in Grammy and Grampa's black and white station wagon. The sun above beat down upon the roof of the car and would have transformed it into an oven, baking all those inside, if Melody hadn't insisted on leaving the windows wide open. Grampa's hair was a little worse for wear but it was nothing that a comb couldn't fix; Grammy's bouncy curls were no problem, but Melody's . . .; they had wanted to braid it before leaving, knowing Melody's propensity for pretending she was a dog, with her head hanging out the window and her tongue hanging out of her mouth, but there was nothing really to be done about it, short of tying her up and then braiding it. The only good thing about it was that Melody's hair rarely defied brushing, even when it tangled in such a way that it highly resembled those newfangled dreadlocks that a number of people from the Caribbean Islands were starting to wear. All you needed to do was get it wet, and the whole she-bang would just straighten out. Grammy kept a staying hand on Melody's arm because the real danger was that she might lean out too far and fall flat on her face in the middle of the street while the car moved ahead in the busy beach traffic.

When Grampa finally pulled up in front of the big garage, a very rare commodity in that area, Grammy let go of Melody's arm and let out a sigh of relief. She loved the child as she did her own life, but there was no denying that the girl tended to be a little too reckless at times. Thank goodness, they were home at last. Waiting anxiously until Grampa parked the car inside the garage was hard on Melody's system, but she knew it would only be a few more minutes until she could race into the house through the garage door. She had seen Beau sitting on the back of Grammy's green easy chair and then when he had taken off, running toward the kitchen door where she knew he would be waiting for her.

Once inside the door, she knelt down on the kitchen floor and opened her arms to the fluffy gray bullet that shot through the dining-room door. Soon, the miniature French poodle had her giggling hilariously as his sandpaper tongue washed her face at the joy of seeing her. His short pom-pom tail wagged so fast that she could hardly see it and soon the two of them were rolling on the floor in a free-for-all wrestling match.

"All right, you two, that will be quite enough. We can watch wrestling on the TV this evening before going to bed. Mickie, dear, Grampa will carry your suitcase to your bedroom after he takes your bike out of the trunk and puts it in the garage. In the meantime, you can wash your hands and face. Afterward, you can take a walk along the path in the flower garden. Run along now, dear, that's a good girl."

When she came out of the little washroom in her bedroom, she saw that Grampa had already brought her suitcase into her room and that Grammy was busy putting her clothes away in the drawers in the black and white dresser that had been hers since the day that she had come home from the hospital. She loved this bedroom and all the furniture that was in it. The furniture was shiny black and white with a wonderful night-light with a bright red lampshade attached to the shiny black headboard on her bed. There were also two black reading lamps with white shades on the nightstands beside the bed. Grammy gave her a beautiful hand-crocheted bedspread (with two marching horses) that she said her mother had made many years before in England as part of her wedding dowry. The little washroom had been painted bright red, because this was *her* room and red was her favorite color. There was a big window on the wall overlooking the street, along with her own private door that led onto the porch. It was neat, because she could regulate the Venetian blinds so that she could let in as much light and fresh air as she wanted. However, the best part of the bedroom was the neat pinewood wall paneling, the same that could be found anywhere else in the house, too. She and Grammy spent hours looking for new animal faces that might pop out unexpectedly, as well as seeing old faces that they well knew. Grammy and Melody would invent stories about what the animals had done since Melody's last visit. Melody's very favorite character was a very small, fluffy owl that was on the wall right in front of Melody's bed, just beside the door that opened onto the living room.

After Grammy and Melody finished unpacking, they went out into the yard to visit Grampa's flowers. Because the house was situated on a corner, the yard or, more precisely, the garden curved around the entire front and side of the house. It was beautiful, full of all sorts of flowers, but the pride and joy of the entire garden were Bill's roses. Dark red roses filled the neighborhood with their deep fragrance. The pink and white, candy stripers were Melody's favorites, but she adored the yellow and pink ones, too. Honey's favorite was the pure white rose that bloomed toward evening. There was a great variety of other flowers, too;

depending on the season you might find purple and yellow pansies; chrysanthemums; hydrangeas; elegant white Easter lilies; perky yellow daffodils; dark purple irises; and jaunty red, yellow, and white tulips, whose original bulbs had come straight from Holland, but had multiplied beyond measure.

Melody's very favorite flowers were of a less elegant variety and were very much appropriate to her own character: spontaneous and impertinent. That day, there was an abundance of the three colored miniature violets, the purple, white, and yellow Johnny-jump-ups. Every morning when she followed her grandfather around the garden as he watered each plant, she was very careful to stay on the big flat rocks that had been specially placed to form a path, so that no wandering plants would be stepped on before Bill had the chance to transplant them in another, more convenient place.

There was a short, but extremely full, lemon tree in the part of the garden that was in front of Melody's bedroom window, and that was almost always full of bright yellow fruit or sweet-smelling white flowers that would soon become lemons. They were yummy as lemonade or squeezed on sardines, but they always made her mouth pucker if she just ate them alone. They were nothing like oranges, she decided, but they were good anyway.

Alongside of the steps that led up to the porch where she and Grammy spent most of their time together during the summer, there were two very tall cypress trees that had been there at least fifty years. There was another one just like them at the end of the garden, leaning against the garage. There was a series of lawn chairs along the long side of the porch, where Grammy and Grampa would pass their summer evenings watching the sailboats pass by on the other side of the peninsula. Hot-pink and purple fuchsias hung in big metal baskets from the roof that extended over the porch. All things considered, it was a wonderful place for a person, and especially for a seven-going-on-eight-year-old granddaughter to spend a week of full relaxation.

"Mickie, dear, what is this?" Grammy pulled a little ball of fluffy grayish-black feathers out of her pocket. "I found it in the middle of your clothes." Melody didn't have the faintest idea how the ball of feathers had gotten into her suitcase. She hadn't even thought about it since she had put it in her closet a week earlier, not to mention putting it into her suitcase.

"I don't know, Grammy. I found it in the backyard last week, but I forgot all about it. It's kind of interesting, though, isn't it?"

Grammy held it for a few seconds, and then agreed with her granddaughter. "You're right; it almost seems alive, even though it hasn't got any of the essentials. It's just a ball of feathers. Well, if you want to keep it, we'll just put it here on top of your dresser; that way you can keep track of it. Now, would you like to go to Bill's market with me so we can get your favorite sourdough bread and some sardines for your lunch tomorrow?"

After giving her grandfather a peck on the cheek and a big hug, Melody raced to the small gate at the front of the garden in two gleeful leaps. The small, local market was only eight blocks down, but they were fairly long blocks, and it was great fun walking down to the store with Grammy. There were always people to greet, and you could see the giant Ferris wheel about halfway to Bill's. The Balboa Peninsula wasn't very wide—the Pacific Ocean, with its wonderful sandy beaches, ran along the southwest side. The main road, with all its little side streets, ran down the center of the peninsula, while the canal was separated from the main road by a minor road and a small port. It was also on this side that the Tenth Street Bay was found, the one where Melody and all of her brothers and sister had learned how to swim. It was the selfsame bay where the McDonalds continued going during the summer weekdays.

Farther ahead, shortly after the Balboa Pavilion, the peninsula ended in a smooth curve. Every year several famous, traditional sailboat races took place along this long coastal area; part of these regattas could be observed from the Jenkinses' porch; Grampa liked to use his binoculars, because that way he could see the sailors as they worked together. After the last boat passed in front of their house, Melody liked to run to the beach on the other side and run to the end of the cement walk way that led from Grammy's street across the sand until it tapered away at about fifteen feet from the shore. There, she could easily watch another long stretch of the race. Sometimes, Grampa would go with her, and she would race back and forth until he caught up with her.

Today, however, there was no such race, and in fact, most of the sailboats at the Balboa Yacht Club had their sails either furled or completely taken off of the mast. It was not a day for sailing; the bright blue sky was completely unmarred by scudding clouds that would have announced the presence of wind. The bay and the canals were completely still, and none of these signs were conducive to good sailing weather. The few sailors that had taken their boats out of the harbor were now floating them in place, or slowly pulling them along by the current as they absorbed the hot, late-afternoon rays of sun. However, the Yacht Club's parking lot, which at one time had held the house where Melody had spent the first four years of her life and was kitty-corner from Grammy's house, was full of cars, a sign that there would probably be a big hubbub at the club.

"Hey, Grammy, look, there are some of those funny-looking cars that Daddy has us look for when we come down here to see you or go to the beach. You know, the ones they call the 'bug.' That sure is a funny name for a car, huh?" Melody pointed toward a rather small white, hump-backed vehicle parked right on the edge of the lot. "It's so dinky; where do the people sit, anyway? It sure wouldn't be big enough for us, anyway."

"Well, yes, dear. It's a foreign car and the roads in Germany aren't very big, so they make small cars like that. But yes, you're right—it really is quite a tight squeeze, I'm sure."

With that, the two of them took off down the street, walking on the right hand side (which was the side Grammy's house was on) because that side was in the shade. Melody thought that they might never make it; she ran the whole distance several times, waiting impatiently for her grandmother at the end of each block: she knew better than to cross the street without Grammy; it wasn't really dangerous, but some weirdo might turn without signaling or something. You just never know what people are going to do. And that was why she ran up and down each block, waiting for Grammy.

Fortunately, there were only six blocks between Grammy's house and Bill's Market, and Melody soon calmed down enough to walk the two blocks while holding Grammy's hand. Most of the small yards adorning the houses along the street were full of plants, but none, of course, were as beautiful as Grampa's. Melody loved stopping in front of these houses and smelling the flowers on the plants. None of them had roses or tulips, but several had hydrangeas and a few even had some snow-white camellias. Every once in a while she could see a butterfly and a large number of bees, but, to her great dismay, there were no frogs or lizards. She couldn't actually remember having seen them in Grampa's flowers, either, and she thought this was very strange. But then, there wasn't much grass there either. She didn't really have any idea what that could mean, but it seemed important to her. *Oh, well,* she thought, *we don't have shells or sand crabs at our house, even if there is sand under the house. I guess we can't have everything everywhere.*

There was one house in particular that attracted her attention along the way. Every time they passed it, she asked Grammy or Grampa how the word on the sign hanging from the eaves was pronounced. It looked like a foreign word, although they assured her it really was an English abbreviation. THE FO'C'SLE, it said. Not only couldn't she pronounce it, but she didn't know what it meant. She figured it probably had something to do with boats, but she had no idea what. "Grammy, how do you say that word again? I can't ever remember."

Grammy, as a true Englishwoman, pronounced, as only they can do, it as "fo-cuss-ell." She said, "Now, dear, it's really not that difficult. It's the abbreviation for 'forecastle.' "

"But Grammy, what is a forecastle and wouldn't it just be easier to say 'forecastle'?"

"Well, actually, dear, that's how they pronounce it in England, you know. That's why it's written that way. A forecastle has nothing to do with the first part of a castle, as it could seem, but it's really the front part of the deck of a ship."

"Oh, I see, I think." She really didn't, because she didn't understand how something could be called part of a castle, if there was no castle, but she was sure that someday she would figure it out. Maybe.

On the way home, after buying their reserves for the next couple of days, Melody stopped short in front of a building that had captivated her attention. It was built of red bricks and covered with ivy. They had ivy at their house, but it didn't cover the whole house. "Grammy, what's this building? I've never seen a house all covered with ivy before; it looks neat."

Knowing her granddaughter's tastes, Edith had somehow managed to avoid this particular building—not so much because it was distasteful, but because she knew that once Melody knew what it was, she would have a hard time keeping her from coming here all alone. This was something that should be avoided at all costs, at least for the time being. After all, it was a busy street, especially in the summer, and Melody was a little reckless at times; even a doting grandmother could see this. However, the girl had caught sight of it, and the time had arrived in which the nature of the public library could no longer be hidden. All things considered, she didn't spend that much time with her grandparents, and so maybe it wouldn't interest her that much.

"It's the public library, dear."

"No, not that building; I already knew about that. You can see the rows of books from the window, plus there's a big sign on the front that says, BALBOA PUBLIC LIBRARY. No, I was talking about the one next door to it. The one without windows and with the long driveway."

A ten-foot wave of relief flooded Edith's entire being. "Oh, that's the Fire Department. Maybe someday we can come by and visit it. They don't usually let people go through, except on certain days, but Grampa is friends with the chief. You know, working with the police, he sometimes has dealings with the Fire Department, too. Oh, look, there's their mascot," she concluded as a big black-spotted, white dog came bounding out of the station.

"Wow, a real dalmatian. I never saw one in person before. Here, Sparky," she called out to the dog. Hearing its name, the dog perked up its ears and went to lick Melody's face.

"Mickey, you never fail to surprise me. How did you know that the dog's name is Sparky? I didn't even know that."

"Well, it just seemed the logical name for a fire station mascot. It could have been Spot, but that didn't sound good enough for an important dog like this one." She giggled as the big dog snuffled in her ear. "Okay, boy, it's better if you go back into the station. We have to go home now." She giggled again as Sparky offered his left paw. Shaking it, and doing it solemnly, she added, "See ya later. Be good, okay?" With that, the three of them separated, Edith and Melody going toward home and Sparky back to his fire engine.

Saturday at Grammy and Grampa's house was a lot different than at home. First of all, it was a lot quieter, at least at the beginning. Of course, things did kind of change after the TV had been turned on for about ten minutes, because there was always a big bet as to who was going to win the boxing match. The event became quite vocal at times, first with Grammy, then with Grampa, and then all three together. Melody didn't really care who won: she won in either case, because Grammy and Grampa both had her, and the three cents were always a big help. Afterward, there was professional bowling, in which Melody was particularly interested, because both Ross and Honey enjoyed bowling, even if

128

Daddy was really good. She always hoped that someday she would get to see her daddy on the TV as he bowled with his team in some championship. He even had a plaque at home from when he had had a perfect three-hundred-point game. Melody had tried once to throw the ball down the lane, but her fingers had gotten stuck in the holes, and if it hadn't been for the fact that the ball weighed way too much for her to throw it, it would probably have dragged her down the lane with it. Of course, then she had tried to just push it, but that was no good, either, because it just ended up in the gutter. The only time it really got anywhere was when, to her great embarrassment, it stopped halfway down the lane and wouldn't budge, even when they jumped up and down. They had to get one of the alley's workers to go push it into the gutter. She decided at that time that bowling just wasn't her thing. Maybe they'd let her keep score when she was a little bigger; that wasn't too hard, and the scorekeepers always got paid for their work.

Of course, they always watched the Million Dollar movie on Saturday nights. Sometimes there were scary movies, but mostly they showed musicals or other movies that didn't cause nightmares, but it finished late, and it was hard to stay awake so that they could see the end. Being cuddled up on Daddy's arm was very conducive to sleep, even if you had to struggle to get the best position: there were three other kids who wanted the same place. Watching TV with Grammy and Grampa was fun because she got to sit on the sofa between the two of them, with her feet perched on Beau's back, or at least they were when she leaned forward to get her glass of pop from the coffee table in front of the sofa. She supposed that the reason that Daddy didn't watch bowling on TV was that he had enough of it in real life, and anyway, he was a lot better than the guys on TV; none of them ever got three hundred points.

Things were a little different that evening, though; Beau was mad at her and wouldn't even talk to her. He knew she had been talking to another dog, because he had run to her when they arrived home, but stopped abruptly when he smelled Sparky's odor all over her, and was jealous. Now, instead of lying down under her feet, he was stretched out at Grampa's end of the sofa, near the green and white hi-fi/record player. His position was rather odd, unlike any position that Melody had ever seen for a dog.

"Grammy, what's wrong with Beau? He looks like a frog with his legs out in back like that. Did he break them or something? He's not hurt, is he?"

Edith looked down at the huffy gray dog and laughed. "Oh, don't worry about him. It frightened me, too, the first time I saw him lie down like that, but the veterinarian said that was just something that only purebred dogs can do. And don't you worry about him not paying you attention; you'll see, he'll be over it by tomorrow morning."

At that point Bill nudged his "girls" and shushed them; the boxing match was about to begin. "Okay, I think I'll take the guy in the white shorts—he looks like a better boxer than the guy in black."

"No, you just think he's better because he's stockier than the guy in black. You're on. Ten cents says that the guy in black will win."

And so began the evening fight (on TV, not between the observers), with Grammy, Melody, and Grampa sitting and urging on their chosen color, Bill and Edith each nursing their glass of beer, and Melody drinking her ginger ale with a special Mickey Mouse–shaped straw. The winner was the one wearing black shorts—Melody could have told Grampa that great things often come in small packages—and Grampa had to cough up thirteen cents. Bowling was less competitive than the fights, because there were no official bets; this didn't mean, however, that it was less noisy. Every time one of the bowlers got a strike, all three observers threw their hands in the air and cheered on the bowler. It was a good evening, and while none of them got full points like Ross, some of them got pretty good scores, way over two hundred.

There were no discussions when Grammy announced it was time for bed; it had been a long day, what with working in the backyard, riding the ponies, and running up and down Balboa Boulevard so Melody was more than ready for bed. Six o'clock in the morning came early, and while she knew that she couldn't go running around the house until she heard Grammy stirring in the kitchen, getting her and Grampa's tea ready, she could always turn on her lamp and read.

After she slid into her new baby-doll pajamas, Grammy came in and brushed her long, silky blond hair, one hundred strokes, and then listened to her prayers. Just before Edith turned out the light, Melody looked at the pinewood wall in front of her and let out a little shriek. "Grammy, look, the little owl has been swallowed by an ostrich. When did that happen? The owl was okay this afternoon when I got here. Oh, poor little thing."

"You're right, dear; I remember seeing it this afternoon, too. Oh, well, don't worry, because I'm sure that it will be alright. If you can still see it, nothing will happen to it. Okay, close your eyes now and go to sleep. Nighty night, sleep tight. Don't let the beddy bugs bite."

The advice was unnecessary. Melody was already asleep before Grammy had touched the light switch.

Melody awakened bright and early the next morning, and was raring to go. She could hear the pounding of the surf on the sandy shore not fifty yards away. It was still too early, though, to get up for good. Grammy left a night light on for her in the living room in case it was needed during the night, but the sun was already on the rise, and she didn't really need the light. She got up and tiptoed as lightly as she possibly could, turning out the light as she passed. Grammy had closed the curtains the night before, but the early-morning light filtered through enough to let Melody pass without knocking into anything. While she was on her way back to her bedroom, Beau, who was sleeping at the foot of Grammy's bed, lifted his ears at the sound of her passing, without bothering to open his eyes. He let out a low woof in acknowledgment of her presence and instantly returned to his dreaming. Melody wondered what he could be dreaming of—maybe some poor, hapless cat that wandered not so innocently into his garden.

For the next hour or so Melody lay down on her bed and began reading one of the new library books Daddy had brought her the other day. It was about a man who was kind of like her: he could talk to animals and they talked back to him. The only difference was that when she talked with the animals around her, she usually just thought what she wanted to say while he and the animals he talked to talked aloud. It was pretty neat, though. She was so immersed in her reading that she almost didn't hear Grammy go into the kitchen. In fact, she only knew that Grammy was awake because she heard the teapot whistle when the water was ready. She quickly closed the book and set it on the little table next to the bed.

Grammy was already back in the bedroom and sitting on her bed, drinking her tea with Grampa by the time Melody made it into their room. It was an every morning ritual that was rigidly followed. While her grandparents drank their tea, Melody would sit at the foot of Grammy's bed and they would talk about their dreams and their plans for the day. It was fun, because she always got to participate in the conversation. When the tea had all been drunk, Melody went into her room to change her clothes while Grammy began to prepare breakfast and Grampa put on his wooden leg (he had been seriously injured during World War One, and they had had to amputate his leg; his wooden leg looked so real that, except for his slight limp, it was almost impossible to see that he had a problem).

By the time Melody emerged from her bedroom for the third time that morning, there was already a nice bowl of cereal at her place, and Grammy was already busy preparing her toast and eggs and bacon. A big glass of ice cold orange juice was ready to be carried to the table, together with the rest of the meal. At times it seemed impossible that such a skinny child could be capable of eating such a huge breakfast, but she was the granddaughter of an Englishwoman. She was also very active, and it wasn't all that unusual for her to be extra hungry after a couple of hours. Besides, lunch was a much simpler affair, with only a sandwich and a few sardines, or something else equally simple. Therefore, Grammy was always happy to fix this first meal of the day, while the three of them sat together at the beautiful polished pine table that Bill himself had made.

This morning, as soon as breakfast was over, Melody and Bill would take off for the beach while Grammy stayed and washed dishes. It was a perfect morning for fishing, slightly overcast with a slight breeze. Melody's bathing suit was ready to put on—it would only take a minute—and then they would be off.

Melody and Bill walked together down the walk, waving gaily to Edith as they went. Bill was carrying his fishing pole and his tackle box while Melody had his bait bucket swinging from the crook of her left elbow, which is where she usually carried anything that could be hung; it was useless wasting a good arm and this left her right hand empty, ready to gather whatever was ready to be gathered. At the moment the bucket was empty; it would be Melody's job to fill it up with the kind of bait that was most popular amongst the fish waiting to be caught in the early morning surf.

"Grampa, what if I can only find hard-shelled sand crabs today? You know the soft-shelled crabs are kinda hard to find sometimes."

"Don't worry, there are always some around, and you're an expert at finding them."

When they got to the edge of the shoreline, Melody bent down and filled the bucket halfway with water, making sure to add a little sand, too, so that the crabs wouldn't dry out. While her grandfather began setting up his pole Melody, after setting down the pail beside her, knelt down just where the waves rolled onto the sand and quickly stuck her hand into the still wet sand. After digging around for a few seconds she let out a sound of triumph as she pulled a fairly large sand crab out of its hole in the sand. It was a whopper, according to sand crab standards, almost as long as one of Melody's fingers, and obviously well-nourished.

"Look, Grampa, it's a giant," she yelled happily. But then, a note of disappointment entered into her voice. "The only problem is, he's got a hard shell."

"Well, don't worry, the beach is full of them and so are the waves, and sooner or later you'll get what you're looking for. Just keep trying. Keep him, though, for the moment; we might be able to use him anyway." He hadn't really expected her to catch a soft-shelled crab on the first try and had brought some rubber imitations that gave the general idea to tie onto his hook. They worked pretty well, but sand crabs were much better, because that was the main diet of the fish that swam so close to the shore. After attaching one, he launched the line far beyond the breaking waves where it would float in relative peace—broken, he hoped, only by the tug that would announce the imminent capture of a fish.

Half an hour later, Melody had already caught five medium-sized, soft-shelled sand crabs and had let the hard-shelled crab loose again, slightly farther away than where they were fishing. Bill had already substituted the rubber bait for the real thing; Melody was intent on watching the holes in the sand that showed where the sand crabs had hidden themselves, hoping to catch planktons as they passed by without being caught themselves. It would seem a simple thing to do as there were holes everywhere in the sand, but the problem was that there were too many dinky ones—millions of them when compared to only hundreds of the really big ones—and you only knew which was which after you stuck your hands into the sand. Then, it seemed like they could figure out that Melody was there, so they kept changing feeding spots along the beach.

"Grampa, there aren't any more sand crabs here; may I go down that way a little," she said, pointing her finger toward the Balboa Pier, "and see if there are any that way?"

"All right, just don't go too far, and don't go into the water without telling me first," he warned. "The tide is receding, but the waves are getting stronger and they could pull you under. I know you can swim almost as well as a fish, but they have gills, so they can breathe underwater, but you don't. Just stay within hearing distance; if I'm lucky, I may need another one of those crabs soon."

"All right, Grampa, I'll be careful." Taking the bucket in her hand, she walked down the beach another ten feet or so. Grampa was right—the waves were getting higher, as was the sun, and soon the beach would be filling up with sunbathers and swimmers. Board surfers weren't allowed in this portion of the beach because there were too many other people around. They weren't really too worried about it, though, because the waves were a lot better in the zone just before the Newport Pier, anyway.

An early morning beachcomber walked slowly down the beach, moving his metal detector from one side to the other as he searched for metal items, either left on the beach by unwitting beachgoers or else carried there by the preceding evening's high tide. His leather pouch jingled with the items he had already found. When he was about two feet away from Melody, the detector began beeping, indicating some unknown treasure buried in the sand under the man's feet. As he pulled his shovel from his shoulder, a very curious Melody came up to see what he was doing.

"Hey, mister, what are you looking for? I'm looking for sand crabs—that's my Grampa there who's fishing. Are you looking for sand crabs, too? There's lots of them around; I don't even need to use that vacuum cleaner thing you have there. Look, that's what all those little holes are. When the water passes over the sand, they go in them, see, and then they try to catch something to eat. That's what my Grampa says, and he knows everything about sand crabs, 'cause he uses them for bait."

She stopped to catch her breath and the surprised stranger took the chance to answer her question. "Uh, I'm looking for things that people leave on the beach or that get washed up on it, like bracelets or earrings. I even find coins, sometimes. I can find just about anything that's made from metal, if it's not buried too deep."

"Neat! Do you take them to the lost and found department at the police station so that the people that have lost them can have them back?" She tried to encourage him with an engaging toothy grin and looked up at him with big, innocent blue eyes.

At a loss for words (something that happened quite often to people in their first encounter with Melody), the young man started, "Uh . . ." Fortunately for him, Bill called his granddaughter just at that moment, saving him from either having to tell a lie or else explain an embarrassing truth.

"Bye, mister, good luck in your hunting. I'm coming, Grampa." She turned to wave at the bewildered beachcomber and then galloped toward her grandfather, hurdling over a mass of gnat-covered, dried-out seaweed that had somehow been missed by the beach patrol that morning. Another time, she would have been interested in popping open the dried pods, but she could see now that Grampa had a fish hanging on the end of his line. She hurried even faster, the bucket banging into her legs as she ran.

"Grampa, you caught a fish already. Boy, it's a big one, isn't it?" Reaching him, Melody took a closer look at the fish and asked, "What kind of fish is it, Grampa? Can you eat it?"

Bill held the seventeen-inch, three-pound fish up proudly and told her, "It's a croaker. They like worms, so I guess he was pretty much fooled by that rubber one I had there on my hook. But, if we want to get some other kinds, we'd better use some of those sand crabs you've got there in your bucket."

While Melody was engaged in searching through the sand in her bucket for the best of the sand crabs, Bill gently took the large croaker off of the hook and placed it into his creel. "Grampa, why do they call it a croaker? Isn't that what they usually call frogs, because of the sound they make?"

With great care, Bill rubbed the underside of the fish, and it emitted a very strange sound that almost seemed like the sound that balloons made when she and her siblings rubbed their hands against them. "Wow, I thought fish didn't make noise, but this one sure does. Cool. Here's the sand crab. Are you gonna catch another croaker?"

"Well," he said, putting the crab on the hook, "if I don't catch another croaker, I hope I catch something. These crabs of yours are really special, so they should also catch a special fish."

"You mean like a swordfish or a marlin? Swordfish is my favorite kind, after tuna, sardines, and that neat pink salmon Grammy gives me. That's really yummy, 'cause you can eat the bones."

"We-ell, I don't think I'll be able to catch one of those, because they live in really deep water, and you catch salmon farther north, but I might be able to catch a halibut or maybe a surfperch. Those live in this kind of water, here by the beach. It's a little late in the year for surfperch, but it's possible that I can get a halibut. We'll just have to wait and see."

Melody stood next to him as he cast his line beyond the incoming surf, burying her toes into the wet sand as the next wave came up and rolled up to just under her knees. The water was cold, but the haze had lifted, and the cool water felt good. She wished she could go swimming, but she knew that she might scare the fish away if she did.

"Grampa, can I go look for some more sand crabs? There are only four left, and I hope you catch a lot of fish."

He looked down the beach to where the beachcomber had been, but he was no longer anywhere in sight. "All right, just don't go talking to strangers, okay?"

Melody nodded her head and then took off up the beach, in the complete opposite direction. She had noticed, while talking to her grandfather, that the tiny holes had started going north, and she knew that the prey was heading in that direction. As she neared the area, something unexpected, halfway buried in the sand, caught her eye. Thinking it was just a broken shell, but interested all the same, Melody knelt down and pulled the shell from the sand. It wasn't just any old shell, and it wasn't even broken: it was a complete sand dollar! Wow, she usually found only bits and pieces here at this beach. Sometimes they found a live one at Little Corona beach, in the middle of the tide pools, with its fuzzy purple skin, and sometimes they even found a dinky one that looked like a quarter, but this one was big. She studied the rough sandpaperlike bone. It was kind of a dull, grayish white and there was a form that looked like a starfish on the top. When she turned it over she saw that there was a tiny hole in the center. She supposed it was so they could breathe, when they were alive. *Everyone* knew that the gray form she now held in her hand was just the skeleton. She looked around excitedly to see if there were others, but this seemed to be the only one in the zone.

Once again she hurried back to her grandfather, just in time to see him pull another fish toward the shore. This one was much different from the first. The croaker had a normal fish body—oval shaped; with one eye on each side of his head; with fins on its back, sides, stomach, and tail—while this new fish was completely flat, but almost circular, and a whole lot bigger. It had both eyes on one side, which made it look really weird. The side that had the eyes was a kind of muddy brown, while the other side, which looked almost normal except that it didn't have eyes, was a lardlike white.

"See, Mickey! I told you your crabs would get us a special fish. This," he said, indicating the newly caught fish, "is a halibut, and it's a real doozy. Look how big it is; it must weigh at least ten pounds. I think we can go home now."

"See, Grampa, I found a silver dollar at the same time you caught that big fish. This must be a lucky sand dollar." A look of wonder passed over her face as she looked happily at the two fish in the creel. It was a good thing that the creel was big, because the halibut almost didn't fit in. As Bill gathered up his gear, Melody carefully put the newfound treasure in her pocket, feeling quite rich (wow, a whole dollar) and very lucky (Grampa caught that great big fish just when she found the sand dollar). She didn't really like fish, but Grampa had caught it for her, so it was probably good; she'd eat at least a little bit of it, anyway, just to make Grampa happy. When everything was packed up tight, the two of them took off toward home; they were halfway up the walk when Melody turned around and trotted back toward the shore and gently tipped over the bucket into an incoming wave. They certainly didn't need the sand crabs anymore today and they wouldn't survive the night in the bucket, as Melody had already learned from sad experiences.

The halibut wasn't as good as swordfish or salmon; it left a kind of flaky taste in her mouth, and it had a lot of bones that you couldn't eat; if they got stuck in your throat, they weren't very easy to get out and they made you cough a lot. She figured that if she ate the fish like Grammy showed her, it wasn't too bad, but nothing could make her really like it. She put a little more of Grammy's fresh lemon on it, thinking that might help it out a little, and she took a bite of fish, a forkful of succotash, a forkful of mashed potatoes, and then another bite of the fish. Yes, that made it taste a little better.

After Grammy had washed her hair in the big washtub on the service porch in back, she had followed Grampa in the garden as he watered the plants and filled up the birdbath. Two sparrows immediately flew in and began their daily ablutions, cheeping happily as Melody helped Bill out by pulling the weeds that had popped up stealthily through the gravel during the night. Fortunately, they hadn't been the only things to grow during the night: there were also two new bright pink roses on the bush nearest the birdbath. Personally, Melody thought that they were perfectly splendid, pink being her favorite color, along with red. She would have liked to stop right off and look at them, but hadn't wanted to frighten off the birds before they finished their bath.

That afternoon, after lunch, she and Edith had taken a deck of cards out onto the porch and played several hands of rummy, using the new card holder that Grampa had carved out of some spare wood—which he had in the garage—so that Melody could see her cards without everyone else seeing them, too. Grammy hardly ever won, but she didn't seem to care all that much; she was always just as happy when Melody won as when she did. In fact, it seemed like she was happier when her granddaughter won. She would throw her arms up in the air, laughing, and give Melody a big hug. Then, she would lay her cards down on top of the pack and shuffle them all again, and the game would begin all over again. It was a fun way for the two of them to pass a little time together and enjoy each other's company. It also gave Grammy a chance to make sure Melody rested up a little before meeting the world on her bike or skates.

After dinner, Melody pulled out her superdeluxe animal scrapbook and began to study its contents. It was full of pictures of almost every kind of animal in the world and it was her pride and joy. She and Grammy passed hours together reading through old magazines, looking for photographs of animals of all kinds. There were a number of drawings, too; many were advertisements for any number of items, including some weird thing called "whiskey" that came from a far-off country called Scotland. Grammy told her that Scotland was near the country she came from, although it was on the top part of the island. There were two cute little Scottish terriers, one black and one white. There were also, naturally, lots and lots of horses of all colors and sizes. There was one, in particular, called Man o' War that was really neat. Grammy said he was already dead, but had been so famous that people still wrote about him in magazines and stuff. They said he had been the best racehorse in the world. Be that as it may, Melody was convinced that the best horse in the world was Fury.

Grammy had lots of magazines in her house and Melody could cut up any of them that she wanted to. The only exception was the one that Melody would have liked to cut up the most because it was mostly about animals: *National Geographic*. Oh, well, if she couldn't cut it up, at least she could look at it whenever she wanted to. And maybe it was better if she couldn't cut it up, because she would have ended cutting up some animal that she would probably have liked to cut out instead. Animals were the best people in the world, except for her family, of course.

The fire engine's glossy surface gleamed in the soft morning light in the Newport Beach Fire Station garage. It was Bill's day off, and the Fire Department's chief had finally given them permission to come there and take a tour of the station, and so Melody was in seventh heaven. They had just started out, and Melody was already completely enthralled from all that she had seen, from the high-flying American and California State flags to Sparky's immediate obedience when Chief O'Shea had told him to let go of Melody's braid. She was of the opinion that no vehicle could be as beautiful as the shiny fire truck, with its black upholstery that contrasted so nicely with the bright red exterior. Chief O'Shea had let her climb up on the truck and turn the steering wheel (it sure was a lot harder to do than moving the steering wheel on Daddy's MG) and even honk the horn, but he did draw the line at sounding the siren. Not only would that have bothered all the dogs on the block, but it would also have constituted a false alarm, which would doubtlessly annoy the other firemen on duty. He didn't bother telling her that it couldn't be turned on anyway without turning on the truck's motor.

Before going on to the next part of the tour, Fire Chief O'Shea allowed Melody to meticulously examine every inch of the fire engine. She closed her eyes and imagined climbing quickly up the sides and holding on with all her strength as the driver raced to the fire scene. She supposed she wouldn't be able to drive, since she had a real hard time turning the steering wheel, but it would have been nice with good old Sparky sitting next to her, his ears flapping in the wind. She stared hungrily at the collapsible ladder on the side, thinking how nice it would be to have one like it, so she could climb up on the roof and jump off, like they did from the tail of that old World War II airplane there at the Costa Mesa

Park. It would make it easier to visit the couple of pigeons that lived under the eaves of their house, too.

But the thing she liked the best was the long, brownish gray hose that was rolled up on the back of the truck. It was bigger around than her body, and just the thought of all the water that she could spray on a hot summer day like today already made her feel that the temperature had dropped ten degrees lower than it really was. And, to top things off, she was now ready with her first question; her grandparents had wondered at her self-control.

"Chief O'Shea, how do you get water out of that hose there? It's all flat right now, and it's not hooked up to anything. Where does the water come from?"

The man was used to answering the questions of inquisitive children, and this really was quite a simple one. "Well, Melody, have you ever noticed those red fire hydrants placed along the boulevard here? When there's a fire, the first thing we do when we get to the scene is hook up the hose to the closest hydrant; see this end here with the reinforced opening? It's called a 'connector.' We can even add more hoses to one, depending on how far away the hydrant is from the fire. After opening up the hydrant's pumper cap, we screw this end to it. We screw a nozzle onto the other end and open the hydrant's pressure valve. Once the valve is open, the water comes out in a very powerful stream."

Melody's mouth formed a silent "oh" as she gazed in awe at the workings of the fire truck and the hose. At the same time, her mind was forming her next question. "If there's so much pressure in the hydrant that it can shoot out so much water, how come the fire hydrants don't explode when you're not using them?"

Chief O'Shea stared blankly at the little girl—momentarily at a loss for words—and then shot a furtive glare at her grandparents, who smiled sweetly in return. However, Chief O'Shea, being Irish and never long at a loss for words, came up with a solution. "Well, Melody, the pressure never really gets heavy enough to explode because it continuously flows in long pipes, but we do open the hydrants from time to time, just to let a little of the water out. Is there a fire hydrant somewhere on the street where you live?" Melody nodded her headed, concentrating on his answer. Picking up speed, the fire chief continued, "I'm sure that you've noticed that from time to time a technician comes and opens it up and lets the water run down the street." Melody's head continued to bob up and down. "This is just one of the ways that we use that enables us to keep the water pressure under control." It wasn't completely true, but Melody seemed to absorb every word and accept what he said.

"Now, let's climb this stairway and we'll come into the entryway of the complex itself." He guided the three visitors up the stairs and into a large foyer. "Here on the right, we have the visitors' entrance or exit. Normally, this is the door you would use to obtain information or to report a fire. The main office is here on the left." As Melody looked toward the right, she saw a well-known figure: Smokey the Bear, with his motto, "Only You Can Prevent Forest Fires." She tugged her grandmother's sleeve excitedly, but Grammy put her finger to her lips and said, "Later."

They turned and walked down a corridor, Chief O'Shea pointing out several doors, saying that these were the sleeping quarters of the firemen on duty. At the end of the hall they came to a big room, completely decorated in red, with a big round table and several red-backed chairs around it, three plush, red easy chairs, and a bright red refrigerator. Seated at the table were four men, deeply engrossed in a card game. Others were sitting in the easy chairs watching a baseball game—it was the Los Angeles Dodgers against the New York Yankees. Melody was about to sit down on the wooden floor in front of the TV and watch her idol, Mickey Mantle, as he brought in four more runs for the Yankees, but her eyes caught sight of a big round hole right in the middle of the floor, almost where she had been about to sit down.

"Wow! What's this for," she asked, pointing at the long, shiny pole that ran from the ceiling right on through the hole to the floor in the room underneath them.

"Barney, Fred, would one of you two Dodger fans like to show this young lady and her grandparents what this pole is for?"

Both of the young men stood up and, after grabbing a red fireman's hat from a peg on the wall and pulling black gloves onto both hands, ran and jumped, one after the other, onto the pole and slid quickly down it, landing lightly on their feet at the bottom. Inspired by the vision, Melody started to jump in the direction of the pole, but Chief O'Shea caught her just in time.

"No, you don't, young lady. You need to have special gloves to be able to slide down that pole; if you don't have them, you'll burn your hands, because the fall is very fast. We don't have any gloves your size, so you'll just have to wait until you're grown up, and become part of the force," he said, echoing her earlier fantasizing. "Now, as you see, this pole is placed in the middle of that big hole in the floor so that our firefighters can get to the trucks faster, and in this way arrive at the scene of the fire sooner, which makes for a better chance at putting the fire out quicker, and possibly saving more lives."

They all said their good-byes to the men that had remained in the club room and their guide ushered them out into the main corridor. On their way to the front exit, they encountered the two sliders and Melody solemnly shook their hands, telling them that in the meantime the Dodgers had two outs and the count was two and one, with Don Drysdale up to bat. They ran back to the room, just in time to let out a very audible sigh of relief.

"Chief O'Shea, sir," began Melody just as Sparky came to say good-bye, "why do the firemen use dalmatians for their mascot? I mean, Sparky is really neat and all," she bent down to take his proffered paw—"but couldn't just any kind of dog be just as good?"

The fire chief/tour guide didn't miss a beat, this time. "There are a lot of stories as to why the first firefighters chose dalmatians as their mascot. Many people think that dalmatians are able to see the color red and smell smoke fumes better than other dogs; this may well be true, but I don't know. As far as I know, the real reason is that for centuries horses were used to pull the carts that carried buckets of water to the fire scene, as well as the fire brigade. Now, dalmatians get along very well with horses and because of their affinity with these animals, they were able to guide them to the scene of the fire and also keep them calm; horses are very frightened of fire. And so now, even if our carriages are motor-driven trucks, we still keep dalmatians as our mascot, because they are intelligent, loyal, and very obedient." The man bent down and scratched the dog behind the ears.

After everyone shook hands with their special guide, thanking him for the wonderful learning experience, Bill slapped him on the back and whispered, hopefully out of Melody's hearing range, "You did that very well, old boy. Not everyone could do such an expert job at answering Melody's questions."

"Well, buddy, next time we're together at a fire scene in an official capacity, I'll let you do all the paperwork."

"Yes, well . . ."

When Melody went to bed that night, her dreams were full of

galloping horses, with big black and white dalmatians running along beside them, trying at every turn to offer them their paw in a silent offer of friendship.

8

Proud to Be American

Saturday morning arrived and Melody got out of bed rather more reluctantly than she was wont to do. She was happy, for a change, that Grampa wouldn't be at home during the morning, because that meant that she could prolong her stay for at least a few more hours. She waved listlessly at Grampa as he drove by on his way to the police station and then bent over to give Beau a big hug. Grammy had been right: he had forgiven her very quickly for her supposed defection, although yesterday he had looked at her very suspiciously when they had returned home from the fire station. It wasn't her fault that she got along so well with animals; it was just a part of her makeup.

The day passed quickly, and all too soon it was time for her to repack her suitcase. One by one, she placed her clothes haphazardly in the suitcase, along with her scrapbook and her reading material, until there was only one thing left in the drawer: the little ball of feathers. She had hardly thought about it during the week, although it had popped up in some very strange places and at some very strange times, like, for instance, the time when she was getting ready for her bath and had found it inside the soap dish, on top of the soap. Another weird time was when she found it next to her breakfast plate just before going to the fire station yesterday. As she put it carefully into her suitcase on top of her bathing suit, it came to her mind that it was almost as though it had been trying to capture her attention.

After lunch, the three of them lifted Melody's various items into the back of the old station wagon, and, with one last glimpse around the garden and a sad woof from Beau, Melody climbed into the backseat of the car and the return trip home began. Melody waved good-bye to Beau, who had climbed onto the back of the old couch that served as his personal bed.

For some reason, the trip home wasn't as much fun as had been the trip to her grandparents' house. She didn't even feel like sticking her head out the window, until they had driven far enough along that the view of the ocean was just a memory; then the heat got much too oppressive, and sticking her head out became a necessity. As they drove down the familiar main street of Costa Mesa, though, Melody suddenly slipped out of her unnatural apathy. She hadn't noticed that they had changed months while she was at Grammy's house and that today was already the second of July, but the beautiful red and white striped flags, with the blue square and the fifty white stars, hanging from every lamp-post along the way, brought vividly to mind that the day after tomorrow would be the Fourth of July, one of the U.S.'s most exciting holidays.

From that moment on, Melody suddenly became her usual exuberant self. It's not that she wasn't still unhappy at having had to leave her grandparents' house; it's just that something new had trapped her interest. Visions of swirling colored stars filled her mind's eyes, and she could almost taste the roasted hot dogs that they would surely eat at their picnic at the beach. However, the best was yet to come. Distracted by her colorful thoughts of the following Monday, she almost missed seeing the billboard just before their turn-off—almost, but not quite. As she looked up at the stoplight, she almost slipped off the backseat of the car in her excitement. What a neat week she had ahead of her! Not only was Monday the Fourth of July, but next Friday was the first day of the Orange County Fair. Oh, wow!

Whereas before seeing the flags on the trees in Costa Mesa, Melody had been immersed in the deepest of the doldrums, her present state was a complete about-face; in fact, she seemed an entirely new person, full of vital electricity. She could hardly wait to get home and tell everybody about the fair next week. She was pretty sure that everyone knew about the Fourth of July—there were two calendars in the kitchen, one on the wall by the phone and one on the fridge, where all of their school events were listed—but surely no one knew about the fair yet. She was so excited that she hadn't even noticed that they were home until Grampa got out of the car and went to open the door for Grammy.

While Grampa lifted her bike out of the trunk, Melody grabbed her suitcase and skates and took off running toward the house. About halfway there, however, she stopped in her tracks: whoops of laughter and the sounds of loud splashes reached her ears from the backyard. The laughter she could understand; it was Saturday and Daddy was surely at home—she could hear his booming laughter, too—and it was almost always fun when he was home, but where were the splashes coming from? There was a lot of water with the slip-and-slide, but not enough to make splashing sounds and you didn't make splashing sounds running through the sprinkler, either, just a sploshy sound when the mud sucked around your feet. No, the only way that sound could be made was either with a bathtub (and she was sure there was no bathtub in the backyard—no one would take a bath in public) or else a swimming pool, but they didn't have a swimming pool, either. Or did they?

The three of them entered the strangely silent house so that Melody could put the suitcase and skates in her bedroom and then they followed the shrieks and whoops of delight into the backyard patio. There, to her immense surprise, Melody found the entire family—with the exception of Chas, who didn't know how to swim yet and was therefore sitting in his stroller—romping in a great big swimming pool full of enticingly cool blue water. She was suddenly filled with righteous indignation; here she was, planning on giving them some really neat news, and they were all out here swimming in a great big swimming pool *without her!* There was no justice in life. Of course, the idea that she had just come home from a week at their grandparents' house at the beach didn't happen to enter her mind at the moment. However, she decided to be forgiving in this instance.

"Hey, you guys, I'm home, and Grammy and Grampa are here with me, too. Hey, stop, you're gonna get us all wet."

All splashing and whooping stopped, and a slightly guilty silence momentarily took over. It only lasted a moment, because everyone in the pool had already taken into consideration the fact that Melody had just spent a wonderful week with Grammy and Grampa and had probably gone swimming in the ocean every day, too. The ocean was loads more fun, with its waves and all, but the pool was neat, too. This, of course, was the general consensus. The pause slipped by quickly, and in the next moment, all and sundry clambered out of the pool so that they could all go and hug the Jenkinses. Of course, in the flurry of the moment, a few heads got pushed underwater; said heads, not having had time to catch their breath before going under, spluttered breathlessly as they emerged, spitting out water from nose and mouth. These unfortunates, after being pulled out by Ross, shook themselves like overgrown, very wet puppies, splattering water over everyone, and then ran to hug the elderly newcomers. Honey was more upset about her parents' wet clothing than they were themselves; they knew that a grandchild's hug was infinitely more important than wet clothing; their clothing would dry quickly enough anyway, in the suffocating California heat.

While everyone else's attention was thus employed, Melody edged silently toward the pool, and stuck her hand into the water, discovering that it was fairly warm. *Hmm,* she thought, *they've already had it at least since yesterday.* She was more than a little jealous, but decided it wasn't really worth saying anything. They might not even let her swim in it if she complained too loudly.

She interrupted her reverie when she heard Ross say to Edith and Bill, "Okay, we'll keep your places for you on Monday, so you won't have to come until just before the parade. We'll go early enough that Honey and the kids can get a place in the front, so that the two of you won't have to stand up all morning until the beginning of the parade. They say that the grand marshal of the parade is going to be a very famous Western actor, and that there will be a number of very famous people there this year."

Parade? There was going to be a parade on Monday? And with famous actors? Wow! Who cared if we had to get up early? I always get up early anyway. Man, maybe Fury would be in the parade, too—there are always lots of horses in parades, and he for sure is famous. And maybe even Joey Newton would be there, too. Cool.

Her reveries were once again interrupted. As though she had been able to read her earlier thoughts, Grammy said, "Mickey, dear, Grampa and I are going home now. The fights are on tonight, and we need to have dinner before they start. We sure are going to miss you. Be good now, and don't make your parents become angry with you, or they won't let you come visit us anymore. We'll see you on Monday." She and Bill started out toward the car, with a whole pack of grandchildren trailing behind them. They hugged each of the McDonalds in turn, and then climbed into the car. The younger members of the family followed them to the end of the street, waving until they could no longer see the black and white station wagon as it disappeared at the end of Orchard Drive.

"Melody, what in tarnation are you doing out of bed at this hour?" Monday morning dawned even earlier than Ross could have imagined. He had gotten up earlier than usual so that he could go to the Donut

Shop, so he could be sure to get doughnuts for the holiday breakfast, and he had found the little girl sitting at the kitchen table with a stack of paper napkins to one side and her box of crayons on the other. At the moment she had a red crayon in her hand and was intent on coloring the diamonds that framed an open napkin. A blue crayon was waiting to be used on alternating diamonds.

"Oh, I'm decorating these napkins for the Fourth of July picnic after the parade. See, the napkins are white, and I'm coloring the diamonds red and blue, just like the American flag. Neat, huh?" With that, Melody turned her attention back to her napkin decorating and Ross, shaking his head, continued on his way to fulfill his task.

When he came home forty-five minutes later he found Melody still at work on the napkins, but now she was assisted by Mark, Kenny, and Jan. The two boys were hard at work coloring the diamonds on the napkins—Mark with the blue crayon and Kenny with the red—while she and Jan were busy drawing American flags and fireworks on the ones that had already been framed. Ross realized that it would be completely useless telling them that the napkins thus decorated were no longer very hygienic.

An hour and a half later, the whole troop was lined up on Costa Mesa Boulevard, waiting for the beginning of the parade, which would take place in about another hour. All of the children were wearing red, white, and blue clothing, in celebration of this national holiday, and Jan and Melody had little flag pins that they had gotten as a prize at the Fish Fry. The boys had them, too, but they wouldn't have been caught dead wearing "girls' stuff," even on the Fourth of July.

There was a great deal of excitement in the air; between the parade—who doesn't get excited at a parade?—and national pride at being an American, and trying to guess who the famous guest would be, most of the watchers couldn't stand still. Melody was absolutely convinced that Fury would be the number-one guest, maybe with Joey Newton as his rider. Everybody knew that the best part of a parade was all the horses. Of course, they had to have riders because most people thought that horses wouldn't know what to do if they didn't have some person on their back telling them what to do and where to go, but Melody knew much better. According to her, horses were smarter than most people. Oh, well, horses couldn't wave to people while they walked, so maybe that was why they had riders in parades. Of course, she supposed most people liked to watch the actors, too.

Grammy and Grampa arrived about ten minutes before the beginning of the parade, just in time to settle themselves in their folding chairs on the edge of the curb. It had been decided that Mark and Kenny would take turns sitting on Ross's shoulders so that they could see a little better as others began to fill in empty spaces and even spaces that weren't all that empty. Some of the more overbearing adults even managed to push in front of Ross, who, fortunately for his children, was slightly taller than the norm. There was a cord lining the street that served the dubious purpose of keeping people out of the street and out of the way of the parade's participants.

Just as Mark climbed upon Ross's shoulders, someone shouted and the first notes of a band playing *The Star-Spangled Banner* could be heard over the roar of the crowd. Those who knew the words sang with great gusto. The closing notes signaled the beginning of the parade and the crowd applauded and cheered the passing of Old Glory as it was held high by the parade's grand marshal, John Wayne. Like the good scout that she was, Melody placed the first two fingers of her right hand to her temple and saluted the flag with pride, as she felt honored to live in the United States of America. As the grand marshal passed, Melody observed his beautiful steed, a tall bay—as was fitting for a cowboy like John Wayne—with a long, flowing black mane and tail, black stockings, and a bright white star on his forehead. His large brown eyes flashed with intelligence and pride, showing off his fiery spirit.

Floats with patriotic themes passed by, followed by loud marching bands in their best parade finery, led and directed by a drum major in a flashing white uniform. On this important day, none of the musicians were out of step, and no discordant notes were to be heard. When the Newport Harbor High School band marched by, playing "Yankee Doodle," all the McDonald children (well rehearsed in this particular piece by Ross) roared out their approval, singing right along with the music. Little Kenny had some problems with the words, so he opted to whistle right along in tune with the others.

The marching bands were followed by smartly stepping drill teams that twirled their batons through their fingers with great precision, swirling them from one hand to the other and back again; and then, in perfect unison and with a whooshing flourish, they threw the twirling, glittering rods into the air. The batons spun blindingly in the blue sky under the summer sun, coming to land as one in each outstretched hand. Deafening applause greeted each of these flawless drills, for the skill and grace of the girls. As in the splendidly played music, no baton had fallen to the ground, and the girls marched proudly on.

Closely following the thrilling performance of the drill team, and wishing that she, too, could twirl a baton like that, Melody hadn't noticed that the group following the team was comprised of five strutting horses. But then Jan called her attention to the beauty of the finely chiseled saddles and the brightly shining silver inlays in the saddles and bridles.

"Melody," she said in a theatrical whisper, "look at those neat saddles. Wow!"

Melody shook her head and looked in the direction indicated by Jan's pointed finger. "Wow! They could all be Fury's brothers and sisters." In fact, Melody had finally noticed, not the artistically made saddles and bridles, but the beautiful horses that wore them. All five of the steeds were a pure, shiny black, from the tip of their long, flowing tails to the tips of their noses, their nostrils flaring as they nodded their heads at the onlookers. At an unseen signal, all of the horses stood up on their hind legs, wavy manes flying and front legs slashing in the air in a salute to the American flag. It was an awesome moment as the horses and their riders moved in one fluid motion. Melody felt her heart skip a beat as it leaped into her throat at the joy and beauty of the moment. She wished that she could have been one of those fortunate riders, but then again, had she been, she wouldn't have been able to witness the sheer magic of the group. She decided that she couldn't have everything at once.

The rest of the parade continued in the same vein—two exciting hours of patriotic celebration. When the last event rode onto the scene, Melody thought she was had died and gone to heaven. No, it wasn't Fury, but the pink flanks shone like a new copper penny in the sun and the long, gold mane and tail flowed like ripened wheat in the wind. The most famous palomino in the world marched side by side with the light-colored buckskin that was his eternal companion. Had there been any doubt as to their identity, the big German shepherd that ran beside them clinched it. Trigger, Buttermilk, and Bullet were among Melody's favorites, even better than Flicka and Silver. Roy Rogers and Dale Evans waved their cowboy—and cowgirl—hats in a greeting to the paradegoers. On their part, the crowd roared out their own greeting and approval.

The parade ended on the notes of "America the Beautiful" and the crowd began to disperse. The entire parade had been wonderful, from the grand marshal at the beginning to the last big surprise at the end, but Melody was a little disappointed. "Jan, did you see anything weird about Trigger?"

"No, he sure was pretty. So were Buttermilk and Bullet. I was sorry that Pat and that funny old car they have weren't there, but at least the others were."

"You didn't notice, I guess, that this Trigger had white stockings while he doesn't have them on TV. I don't think he was really Trigger."

"Aw, Melody, you're nuts. No way can they exchange another horse for Trigger; how many smart pink horses do you think there are walking around? And there was Roy Rogers, and he wouldn't ride any other horse but Trigger. That wouldn't be loyal, and Roy Rogers is *always* loyal, isn't he?"

"Yeah, well, I guess so, but he didn't bring Pat Brady or Nellybelle, either."

"Gee whiz, Melody. Why do you always have to invent problems where there aren't any? Man! Did you see any other cars in the parade?"

"No, but I did see a lot of other horses. He was almost as neat as Trigger, but I'm tellin' you it wasn't him. I'd never make a mistake with a horse."

"Hey, you two; when you finish your earth-moving discussion, do you think you can join the rest of us in the car? We've been waiting there for you for at least five minutes. If you don't hurry, you can walk to the park by yourselves, and I won't guarantee there will still be something left for you to eat, once you get there. So, get a hustle on!"

The two of them hurried to reach their father's side. As they ran, Jan grumbled from the side of her mouth, "See, now they're starting to forget me, too; it's all your fault."

Melody shrugged her shoulders as she mumbled, "Well, it won't hurt you for once. It happens to me all the time, and I'm still alive. Anyway, the park's only just across the street and down a block on the next street over. We could all walk and not even have to look for a parking place."

"Yeah, well . . ."

151

"And," she continued, "that was a fake Trigger."

In the end, that's exactly what they did. Either Ross had overheard Melody or that's what he already had in mind, but once they reached the car he began pulling out all the items that were necessary for a good picnic. By the time they were ready to head over to the park, everyone except Grammy, Grampa, Honey, and Chas had been loaded down "like a pack of mules," as Melody put it. She had carried the big plaid blanket that they would all sit on at lunch. It was nasty because, being made of wool, it scratched and itched and made her perspire in the hot July sunshine.

It was just as well they had walked, because there wasn't another parking place within a mile of the park. Unfortunately, they hadn't been the only paradegoers with the idea of having a picnic at the Costa Mesa Park, which had constituted the main reason there were no parking places to be found. After having looked disconsolately around and noting that there wasn't even room enough to put a napkin on the grass, not to mention an empty picnic table, the group trudged back to the car. They didn't leave alone, however; several ants, finding that there was no longer any space on the grass, even for them, had hitched a ride on Mark's leg (having sensed the presence of food in the bag he was carrying), causing an even greater discomfort than that which he had previously experienced.

They had all decided that they should go have their picnic lunch at home, around the pool. Then they could all take a nap—an announcement that had been greeted with a loud groan from all interested parties—because they would pass the evening at Huntington Beach watching the fireworks that would be shot off from the end of the pier. Since it would finish quite late, it was necessary that everyone get enough sleep during the afternoon.

And now, here they were. Gramma Mary had joined them later on at the beach. She had brought her famous barbecued chicken wings, to everyone's great joy. Ross had built a fire so that they could roast hot dogs and toast marshmallows on sticks that Ross had taken from the eucalyptus trees along the fence in the backyard.

In the meantime, Honey was having a hard time keeping track of her very active children as they ran back and forth across the sand, down to the shoreline and back. The only two that had really had any experience with waves were Melody and Jan, and they were having a blast teasing their two younger brothers, pretending that they were drowning under the waves, and then coming up behind them and grabbing them by the ankles. After two or three such episodes, the boys had learned the lesson, and were now ready to turn the tables on their sisters. Of course, they still weren't ready to jump under the waves like Melody and Jan, but they could grab *their* ankles as they rode by with the waves. Soon, all four of them were splashing each other, completely unperturbed by the waves that occasionally knocked them over. They were close enough to the shore that the water couldn't harm them, and they were immersed in the joy of their watery playground. Of course, none of them had noticed that they were being pulled farther and farther down the beach by the tidal currents until they looked up and saw Honey waving her arms as she ran toward them, from much farther up the shore than they had thought possible.

"Hey, you guys, what in the world are you doing way down here? Didn't Daddy and I tell you to stay in front of us and to not go off on your own without telling us where you were going? Now, come on, all of you; Daddy's got the fire going, and it's time to start roasting the hot dogs."

At the beginning of Honey's scolding speech, the children had looked at each other with guilty expressions—it hadn't really been their fault, but they admitted among themselves that they should have been more careful and should have watched where they were going—but at the mention of roasted hot dogs, they suddenly discovered that they were dying of hunger, and all guilt complexes disappeared.

All in all, the afternoon had been wonderful. They had come early, but it was, in the opinion of the McDonald children, never too early to go to the beach. However, by the time they arrived back at the towels, the sun was no longer high, shining brightly in the turquoise sky, but had settled in a golden glow to rest on the peaceful Pacific Ocean. The sky itself was now a glorious explosion of color, from the bright crimson immediately surrounding the sleepy sun—which, all observers agreed with relief, deserved its rest after a long day of work at warming the earth—to every shade of pink, orange, and yellow to the darkening shades of blue, with purple fingers pointing toward the oncoming night. The exaggerated heat of the day had given way to an evening coolness, heightened by the breeze rising from the beating waves.

It had taken a while for the four of them to reach their place on the beach because they had splashed gaily through the foamy-root-beer edges of the advancing waves. They found Honey standing over the fire rings provided by the city, poking at the burning embers, keeping the coals alive while waiting for the rest of the family to arrive. Gramma Mary and the Jenkinses were sitting on lounge chairs, taking advantage of the heat from the fire. Ross was nowhere to be seen.

"Hey, Mommy, where's Daddy? How come he's not here? We wanna eat!" inquired Mark. "How can we start cooking if he's not here?"

"Daddy had to go get something he forgot to bring, but he'll be right back. Hey, what took you guys so long? I called you half an hour ago, and it seemed as though you took right off. You sure took your time getting here."

"We-ell," Melody started off, "we, uh, didn't want to get sand all over people, so we couldn't cut across the sand, so we kind of, uh, waded along the shore, and then we walked really slow, so we wouldn't kick sand all over everywhere. There sure is a lot of people here tonight, huh?" she added, trying to change the subject.

Her mother, equally shrewd, countered, "You may not have wanted to kick sand on the others, but you sure got a lot on yourselves. I don't know how you guys do it; you just got out of the water, and you're still covered with sand. You are really an incredible bunch. Go rinse off before Daddy gets back, and try not to get lost and all sandy again. Do you hear me?"

"Yes, Mommy," the chorus reached her as the four of them took off, heedless as to whether the other beachgoers would be covered with sand or not.

"Yeah, sure, and my name is Tinkerbelle," she muttered as their grandparents chuckled at the excited antics of the children.

When they returned, she had to admit that they had been fairly quick, and though they weren't completely sand-free, at least the sand only came up to their knees, and their hands were visible. It was better than nothing, she supposed. They were back none too soon, because just after they arrived, Ross showed up, sliding through the sand and carrying a humongous box of Safe and Sane Fireworks. A shout of approval rose through the McDonald ranks and even Edith, Bill, and Mary clapped their hands in agreement with the others. The great amount of noise had finally awakened young Chas, and his curious cooing added to the general hilarity of the moment. It was, of course, his first Fourth of July, but even he could tell that the day was an important one and so he didn't complain at his abrupt awakening.

By the time the McDonalds had run the roasting twigs through the hot dogs and begun to hold them over the burning coals, the sun had completely disappeared; the night was as black as pitch and only the first star had shown its face. But there was another spectacular sight that illuminated the beach and continued to display nature in all her original beauty.

"Daddy," an awestruck Jan whispered, "look out there at the waves. They *glow in the dark*, just like the nightlight we have on the light switch at home."

Until Jan's whispered announcement, everyone had been busy turning their hotdogs over and over in the bright orange flames in order to avoid burning them to a crisp, but at her words, all eyes turned toward the crashing waves. The color was more bluish than the phosphorescent green of the said nightlight and its dreamlike quality evoked thoughts of fairies or fireflies flitting through a forest in the dead of night. It was truly a glorious vision, and they were completely mesmerized by its unearthly beauty, until a slightly more earthbound sizzle called their attention back to the roasting hot dogs. Mark, who had been the first to put his hot dog over the fire, was now the proud owner of a block of charcoal. At that sight, everyone else quickly removed their hot dogs from the flames, before those, too, reached a similar state.

"Hey, guy, take this and toss that burned one in the fire. I guess we all got a bit distracted," Ross said, handing another wiener in Mark's direction.

"No, I like 'em this way; they make a really neat, crunchy sound when you bite into 'em. Can I have some mustard an' ketchup an' pickle relish on my bun?"

"Mark, that's disgusting. How can you eat it that way!—it's just like the charcoal Daddy put in the fire pit. Yuck!" Mark wisely pretended not to hear Jan's finicky comment and chomped crunchily into his hot dog.

Once all the hot dogs were off the twigs and ready to eat, all discussions of any type came to a stop as they concentrated on eating the typical Fourth of July beach fare. Of course, Gramma Mary's chicken wings were also welcome, along with Honey's potato salad. In a lull between eating the first round of hot dogs, and putting the second round on the twigs, Melody crept closer to her father and asked, "Daddy, why are the waves shiny blue like that? Are there fireflies swimming around in the waves?"

Chuckling at her innocence, Ross answered with another question, "When you guys were out there playing in the waves, did you notice that the water seemed kind of reddish?"

"A little, yeah, but not too much. There was a lot of seaweed out there. Is the red what makes the waves turn blue?"

"We-ell, that's part of it, I guess. But what really does it are a bunch of little animals, smaller even than fireflies—so small, in fact, that you can't see them without a microscope unless they're in big groups that turn the water red during the daytime and phosphorescent blue at night. It's beautiful, isn't it? But, if you're not careful, it can be dangerous and you shouldn't stay too long in the water."

Melody had known that asking her Daddy was the best thing she could do; he knew just about everything there was to know or, at least, more than most grownups did. She had, of course, another question to be answered: "Daddy, how can red turn blue? We learned at school that red and blue are both primary colors and that they can be mixed to make new colors, but there isn't another color that goes with red to make blue, so how do they do it?"

Ross, who had already started to give himself a figurative pat on the back for his quick reflexes, was jolted back to reality by this question. He searched desperately in his memory banks for an answer that might reasonably satisfy Melody's unquenchable thirst for knowledge. And then it came to him. He started off again with still another question: "What color is Jan's nightlight during the day?"

"It's red and yellow and pink and green. You know; it's a clown with an orange umbrella."

"That's right. And what color is it at night?"

"It turns green and glows. But, why does it glow?"

"There's a substance that transforms the clown at night. It doesn't have a color, and that's just what happens with these little animals. They're red during the day, but at night, the same substance that's on the clown turns the animals blue. It's pretty neat, huh?"

Seeing Melody begin to open her mouth to ask another question—he knew that there were never two without three, in Melody's book—Ross hurriedly continued, "And the reason that you can see their

156

red color, even though they are almost invisible, is because there are so many of them that their color becomes visible. It's just like dirt; you can't see just one grain, but with a bunch of grains together, it's easily seen."

He watched Melody nod as she rolled this over in her mind. Hoping to avoid any further inquiries on her part (he couldn't be lucky forever, as had been demonstrated in the past), he stuck a big, fluffy marshmallow on her roasting twig. After all the others had been served their marshmallows, Ross began rummaging through the box of fireworks and pulled out three much smaller boxes, each containing a different color of sparklers that could be held by the children and waved through the air. Having finished eating the mushy, burned (and, in Mark's case, charcoallike) marshmallows, Ross let them choose three sparklers each, which they pretended were fairy wands. In the wait between the sparklers and the Huntington Beach fireworks display, they shot off the cones, with their volcanolike fountains of gold and silver stars, followed by a Piccolo Pete; a Smokin' Sam and his smelly smoking cigar that whistled as the yellowish smoke rose skyward; they eyed the cabin, with the smoke that poured out of the chimney, and the worms. These latter particularly interested Melody and her siblings, because they couldn't for the life of them figure out how the long, curling gray worms could possibly be produced by the little black pills. Ross thrust another sparkler in each of his children's hands as he saw them squirming with curiosity. One bout of inquiries in a day was more than sufficient.

At that moment, a terrific boom sounded from the direction of the pier and caused all McDonald ears to perk up and all heads to turn toward that area. With the fall of night, the temperature had dropped quite a bit, and it could have almost been feasible to think that the sound had been thunder; in fact, everyone in the group had pulled on a lightweight sweater to ward off the coolness of the coastal evening. The sight that met their eyes, however, was not a flash of lightning, but a huge red zinnia composed of millions of blinking red stars. The sight was so beautiful that more than one of the children let their sparklers fall heedlessly to the ground, where they were immediately extinguished by the sand. No one noticed the loss.

Only one member of the group was not happily impressed with the display; Chas had fallen back to sleep after drinking his bottle of milk, but the bomblike noise had jerked him out of a deep and very pleasant sleep. He yelled out his disapproval of the unexpected disturbance. Another boom provoked another shriek of fear, but then, the sight of the falling stars of another airborne zinnia hypnotized him with pleasure, just as it had done with his older brothers and sisters. One burst followed another, and Chas slowly began to become accustomed to the noise.

The initial flower had dissolved into a series of brightly colored fireflies that fluttered gaily downward until they disappeared magically with a last poof! into the waiting blue waves, but the swirling knots of glittering red, green, gold, blue, and silver gems continued to shake the air, enchanting all and sundry; whispered "oohs" and "ahs" and a "wow" could be heard from the crowd up and down the entire length of the beach. Each individual star glittered with a light of its own, with all of them working in a joint effort to create a unique work of art against the velvet black backdrop of the night. After too short an interval, three loud cannonlike shots crackled through the air, announcing the end of the show. These weren't followed by the usual lights, and the McDonalds finally let out their held breath in a disappointed whoosh.

They gathered up the trash and tossed it into the appropriate bin on the way out of the beach. Several sparklers had remained, and the children would have the joy of lighting them the following evening, along with several glowworms and a Piccolo Pete. The picnic basket was, of course, completely empty now; unconsciously, little hands had continued to carry food to hungry mouths while avid eyes and thoughts were completely absorbed by the wonder of the panorama before them. Now, however, the excitement of the day had caught up with all of them, and even Melody wished that she had slept a little longer during her afternoon nap. The entire family staggered toward the various cars, carrying much lighter burdens than those that they had carried at their arrival six hours earlier. Melody turned and gazed wistfully at the rolling phosphorescent waves, knowing in her heart that she might never be lucky enough to witness such an ethereal sight again. One last look, and then she climbed wearily into the backseat of the car.

The next morning, the three older McDonald children were out and about at a most unheard hour for most of them. This early morning encounter took place every July 5, because they all had a very important job to do: they always went through everyone's Fourth of July leftovers to see if they could find some unused fireworks that had been inadvertently tossed out with the others. It made no difference if they found some that were of a different brand name than the ones they already had; they got shot off at night with all those that had been left over from their own celebrations, and everyone knows that you can't see the difference in names in the dark. The three of them spread out to different homes on Azure Street to save time and so that their parents couldn't see them; the discovery of their early morning scavenging would have nipped their growing career in the bud. They had to hurry also because today was trash day and they had to finish before the trash truck got there, or their rummaging days were over.

"Hey, you guys, look here: I found a Smokin' Sam that looks like it hasn't been used. See. It still has its cigar stuck in its mouth, and if it had been used, it would have been all burned up." Jan waved the probable firework in the air as the others ran up to her.

She wasn't the only one to have success in her search, though. Melody produced a box of completely unused green sparklers and Mark had found a few stray glowworms on the curb next to the trash cans that were waiting to be emptied. After comparing their newfound treasures, the three of them headed off to new territories, only to stop in their tracks as they heard the unmistakable crash and bang, followed by the whirring and grinding of gears of dump trucks emptying trash cans in the not-too-far distance. As they exchanged a quick glance, they wordlessly decided that it would be best to make a hasty retreat. Hiding behind trees and ducking beneath bushes, they managed to make it back home more or less undetected—the dumpster drivers weren't blind and the McDonald children, despite their Scottish last name, were definitely not James Bond material.

By the time Honey got up and was ready to fix breakfast, Jan and Mark were already back in bed, sound asleep. Melody, of course, had not returned to bed, but was presently in the backyard, dangling her feet in the swimming pool. She had already fed the rabbits, who were as large as full-grown rabbits, which, in actual fact, they were. They had been almost a month old when the Easter Bunny brought them, and they had been members of the family now for almost three months. *They sure are fat*, Melody thought. *I think they eat too much. Or maybe they don't get enough exercise. We don't take them out as much as we used to, because they run too fast and Mommy and Daddy think they're going to get away if we let them out. I don't know where they could go: the whole backyard is fenced in and they're way too fat to get through the links in the fence.*

She pulled her feet out of the pool and was getting ready to jump down from the picnic table they also used as a diving board—so that she could go let the rabbits out of the pen for a quick walk around the backyard—when she heard noises in the house. Changing direction, she rushed in just in time to see Honey putting cereal bowls on the table.

"Oh, well, you certainly are up early this morning. I really thought you'd sleep in for once, after we got home so late last night."

"Well, I tried, but the rabbits called me, saying they wanted to get out and take a walk. They said they're too bored just sitting in that big old cage without doing anything. Can't we take 'em out for a little while today? *Please!*"

"Well, I guess so, but we need to be careful, and we need to have the others, too, so that we can surround them while they're eating. The grass is pretty long; they would probably be too busy to try and escape. Okay," she went on, "when your brothers and sister get done eating breakfast, we can all go out with the rabbits. Then, we can have a nice swim in the pool so we can cool off."

While her mother was talking, Melody filled up her cereal bowl with a healthy helping of Rice Krispies. Honey poured milk over it and Melody gulped everything down as quickly as she could. She would have liked to go wake up the others, but she knew perfectly well that they were tired for two reasons, not just for the one that Honey thought.

As Melody headed toward her bedroom so she could get a book to read, Honey called to her with a different option. "Mickey, would you like to go the minimarket and buy some eggs and milk for me while the others are sleeping? I gave the last milk to you and so we need some more. Do you want to go?"

Did she want to go? What a dumb question; of course she wanted to go! "Sure, I do." She tiptoed as quickly as she could to the bedroom and brought her tennis shoes out as silently as she could. She usually didn't wear shoes during the summer, but the store lady insisted that whoever went into her store had to have shoes on. Honey handed her a shiny half-dollar and she ran out the door and jumped on her bike.

Even though the air was completely still, the motion of the bike created a sort of breeze that ruffled through her hair, cooling off the beads of perspiration that had formed on her face and neck from the effort of pumping the pedals on her bike. It was an exhilarating day; the sun was hot on her face, causing the sprinkling of freckles on her nose to grow in number. It was summer and she was free to go on her bike and fly like a bird. Wheee!

She rolled onto the gravelly parking lot in front of the little neighborhood store where her parents always did their emergency shopping. Mrs. Turner, the store's owner, handed her the merchandise, together with the fifteen cents in change. After thanking her, Melody jumped onto her bike, which was immediately transformed into a galloping mustang. Melody urged it on faster and faster, until both of her legs were a spinning blur. She and her shining steed were home in a flash; she dashed hopefully into the house, being careful to not bang the eggs against the doorway—scrambled eggs were not what she was hoping to eat for lunch—and put the groceries in the refrigerator. No one was in the kitchen, and she discovered that the bedroom doors were still closed. This didn't bode well. Taking her shoes off and leaving them in the middle of the hall, she aimed her steps toward the backyard, where she found Honey hanging the laundry out on the line.

"Mommy, can we take the rabbits out of the pen, now? Those guys aren't ever gonna get up and I'm already bored," she whined.

"I explained to you that we need all four of you so that we can control them better. Look out in back, by the fence. Ian is there with Pansy; why don't you go talk to him and pet Pansy and the lambs?" Honey suggested. "Just look how big they're getting."

In the absence of other ideas, Melody graciously accepted the suggestion (not that she was particularly adverse to the thought; as everyone knew, she was very fond of the three sheep, (and their owner, too, for that matter) and she headed back toward the foursome. "Hi, Ian, what's going on?"

The young man looked up from his work and smiled at Melody. "Oh, hi, Mickey. I'm getting this group ready to go to the fair. It starts on Friday, but I have to have them there tomorrow, because we have to get their pen all ready for the show on Thursday. The judging will be held on Thursday evening. So, would you like to come over and help me give everybody a bath?" At this invitation, Melody's eyes began to pop out of their sockets. Ian continued, "The wool has to be shiny white, and there's a lot of dirt that we have to get rid of. Washing sheep is a lot of work. The lambs are okay, because they don't have a whole lot of wool, but Pansy hasn't been shorn yet and her wool is very thick. I'm sure she'll get first prize. Then, we have to try and brush her. C'mon, go ask your mother. I'm sure she'll say yes, but," he warned, "you'll have to put on clothes that it doesn't matter if you get them dirty."

Of course, Melody didn't need to be asked twice. She jumped to her feet and literally flew across the backyard, begging her mother to let her help Ian with this very important chore. Honey raised her eyebrows and inquired cynically, "And the rabbits? Weren't we supposed to take them out for a walk when the others wake up?"

"Naturally, we'll do that, too. But Ian needs help now, because he has to have them ready for tomorrow, and there's a lot of work to do. Oh, *please*, Mommy," she wheedled. "We can let the rabbits out after lunch."

"Oh, all right. I was just kidding, anyway. You can't wash them if you're dressed like that, though. Go put on your jeans, and then come back. Hurry, I can see Ian there waiting for you."

Melody raced into the house and started rummaging through her dirty clothes, looking for a pair of jeans, without even bothering to be quiet. Of course, she woke up Jan in all the confusion, and she, quite naturally, wanted to know what was going on.

"Mommy said I can go help Ian wash Pansy and her lambs. He's going to take them to the fair tomorrow, and they need to be snow-white, not muddy brown. So, see ya later." And with that Melody slipped on her dirtiest pair of jeans and an even dirtier T-shirt, and dashed back out the door.

Jan yelled after her, "I wanna go, too. Wait up!" Without waiting for Melody's reply, which wasn't forthcoming, Jan slipped on her dirtiest clothes and ran out of the house in her sister's wake, just as Melody had finished climbing the fence, jumping down to the other side.

In the end, all four of the older children ended up helping out Ian. The work would probably have proceeded much more quickly without the help of some of his assistants, but he was a good kid, and understood their need to be at the center of things. He wasn't in that much of a hurry; the day was warm and Pansy would undoubtedly dry off way before the evening came.

By the time lunchtime rolled around, Pansy and the lambs had been completely washed and rinsed, and instead of the balls of mud they had previously resembled, they now shone like balls of newly fallen snow.

The same could not have been said for those who had been actively involved in the cleansing process. They were covered from head to foot with soapsuds and mud. It was a rather incongruous mixture, and when Honey saw them she was hit by a sudden attack of hilarity. She ran to the side of the house, grabbed the hose, and ran back to the fence. Aiming the nozzle at the unwary group—all of whom were looking in all directions but hers—she sprayed them until they were clean, or at least as clean as possible under the present circumstances, and then stood back to admire her handiwork. After their initial shock at having been spray-attacked by the icy needles of water, the five of them also began to laugh. One by one, the four McDonalds climbed back over the fence into their own backyard, Kenny being boosted over by a still-laughing Ian. After promising that they would indeed go and visit Pansy and the lambs at the fair, they parted for their separate destinations—the McDonalds went to dry out under the hot sun while Honey prepared peanut-butter-and-jelly sandwiches for lunch, as a laughing Ian waved to them after crossing the wide yard to then disappear into the house.

9

The Orange County Fair

The next morning saw Melody and Jan busy at work trying to push an unusually stubborn Pansy onto a waiting trailer while Ian was pulling patiently on a thick rope tied around the reluctant ewe's neck. His younger brother, twelve-year-old Rafe, was yanking angrily on another rope while berating himself for getting into that position in the first place. Rafe was not exactly the nicest, or most liked, person in the neighborhood, and his usual attitude toward his elder brother was one of disdain for his gentleness with animals and people alike. His favorite criticism was that Ian was "sweet." However, taking into consideration the importance of the moment, he had condescended to help out with getting "that mangy, cantankerous, smelly old sheep" onto the trailer. After fifteen minutes of fruitless pushing and pulling, Honey came up and suggested loading up the lambs first. Once that had been accomplished, easily done apart from the accompanying bleats and baas on the part of lambs and mother, Pansy docilely trotted onto the trailer.

His eyes popping at the simplicity of the act, Rafe turned toward Ian and glared at him. "Hey, Mr. Know-it-all about sheep! How come *you* didn't think of that idea? We could've saved a whole morning's time and effort, you know. Think about that for a moment, ya dummy!" Having said his say, Rafe stomped off in a rage, neither expecting nor waiting for an answer from his brother. Ian answered him anyway, aiming his words at the retreating figure of his brother. "Perhaps if I were a mother I would have come up with an easy solution, but I'm just a dumb boy." Turning to Honey, he said, "Thanks, Mrs. McDonald. Most of us would probably still be here if you hadn't saved the day. Don't worry about him—he was close to exploding just because I asked him for his help. He would have said no, but my parents said he had to come out. And thank you, you two," he said to Melody and Jan, ruffling their hair affectionately. "You were both a big help, too. If you hadn't carried the twins onto the trailer,

164

I don't know what Pansy would've done. Thanks to all of you." He hugged the two girls and jumped into the passenger seat of the truck.

After waving good-bye, the girls turned and climbed back over the fence, jumping down and landing in cat fashion on their feet in their own backyard. The day's work was nowhere near being over; they had had their fifth-of-July party beside the pool, blowing off all the remaining fireworks. It seemed that Honey and Ross hadn't noticed the addition of several fireworks of a different brand, or even that there were a larger number of glowworms and sparklers than what they had started out with the night before. Now, Honey had enlisted the help of all four of them in cleaning up the backyard. After that, they would have the privilege of supervising the three rabbits while they mowed the lawn. They hadn't had the opportunity to let the rabbits out the day before because Ross had taken the family to the Tenth Street Bay when he returned home from work. It had been almost dark when they arrived home, so it really had been impossible to let them go.

The Chateau girls were out in their backyard playing between themselves, but when they saw that the rabbits were out, they ran over to help in supervising the fluffy animals. When the grass in the zone where the rabbits had been eating was quite a bit shorter, Honey instructed the children to put the rabbits back in their pen, which they did most reluctantly. Melody would have preferred skipping lunch and staying out with the rabbits, but Honey was adamant in her decision. With a last tweak of Pink Ears's ears, Melody allowed the rabbit to hop back into the large enclosure and she closed the pen door, making sure to lock up so that the hoppers would not be able to push open the door and escape. No one noticed the small hole at the other end of the pen.

Among the other delicious details revealed by Collette and Karen was the enticing fact that the FOR SALE sign in the Ortolanis' front yard was no longer there. Melody and Jan wondered if perhaps Tony and his family had changed their minds and had decided to move back. Melody certainly hoped so; Jan immediately pooh-poohed that idea. "Mickey," she declared, "you are crazy! They've been gone a long time; why would they wanna come back now?"

"Well, maybe they couldn't sell the house, or maybe Mr. Ortolani decided he didn't like his new job. Or maybe, just because they miss us; *I* miss *them*."

Jan rolled her eyes in exasperation. "Mickey, what a dumbbell you are! You don' move back just 'cause you miss someone."

The two of them continued to bicker good-naturedly, as sisters are wont to do, as they walked to the edge of the front yard and sat down on the curb, looking at the yard where the FOR SALE sign had once stood. After considering the situation in silence for several long minutes, Jan spoke up, saying hopefully, "It sure would be neat if there were some kids to play with, maybe even a girl my own age. There's lots of kids your age, but only Collette who's mine."

"Yeah," agreed Melody, chewing on a blade of grass, "that would be pretty good, but there'll probably be nasty ol' boys who'll pull our hair while we're playing. It always happens." The two of them sighed in unison.

"Oh, well, who knows when they'll get here and what they'll be like. I guess we'll just have to wait and see," Melody said philosophically.

They continued speculating until Ross drove up into the driveway. As he unfolded himself from the rather small space in the driver's seat, the girls left their seats and went running up to him.

"Daddy, Daddy! Look, the FOR SALE sign is gone. Who do you think will be moving in? We can hardly wait."

"Well, I'm sure you'll have to wait at least one more day, or even more. But why are you so anxious? You might not even like whoever it is."

"No, Daddy," disagreed Jan, "we always like everybody."

"Yeah, sure," said their father with a sardonic grin, "especially Rafe MacKenzie, right?"

"Daddy, that's different," Melody explained patiently, "Rafe isn't a person, he's a bully! And nobody likes a bully."

"Well, we'll certainly hope, then, that none of the newcomers is a bully." Having said that, he reached back into the back of the car and pulled out several big boxes, which the girls immediately recognized as a cake box and two pizza boxes. "C'mon, kids, let's get into the house before everybody else comes out looking for us. If that happens, we'll never get back in, and I have an important announcement to make."

"Is that why you brought pizzas for dinner? What's the cake for? Is it somebody's birthday? Or is it because we're gonna have new neighbors?"

"Whoa! Hey, slow down. The first hypothesis was the correct one,

166

and the cake is for the same reason. When you see it, you'll probably guess what the important news is. The two of you are so smart. So, chop-chop, fast as a bunny hop."

Jan and Melody, flattered by the compliment, and knowing how fast a bunny can hop, stopped asking questions (aloud, anyway) and hurried into the house, ahead of Ross. Their smug, ear-to-ear grin was a sure sign to their brothers that they knew something that boys didn't. Of course, the boys didn't know about the missing FOR SALE sign, either, so the smirk was doubly smug. When Ross stepped through the door holding aloft the boxes, the younger children began to slightly understand the look on their sisters' faces. Ross pecked Honey on the cheek as she stepped out of the kitchen. Strangely enough, she wasn't wearing an apron for once; it was as though she already knew that Ross had brought home dinner.

"Okay, guys, everyone into the bathroom; there's no dinner for anyone until all hands and faces are shining clean." There was no need to repeat the invitation. All four of them were on their way down the hall before the words "shining clean" were out of their mother's mouth. "You know, Ross, maybe you should bring home pizza every night. It would take away a lot of stress on my part and I surely do appreciate the quick obedience that is not an every-night happening." Ross set the boxes on the kitchen table and put his arm around Honey's shoulders.

The children were back in the kitchen in a flash without a push or a shove from anyone. Kenny had even attempted to plaster his hair to his head, but that was an exercise in futility and the result brought fits of laughter to everyone. Fortunately, Ross had remembered the evening meal the day Chas had been born and had bought four pizzas—with olives, pepperoni, mushrooms, and anchovies, all of Melody's favorites. Finding it difficult to choose one kind, she compromised and ate one of each kind. Her parents never had been able to figure out how such a scrawny little girl could pack away so much food without having it show.

After the pizzas had been completely devoured—without a single crumb being left in the boxes—Ross opened the cake box with a flourish. "Okay, you guys, let's see if you can guess what my announcement is about," he invited, laughing.

The cake, like all the cakes bought in this particular bakery, was a work of art. There were a lot of little houses made from candy and cookies, with trees and bushes made of frosting and even jelly bean rocks. In front of a number of the houses were miniature newspapers made of frosting, even a few in the middle of the bushes. There was even a plastic dog in front of one of the houses. There was a gravellike jelly bean street, with a model of Daddy's car on it, in front of one of the houses. Jan and Melody stood and mulled over the complexity of the design, trying to figure out what the message was. Their brothers weren't a lot of help; they kept chanting impatiently, "Cut the cake, cut the cake," as though it were a religious mantra.

Finally, after five minutes of contemplation, an idea came to Melody. "Okay, there are a lot of newspapers and Daddy's car, so it has something to do with newspapers. Did you get me a paper route? That would be neat; can I start tomorrow, and what time do I have to get up? Earlier than five o'clock?"

The table began to shake so hard from everyone's laughter that Melody feared that the cake was going to fall to the floor. She asked confusedly, "Did I say something wrong? If I have to get up earlier, I will. I like getting up early." That raised the sound level of the laughter, and Ross decided to help her out.

"No, Mickey. You don't have to worry about getting up any earlier. You already get up too early as it is. You guessed right about the paper route; I knew you would, but it's *my* paper route, not yours. We, your mother and I, have decided that with the arrival of Chas, we need for me to get another job, so that she can stay home with you guys. I got this job, which is nice and doesn't take much time. So, what do you think? Do we have a reason to celebrate?"

His question was greeted by a moment of perplexed silence. Melody ventured, "Does that mean we would see you less than we do already? If you want, I can do the job for you," she offered valiantly.

He chuckled and said, "No, there's no need for you to do it. I'll be carrying three hundred newspapers every morning, leaving the house at three o'clock in the morning, when even Mickey will be sound asleep. The best part is that you guys can come with me one at a time, once a week, at least until school starts. Then we'll see what happens later. So," he said, "not to change the subject, but what do you all say about cutting the cake and eating it? There's a new movie out, and I'd like to go see it. So, what do you think?" Kenny answered his question by holding out his plate. Without further ado, Ross served up the cake to one and all, and watched as it disappeared in a flash.

168

There were no arguments when the children were sent off to put on their pajamas. It was understood that if they went to see a movie at the drive-in, they would have to put on pajamas. It was possible that a few of them would resist till the end of the movie without falling asleep, but it was probable that they would all, including Melody, be asleep by the time they got home.

There was an aura of excitement in the McDonald family car that evening as they drove toward the outdoor theater. Ross hadn't mentioned what the movie would be; they only knew it was a Disney movie, and they could hardly wait to see what it was, because Walt Disney's movies were always fun. After paying the admission fee—when the family was big, it was always cheaper with a drive-in—Ross drove into the parking lot, where an usher with a big flashlight waved them on to the fourth row. The darkened sky still had a few streaks of light when they hung the audio mikes on the interior of the car window. After adjusting the sound and the position of the cumbersome machine, Ross took off for the refreshment stand. They tried to make it a one-time stop, but little kids are also well known for leaky bladders, especially after drinking a whole glass of soda pop. This necessitated passing through the refreshment stand once again, which, of course, stimulated hunger pangs. It was a losing battle, because the theater itself flashed almost invisible refreshment ads during the film that were noticed only by the subconscious mind. *At least*, Ross reflected, *I'm able to avoid the rush at the break; little kids cannot be put off. When they need to go, they need to go.* When he got back to the car, he distributed popcorn, pop, and candies, just in time for everyone to settle down for the beginning of the movie.

Soon, everyone in the car was completely engrossed in the antics of the forest animals. Shrieks of laughter greeted the grouchy old owl's head spin and irritated hoots at the twitterpated birds as they scattered everywhere in the glen. Melody longed to cuddle and stroke the little newborn fawn; she wondered if she could maybe catch one during their next camping trip at Yosemite National Park and bring it home and keep it in their backyard. The little rabbit—the one that thumped—looked so much like Brownie, she wondered why they hadn't come with the idea of calling him Thumper. When the bunny and the fawn went skating across the ice, Melody felt the pangs of empathy for the little fawn. She had already felt a twinge of familiarity when Bambi and Faline met for the first time, but now she could actually see herself sliding across the

169

frozen lake on the seat of her pants. She was great on a pair of roller skates, but what Southern Californian could skate on ice?

The ice cream bonbons had been finished in a flash—there were only six in a box—but the big bucket of popcorn, eaten with a compulsive frenzy at the beginning of the movie, was still half full. Even the glasses of pop sat forgotten in front of each child as they each chewed a straw, unaware of what they were doing, and watched the drama of life unfold on the big screen. Only when they heard a sob escape from the fold-down seat in back did Honey and Ross remember that there were four children in the car with them. Chas had been left at home with Jessie; he wouldn't have understood, anyway, and the week had already been jampacked enough for him. Looking back, they saw that not only Melody had tears running down her face, but Jan and Mark did, too. But, the sob hadn't come from any of them, but from Kenny. They supposed they ought not to have been surprised—Kenny loved animals as much as Melody—but they had thought he would probably not understand just *why* Bambi's mother would no longer be with him.

Melody was ecstatic when the final scene showed two fawns in the glade. In fact, her sighs reverberated in the car as Ross unhooked the loudspeaker from the car door. After being told that, "No you can't see it again, because they only show it once," Melody gave in to her own private thoughts that if one fawn would be fun, two fawns would be even better. Most of the children were already asleep by the time the McDonalds arrived home, but Melody was still imagining bringing home the two fawns and letting them loose in the backyard together with the rabbits. She didn't even notice when Ross picked her up and put her in bed, and she was already flitting through the Redwood Forest looking for deer by the time Honey settled Jan in her own bed in the room with Melody.

Yesterday, the livestock judging had been held just before the beginning of the county fair, and Melody and Jan were just itching to know how things had gone for Ian, Pansy, and the lambs. The two of them were convinced that all would go well and that Pansy had gotten a blue ribbon, but still, they hadn't heard anything from Ian yet, and they were afraid they might not even get to see him, once they were there. The problem was that almost all of the sheep looked the same, and they didn't want to miss her. Who knew if there would be other ewes with two

170

lambs? The fact that Pansy had two lambs reminded Melody of the two fawns in the movie that they had seen the night before and she began to sigh once again.

"What're ya thinkin' of, Mickey? Is something wrong?" Jan asked.

"Naw, I was just thinking about how Pansy has two lambs and there were two fawns in that movie last night. I sure would like to have one; they're so pretty with those big brown eyes and those cute white spots on their backs that look just like freckles."

"Yeah, sure, and where would we keep it? It wouldn't fit in the rabbit pen and it would eat all the grass in the backyard. 'Course, that might not be too bad, 'cause then we wouldn't have to rake it all up and put it in the wheelbarrow when Daddy gets done mowin' it, 'cause if there wasn't any grass, Daddy wouldn't have to mow it. But then, we couldn't let the rabbits out anymore to eat the grass, because there wouldn't be any more grass left for them to eat. Hmmm."

Jan continued to mull over the question until Honey called them into the house, so they could get ready to go to the fair; Ross would be home soon, and he wanted to go as soon as possible. In fact, if the kids were ready to go, he wouldn't even bother to get out of the car. Everybody was excited: the fair would be even better than the Fish Fry, and that was just about the neatest thing around. In fact, Mark was so excited, he ended up putting on two shirts instead of pants and a shirt, and one of his shoes was brown and the other black, not to ignore the fact that they were, as usual, on the wrong feet. Honey decided that this last problem could be forgiven: the kids hardly ever wore shoes, if it could be helped, and he was therefore out of practice. For the remaining items on the list, she just shrugged her shoulders and helped him get straightened out.

Missy, sensing that something important was going on, thought she might like to accompany the family and she jumped over the fence when Ross honked the horn to let everyone know he was home. In the general confusion that followed, no one noticed that she had decided to come along until she jumped onto Melody's lap. She might still have gone unobserved by Honey or Ross (who was busy putting the baby stroller in the trunk) if Kenny hadn't innocently said, "Hi, Missy. Are you going to the fair with us?"

The children were actually quite happy at the thought that she could come and have fun with them (she absolutely loved herding sheep, and they all thought she could be an immense help to Ian in keeping his small flock in order). Unfortunately for Missy, Honey, who was in the front seat with Chas, turned and glared at all five backseat passengers. "No, she is not coming to the fair with us! Missy, go straight into the backyard and stay there until we get back! Mark"—he was the closest to the door—"take Missy back and make sure you close the gate all the way."

Missy was not at all anxious to leave the car, so Mark had to drag her by the collar. The only problem was that the more Mark pulled in his direction, the more Missy pulled back toward the car. After only a few moments, what had started as a mere walk to the backyard had developed into a full-fledged tug-of-war in which Mark was clearly going to be the loser if he didn't get some help pronto. Even Honey was laughing so hard that she woke up Chas. There was only one thing left to do; Ross, after looking up and sizing up the situation, closed the trunk and went to help Mark. Instead of pulling on the dog's collar, he picked her up and carried her straight to the backyard, where he set her down and told her to stay there. Unseen by Honey, he gave her a doggy treat so that her humiliation would burn a little less.

Once the McDonald family arrived in the county fairground parking lot, they were faced with the exciting prospect of finding a parking place: It was decided at that point that Honey would take the kids and go get in line at the ticket booth while Ross would scout out the lot in an attempt to find a spot as close to the entrance gate as possible. He had been particularly lucky, because they could see him when he stopped the car.

There was no argument as to where they would start out, because everyone agreed that they would go straight to the livestock barns. Unfortunately—or fortunately, depending on your point of view—there were a number of barns, depending on the types of animals. Some, like the cows and goats, had more than one barn dedicated to them. The biggest problem was presented by the fact that they would have all liked to find Ian first, but the first barn was dedicated to the pigs, which were just as interesting as the other animals, even if they were kind of smelly. But the piglets were really cute, and sometimes they even got out of their separate pens. Then the mama pigs would stand up and snort and try to reach the piglet that got away and scattered the other ten or eleven piglets that were attached to their mother's nipples. This was funny, because the whole group would start running all over the pen, their squeals loud enough to be heard throughout the entire barn. Eventually, the pig's owner would catch up with the fugitive piglet and replace him in the pen with the rest of the family. This was never an easy proposition, but it never failed to cause a moment of combined hysteria and hilarity.

This time, however, there were no fugitives, but there was one blue-ribbon sow that had fourteen piglets. Most of them were a lovely shiny white, but there was one that was all black with a white strip around the waist. They were so cute crawling all over each other as they tried to get a position they deemed better than the one they already had. It was a perfect example of the milk that flows faster in the other guy's nipple. The kids had a good laugh as they watched the little animals wind and twist around each other.

The next barn was one of the ones that interested Melody the most—the horse barn. Of course, Melody was in a bad position because of her preference for this particular barn, and Ross immediately took advantage of the fact, teasing her with a very serious face.

"Well, Mickey, I don't think we'll stop off in this barn; if we do, we'll lose too much time, and we'll never get to see the rest of the animals, including Pansy. Then your friend Ian will be very disappointed, won't he? Anyway, all horses look the same, don't they?"

A very discouraged Melody, who was inclined to be very trusting of whatever anybody told her, ignored the last part of the joke, looked up at her father and then at all the others (everyone knows that no two horses are exactly the same; that's how she knew that the Trigger in the parade wasn't the real Trigger). With downcast eyes, she responded, "Oh, you're right, Daddy. I hadn't thought of that. I guess we'd better go there first before it gets too late and we can't see Pansy and her blue ribbon. C'mon, you guys, let's go."

She headed off toward the next barns, but then stopped suddenly. There was just one small flaw in her plan: nobody knew exactly where the sheep barn was; they were all kind of connected, and you never really knew until you got there. It was in that moment that she realized that her father was once again teasing her. In a slightly huffy mood, she stalked back to where the others stood around laughing and glared at all and sundry. "Ha, Ha," she said. "Very funny. Can we go see the horses now? The fair isn't over until lots later, so we'll get to see Pansy, anyway."

With that, she marched haughtily into the horse's stall without a backward glance. The others followed close behind, some continuing to giggle off and on as they walked through the whole building, completely ignoring Melody's baleful glares.

Soon the baleful glances disappeared, for who can be grouchy when looking at the most beautiful animals in the world? Dogs are wonderful friends, but they simply don't have the same beauty and magic as horses. Melody was in paradise. There were horses of every type and color: tall chestnut-colored stallions; short black mustangs; brown and white pintos; proud, fiery eyed Appaloosas, with their black-spotted rumps and waving manes; small Welsh ponies and even smaller Shetlands, with their tufted hoofs. There were huge, sturdy bay-colored Percherons, with muscles rippling, capable of pulling heavy weights. Melody's favorite, though, was a very elegant black Arabian with silver and turquoise trappings. Even though his haughty stance, blazing black eyes, flowing black mane and tail, and flaring nostrils denoted a very impetuous nature, the white star on his nose was endearing, and when he softly nuzzled Melody's hair, chewing it like the straw it resembled, the little girl was in seventh heaven. She reached her arms around his neck, enjoying his warm, grassy breath.

By the time Melody's parents convinced her that she could not take her new friend home with her, the rest of the group had reached the end of the building and were enjoying the antics of a newborn burro. The little donkey still had its fuzzy newborn hair, and was, in fact, trying to convince its mother to let it nurse. She was rather reluctant to share such an intimate moment with a gaggle of giggling children, but the continuing insistence of the tiny baby was so urgent that in the end, she gave in.

It was the call of this particular action that in the end caused Melody to forlornly abandon the big black stallion; the loud sucking sounds called her as no other sound could. With one last hug and a kiss on the handsome nose, Melody ran down the aisle to watch the eager burro as it tugged mercilessly on its mother's teat. It was truly a sight to behold! The mother had turned her back on the observers—what you can't see, isn't really there—but the baby donkey was in plain view of everyone. Of course, it couldn't see anyone, either, because its eyes were closed from the sheer pleasure of sucking the warm milk, but its joy was obvious to one and all, from the closed eyes to the wagging tail and the jerking head movements.

The twitching gray ears of the mother showed her disapproval at having to share the moment with indiscreet onlookers, but she stood still with a mother's patience, turning her head from time to time, rolling her eyes impatiently at the crowd, to give a little nudge to the little brown donkey standing at her side. At long last, the baby burro, having eaten its fill, let go of the teat and turned to look at the growing audience. The sleepy brown eyes looked out at them from the woolly white circle that surrounded them.

The McDonald children had never seen a donkey before, and hadn't known that they could be so small. Of course, Melody had read about burros before in a *Happy Hollisters* adventure, and knew that they were smaller than regular donkeys, but even she hadn't known they could be so tiny. Why, the baby wasn't much taller than Missy, and even the mother was only a tad bigger than Pansy. Of course, Pansy was pretty tall for a sheep, but this burro was only as tall as Melody's shoulder. She wondered how such a small animal could be used to carry heavy burdens up steep mountain trails. She figured that was probably why they were reputedly so stubborn. She was pretty much convinced that she would balk too, if so much stuff got piled on her shoulders when she had to walk like that. In fact, thinking further on the matter, she did grumble for even less. Her heart went out to these poor beasts of burden in a welling of pity.

Perhaps the little animal had felt Melody's feelings for his race, because when the group passed on to look at the animal in the next stall, a big brown mule, the burro began to put on a show worthy of a bucking bronco. He ran around the stall, kicking up his heels, arching his back, twisting and turning; he rolled and barreled and sun-fished, doing all these as he jumped high into the air. The performance ended with a spectacular action as it put all the movements into one burst of energy that ended brusquely as once again it calmly stuck its head under its mother's flank and began to serenely suck the warm, energy-giving milk. This time, the mother had nothing to argue about—their audience was on its way out and nothing would disturb this moment alone, at least until the next group of gawkers arrived.

The mule was a big animal; though not as tall as a horse, it was much sturdier, and had a very stubborn look to its eye. Just looking at it, Melody could understand where the saying "Stubborn as a mule" had come from. He had longer ears than a horse, but not as long as a donkey's and his hair was sleek and shiny, not woolly like the two little burros that they had just seen. There was a sign on the steel bars, warning observers to be very careful because Jesse James, the name of this particular mule, was not very friendly and had been known to kick out from the side, just like cows do, for no obvious reason at all. Kenny jumped down from the fence after Ross read the warning and all of the McDonalds, Melody included, took a step backward before continuing on to the next barn. He curled his lip in an amazingly humanlike sneer and let out a big horse laugh as the seven humans headed out the door.

The sounds arising from the next barn alerted the McDonalds to the fact that they had finally found the section they had been, for the most part, waiting for. As they walked through the wide-open doors, they heard a triumphal shout; looking up, they saw Ian running toward them, holding a big blue ribbon in one hand and two smaller red ones in the other. The excited boy jumped from one foot to the other as he led his friends to the pen that had been reserved for his small "flock" of sheep.

"Look, you guys," he greeted them happily, "I got another blue ribbon for Pansy's wool; I've already got a buyer for it. We'll have to shear her at the end of the fair. She's not real fond of the shears—it's worse than trying to get her on the trailer—but I've been offered a lot of money, and this means I don't have to sell her, yet. The twins got second place for newborns, because they're too small to be blue-ribbon material. That's because there're two of them. Somebody wants to buy them, too, but they want to wait until the end of the summer, when they'll be fatter. That will be better for me, too, because I'll get paid more."

He stopped a moment to catch his breath while the human kids ran and gave him a big hug. Everyone was very happy for him, because he had worked hard for this honor and also because he wouldn't have to get rid of Pansy. She had become a regular fixture in their neck of the neighborhood, and they were very fond of her, too. They went to pet her and the lambs before going on to visit the rest of the participants in that particular area. There was a general concurrence that, while almost all of the other animals were very nice to see and pet, none of them were as beautiful or as personable as Pansy and the twins.

There was one enormous black ram, with huge winding horns, that they found very interesting as a possible husband for Pansy, but they decided that he was probably much too big for her. He weighed more than four hundred pounds. They were astonished that any animal that wasn't a whale or an elephant could possibly weigh so much, but Ian assured them that it was quite normal to find a ram that big; sometimes they got even bigger. The children turned back to look at him again with awe. He, too, had a blue ribbon hanging in his pen, which reinforced their idea that he would indeed make an excellent husband for Pansy. Jan mentioned the idea to Ian, who laughed and said, "Well, you never know. He really is a fine specimen, but look at him: he's all black and Pansy is all white. What a mixture that would be!"

Mark's considerations of that matter, "Gee, maybe they'd come out white with black polka dots on them, just like Mickey's Easter dress last year," caused such an uproarious laughter that onlookers from several barns came to see what was so funny. Mark, who had been quite serious in his considerations, also wondered what he had said that had brought on such a reaction; he thought that if his parents were laughing, too, though, whatever it was, it must have been really funny and he joined in with the crowd. At least they weren't yelling at him, this time. Soon, the whole group had tears running down their faces, and some of them were even clutching their sides, while the sheep and lambs watched and peered curiously at these very strange human beings, wondering what in the world was going on. Human beings were so hard to understand.

Staggering to his feet, Ross shook Ian's hand, congratulating him for a job well done, before gathering up his tribe and heading off toward the last building. The other members of the family tried to dry their eyes before hugging Ian and taking off behind their father. Even Ian considered this one of his more eventful successes, not least because of the love and friendship offered him by people that weren't part of his immediate family. These latter had been there to see him, but their presence had not been as heartwarming as this last visit. They had congratulated him, but nothing more than that. Nothing had been said about the lambs, but he knew that they had been disappointed that they had only brought two second-place ribbons; he was a MacKenzie and nothing less than perfection was expected of him. Rafe hadn't shown up, but then, Ian hadn't expected him to. Shaking his head as he watched the McDonalds enter the final building, he turned and went back to cleaning out the assigned pen. Tomorrow would be another day.

The last building consisted of smaller barnyard animals such as rabbits, chickens, ducks, and some strange-looking animals that looked like a weird cross between a rabbit and a rat. The sign said that they were called "guinea pigs." There was one rabbit that made Melody think of Pink Ears, although it was nowhere near as pretty as her particular rabbit. Its ears didn't stick straight up in the air like a regular rabbit's ears should; they looked as though someone had broken them—they flopped off to the sides when the rabbit hopped around. She thought it looked funny, and couldn't understand how a rabbit with broken ears could possibly win a blue ribbon. Its fur was different, too, because it had swirls in very odd places. She supposed it was interesting, but she was of the opinion that if that rabbit had gotten a blue ribbon, then her Pink Ears would most assuredly have gotten two!

Once the group exited from the livestock exhibitions, they headed off toward the other exhibits in other buildings, after grabbing a quick corndog. Melody was a collector—of anything and everything, especially if there was anything to read—and the next building really interested her. It was the forestry building and there were pictures and pamphlets explaining everything about the California Department of Parks and Forestry. She was already in heaven, she thought, as soon as they walked through the door. There, walking up and down the center aisle was the living version of her old friend from the week before, Smokey the Bear. He was handing out pamphlets and shaking hands with everyone, talking about the necessity of preventing forest fires, and saying that only people could do it.

After having their picture taken with Smokey and accepting his pamphlets on fire prevention, the McDonalds headed on to other exhibits in the building. The Yosemite National Park exhibit was of particular interest to the whole family because in just another couple of weeks they would be going to the park for a camping trip, and this would give them an excellent chance to see a lot of things that were offered there. Among the other available visual aids, there was also a short slide show showing the great natural beauties that the park had to offer, along with modern camping amenities. They had, of course, gone camping there other times, but it was always neat to see nature at its best. There were so many other exhibits to see in the building, however, that they didn't stay and browse as long as they would have liked, but they did gather up at least one of every pamphlet so that they could pore over them at their own leisure in the comfort of their own home.

Another exhibit that was greatly to everyone's liking was the one talking about the trout hatcheries that were found in various locations around the state. They were pleasantly surprised to discover that there was one near Yosemite, at Mammoth Lakes. It was only about forty-five minutes away and, as they had never seen it before, Ross and Honey felt that that might be an interesting item to see while they were there. With a silent nod, they added it mentally to their list of things to do. They gathered up the reading material and then immediately put it back down again; Melody had already provided material, and knowing the youngster's propensity for not missing anything that could be construed as reading material, they felt that whatever they might try to add would only be superfluous.

The rock-hard objects that Mark discovered at the Sequoia National Park exhibit turned out to be petrified wood, or at least, that's what the Rangers told them. Since Ross was inclined to disbelieve them, Melody was, too. Her question was, "If wood gets all rotten after leaving it out in the rain, how can it stay outside and still turn into a rock?" The young ranger was momentarily taken aback; he was, after all, concerned with animal life and preservation of the park's ecology and hadn't actually studied geology. He knew, however, that in a certain way the things were connected, and so he bravely attempted to set the little girl's mind at ease about the truthfulness of what he had said.

"Well, you see, it's like this. When the wood gets buried underneath the soil, it does tend to rot, but there are certain minerals in the soil that take the place of the rotting plant material. In the end, what remains is wood that has become a type of rock." He wasn't sure that he had been able to completely explain the transformation that takes place during the petrifaction process, but he had wanted to try to explain it in a way that all of the children would more or less be able to understand. Most of them were, in fact, convinced that this was the exact way that it happened, but of course, Melody voiced another of her famous objections.

"But, if the wood rots and if everything becomes minerals and they make a rock, then it really isn't wood anymore, is it?" she inquired, confused.

The young man had to concur with her that technically she was correct, but continued to insist that since the original form, and the material, were that of wood, it was wood that had become a rock through the petrifaction process. The usually alert Melody was uncommonly obtuse on this occasion. The family left the stand with Melody and the park

179

ranger shaking their heads in total confusion. The latter had never before met up with anyone quite like Melody, and he sincerely hoped that if he ever did again, he would be able to escape before they started asking questions without answers.

The next morning, at the break of dawn, Melody raced silently out of the house with her new chameleon attached to her red T-shirt. The lizard was brown for the moment, but she was taking it outside so that she could put it on the grass and watch it gradually turn green. She had seen the reverse process last night; it had been green when Ross had bought it at one of the booths scattered around the fairgrounds, but as soon as it had been put on Melody's T-shirt it had turned this odd bronzy brown. To tell the truth, Melody much preferred the bright emerald green, but it was a lot of fun watching it change. She'd never seen anything like it before. Of course, if her parents knew that she had brought the lizard outside, they probably wouldn't have been very happy with her. This was the reason that she had come out with it so early.

True to form, the little lizard once again turned green once Melody placed it onto the grass, but it still retained a portion of brown on its skin. Melody was worried that perhaps she had tried to make it change color too often, but then she noticed that there was a smidgeon of plain earth underneath its belly. Still marveling over the magic of nature, in the form of a color-changing lizard, Melody turned to go out to see the rabbits and tripped over Missy, who had arrived just as noiselessly as had Melody. The girl fell flat on her face, landing with her arms and legs sprawled in all directions. Momentarily stunned, she opened her hand and then had to scramble quickly after the now bright green lizard as it hastened to take advantage of Melody's relaxed grip. She grabbed it just in time, before it disappeared into the rambling honeysuckle vines growing on the side fence.

"Oh, no, you don't," she whispered to the escapee. "I just got you and Daddy would be really mad at me if I let you get away." She took the six-inch-long lizard into the house and put it on the living-room curtain, together with the other three. She put the little leash back on it and then headed back out into the backyard. After seeing that strange rabbit last night at the fair, she was quite ready to go and cuddle her own cute rabbit waiting for her in the cage together with Blackie and Brownie.

Looking into the pen, her heart slipped down into her stomach and then began its climb upward in an attempt to flee. It was accompanied by a sound that, at the beginning, was a mere rolling, bubbling sound of boiling water, which rose in volume as it climbed resolutely toward her vocal cords. In the end, regardless of her attempts to keep it in, it escaped with a shriek that highly resembled the whistle of a boiling teapot. In a vague attempt at calming herself down, she looked once more into the darker regions of the hutch, but the result was always the same: there were no rabbits remaining inside the hutch. Frantically, two endless tears streaming down her cheeks, she turned over every food and water dish in the pen, hoping against hope that, by some strange stroke of luck, they were hiding underneath one of them. Unfortunately, the only signs that there had ever been rabbits in the pen were big globs of black fur all over the inside of the hutch. There was also a shred of white and brown fur entangled in the chicken wire and a drop of still-wet blood on the wood near a big hole in the ground.

In the end, in the face of the almost inevitable cause of their disappearance, an unconsolable Melody sank to her knees in the long, uncut, brown-tinged grass and sobbed until she thought her heart would explode with the pain of her loss. She could vaguely hear Missy barking somewhere in the distance; after what seemed an eternity, she could feel the loving dog try to offer solace to the white-heated pain that wracked her existence by licking the tears from her face, but in that moment she was beyond consoling. She threw her arms around the dog's neck, and buried her face in the soft hair.

Honey found her in that position when she came out later to call her eldest daughter into breakfast. She looked at the little girl's tear-streaked face and saw the devastation in the rabbits' pen and had an uncanny intuition as to what probably had happened. When Melody felt her mother's hand on her shoulder, she looked up and said tearfully, "Mommy, the rabbits aren't in their pen and I looked everywhere for them, but they aren't anywhere around. Why did they go away and leave us alone without them? Didn't we treat 'em good enough?"

Honey drew Melody into her arms, cuddling her as she said, "Mickey, those rabbits probably just managed to get out of their pen and have just decided to take a walk around the neighborhood. You know that there are lots of vacant lots that are plumb full of all sorts of plants. Don't worry; I'm sure that they'll come home soon, fatter than ever from all the stuff they'll have eaten. Don't cry, now, sweetheart. You'll see."

181

She truly hoped that what she had said to her daughter was true, but she had very serious doubts as to that. Saying a silent prayer in that regard, she dried Melody's tears and led her back to the house. There was also another problem to consider: Mark and Jan also had to be told that Brownie and Blackie were missing. It was bad enough that Melody had discovered it on her own, but telling the other two was going to be a real mess. She wished that Ross were here to help out, but he had already left half an hour ago to go to his regular job. *Sometimes,* she thought to herself, *this job is terribly underpaid, and much tougher than it seems.*

Four days later, four very subdued children watched with a remarkable lack of interest as the long-awaited moving van pulled up in front of the empty house that faced their own abode. They had spent the last four days looking in every possible (and sometimes not so possible) hiding place in the entire neighborhood. No one had seen them, nor had they seen any stray dogs that could be blamed for the rabbits' disappearance. Now, in a fit of very unusual shyness, the foursome was hiding behind their father's old Chevy, waiting for the arrival of their newest neighbors. Only when the new owners drove up in their old beat-up pickup did a spark of their customary curiosity flicker in their eyes and in their heretofore listless manner.

"How many people are there in the car? Of course, the daddy is driving and the mommy is sitting next to him, but can you see if there are any kids?"

Melody stuck her head around the old car's bumper, trying to get a good look at the newcomers without being seen herself. To be seen would be very rude, as everyone knows. Unfortunately, the car's tail fins got in the way and she could get only a quick look, but she thought she had seen three people in the backseat. "Well, I think there are three kids, and they all have black hair. One looks bigger 'an the others and is kinda fat. Two have short, curly hair and . . ."

"How do you know all that stuff? You only looked for a second and the windows are closed. I bet you didn't see any of that stuff you're tellin' us."

At that moment, the car stopped and the doors opened, releasing the driver and passengers from their temporary prison. The first person to emerge was a short, muscular man whose face and head were of the same leathery brown; they could tell the color of his head because there was not even one strand of hair to cover it. He stretched tiredly and then pulled up the front seat so that the backseat passengers could crawl out. Having done that, he walked to the other side of the car and opened the door, revealing what all four Peeping Toms deemed to be the most beautiful woman they had ever seen, with the obvious exception of their own mother, who could have won a Miss America Contest, if it weren't for the fact that she was married.

"Wow, look at her hair! It's even longer than yours is, Mick, and look how it shines. I bet the only reason you can see it at night is 'cause it shines so much, just like her eyes."

"Yeah, they look almost like glittery glass; ya almost have to look at her, just like when those guys wave that gold coin in front of yer eyes and make ya do whatever they want ya to do."

"Uh huh, and look how she holds her head. She looks like she could be one of those Spanish dancers we saw a couple of weeks ago on the *Ed Sullivan Show*. All she needs are a couple of castanets and a bright red dress with all those frills." Melody's eyes took on a dreamy quality, until the woman turned to show her profile.

"Man, is she ever fat!" she whooped. "She's even fatter than Mommy was when she was getting Chas ready to be born. Who knows, maybe she's gonna have a new baby, too."

While the new adult neighbors turned and gazed toward their new house, a sudden movement recalled the quartet's attention to the occupants of the backseat, who had already begun to get out of the backseat. As the McDonalds knew, getting out of the backseat of a two-door car tended to prove difficult at times. They no longer made any pretense of secrecy; their curiosity had reached such a level that, for the moment, they weren't even overcome by the melancholy that had reigned supreme since the loss of their beloved rabbits.

The first person to roll out was a little girl, about the same age as Jan, whose short black hair was as curly as Jan's was straight, and shone as blackly as her mother's and seemed to almost have a slightly blue glow to it when the sun hit it in just the right way. "Hey look, Jan; it looks like your wish for a girl your age came true. See, I was right; she does have short hair."

"You never said she had short hair. You said there were two short-haired people in the back."

"Yeah, maybe because you didn't let me finish what I was saying.

You stopped me in the middle of my sentence. Anyway, shh, we don't want to let them know we're spying on them."

A boy of about ten climbed out of the car, following his sister, and glanced around the street, as though looking to see if there were other children his age. He had a rather cynical look on his face and Melody exclaimed, "Oh no, another boy. Gee willikers, he looks just like Rafe, except with curly hair. Just what we need, another bully in the neighborhood."

Just then, as though he could hear her (which he probably did; the street wasn't *that* wide), he turned in their direction and gave a sneer worthy of Snidely Whiplash. She knew then that, from that very moment on, their life would no longer be the same.

Now the group waited anxiously to see if Melody was also right about there being a third person with long hair in the backseat. They didn't have long to wait, because the last occupant finally pushed its way out of the car. Its long, pinkish tongue hung from its mouth, sending a long string of slobber flying in all directions, causing a general uproar of "How *gross!*" All four McDonalds, Melody included, took several steps back; it was obviously a dog, for no one would bring a full-grown bear with them and let it sit in the backseat with their kids.

"See," Melody said triumphantly in the midst of everyone's laughter, "I told you it was bigger than the others and that it had long hair. Although," as she stopped to consider the idea for a moment, "I guess I was a little bit wrong there; its hair just looked long."

Still giggling for the first time in days, the four of them came out of hiding and went to introduce themselves to their new neighbors.

10

Sleeping under the Stars

They knew that they were in serious trouble as soon as the head of the new family in town opened his mouth to speak. The little girl hid behind the bear-like dog, while the boy stood with his arms crossed across his chest, with a cocky, self-satisfied grin smeared across his broad, tanned face. Jan tried to coax the little girl away from the dog while Melody attempted to initiate a sort of conversation with the parents. Unfortunately, it seemed as though the kindly looking man had a mouthful of marbles and no one was able to understand his seemingly garbled speech.

Just then, Ross drove up into the driveway with his little MG and the children knew that there was only one thing for them to do; after shrugging their shoulders, they ran over to their father to ask his advice.

"Daddy, Daddy, come meet our new neighbors!" Jan said, hanging from her father's arms. "They seem really nice; at least most of them do, but we can't understand what their daddy is saying. Can you come help us?"

Ross took a quick glance over toward the newly arrived family and said, "We-ell, you might want to try talking to them in Spanish. They look like they could be Mexican."

"But Daddy! We don't know how to speak Spanish. Do you? Can you teach us some words? We wanna make friends with them. There's a girl that looks like she's Jan's age, and there's a ratty-lookin' boy, too."

"You speak Spanish just like you speak English—with your mouth."

"Daddy," an exasperated Melody replied, "we know that, of course. Please teach us how to say 'hello' and 'How are you?' and 'What's your name?'"

"Well, I guess I can tell you those words, at least. But, Mickey, didn't you learn anything from your friend at school?"

Melody rolled her eyes at her father and answered, "Of course not;

185

they always make us speak in English to him, and he mostly talks in English, anyway. He only says something in Spanish when he's excited. C'mon, Daddy, tell us how to say those things, *please.*"

Melody and Jan took several long minutes trying to pronounce the unfamiliar phrases until Ross thought they could get by well enough. Unfortunately, he didn't take into consideration the nervousness factor and the children were back faster than the Flash, asking him to please repeat what they were supposed to say.

"Oh, all right, first say, *Buenos dias.* Okay, repeat." The girls repeated the phrase and Ross went on to the next, slightly more difficult phrase, *¿Como está Usted?* After several tries, that, too, came out fairly well. In the end, they tried the last, and most complicated question, *¿Como se llama?* After assuring themselves that they did, indeed, remember everything they had just practiced, they galloped back across the street to try out, once again, their newly learned linguistic skills.

Their efforts were at first greeted with complete silence as their listeners tried to sort out their rather unusual pronunciation of the unwieldy Spanish words. (It helps to remember that they were just little girls, not distinguished polyglots.) After an uncomfortable interlude on both parts, the new girl lifted her head over the shoulders of the panting dog and began to giggle. "We speak English okay; in fact, our daddy won't even let us speak Spanish out of the house. My name's Luz Ybarra. My dumb old brother's name is Juan and he thinks he's really great because he has the same name as a famous saint, just like the one our last city was named after." As an afterthought, she added, "We call him Juanito, or little Juan." The grimace that the curly-haired boy made was anything but saintly and Melody foresaw great difficulties ahead with this one; oh, well, if she could handle Rafe, she could handle anyone, for sure. "My daddy's name is Juan, too and my mommy is Consuelo. And this," she continued, pulling the big dog's ears, "is Oso. It means 'bear' in Spanish," she added unnecessarily—the fact he was more a bear than a dog was rather obvious to everyone.

Once Luz had opened the dam, the words flowed unstoppably like a rushing river. She had also subdued everyone's shyness, and the children. By the time dark rolled in around them, Luz and Jan were the best of buddies, as though they had known each other for a lifetime, brief though their lives had been up to that moment. It was really a big help that they both were the same age, too.

186

Juan Senior—or Big Juan, as everyone called him—was the nicest person they had ever met. He was hard to understand sometimes, not because he had marbles in his mouth, as Melody had first thought, but because he was very soft-spoken. He took the entire McDonald family under his wing from the very start, and they all admired him greatly. His family, like Mr. Chateau, also came from Europe. In fact, their origins were from bordering areas, separated by the Pyrenees, a mountain chain that divides France, Mr. Chateau's homeland, from Spain, Big Juan's homeland. He did speak Spanish, but not here, because he was in America, and they were all Americans.

Consuelo was indeed expecting a new member of the Ybarra family, and his arrival would definitely not be too far off. She was very tired at the time of their arrival and, after directing the moving men as to where the furniture should be put, at least temporarily, she plopped down on the comfortable sofa to rest.

Juanito, true to form, disappeared as soon as he possibly could in search of adventure. No one seemed to miss him, and Melody was sure that she was right in her idea that he was not the kind of person she would like as a friend. Oh, well, her brothers had already disappeared, too, but they were at home, not out getting into trouble.

Luz, Melody, and Jan sat on the porch and chattered away like three cocky little sparrows until Honey called out to them to come home and eat dinner. Big Juan had already gone into the house to try to make headway in the kitchen and prepare something for his family to eat. The girls giggled and made promises to come back the next morning to play. "I'll show you my new dollies that my Daddy bought me just before we left San Juan Capistrano," she promised. "They should be unpacked by then; I can't sleep without them."

"And we'll show you our bunnies when you come over to our house. We live there, right across the street in that kind of pinkish house." Then, Jan's and Melody's eyes crinkled with pain as they remembered that the rabbits had all disappeared. "Well, I guess we won't show you the rabbits; they disappeared," Jan managed to get out before sobbing. The three of them said good-bye and Melody and Jan trudged sadly back home. They'd been having so much fun getting to know the Ybarra's that they hadn't even thought about their terrible loss.

"Hey, Ybarra, let's see who can throw a rock farthest—you or me. I bet ya that ya can't even throw as far as those two dumb girls there in the middle of the street and I can." Melody's worst scenario had just come true. The Ybarras had been here only for an hour or so and Little Juan had already met up with that darn stinkin' Rafe. Man, how did he do it? The ratty types must have some kind of magnet or something that attracts others to them. Oh, well, life was really going to be exciting, now.

"Hey, man, you're wrong. I'll take you on in a minute. Watch me!" He raised his arm and began to wind it around, just like the pitcher Don Drysdale, preparing himself for the throw. Honey walked through the front door as he was winding up and, screaming angrily at him, ran to him, puffing up just like Rebecca, the hen, when protecting her little chicks, and grabbed his arm just as he was preparing to let go of the rock. He did let it go, but instead of it arcing through the air at breakneck speed and landing on top of someone's head, it landed heavily on Juanito's own foot. Hoots of derisive laughter greeted this aborted attempt at masculine supremacy as Rafe and his cohorts took off running.

"Good show, Ybarra. We'll see you tomorrow and you can show us your stuff. Hope it's better 'an what you showed us today. *Hasta la vista, amigo!!!*" The three boys disappeared around the corner, the echoes of their laughter and catcalls still lingering in the shadowy atmosphere as the newcomer slinked grumpily toward home. As he stomped up the steps onto the porch, the McDonald women could hear a small girl's voice snicker, followed by an embarrassed grunt as Luz stuck her thumb into the air in approval of Honey's quick thinking and Little Juan slammed the front screen as he entered the house. A giggling Luz followed him in as their father turned on the outdoor light and Honey gathered her little chicks under her wing and guided them into their own waiting home.

Jan ran excitedly into the house, carrying a small package that the mailman had just left in their mailbox. She had been playing with Luz in her front yard when the mailman had come, so she had also been first on the scene. She knew perfectly well what was in the package; it was the second to arrive in the last ten days, since Gramma Mary had left for her vacation in Europe the day after the big Fourth of July celebration. She could hardly wait to see what dolls were in there this time: the last two had been a French boy and girl with their native folkloristic clothing, sent straight from Paris, complete with a small metal version of the "Awful" Tower. She didn't think it was all that awful, but maybe there was something about it that didn't show up unless you were really there. Mommy and Daddy had put the dolls on the high shelf that ran all around the bedroom wall. Why they put them up so high, she couldn't figure out at all, but Melody thought that *they* thought that the two girls would destroy them if they handled them too much. Of course, that was absolutely ridiculous to even consider, but then, adults just didn't understand the workings of a young person's mind. She'd heard that grownups had been children, too, at one time, and maybe it was true, but they sure as heck didn't remember what it was like to be a kid. Well, yeah, sometimes they did, but only when it was convenient for them, like, for instance, when they wanted to play on the slip-and-slide or swim in the pool. Of course, it was a lot of fun when Daddy played in the pool with them, but still . . .

Running into the house and slamming the front door, she called breathlessly, "Mommy, Melody come quick! I think there's another package from Gramma Mary! Hurry, I wanna see what's in it *this* time." The words had barely been uttered when Melody appeared from the bedroom doorway, trudging listlessly into the living room; she had been up before dawn, thinking to maybe find the lost rabbits eating grass in the predawn light. She was just as anxious as Jan to see what was in the package, though. Strangely enough, the boys were nowhere to be found, but then, it didn't really matter, because they weren't particularly interested in the dolls, partly because they *were* boys, and mostly because they were too little to understand about other countries. Jan didn't worry too much about that, either, except she did think that the clothes were very interesting and pretty. Melody was interested, though; she had just read some interesting books about children in other countries that had belonged to Honey when she was a little girl. It was funny how she had just finished reading about a little girl in France on the same day that the French dolls had arrived. Now she was reading about a boy from Spain. Wouldn't it be funny if these dolls came from Spain?

"How do you know it's from Gramma Mary? You don't know how to read. Lemme see it." She reached out to grab the package from Jan, who quickly moved out of the way and said, "It looks just like the other one, same size and stuff. Where's Mommy? We can't open it unless she's here. What if we tear it?"

"Mommy's in the bathroom and don't worry. We won't tear it. Man, Jan, you know I never tear paper; I always take it off real slow and careful-like. You guys are always yelling at me on my birthday, and on Christmas, too. C'mon, let's take a look."

At that precise moment, Honey walked out of the bathroom and deftly took the package out of Jan's hands, in a move that would have made her basketball-playing husband green with envy. "Okay, girls, let me see just what we have here." With that, she opened the package with a quick slit with a handy kitchen knife. Oh, look, there's a letter to me, too. I'll have to read it later, since I have two very curious daughters with whom I must contend. Now, let's see. There are three separate boxes. What do you say, shall we open one each?"

Without waiting for an answer, which was quite unnecessary anyway—as the question had been rhetorical—she extended one box to each of her female offspring and began to open up the third. She gasped when she saw what it was, but refrained from pulling it out until the other two boxes had been opened. True to form, Melody was taking her time about getting the nondescript brown wrapping paper, but Jan had already torn the paper off of her box even before Honey had finished unwrapping hers. She, too, waited impatiently for the slow, meticulous unwrapping done by her exasperating sister before pulling out her doll. Her eyes sparkled with the anticipation of being able to show off the doll—in her beautiful, bright orange, flamenco-dancer costume—to Luz.

Finally, Melody was ready with her doll, and the three of them pulled their dolls out simultaneously on the count of three. Of course, the perfect companion for a flamenco dancer would have been a bullfighter, and that's exactly what Melody pulled out of her box. Carmen and her matador were a perfect set, but when Honey pulled out a perfectly formed black Spanish bull—complete with festooned spears jammed into its shoulders—to finish the set, both Jan as well as Melody let out a shriek of ecstasy. Then, Melody looked at the set with wonder.

"Wow, that's weird," she murmured. "French dolls after reading a book about a French girl. Now, Spanish dolls while I'm reading about Spanish kids. Is Japan in Europe?" she asked, turning to her mother.

"No. Why do you ask?"

"Because the next book I have to read is about a girl named Kumi San, who lives in a place called Tokyo, in Japan. I guess that means we won't be getting a doll with Japanese clothes, huh?"

"No, I suppose you won't, seeing as how your grandmother isn't going to Japan on this trip. Japan is in Asia, not Europe, and they're not all that close to each other."

"Mommy," Jan began meekly, "can we show these dolls to Luz before we put them on the shelf? They're so neat, and she's always showing us all her dolls. Please," she wheedled.

"Well, you can bring her over here, but I can't let you take them out of the house. We have to wait until Daddy comes home before we can put them up, anyway. He's the only one who's tall enough to reach the shelf."

"Yeah, silly. You wouldn't want to take it over to Luz's house. I mean, okay, she's all right and all, but you never know what that dumb brother of hers is gonna do. He's such a rat, and he's usually hanging around with that dumb Rafe. You can't trust either of them. They're both bad news."

"Yeah, you're right." Jan looked around with alarm, as though she might find the two boys hanging around in the kitchen. "I better ask Luz to come over here. She's never been here before, anyway, and I bet she'd like to see the French dolls, too. She probably never saw the 'Awful' tower before, either."

Honey lifted a quizzical eyebrow at her youngest daughter's comment. "The 'Awful' tower? What in the world is that?"

"You know, Mommy, that metal tower that Gramma Mary sent with the French dolls."

Recognition dawned on her. "Oh, you mean the Eiffel Tower, not the 'Awful' tower. C'mon, you two, let's go get lunch ready, and then, after your nap, you can go call Luz to come over and look at your dolls."

She smiled at her two daughters as Jan, while walking into the kitchen, exchanged a puzzled look with Melody and asked, "Why do they call it that? There aren't any eyes all over it."

Melody, with all the cosmopolitan knowledge she had at her disposal, answered haughtily, "It's because just trying to see the whole thing at once is a real eyeful."

"Ross, you really have to take a look at this letter from your mother before you fall asleep. It was in the package with the dolls; I don't think the girls saw it, because I tried to hide it before they did, but that doesn't necessarily mean they didn't see it. I can't even think why I did hide it, although it was actually a pretty good thing that I did, at least for the moment." While Honey stopped to catch her breath, Ross whisked the letter from her hands.

"The first part is actually something that could be read to everyone, even if I can't imagine them being particularly interested in what she had to say about hoping to buy a new car when she gets to Germany. She did talk about hoping to ride a bicycle across Holland, and I'm sure that Mickey and Jan would doubtless be eager to hear about that project and perhaps even wish to send some kind of advice, but the important part is where she talks about what she'd like to do after landing in New York. It has a lot to do with Mickey, and oh, my goodness, whatever are we to do?"

"Perhaps if you would let me read the letter myself, I might be able to answer your question. At the moment, I have absolutely no idea what it is you're talking about." A quick reading led to a more lengthy perusal of the stunning *lettre*. In fact, the length of the study was so extensive that Honey began to wonder if perhaps her spouse had fallen asleep with his eyes open. It would not, of course, have been the first time that he had done so, but the question at hand was of such import that he absolutely had to stay awake long enough that they could discuss—at least briefly for the moment—the issue. In the end it would necessitate a long and in-depth discussion, but for the moment, all that was necessary was a preliminary impression.

"Oh, Ross, are you here?"

He looked over the page with a stunned expression on his face and said, "She's joking, isn't she? Please tell me she called to tell you it's only a joke. No, don't bother to answer; I can tell from the look on your face that no such phone call has come through, not today, or any other day. Is she crazy? Who in their right mind would want to take one of our kids on a car trip all the way across the United States? And, in particular, Mickey. She must have fallen off her bike and bumped her head."

"No, I don't think that could possibly have happened; she hasn't ridden her bike across the tulip fields yet. That comes up next week, *after* she buys the car in Germany. Well, now that we've established that she must have eaten something that disagreed with her, we need to ask next, What do Sonja and Todd think about this? I mean, they'd have to travel across America with Mickey, too, wouldn't they?"

"I imagine so, but you know how Mom is. And anyway, for some strange reason, Sonja likes Mickey. Who knows, but maybe she has more answers to Mickey's questions than we do. You know, it would undoubtedly be an interesting experience for her to travel across the country like that, and she would certainly see some very interesting things during the trip, and someone else could answer all her questions for once."

Caught up in Ross's imagined scenario of eighteen days in relative peace, Honey murmured, "Yeah, just think about that. You know, I'm beginning to like the idea. My only question is, Is the rest of America ready for the likes of Melody Erin McDonald?"

"I think we need to study the issue a little deeper, as you said before. Let's go to sleep on it and maybe we'll have a better idea as to what to do in the morning. They say that the night brings good counsel. Is that okay with you?"

For once, it was Ross that received no answer to his question. The day's excitement, and the prospect of eighteen Melody-free days, had led Honey into a deep, contented sleep. Ross grinned sheepishly and snuggled up against her under the cool sheets.

"Would I get to go on an airplane all the way to New York?" As she thought about the idea for a moment, another question came to mind. "Where *is* New York? Is it very far from here?" she asked. "If I get to go on an airplane, that might be okay. But then, we haven't found Pink Ears yet, and I don't wanna go anywhere until we do."

The night had brought some kind of counsel to the McDonald parents, and they had decided that the best thing would be to ask Melody if she even wanted to go. From there, they could make any plans that were necessary. They had been convinced that the idea would be pleasing to her, but they hadn't considered her stubbornness regarding the missing rabbits. They rolled their eyes at each other over the head of daughter number one, each one convinced that the child's strange idiosyncrasies had been inherited from the opposite parent. Once again, they tried to convince the dear child that it would be in her best interest for her to go.

"Of course, you would go in the airplane. How else do you think you could go all the way across America all by yourself? Gramma Mary certainly didn't ask us to take you there, and if she had, we would have to take your brothers and sister with us. That would certainly not be possible. So, would you like to go?" It didn't really matter what she said—she was going. Mary had called very early that morning and they had told her that Melody would be on the airplane leaving L.A. International on July

29 for La Guardia Airport in New York City. She really hadn't given them much of a choice; she had already bought the ticket, because she knew that Melody would be excited at the idea.

"And, if you want to find your rabbits before you go anywhere, you'd better get a move on—we're leaving tonight to go to Yosemite, as you'll remember, and you are definitely going with us, whether you want to or not." Ross really wasn't in the right mood to be contradicted at the moment; he still had too many things to do before taking off. "Have you gotten your clothes ready yet? You don't have to bring along too much stuff, just jeans and T-shirts and that new windbreaker that we got last week. And don't forget your bathing suit. When you're done packing, you can go take one last look around the neighborhood to see if you can find your rabbits. Any questions?"

Melody folded her arms and grumbled, "I don't wanna go without our rabbits in their pen. They might come home and not find us here and go away again."

"Just do what you're told, please, without arguing, and we'll all be much happier. Go."

Melody walked sullenly down the hall, kicking at imaginary rocks, wishing that there had been real rocks on the floor that she could pick up and throw at someone. Everything about her oozed disapproval at her parents' decision to go on vacation that night, especially without the rabbits being back home yet. It just wasn't fair! Her long hair bristled with disdain at the indignity of not even being able to decide what she would or wouldn't do. What the heck did they know about pain and loss? They could do whatever they wanted, and they even got to tell everyone else what they had to do. Well, she'd show them! She'd pack her suitcase, all right, but not to go on the camping trip with them. She'd pretend to go, but she'd disappear with all the confusion of getting everything and everyone loaded into the car. They would never notice her not being there—they never did anyway. Secure in her way of thinking out her plan, and secretly smiling at her cunning scheme, Melody stomped off to her bedroom and began to pack her suitcase.

The day passed quickly, notwithstanding the little quirks of fate that always seem to pop up when you are preparing for a vacation: the car ran out of gas as Ross was driving to the gas station to fill up the tank (the two-mile walk under the sweltering sun, of course, did nothing to better his temper); Honey discovered that the ice trays were empty when

194

she went to fill up the icebox (thank goodness, they had to go to the grocery store to buy other food items for the trip); two of the tent stakes were missing, even after they counted and recounted five times (they finally found them in Mark's little toolbox—he'd used them as levers in trying to open Melody's ant farm); and the only pair of tennis shoes that Jan could find were a pair that Missy had chewed up when Oso had stolen her bone (they finally found the rest when Honey went to help her pack her bag: Melody had put them there that morning when she had tried to help packing up Jan's bag, too. No one could figure out, though, why she didn't say anything when everyone was screaming at everyone else).

Finally, though, everything was packed and put onto the rack on top of the car. Blankets had been placed in the back of the car, for the kids to sleep on and under. The cooler was on the floor at the front, with sandwiches and soft drinks for everyone. They would, of course, stop from time to time for the necessities of life, like visiting a toilet and taking short walks for loosening cramped-up muscles. None of the McDonalds were particularly used to sitting still for long periods of time, but Mommy and Daddy McDonald were more than a little leery about stopping for long periods of time, for obvious reasons. Still, some stops had to be made.

Melody was still sulking. She had looked everywhere for the missing rabbits that morning without finding even the smallest trace. She was really worried, because that darn Juanito had walked past her during her search, swinging a white rabbit's foot on a small gold chain while whistling "Here Comes Peter Cottontail." If possible, he was even meaner than Rafe and after that episode, there was absolutely no way that she was going on that camping trip without first finding her fuzzy friends. She didn't think he would transform her Pink Ears into a stupid good-luck charm, but you never could tell with the likes of those neighborhood bullies. She had decided, anyway, to try to distract her parents from thinking that she might pull some kind of trick by telling them that she could hardly wait to leave for her cross-country trip with Gramma Mary. She was pretty sure that her act had worked, but you could never be sure; her mommy and daddy were a lot smarter than it sometimes seemed, and at times, it even seemed to her that Mommy had eyes in the back of her head. Only time would tell.

Melody wasn't the only member of the family who was sulking.

Missy, who had been watching the day's events all afternoon with ever-increasing excitement for the upcoming trip, had been sent over to the Ybarras' house, where she would be spending the next week together with Oso. She was now in a black funk, and when Melody came to say good-bye (in keeping with her act not to let her parents catch on to her plan), the unhappy dog just turned around and hid her head under her paws. She was having nothing to do with those conniving humans, and Melody, her head hanging in shame, left her where she was. There really was nothing else she could do; she had tried to tell her that she wasn't really going, either, but for some reason, Missy didn't want to even listen. Oh, well, she would just be that much happier tomorrow morning when she woke up and found Melody still there.

Or, at least that's what Melody thought was going to happen. The entire family had gone to bed early that night, in view of the fact that they would be leaving at about three A.M. Ross and Honey wanted to get enough sleep in bed before leaving so that they wouldn't fall asleep behind the wheel. The sun was still shining fairly brightly through the bedroom window, and Melody, in keeping with her plan, had read until there was no longer sufficient light to read by. She had tried reading with her flashlight (which Honey had bought for all of the kids so that they could go to the bathroom during the night without having to turn on the big light; Melody never used it for that purpose—her eyes were almost as good as a cat's in the dark—but it was a little too dark to read without some kind of light); but the batteries now died and Melody slowly drifted off to sleep.

Something had gone definitely wrong. When she woke up, she discovered that she wasn't where she thought she'd be. Actually, she hadn't even planned on falling asleep, if the truth were to be known, and there she was—flanked on both sides by sleeping siblings—lying on a blanket in the back of the car. How she got there, she didn't know for sure, but it didn't take much thinking to figure out that she had been carried there while she slept. Usually, they woke her up in analogous situations, but they must have guessed what she had had on her mind. Well, just because they had won the skirmish, it didn't mean she would make it easy for them to win the battle. Well, on second thought, maybe she would. She may as well take advantage of her position and just have fun. She decided that it was just as well that Missy hadn't listened to her, though, because then the dog would never have trusted her again. Phew! What a mess. Thank goodness, she had put the *Weekly Readers* that she had gotten up till then in her bag, together with a stack of *Superman* and *Richie Rich* comic books. At least that way she wouldn't get too bored during the long trip to the camping site. Resigned to her fate, the little girl snuggled up closer to her brother and sister and fell back to sleep.

After filling up the gas tank and buying soft drinks for the whole group—thus making sure that they would soon be stopping once again—Honey felt that making a head count before taking off would be an excellent idea. In the light of the fact that a certain member of their somewhat numerous offspring had the uncanny habit of disappearing just before an imminent departure, not to mention the fact that they had a pretty good idea that she had planned on doing that just before leaving in the first place), Ross agreed with his wife unconditionally. After rounding up as much of the group as they could find, Honey counted heads. As was to be expected, one was missing, and there were no doubts as to who it was.

Fifteen minutes after the hunt had begun, the sun was high in the sky, and the little people standing underneath it were becoming more than a little cranky; the early departure and the heat were more than they could stand. Ross had looked everywhere possible for the missing girl while Honey stood near the children, trying to calm their whines and grumbles. There was a general feeling of mutiny in the air; the soft drinks that were to have lasted for at least the next fifty miles had already been consumed and the children were once again ready to visit the toilets. After a Mommy-to-Daddy conference, it was decided that Honey would accompany the troops to the toilets and that then they would lay the backseat of the car down so that the children could lie down and take a nap. In the meantime Ross would continue his search for their AWOL daughter.

The sultry air rang with her sudden shriek. "Melody Erin McDonald! What are you doing here? We've been looking everywhere for you for the last half hour. Where have you been?!"

When Honey brought the kids back to the car, she found an unexpected surprise waiting there in the center seat. Melody was calmly working on a crossword puzzle that she had found in her *Weekly Reader* that week. She, too, was surprised that her mother had asked that particular question; they had all been told by their parents to return

197

immediately to the car as soon as they had finished in the bathroom, and she had. It was too hot to stand around outside and the car was in the shade and it was relatively cool there.

"I've been here in the car, waiting for you guys to get back. You told us to come straight back here, and I did. It's too hot outside anyway. Are we almost there?"

A flabbergasted Honey called her husband back to the car. The vain twenty-minute search under the broiling sun had done nothing to sweeten the man's already tried temper. He glared at his supposedly errant daughter; she stared back at him with indignant innocence. She had done nothing wrong; her parents had told everyone to come straight back to the car, and she had. So what if she had a tendency to dawdle and get left behind. It didn't happen all of the time, just most of it. They could have looked in the car before taking off in all directions to look for the nonmissing missing. Oh, well, there were just no understanding parents; they didn't think logically like little kids did. She'd just have to forgive them, she supposed. With that in mind, she smiled at him with a toothy grin.

Wordlessly, an exasperated Ross strode to the front of the car and got into his seat. He was not really angry with Melody, but rather with himself. They had all been rather stupid; they could quite easily have put the kids into the car without making them stay out in the sun. That way, they'd have found Melody right away and they'd already be about thirty miles farther along the way to the peace and quiet of the Yosemite camping grounds. There were still another three or four hours left to drive before finally making it there.

Honey climbed gingerly into the front seat next to Ross. How she had managed to keep Chas asleep during all the confusion, she didn't know, but she was surely glad for small miracles. He had had his bottle a couple of hours ago, and she hoped that her luck would hold up until they got safely to the campsite.

As soon as Honey buckled up her seat belt, Ross took off at a rather faster speed than was permitted by the law, but he truly enjoyed racing around the mountain curves at a pace that even Mario Andretti would have envied, and he hoped to make up for a little of the time they had lost. Of course, it would have been much more exciting with his little MG than it was with the bulky station wagon, but one of his favorite dreams was to drive at least once in a Grand Prix race or in the

Indianapolis 500. Oh, well, that dream was more or less out of the question, now that he was a staid father of five. It was certainly a good thing that none of his children suffered from car sickness, because most of the road ahead was twisting and turning, like most of California's mountainous coastline. Actually, some of them even seemed to thrive on this kind of road.

An hour later, they made the last stop (he hoped) along the road so that Honey could pull out the sandwiches that had been prepared. He had wanted peanut butter and grape jelly, but Honey had vetoed that idea as being too messy. Instead, they were now eating baloney-and-cheese sandwiches. He couldn't see that they were that much neater, but he did concede that at least baloney wouldn't drip.

The pit stop lasted a little longer than had been hoped for, because Chas had finally woken up and was demanding that he, too, be fed. He also had the inconvenient surprise of needing to have his diaper changed. Honey really regretted in that moment that her free diaper service had ended. She was really looking forward—ha, ha!—to a week of washing diapers in the icy river. Well, at least she would be able to keep her hands cool.

The scenery had changed rather quickly as they left the coastal highway and headed straight up into the mountains. The traffic was much lighter now, but they were surrounded by tall pine trees, firs, and other evergreens that tended to cool down the atmosphere. The children began to look more closely at the flora along the way—you never knew when they might see Bambi and his family, or some other denizen of the woods. Even though the traffic was not quite as heavy as before, Ross decided that it was probably a good idea to slow down. Wild animals—either frightened by the noise of the charging cars or else following some unseen path, known only to themselves—were known to cross the road without advance warning. Many drivers had become unwitting poachers by hitting running deer that came upon them unexpectedly as they hurtled from the woods. Other than the heavy fines paid by these nonproclaimed hunters (who didn't even get to keep the meat), a great deal of very costly damage was usually inflicted on the improvised weapon, sometimes rendering the machine unusable. Ross most assuredly didn't need any of the above, and so he drove rather less quickly than he had before.

Although driving along at the snail's pace Ross had chosen, the

McDonalds soon met up with another car that was going even slower than they were. The reason for the sudden slackening of speed was soon understood. Along the road, just before the mouth of the long tunnel that stretched out in front of them, a family of rabbits was taking its time getting from one side of the street to the other. Noticing Jan, Mark, and Melody's stricken faces as he took a quick look at the backseat through the rearview mirror, Ross realized that the moment had arrived for drastic measures.

Several yards into the long tunnel, Ross rolled down the window and, sticking out his head, shouted, "Hoo, hoo, hoo, hoo, hoo, hoo; hoo, hoo, hoo, hoo; he, he, he, he, he, he." The unsuspecting children were startled out of their pessimistic reveries, and they started to giggle as the world's most famous woodpecker's crazy laughter rang out and echoed along the length of the gallery. A number of cars that had been stuck in the block-up caused by the rabbits slowed down once again, looking wildly around to try to discover from whence the wild laughter came.

Ross looked sheepishly around from his glaring spouse—who was not exactly thrilled by the fact that the sound had awakened their youngest offspring—to his older children, who were staring at him with undisguised delight. All four of them clapped their hands with excitement and yelled, "Do it again, Daddy! Do it again!" Deciding that since Chas at this point was already wide awake, he shrugged his shoulders at Honey—who rolled her eyes toward the top of the car—and, sticking his head out the window, he let loose with the loony woodpecker's maniacal laughter.

This time, his imitation was greeted in a completely different manner. Several drivers in other cars gave him the thumbs-up sign, while the rest just drove on as though nothing unusual had just happened. His own car rocked with the children's hysterical laughter, as they, too, attempted to imitate their father's imitation.

Almost immediately after leaving the tunnel, they entered into another, albeit much shorter, tunnel. In fact, they entered into a series of tunnels before finally arriving at their destination point. The sun was just beginning to sink beyond the horizon, but its particular position framed the dark-green evergreens in such a way that they seemed to be surrounded by a blazing fire. As the McDonalds neared a grove where a group of very tall redwood trees grew, the sky grew darker and the trees taller; the trees were so tall, in fact, that they couldn't decide if it was dark because you couldn't even see the sky, or if it was actually getting late. A quick look at Ross's watch showed that it was indeed late afternoon, but not quite late enough for it to be totally dark. He stopped for a moment to let the children take a look at the trees, because these were among the tallest trees in the world.

Melody looked up with awe at the tree nearest to the car; she didn't bother to cover her eyes with her hand because the sun wasn't able to penetrate through the high umbrella of the redwoods. "Wow," she murmured, wonderstruck by their gargantuan height. "I don't think I would want to jump from the top of one of them. I might like to try and climb one, though," she added thoughtfully. "Me too!" chimed in Mark.

Recognizing the belligerent look on Melody's face, and hoping to avoid an argument over who could climb the trees and who couldn't, Honey moved closer to a tree and said, "Hey, kids, did you look at the neat color of these trees?"

The children gathered around her so that they could inspect the odd color of the wood. They had never seen wood that had that reddish glow before. The eucalyptus trees near their home were a rather grayish-beige color, while these seemed much different; in some places it even seemed as though they were a pinkish-gold, although they conceded that this could possibly be an optical illusion caused by the failing light.

"Hurry up, you guys, and get back in the car. If you don't, we'll have to set up camp in the dark, and believe you me, that will not be the least bit of fun," Ross exhorted the rest of the family. Reluctantly, they all climbed back into their respective places and Ross took off: first, toward the ranger station, so that they could confirm their camping reservations, and then, off to their assigned site.

"Hey, guys, look how neat this place is! Did you see all the waterfalls along the way? And another good thing," Honey added, "is that we're not too far from the toilets." This, she thought to herself, is probably one of the best parts of the site; with five small children, the proximity to a bathroom, on any campout, was essential. Of course, they probably wouldn't be spending all that much time there, but children are children and they always have to go to the toilet at the least opportune moments.

"And look over there, through those trees," Ross put in. "Do you see that big old rock that looks like it has been burned?" he asked, pointing toward Glacier Point. The children all turned in that direction, and nodded solemnly. They could indeed see the cliff that their father had indicated. "Well, it doesn't just look burned, but it has been burned many times, in fact. In about an hour they will put on a very beautiful show that I doubt you will ever forget. It's exciting, because the other name for that place is Fire Falls. And, do you see how high up it is? Well, just think, Grampa Mack did a handstand up there, right on the edge. We'll go up and see the place where he did that, one of these days while we're here."

He stopped bragging about his own father as he felt a tug on his arm. Looking down, he noticed his second son hopping back and forth with a very pained expression on his face. He also noted that none of his children were still looking at the historic site he had been talking about, but that all were giving none-too-subtle glances toward the very toilets that Honey had referred to. Thinking guiltily that a good deal of time had passed since the children had been taken to the toilet, he said to Honey, "You take them to the rest rooms, and I will set up the tent." Looking at the children, he said, "Try to hurry, will you? I need you guys to help me put the stakes into the ground around the outside of the tent."

The family was back much sooner than he had anticipated, but he was glad to see them. Raising the tent on the central pole had been okay, together with the frame around the top of the shelter, but without someone to hand him the other poles that went into the corners, the tent itself kept crashing down around him. However, the first words that his loving family pronounced, as they came up to him, were not the offers of help he had been hoping to hear.

"Man, Daddy, that place really reeks. They don't even have a flusher so you can get rid of the stink; there's just a big seat you sit on with a big smelly hole underneath. You can even hear everything as it falls, and it falls a long way. Ugh! Do we have to go there every time?" Melody shivered at the very thought of it. It really was too disgusting an idea to even consider.

Her brothers and sister echoed her impressions, but their hopes of a sweeter-smelling and more hygienic place to relieve themselves were soon dashed to the ground by their father. "Well, you all have a choice. You can either go there, or you can hold it until we get home next Sunday night. The others are just like this one or worse, so it's up to you. Now, do you all think you can give me a hand here, so we can get this tent up, eat, and get to bed? I don't know about you guys, but it's been a very long day for me."

With help, the tent went up quite easily, and soon the children were roasting hot dogs over the bright, warm fire that Ross had built in the fire pit that accompanied their space; Honey was frying French-fried potatoes over their little camping stove.

As twilight shifted fully into night, crickets hidden up in the bushes and grass surrounding the camping area pulled out their fiddles and began their evening concert. It was a most fitting accompaniment to the hushed lullabies of the mother birds as they sought to sing their young to sleep. An occasional rustle in the bushes and grass gave notice of unseen nocturnal hunters and scavengers, but the McDonalds were only marginally aware of these wilderness sounds. Together with their next-door campsite neighbors, Maggie and Sam, they sat entranced by the scene that unfolded before them on the Glacier Point cliff as the burning coals of the Fire Falls tumbled down the long precipice. In the distance, it truly appeared as a burning cascade, or perhaps a river of falling lava from an erupting volcano.

"Daddy, do they show this every night, or just on the nights that someone new gets here?" Melody asked innocently.

"Well, they only show it on the nights that someone new arrives, but since someone new arrives every day, I suppose you could say that they show it every night."

Once again, Honey and Ross could tell that Melody was revving up for a new barrage of questions. Much too tired to get immersed in a discussion of the whys and wherefores of Fire Falls, Honey announced, "Okay! The show's over. Everybody say good night to Maggie and Sam. We'll take one more walk down to the rest rooms, and then we'll be off to dreamland."

Despite the chorus of protests, Honey and Ross accompanied the troops to the end of the gravel road and then settled everyone down into their respective sleeping bags. Not long after, the only sound, other than the crickets' song, was that of seven people sawing wood in their dreams.

Unfortunately, the idyllic interlude did not last as long as had been hoped for. Around midnight Melody, having learned the road to the rest rooms left on her own while all the others were still deeply immersed in their dreams. Although she had not been gone long, there was a great deal of commotion going on in the tent when she returned. Perhaps due to the excitement, or perhaps due to the amount of sun that had been absorbed by the other children while they were waiting for the return of Melody (who had, as we know, already returned), or for whatever reason, the three middle children had taken sick. Sounds of retching and coughing could be heard coming from the interior of the tent, and Melody had a pretty good idea that she did not want to spend the night with her brothers and sister. Fortunately, Maggie, having been apprised of the situation, had obtained permission for Melody to come over and sleep in the hammock in which Sam spent the better part of his afternoons.

In spite of her excitement at sleeping in a hammock for the first time and her worrying about the other kids, Melody was soon back to sleep, a deep and profound sleep from which she was rudely awakened only at the first light of dawn.

11

The Force of Nature

Startled, a clumsy, sleep-ridden Melody tried to climb out of the hammock; her endeavors only succeeded in getting her further rolled up into the hanging bed and she vowed to herself that it would be a long time before she would attempt to sleep in one again. At first, she was rather annoyed by the fact that she had been awakened so abruptly and then had made a fool of herself. Then, she became annoyed with herself because she hadn't awakened earlier. All this rigmarole had taken place in a matter of a moment, and when Melody finally got the hammock straightened out again, and her eyes open, she was more than happy to be awake.

There, standing before her, in all its glory, was a magnificent five-pronged buck. It was, in her opinion, the most beautiful and wondrous thing she had ever seen (except for maybe Fury). The most astonishing thing about the whole event was that it hadn't awakened anyone else in her family. It was also one of the most hilarious things she had seen during the trip up to then and she squelched a sudden desire to laugh—incredibly, the deer was there in the tent's front opening flap, with the top of the tent clutching the animal's antlers in the same way a shipwrecked person would hang on to a passing beam from the ship's mast. Of course, the deer wasn't particularly happy about the position, and was trying desperately to rid himself of the highly cumbersome weight that was keeping him from going peacefully on his way. One abrupt movement of his head brought him face-to-face with Melody's fascinated stare; the girl managed to slide almost gracefully from the hammock—with the innocent idea of trying to help the deer disentangle himself from the tent—but the buck, misconstruing her intentions, stepped back, gave a strenuous jerk of his head, and, finding himself free of all constrictions, took off, running as fast as he could from the

205

presence of "those pesky human creatures," as Melody heard him mutter on his way past.

Deciding that it was, perhaps, a little too early to disturb the rest of the family (she could still hear Jan gritting her teeth), she took off down the now familiar gray gravel road. Five minutes later—deciding, for her personal safety, that it was better to get things done quickly—she was back at the campsite, just in time to see a dismayed Honey looking around the partially dismantled tent.

"Oh, good, you're still here," Honey murmured. "When I didn't see you hanging there in Maggie's hammock, I thought you might have been carried off by the same tornado that went through our tent. You do look like it kind of whipped you around a little; you've got grass all over your hair, and one of your braids is completely undone. You didn't happen to hear it, did you? I was so tired, I didn't hear a thing, but I wanted to see how the little kids're doing; they were awake all night. Your daddy's going to flip his wig when he sees this."

Naturally, Melody giggled at the weirdness of her mother's monologue. She responded, of course, to the most important part of Honey's meanderings. "When did Daddy start wearing a wig? I always thought that was really his hair. Anyway," she continued, giggling even louder, "there wasn't any tornado that went through here to take us to Oz; this isn't Kansas, you know. There was a nutty deer—who looked like the grown-up Bambi when he got all twitterpated because of Faline—who got all tangled up in the tent flap and when he took off, he kinda tried to take the tent with him."

Honey stared at her firstborn, her eyes popping from their sockets with astonishment. "You're just making fun of me, aren't you? What in the world would a fully grown buck be doing here in our campsite? They're very timid animals who, since they eat grass, don't depend on human beings for their food, and usually try to stay away from the campgrounds. You're sure it wasn't a tornado or something? Although . . ." Honey puzzled over the situation for a moment before continuing, "I guess there's not that much difference in a deer coming uninvited into a campground full of people and a tornado in the middle of the California mountains."

"Nah," replied Melody, "it was a deer: look, he even left his hoof prints here in front of the tent to prove it." She looked up curiously at her mother as another thought came to mind. "How come there aren't any tornados in the California mountains?"

A still bemused Honey was saved from trying to find an answer to Melody's inquiry when Ross's complaining voice came from the tent. "Isn't anyone going to start breakfast out there? It's time to get started, or we're never going to be able to do any of the stuff that was planned for today." A chorus of smaller, pining voices joined his. "Yeah, we're dying of hunger; what's for breakfast?"

Relieved by what would have really annoyed her in normal circumstances, Honey jumped to her feet and turned to the small camping refrigerator. Soon, the tantalizing aroma of sizzling bacon filled the entire camping area as Honey scrambled the eggs that would be cooked along with the bacon on top of the tiny green Coleman cook stove that was their very handy friend on all family excursions.

Melody set the table, while her other sleepyhead family members rolled unceremoniously out of the tent. It seemed that their bout of sickness during the night hadn't hampered hunger pangs; in fact, the three middle children were more or less as ready as Melody to get on the move and investigate the beauties that the park had to offer. On the other hand, Honey was already having misgivings as to whether they had done the right thing bringing their offspring to Yosemite. She had an inkling that their rather turbulent presence might cause a rather unusual change in the normally placid tranquility of the forest's primordial life. *Geez,* she thought, *we haven't even been here twenty-four hours, and things are already starting to go funny. Whoever heard of a buck visiting a tent full of people? Who knows what's next?*

She didn't have long to wait to find out. After taking turns at the fountain, washing dishes and faces, the McDonalds returned to the campsite in time to encounter another of the forest's denizens hard at work trying to open the refrigerator. Of course, it wasn't all that unusual to find a raccoon trying to open up a refrigerator and this one had probably felt attracted by the enticing odor of the frying bacon; years of somewhat peaceful coexistence with man had slightly altered the clever animals' outlook in this particular sector, and they had indeed had a great deal of practice in overcoming obstacles that man stubbornly tried to put in their way (like opening supposedly tightly closed refrigerator doors). What was highly unusual behavior, however, was the way this particular raccoon, upon discovering that he was no longer alone, slid down from the table and waddled toward the extended hands of the excited children. Perhaps it thought they were offering food in a much more easily obtainable method than picking locks; it seemed, however, that it changed its mind after looking up and seeing Honey's incredulous glare. Where before it had edged its way obsequiously toward the children, it now took off, running as though its very life depended on the speed used to distance itself from the campsite.

"Wow, a real live raccoon," shouted Mark. "This is for sure going to be the best vacation we ever had. C'mon, you guys, hurry up. There're a ton of animals out there just waiting for us to come and find them." *You don't even know the half of it*, Honey and Melody thought at the same time. They looked at each other and started giggling about their secret.

Naturally, they couldn't leave right away, because the tent had to be set up again, but they were out and about way before most of the campers had even started cooking breakfast. Of course, there were a few early birds seated around the lake that wasn't too distant from the campground. The day promised to be warm, with clear blue skies, and long shadows from surrounding trees sprawled out over the lake, hiding the fishermen from the suspicious eyes of giant rainbow trout. A slight breeze rippled the water in the center of the lake, offering a sense of coolness that wasn't really there. Ross looked yearningly toward the fishing poles scattered along the bank of the lake; a few of the old-timers nodded knowingly toward him, as they glanced sympathetically at the group of kids that followed behind him. Honey had decided to accompany the group during this first excursion, because, as she admitted to herself, if there were any more unusual, uninvited visitors, she didn't want to be alone when they came (who—except perhaps Melody?—would believe her; Chas certainly wouldn't be a very good witness) and she really didn't want to know, either. Her presence increased the old fishermen's concern for poor Ross. It must be a real drag having her along, but then again, with all those kids . . . someone has to take care of 'em. A few of them gave him a thumbs-up gesture and Ross, thus strengthened, looked resolutely ahead and took off down the trail with his group of followers. To tell the truth, it must be admitted that Ross liked the role as head honcho as he led his family along the woodland paths, but since the idea of being considered a martyr by the fishermen of the world (who could ever pass up such an opportunity?) also appealed to him, there was no way he would ever let on that he was having a blast.

The day was warm, but the tall pine trees that bordered the path provided a relatively comfortable shade. The children were wearing their shabbiest tennis shoes, but this didn't hinder them from running up and down the hill, yelling at their parents to hurry up; it made Honey tired just watching them. Two hours after they had left the oh-so-inviting lake, the hikers unexpectedly came upon a lovely, level glade that seemed appropriate for a picnic lunch. A series of smooth, slightly raised rocks appeared to be created for a family of seven; in this case, however, the seventh, slightly concave rock served more as a handy bed rather than a seat for hungry hikers. Little Chas, his most urgent needs taken care of, quickly fell asleep—in his stroller, however, which could be positioned under the shade of the nearby pines and firs.

Giving in to parental pressure, the older children also lay down to rest in the long grass. They weren't used to the higher altitude; while they were on the move, they hadn't noticed any difference, but once they had settled down to eat, a certain fatigue overcame them; even Melody was more than content to lie down for a little while, at least.

A sudden wail woke the entire family up from their "brief" nap. The sun was no longer high up in the sky and the shadows stretching from the trees across the glade did nothing to enhance the McDonalds' sense of welfare. Lifting herself up from her prone position on the soft grass, where she lay hugging a smaller stone, and turning toward the source of the wail, Honey joined her voice to that of her youngest son. There, sitting on the top of the stroller and looking down at its inhabitant, was a large gray squirrel. It wasn't so much the squirrel that had caused Honey's extreme reaction; no, she knew perfectly well that the small curious creature wouldn't have hurt Chas. It was just, well, that it was there. It absolutely was not normal for a wild squirrel to sit on the edge of a baby stroller, looking placidly down at the occupant of said conveyance.

Struggling to her feet, Honey jumped toward the carriage to the accompanying snorts of laughter from the rest of her very understanding family. Only Melody had a vague idea of what was passing through her mother's mind at the time, but she, too, was rolling around in the grass and wishing it was she that had been awakened by the chipper little squirrel. The unwitting perpetrator of all the confusion was startled into action and scampered off toward the nearest tree just as Honey reached the now cooing baby.

It took some time to reestablish order; the long nap had hyped up the kids and they were more than ready to continue their hike, but the sun was already heading steadily toward the western horizon, and they still had approximately two hours of road travel back to the campsite, and Honey was already shooting poisoned darts at all of them with a look that could kill by itself. Secretly, Ross was rather pleased by the fact that it was now time to head back, because he could pull his fishing pole out of the back of the car and bring in a few fish while the kids were washing up and Honey was setting up to cook dinner. He would even clean them so that all Honey would have to do was put them in the skillet to fry. He knew perfectly well that it was she, not he, who was the real martyr today, even though he hadn't really understood the undertones which had colored her every movement that day. It had something to do with the animals, he was quite sure, but he couldn't quite place his finger on it.

The walk back went much quicker, basically because it was mostly downhill, which made it simpler to push the stroller. The children took even less time because, instead of running down the hill, they *rolled* down the hill like barrels. Of course, there were a few minor accidents along the way, with some of them rolling down the wrong hill and finishing up against a tree, but other than a scratch or two, no harm was done. Once a tree stopped their unwieldy descent, they jumped up and ran back up the hill again, ready to begin again, hopefully on the right track, this time. It didn't really matter to the children which slope they took, because the wrong ones were much more fun, but they decided it was better to take the right one if they ever wanted to get back to the tent, especially after glancing at Honey's face; the faintly green shade of her skin was *not* an optical illusion resulting from the sunlight filtering through the green of the tree branches along the way.

They finally got back to the tent without further mishap and in three quarters of the time they had taken to get to the meadow, despite the children's frequent deviations from the main path. Once the others were completely occupied with their various tasks, Ross put his own plans into action. Only Chas saw him take off, but with typical masculine complicity, he didn't say a word to the others about it.

During the short passage from the campsite to the lake, Ross felt the weight of the day's activities slip off his shoulders and, positioning himself in his favorite fishing site, he felt as though he didn't have a care in the world. The day was still sufficiently warm that he could sit in the shadows offered by the trees without feeling cold; in fact, had there not been the problem of frightening the fish, he would have stuck his weary feet into the cool, soothing water. He hastened to put the bright pink salmon egg that served as bait onto his dangling hook—right there, at one foot from the shore, was a big fat rainbow trout just waiting to be caught. It was an auspicious beginning to what he hoped would be a relaxing and fruitful visit to the lake.

A half hour later, the fishing pole hanging from his shoulder and the creel clutched in his right hand, Ross headed once more toward the camp as he whistled a cheery tune. He had every right to be merry: the once empty creel now held six fat trout. The other men seated around the lake had watched him unpack with knowing grins—it really was a bad time of the day to start fishing—and had watched him reluctantly pack up and leave, their envy shining in their eyes. Turning around to wave good-bye, he noticed that several of the men were eying his empty spot with interest, while others were collecting their fishing gear and already making their move. He supposed that tomorrow he would have to be up and at 'em earlier than the birds if he wanted to find a good place. Maybe he could have Melody wake him up, although it might be better not to, because then she would want to come with him, and he only had one pole. It would be interesting, though, to see someday if she had his skill.

Coming through the bushes around the site, Ross was rudely called from his reveries as Honey caught sight of him. "Where have you been? I just sent the girls looking for you at the fountain; I thought you were getting cleaned up, but now I see you still have that chore before you."

"Look what I've got: fish! One for each of us, although they're so big I imagine we can put some in the freezer." He held out the open creel toward her. She crinkled her nose at the fishy smell, but Ross had already gone ahead in his enthusiasm. "I'll go get 'em cleaned, so we can have 'em for dinner. I'll be right back."

She glanced up at him in amazement. "You caught all these since we've been back? Ross, we've only been here slightly more than half an hour. Were they, by chance, just jumping out of the water right into your basket? Not even Dad could have done better than that, and he's a great fisherman. Wow," she concluded with awe in her voice.

211

"Well, no, they weren't really jumping. I just kind of judged from the angle of the light and the shade from the trees where the best place was," he said, his chest puffed up with pride. "Then," he continued, a little more humbly, "it was the only place left that was fishable. And, I just kind of lucked out: there was already a big old trout treading water there in the shade, just waiting for my hook and bait. I guess the others just happened along, looking for the first one, and decided that my bait was what they'd been waiting for all day."

"Well, that's good for us. You go get them all cleaned and I'll get the frying pan and everything ready for when you get back. If you see the girls," she called out to his retreating back, "tell them to get back here as fast as they can, so they can help out. I can just imagine Mickey's reaction when she sees those fish," she continued, to herself. "She's going to want to take them home and let them swim in the swimming pool. She hates eating fish."

Melody really did try to convince Ross that it would be a wonderful idea to take at least three of the fish home to the swimming pool (seeing as how they'd be eating only three of them for dinner). "It would be great for ecological conservation of the species," she argued, "and then we wouldn't have to go fishing for them so often—we could get them straight from the swimming pool anytime we want to." Only after showing her that they were, unfortunately, already dead, did the little girl give in. She had very few compunctions about eating them, though. "They're okay, I guess. They'll never be my favorite food," she had to admit, "but they're tons better than the stuff Daddy gets when he goes fishing at the beach."

The others had absolutely no problems whatsoever eating them, although Jan did mention that she liked shrimp better. The real problem was something altogether different. "Daddy, can we go fishing with you tomorrow?"

"Yeah! That way I can try and keep some of 'em alive for when we get home. Neat idea, Mark."

Of course, the kids were disappointed by his answer: "I'm sorry, kids, it's no go. I only brought one fishing pole with me, and it's that big one that only big people can handle." Unable to stand the hurt look in his children's eyes, he came up with an improvised solution. "I'll tell you what we can do, though. We can go to the side of the lake where swimming is allowed. There's a bunch of little baby fish, like the ones that

Mickey catches at the beach, and sometimes even some big ones show up. You can have fun swimming, plus you can try and catch fish with your hands. They let you do that there, and you don't even need a fishing license." It wasn't quite what they had had in mind, but it was, they decided, better than nothing.

Certain heads began to nod in a very agreeable manner shortly after they all finished eating their fish and French fries. The agreeability was due not so much to the bounty of the delicious dinner and the excitement about the following day's fishing plans as it was to the fact that the day had been a very long, very active one, despite the long rest after lunch. One by one, the children fell asleep and were carried off to their sleeping bags; as each one was carried off, the remaining youngsters fought their way back to wakefulness, but it was a battle lost in the beginning. The only reason that their parents hadn't yet succumbed was because Melody hadn't, either. She was the only one left to stare glassy-eyed at the Fire Falls as the burning coals were tossed over the edge of the cliff. Only after the last fiery coal had burned down to black ash at the foot of the hill did she slide sleepily off the camping chair, much to Ross and Honey's relief.

Once the two of them got their last child into her sleeping bag ("I can do it by myself, you know, I'm not asleep *yet*"), they threw away the paper plates and washed the pans and silverware. Honey had finally revealed to Ross what had been troubling her all day long, and though he was quite convinced that the buck had just wandered in by mistake (he felt much better knowing about the deer: he had been convinced that he had made a mess of putting up the tent), and that the raccoon had probably been attracted by the smell of food in the first place, though he had to admit that the latter's consequential behavior, and that of the squirrel, were in fact quite bizarre. *Oh, well,* he thought, *tomorrow's another day. And then, with certain members of the family, these things are to be expected.* On this happy thought, he became the last of the McDonalds to fall asleep.

The next morning found a well-rested Ross sitting in his chosen spot on one side of the lake, with its crystal clear water, while he kept an eye on his tribe of wild Indians on the other, sandy side of the lake. Their excited shrieks kept disturbing his train of thought, and he couldn't concentrate on the task at hand.

213

"Hey, you guys, look at that one there; it's gigantic! Let's see if we can catch it."

"Shh! Don't yell, dummy. They're not deaf, you know, and if you yell, it'll take off before we even get a chance to get near it." As if on cue, the beautiful, silver fish with the reddish-rainbow stripe on its side darted off toward the center of the lake until the children couldn't see it any longer. "Man, that's the fifth fish you guys have scared off this morning. Can't you do *anything* right?"

"Ah, shut up, Mickey. It's your fault; it took off when *you* moved. Nobody else moved yet; they're not even in the water yet."

At that moment, a flurry of movement from Ross's side of the lake saved the day by avoiding a full-fledged battle. A fountain of silvery water erupted into the air, framing what seemed to be the very same fish that had caused the disagreement between the children. It looked magnificent, sparkling silver in the sun, as it gathered its strength for the battle against the invisible thread that connected it to the fisherman hiding on the shore. The battle lasted fifteen minutes, but to the group of children standing knee-deep in the lake, their eyes riveted on the scene, it seemed to last an eternity. In the end, however, the inevitable happened and Ross, amid resounding applause from the onlookers—fishermen and swimmers alike—reeled the hapless fish ashore.

All four of his older children circled the body of water as quickly as they could so that they could congratulate their father and inform him that it was because of them that he had been able to catch that particular trout. They got there just as he was enjoying a round of rousing slaps on the back and congratulations from the other fishermen who had gathered around him. One grizzled old-timer commented on Ross's uncommon good luck, "Man, I've been trying to get that thar fish for years. He's gotta be ten years old ifn he's a day. Yessir, he's the ole granddaddy of all the other trout in the lake." He looked grimly around at his fellow fishermen, who all nodded in simultaneous agreement.

Ross, also, looked around the crowd that had gathered around the spot. He noted their excitement at someone who had finally had a combination of enough luck *and* enough skill to catch the fish that had been making fools out of all of them for the past ten years. He also noticed that their excitement was slightly tinged with a touch of regret for the capture of a very wily adversary. He also noticed that, after the old-timer's statement, the look on his children's faces had transformed

214

from glee to distant reproach. And then, Ross did something unexpected: he turned the now gasping fish loose in the now murky water and waited until it had swum unseen into the depths in the center of the lake.

A stunned silence filled the air following this "fool-crazy" act and then Melody, followed by her brothers and sister, ran and hugged their Daddy. "Yea! Daddy, we knew you would do the right thing; you're the best daddy in the world!"

The crowd dissipated, many heads shaking in incredulous wonder. Suddenly, another shout rent the air as one more pole bent ominously toward the lake. Its owner arrived just in time to reel in a giant rubber boot. Hoots of laughter that greeted the scene mutated into guffaws when, disgusted, the man dumped out the water and, with it, came a big green bullfrog. The laughter lifted the nervousness that had previously spread across the area like a fog, while Ross and the kids skipped around the sparkling lake in time to join Honey and Chas in their triumphant splashing in the shoals on the beach side of the lake.

The next few days flew serenely by for the McDonald family. No more strange happenings on the wildlife level occurred during these days, which the family dedicated to hikes, souvenir-buying, swimming in the lake, and even a visit to the site where Grampa Mack had done his family-famous handstand on the edge of Fire Falls. There were benches all along on both sides of a clearing, with a large black area where a large bonfire was held every evening before the still-burning coals were tossed over the edge. The children moved as closely as they could get to the edge and looked over the side. They were petrified by the distance, and even Melody—whose stability in accomplishing handstands was not legendary, although her daring was—declared that she was quite sure that she would not want to do a handstand, or even a headstand, on that edge (or at least not at the moment; maybe she would in a few years, but definitely not now).

The day before they were scheduled to leave, they opted to take one last hike. The path they followed was the one they had followed the first day after arriving. Honey had decided that she would stay in camp and begin preparing their baggage for the return home tomorrow, so they were able to move much more quickly, not having to contend with the stroller's wheels getting stuck in ruts along the way. After eating a hurried lunch of peanut-butter-and-jelly sandwiches they continued on their way until they met up with a small waterfall that fell into a fairly deep pool that leveled out into a steadily flowing stream. As the hikers bent over the pool of fresh, very cold water, they noticed several fish hovering at the bottom of the pool in a small area almost unseen behind the cascade of water. Naturally, none of them had a fishing pole, so, after sticking their faces under the water and gurgling at the fish, they took off once again, this time walking along the stream, instead of crossing it.

The flowing water resembled a patchwork quilt: here flowing smooth as satin, without a wrinkle; here, a highly stitched pattern of golden diamonds, glowing brightly in the sunlight, and interspersed here and there amongst the other patterns, the fluffy white cotton of the rapids. Further along, greener sections, dappled with golden sunshine glimmering through leafy trees created an artful counterpoint to the other patterns. Here and there, little flecks of gold flickered through the intermingling of diamonds, cotton, and satin.

"Daddy, looky there, there's gold shining in the middle of the gravel."

"Well, yes, I suppose you might call it that. It's not really, but it's called 'fool's gold.' Its real name is pyrite, but it's a mineral, not metal. Why don't we stop and gather a few pieces while we're here? You can show them to your friends when we get back."

There was no need to ask them twice, and soon they were all ankle-deep in the water, sifting the gravel through their fingers, trying to separate the pyrite from the rest of the particles. And it was there that Melody saw it. There, in the middle of the black, gray, brown, white, and gold particles, a bright pink ball, hardly bigger than the stones and gravel around it, stood out as plain as day. The incorrigibly curious Melody took it in her hands and let out a muffled yelp as something hidden in the salmon egg pricked her finger. Upon further inspection, she discovered that there was a hook attached to a long piece of line. Pulling it revealed that it was attached to a branch that had broken off from a tree.

"Hey, Daddy look at Mickey! She just found a fishing pole floatin' along here in this stream. Neat, huh?" Mark looked with great envy at his elder sister. Fishing was something boys were supposed to do, not girls, but then, Mickey wasn't exactly a normal girl like Jan was. Jan became all fussy even when she saw a little garter snake. Some girls sure were weird, but not Mickey; she liked all kinds of neat stuff.

"Daddy, can I go fishing with you tonight? I sure do wanna try and use this fishing pole before we leave. C'mon, ple-e-ase," she wheedled, looking up, her eyes wide with innocent excitement. "Then we can put my fishes in the bucket and let them go in the swimming pool. It would be just like swimming here in the lake, except without the gravel. Or," she added thoughtfully, "I guess I could eat it; I do kinda like trout. You said before we couldn' come before because we didn' have a pole, but now I do. Please!"

Ross glared at his eldest daughter with an exasperated expression on his face. "Now, Mickey, you know perfectly well that none of us is going fishing this evening. We're going to the trading post when we get back from our hike, and then we have to help Mommy finish packing up, so we'll be ready to leave early tomorrow morning. You may as well leave the pole here for some other little kid." Melody's lower lip quivered dangerously, so Ross had to think quickly. "Look, why don't you put the line, with the bait, in that pool there underneath the waterfall and fish while the rest of us are looking for 'gold'? You remember that we saw several different fish there, don't you?"

In the excitement at finding the little fishing pole, and in the hope that she could finally go fishing with Ross, Melody had forgotten all about the pyrite she had been so avidly gathering with the idea of impressing all of her friends with her great "wealth." Now, she couldn't care less; all she really wanted was to go fishing with her daddy, and he didn't want to go fishing with her. What was worse was that he hadn't even waited for her answer before lying back down on the bank of the stream. She felt as though her heart was going to break in a million pieces. She sat down on a handy rock in the middle of the stream, bending her knees until her feet were touching her seat. Folding her arms on top of her knees while still clutching the little homemade fishing pole, she sat with her head and face hidden from view (and in such a way that she couldn't see the others, either). Rocking back and forth on her precarious seat, she tried to calm her anguish at being rejected; not even the freezing spray that reached her from the white water, as it rushed against the surrounding rocks, could cool the burning sensation in her heart.

Several agonizing moments later, she decided that everything had happened because she had found that stupid fishing pole. *Really!* she thought, sniffling, *it's only a stupid branch with some string and a fishhook tied onto it. We coulda done the same thing before if Daddy really wanted us to go fishing with him.* Considering the matter further, and wanting to be generous, she decided that he might not have thought of the idea, either; she hadn't, had she? *I guess it doesn't really matter.* Having reached a decision, she let the pole slip through her benumbed fingers and stood up resolutely. She stepped leadenly from the water and began to retrace her way up the path that they had just taken back toward the campground. She stuck her hand into her pocket and discovered the small ball of feathers that sometimes appeared out of nowhere. It seemed strangely warm to her touch and she felt slightly comforted by its soft presence.

Only Mark noticed at first that she had gone and he went to pick up the rejected pole that had been the source of so much hope for his bigger sister. He knew exactly how she felt, because he would have felt the same way. He figured she could have at least tried to fish in the little pool, but then he thought the fish probably wouldn't even have seen the bait because the water came rushing down way too fast. He thought a moment, and then, his pockets weighed down with all the gold he had found (along with a good deal of useless gravel), he took off up the path after his sister. He thought he might be able to get away without being seen, like Mickey, but his hopes were soon dashed as he was called back to reality by his father's voice.

"Hey, young man, where do you think you're going to all by yourself?" He may not have noticed his firstborn's disappearance, but he most assuredly did take note of the fact that his firstborn boy was going off in the wrong direction all by himself; it was hard not to notice, since the boy had been leaning on him up until that moment.

"I'm not going anywhere by myself," he retorted, "I'm following Mickey. *She* took off by *herself.* She was crying and let her new fishing pole fall into the water. I'm taking it, so I can give it back to her."

Ross looked around in consternation as he realized that he was guilty of what he had always considered neglect and that, even worse, it was his own darn fault. "Okay, kids, everyone out of the water. Let's get going back, and maybe we can catch up with Mickey and then help Mommy get everything packed up."

Rolling his eyes at his own stupidity, he took the pole from Mark and carried it with the same care as though it had been one of his own prize-winning fishing rods. "Okay, guys, take hold of one another's hand, and let's go see if we can catch up with Mickey."

Kenny and Jan dragged themselves reluctantly from the flowing stream, their pockets bulging with their newly acquired treasure; Kenny's consisted of a heterogeneous mixture of gravel, algae, and several large stones, along with a couple of water beetles that he had seen darting through the rocks. Jan, precise collector that she was, had both pockets filled to overflowing with fool's gold only. There was no telling what those of the group were carrying in their shoes, but it was really a matter of little importance: they would be dirty anyway by the time they got back to the tent.

Despite the fact that she was hurt to the very depths of her soul and was completely immersed in her mourning, Melody walked very quickly, and the others were hard put to catch up with her. Part of the reason was that for them the hike was still a lark, and they ran left and right, often bumping into their father and almost mowing him down. They were very careful to never let go of one another's hands, and this fact added greatly to the hilarity of the adventure. They finally reached the fugitive shortly before arriving at the lake. By this time she had calmed down a bit, and when the others called her, she was almost glad to see them. Being left alone in her own gloomy company had not been comfortable and she was happy to walk back the rest of the way with the other kids. She was not quite ready, however, to forgive Ross, and she gave him the cold shoulder for the rest of the trip back. He didn't complain: he figured he probably deserved it.

That night, the children were sent to bed shortly after dinner; tomorrow would be another long day of travel, and grumpy, cranky children were the last thing that Ross wanted during the fourteen-hour trip. Besides, he had another plan that included waking Melody up before the sun rose. He hoped it would help iron out some of the problems that had arisen during their last hike. He hadn't taken into consideration, however, the necessity that girls have of discussing things that have happened during the day. The situation was further complicated by the fact that the boys, too, had a lot to discuss.

"Man, Mickey, did you see the way that Mommy threw away my water beetles?" whispered Kenny. "They were so cute, and I wanted to take 'em home an' put 'em in the swimming pool. Then we coulda pertended that they were pollywogs and try to catch 'em. She even threw away my water grass I got for 'em to eat."

"Natcherly, she did. If you don' have the bugs, what do you need the grass for, dummy? How come you didn' get any gold? She threw away all your other stuff, too, didn' she, even those neat rocks."

"Naw, she let me keep my rocks. She didn' throw any of Jan's stuff away. Mark hid his stuff, so he's still got some of it left, anyway. Jan, show Mickey all yer gold."

"I can't," Jan complained. "Mommy already put it in the suitcase to take home. I bet Mickey didn't find very much gold; she didn't stay with us very long. How much did ya get, Mickey?"

"Some. About twenty big pieces. Maybe we can play pirates and look for pirate treasure when we get home. I know a place at school where we can find rocks that're full of silver. If we can find some itty bitty white rocks in Mark's gravel, we can pretend they're pearls and have a real treasure trove. Mark," she said, "do you have any pearly rocks in that gravel of yours?"

The only answer she got was a sniff and a small snort. The giggles that followed were silenced by their father's warning: "Go to sleep or you're all walking home." Soon, the only sound coming from the McDonalds' tent was silence.

"Mickey, wake up. C'mon, we've got to go before the others wake up. Put on your jeans and a sweater, because it's still a little chilly outside. Hurry, I'll be waiting for you outside the tent."

Still half asleep, she wasn't sure she had heard right, but she sure as heck wasn't going to tempt fate and not do anything. She quickly slipped into the jeans that had miraculously appeared by her pillow—the last she knew, only shorts had been left out of the suitcase for the trip home—put on her T-shirt, pulled on her sweater, and bounded out of the tent opening, tripping over Jan's feet on the way out. Her sister grunted and gritted her teeth without ever knowing that she had been tripped over.

"Huh-uh-uh-I, Daddy," she stuttered, stifling a yawn. "How come only you and me are up in the dark?"

"Shh! Don't talk so loud or you'll wake up everyone in the campground. You and I are going fishing, but we have to hurry, so we can be back by the time everyone else is ready to leave. So, grab your pole and let's go. Quick!"

He grabbed his creel and handed it to Melody and then gathered his own rod and tackle and the two of them took off along the path leading to the lake. There was no one else there yet, so they had the choice of all the spots along the shore. Looking around and judging which would basically be the most comfortable spot for Melody, he settled her down on a large rock not far from the spot where he had caught the granddaddy fish the other day. There was an ample section of sand and a great overhang where the rippling water had eaten away at the shore and left bare the roots of a majestic pine. He knew that it was a perfect hiding place for wary fish, but he was also pretty sure that those same fish wouldn't be terribly wary at that time of the morning. He had serious doubts about Melody catching anything, but it wouldn't be his fault, at least. "Okay, you sit here; it's a real good place, and if you are going to catch a fish, this is where it will happen. I'll be right over there," he said pointing to a tree trunk about fifteen feet away. "If you need me, just call and I'll be right back." So saying, he settled her down on the rock, showed her how to put the line with the bait into the water and swish it back and forth so that it looked like a swimming insect, and he headed off to his chosen spot.

Melody swished from time to time, but either the fish were warier than Ross thought and they weren't biting or else they weren't even there. As often happens with a typical seven-year-old, Melody soon became bored with the lack of action and her thoughts wandered off to other horizons. Her line, short though it was, also wandered off on its own and soon became entangled in one of the tree roots hanging off the bank. Trying to make a swishing movement, Melody discovered that the line resisted every effort; convinced that there was probably a fish on her line, too big of course for her to fight alone, she called, "Daddy, I think I've got a fish."

Unfortunately for Ross, a real fish began nibbling interestedly at his bait right at that moment, but the man let it go in favor of Melody's seemingly more important battle. "See, Daddy, when I try to move the string, it doesn't move." She tried moving it once again to show him. He had a sneaking suspicion that there wasn't a fish on her line at all and when she handed him her pole, he gave the line a tug and ascertained that it was indeed not going to move.

The early morning sun had sent out tentative rays and the black lake was slowly beginning to take on a lighter color, revealing some of the secrets that had hitherto been hidden by the dark. He could now clearly see the pink salmon egg floating dangerously close to the bare roots. He

221

hoped he would be able to untangle it without breaking the line. Even if he did, he would probably frighten off any fish that might possibly be lurking in the area. *Oh, well,* he thought, *it's a chance I'll have to take.* Fortunately, it wasn't too badly tangled and after a few light tugs, the line came loose. They lost the bait, however, and Ross went to get another one for his daughter from his tackle box. After moving the little girl to another rock, slightly farther away from the overhang, and warning her to be a little more careful, he went back to his own spot once again.

The tip of the sun itself had finally arrived at the opening between two mountains, turning the lake into a valley of molten gold. It was hard on the eyes, but Melody kept hers glued to the little pink ball on the end of her fishing line. The sun rose higher; other fishermen had come to test their skill and still nothing new happened. She was beginning to feel drowsy and knew that soon Daddy would be calling her to pick everything up and head back to the camp so that they could head on home. She looked up and exchanged a wave of the hand with Ross to let him know she hadn't fallen asleep and that everything was still the same.

Just then a sudden, almost imperceptible movement near the bait caught her eye. Crouching down low and trying not to make a shadow herself, she caught sight of the shadowy figure of an enormous fish hovering near the line, as though trying to decide whether it should partake of the offered meal or not. She swished the line slightly in the hopes of convincing "Mr. Fish" that the succulent salmon egg was exactly what he had been waiting for all of his life. After a moment of indecision, he decided that she was probably right and before either of them knew what had hit them, he grabbed the bait, hook and all. Overcoming its surprise, the trout took off like a bolt of silver lightning and soon it had pulled the string to its full length. As Melody rushed into the water after it, Ross saw her predicament and, once again, left his rod, with its own prospective fish waiting a short distance away, and ran over to help her bring in the fish.

"Daddy, look, it's gigantic. Well, not quite as big as the one you let go the other day, but almost. See it over there?" Melody jumped excitedly up and down; it was the very first fish she had caught with a fishing pole and she wanted to do it all by herself. She supposed it would be okay, though, if Daddy held on to her so that she wouldn't get pulled into the lake when the fish started pulling hard while trying to get rid of the hook.

Ross guided her safely through the fight, telling her exactly what direction she needed to go so that the string wouldn't get tangled up in the tree roots again, which is exactly what her prey seemed to have in mind. When "Mr. Fish," as she called it, zigged right, she leaned to the left or went a few steps farther into the water. When he went too near the roots, she bent closer to the water and pulled it away. Finally, when she thought she could move no more and would have to relinquish the pole to her father, the fish gave up the fight and she pulled it in to shore.

Tired though she was, she held the fish as high up in the air as she could, and received the cheers and applause of all the observers. It had been a hard fight, but she was very proud of her very first fish, a very fine four-inch-long rainbow trout. Of course, as Ross mentioned later on to Honey, he wasn't sure it entered into the legal length, but Melody was only seven and a half and she was small, too.

The return trip home seemed much shorter than when they had been coming; this was probably because everyone, except Ross and Melody, was well rested. Melody, though, was so pleased with herself that she didn't even notice that she was tired anymore. Honey had added her congratulations to those of Ross and the fishermen and, naturally, the other kids had overcome their own envy long enough to insist that next year they, too, deserved to have a chance to show that they were better fisherkids than Melody. Ross took a mental note that he would have to remember to pack up more fishing poles next year.

Missy heard the McDonalds arriving way before they actually appeared, and when they drove up into the driveway, she escaped from Juan, who was very reluctantly taking her for a walk, together with Oso. Melody jumped out of the car and ran to hug her four-legged friend; it seemed that she had been forgiven for abandoning the dog, because Missy returned the hug with great fervor. As the two of them turned to run into the backyard to see if the rabbits had returned, she was called back to the car by Ross's commanding voice.

"Hey, Mickey, aren't you forgetting something?"

Unfortunately, right at that moment Juan ran by, trying to catch Oso, who had also managed to get away from the boy. "Mickey?" he mouthed, snickering in malicious delight. With a last, evil grin, he took off after the errant Oso.

Melody had forgotten something: the fishing pole that she had so jealously clutched all the way home from Yosemite was still in the car. This, however, was not exactly what Ross had in mind; the entire stack of luggage had to be taken back into the house before anything else could be done. Shrugging her shoulders, she got in line with the others and held out her arms as Ross gave everyone their first load. After dumping everything onto the living-room floor, they all ran back out for the next load.

In the meantime, Honey distributed all items into different stacks and put each object into its proper place. She looked at the pile of dirty laundry—which was three times higher than any other stack— and sighed; it was a good thing that she had just passed a whole week's vacation in "idleness" because she had about a month's worth of laundry in front of her. She cringed inwardly as Melody brought in yet another load. "Haven't you guys finished yet? You've brought in at least a hundred loads in the past ten minutes."

Melody giggled. "Only fifty, Mommy, and this is the last one. The other guys are standing outside in the sprinkler, so they can get rid of all the dust and sweat."

Ross walked in with the icebox and headed toward the kitchen, where he put the four trout into the freezer. "Mickey, why don't you go out into the yard with the other kids? It's a good way to get cooled off."

"Nah, Missy told me there's something special out in the backyard, so I'm gonna go and see what it is." Saying this, she ran quickly through the house and out the patio door to see what in the world could possibly be so important that Missy would think that she had to go out and see without even playing in the water. In fact, Missy was already out there barking her head off.

What she saw was so astounding that she couldn't believe her eyes. Thinking she might be dreaming, she rubbed them, but her vision was still the same. Out by the rabbit pen was a rabbit; it wasn't the one she had dreamed of seeing again, but someone else was going to be really happy.

"Mark!" she screamed, running into the front yard, "Mark, you will *never* guess what's in the back yard. Ya gotta come and see."

The tone of her voice brought everyone, including several others from the neighborhood, from the yard into the back of the house. She stood there trembling with excitement and envy while pointing at the rabbit that had been missing for such a long time. Mark rubbed his eyes to make sure he wasn't imagining things, and then he ran over to the orangey rabbit and grabbed it into his arms before it had a chance to escape again.

"Where's Blackie?" Jan asked hopefully. "Is he out there, too?"

"Uh-uh. I don't know where the other two are. I was so surprised to see Brownie that I forgot to ask her where they are and she wasn't saying anything. I just saw her out there eating grass like they hadn't been missin' forever. She wasn't even upset by all of Missy's barkin'."

Honey, wondering what all the commotion was about, came out with Chas in her arms and asked, "Hey, what's going on out here?" Mark happily raised his arms in answer to her question, proudly showing her that Brownie had returned home. "Have you found the others, yet? Maybe they're hiding in the grass." She shot a look at Ross and continued, "It has gotten kind of tall again. Well, let's all look around, and maybe we'll find them, okay?"

She set Chas into the backyard stroller and took off with the others, looking for the still-missing rabbits. The seven of them—Missy included—fanned out and in less than five minutes they ascertained that the rabbits were not to be found in the yard, not even in the remotest corners of said yard. Melody even looked under the toadstools that had popped up in their absence, without any luck.

"Well," said Ross philosophically, "if one came back, it's probable that the others will too, sooner or later." *That is,* he continued to himself, *if they haven't been consumed by some hungry stray dog.*

The rest of the week ran by quickly, in a flurry of last-minute shopping sprees before Melody was to leave on her trip across the country. Strangely enough, or so it had seemed at the time, their mailbox was completely empty when they got home; they had expected to find it ready to explode with small boxes from Gramma Mary, but there was nothing there—not even a letter. The mystery had been solved that evening when Mrs. Chateau came over with a bag that was filled to overflowing with the expected packages and postcards. Laughing, she told them that the mailbox *had* been ready to explode, and that she had brought everything in because she had seen Juanito looking at the boxes with a strangely inexpressive look on his face. "That seemed highly suspicious to me, so I decided to eliminate all temptation. I've seen that look way too many times at work, and I'd hate for a kid that young to end up in juvenile hall."

The trip was still on, so Thursday, the day before Melody was scheduled to leave, she and her parents took off for one last trip to the store. New clothes had been bought for the trip and also her new school clothes; Jan had also been included in the school clothes jaunts, because she, too, would be starting school in September. But today's trip would be very brief: Melody needed a book to read during the flight. Of course, she had already read all of the children's books in the house and it was useless to get library books, because they wouldn't be home yet when the two-week time limit expired. So, Melody was looking at every book in the store, trying to decide exactly which one she would get. Of course, it would have to be about animals, but there were so many to choose from. Finally, she made her choice—in view of the fact that she had just gotten back from the forest and seen Bambi for herself, she decided to get the book *Bambi's Children*. She was quite sure it would be just right for the flight. Ross and Honey were equally sure that it would take even more time, because they figured she would probably sleep during the flight to New York, since it would be so late at night.

After assuring herself that the book was safely put into the overnight bag that she would be taking onto the plane, Melody raced out of the house to see if Blackie and Pink Ears had come back yet. She wasn't sure she would be going on the trip across America if they hadn't come back by the next afternoon. She'd been hoodwinked once, but it wasn't going to happen a second time, you could be sure of that. Not finding them there, she walked disconsolately out into the front yard.

Wrapped up in her woe, she didn't notice Juan sneak up behind her until he shouted out in a sing-song voice, "Mickey Mouse, Mickey Mouse, here we have a little Mickey Mouse."

Drawn out of her misery by the rascal's taunting words, an infuriated Melody swung around and shouted back at him, "Take that back!" Her left fist crept threateningly toward her mouth.

Either not noticing or not recognizing the threat, the boy continued his taunts. "Your name is Mickey, ain't it? I heard 'em call you Mickey, so you're Mickey Mouse, Mickey Mouse!"

"I am not Mickey Mouse; I'm Mickey Mantle! I'm gonna play baseball for the Dodgers when I grow up and I'm gonna be just like Mickey Mantle."

The annoying boy gurgled with laughter. "You can't play baseball and be like Mickey Mantle; you're just a dumb girl and girls can't play baseball like boys. Mickey Mouse, Mickey—"

Juanito lay gasping on the grass where Melody had just wiped him out flat. The wiry little girl looked down at him, flexing her muscles, and said, "I'm Mickey Mantle and if I want to play baseball, I will, 'cause I can do anything I decide I want to do." With that, she walked calmly away from the very red-faced, very embarrassed boy lying on the grass. As he watched her go, the suffering bully muttered under his breath, "I'll make you pay for that, *Mickey Mouse.*"

Seconds later, a giggling Karen ran up to her and whispered, "Well done. Hey, guess what; I think maybe I found your rabbits. Yesterday, I was in my daddy's salon, and I heard something chewing on something. I looked around, but I couldn't see anything. I'll bet that's what it is, though. Do ya wanna come tonight and see when everybody else is in bed?"

"Yeah, I wanna see, but let's go now. If it's them, I can hardly wait to find out. C'mon, let's go."

"No, we've gotta wait until tonight, 'cause Daddy's in there now, cutting someone's hair. We gotta go when no one can see us, 'cause they'll get mad if they know what we're doin'."

"Well, I guess it's okay. Jan's gonna want to come, though, 'cause her rabbit's missing, too."

"Okay, I'll come call you when the coast is clear tonight. Man, that Juanito sure is dumb, isn't he? He should of left when he saw you get mad. I sure would of. Well, see ya later."

That night at about ten thirty, Melody heard the sound that she and Jan had anxiously been waiting for: gravel being tossed against their window. "Hey, hurry up, you guys, it's late. I just heard scratching and chewing noises again, so whatever it is, it's still there."

The two girls slipped silently from their beds and, armed with their tiny flashlights that Honey had gotten them for certain nightly walks, they climbed through the screen that they had unfastened earlier that evening. "Man, what took you so long? We were starting to fall asleep. Mommy and Daddy went to bed hours ago."

"Yours. Mine went to bed half an hour ago. Hurry."

Five minutes later, while they were trying to move the chair where Karen thought she had heard the noise, an astounded squawk sounded in their ears. "Karen, Melody, and Jan! What on earth are you three do-ing out here? You should all be in bed at this hour." To the conspirators' surprise the bright overhead light in Mr. Chateau's salon flashed on, blinding them. The little flashlight that they had been shining under-neath the lean-back hair dryer chair fell from Melody's hand with a crash, causing the batteries to slide across the slippery floor.

"Oh, hi, Mommy," said Karen nonchalantly. "They asked me if they could come over and look around, because I told them I heard some strange chewing noises here in *Pere*'s salon. We thought maybe they were their rabbits hiding somewhere in here, because they've been miss-ing for a while."

"Mrs. Chateau, we thought someone had stolen them, or maybe some mean ole dogs had eaten them. See, there are balls of Blackie's hair all over this chair. And Blackie is Jan's bunny, huh, Jan." Melody held out a handful of short, fuzzy black hair.

"Oh, my goodness gracious. Pierre, come here quickly! We have a slight problem, and we need your help. Jan, go call your father, so he can help us, too. This chair is heavy, and we need help turning it over. How you girls thought you could do it alone, I have no idea." Jan took off, run-ning as fast as her chubby little legs could go.

As Jan ran out through the back door, Mr. Chateau stuck his tousled white head through the side door. "Wilma, what is going on here? What are these children doing here at this time of night? Do Melody's parents know she is here?"

"Pierre, we think there is a rabbit or maybe two, here under the chair. Jan has gone to get her father to help us turn the chair over. While we're waiting, we should try to take off the hair dryer so it won't bang against the floor." Without waiting for an answer, she started turning the knobs that would unhitch the machine from the chair. Melody started jumping up and down; the anticipation of what they would find both ex-cited and frightened her. She missed her bunny—she was so soft and white and cuddly—but what if they only found Blackie? It was *his* fur they found everywhere, not Pink Ears's.

Just as Mrs. Chateau finished unhitching the hair dryer, Jan burst through the back door, followed closely by Ross. "Jan says you need my help; what's going on?"

"Daddy, maybe we found Blackie and Pink Ears. We think they're here, inside this chair. Me 'n' Karen heard something chewing and tearing things up there. Hurry! We gotta move this chair."

After confirming Melody's statement, the Chateaus and Ross turned toward the olive green easy chair, now sans hair dryer, and together they heaved it onto its back. Jan pointed excitedly at the coiled springs on the underside of the chair. "Looky, looky! Blackie's there in the stuffing."

Melody knelt down next to her sister and stared into the four bright red eyes that shone out at her from the dark cotton and wool in the interior of the chair. "Blackie! Pink Ears! Finally, we found you. But . . . Daddy, there's a bunch of little rats in here with them, too."

"*Mais no. Se ne pas possible!* Rats in my salon? Impossible!"

Ross knelt down next to his daughters and carefully pulled out the two rabbits, placing them gently into the waiting arms of their worried young owners. Blackie wriggled frantically, trying desperately to escape from Jan's arms and return to her nest in the depths of the chair.

"Looks like your Blackie is a mother, Jan; see how her tummy is all wet from something sucking on it? Let's see how many little babies she has hidden in here. One . . ., four . . ., six . . ., eight . . ., ten. See, they're not rats, but bunnies—lots of them, and all different: Black, brown, gray, white, and spotted."

"But Daddy, Mommy said *Pink Ears* was a girl. And they are so ugly. They don't have any fur and their eyes are closed."

"But Jan, look, they have long ears and almost no tail. Daddy, what's wrong with them? Why don't they have any hair? When Whiskers had kittens, their eyes were closed but they had hair, at least."

"They don't have any hair because they're newly born. In a couple of weeks they will, though, and their eyes will open in about a week. I think we'd better take them home as soon as possible. Wilma, Pierre, do you have a box or something you can loan us, so we can get this group loaded up and take them home? Tomorrow morning we can come and clean up this mess before your first client comes in. Melody, at least, will be up and about." He reached for the box that Wilma was holding out for him and began to load the mother rabbit and her young into it, together with the nest she had made. Blackie began moving the hair, cotton, and wool blend around the ten bunnies so that they were quickly enmeshed in a fluffy, warm, safe web.

"Oh, don't worry about tomorrow morning; Pierre has his first client at eight o'clock, and I think our girls will need to sleep a little later than usual, and you have to go to work even earlier than eight with your newspaper route."

"Well, thanks, but Melody'll be here bright and early, so don't worry. Then, she'll be leaving tomorrow night for a trip with her grandmother."

"Oh, that sounds like fun. Where are they going and how long will they be gone for?"

"The trip'll last for a couple of weeks. My mother's coming home from a trip to Europe and will be driving cross-country, stopping off at a few of her friends' places on the way; she thought Melody would enjoy seeing this country. They'll be home a few days before school starts. Okay, girls, let's get on home; otherwise, *I* won't get up in time for my paper route. Melody, have you got a strong grip on Pink Ears? Pierre, can you help Jan crawl up on my shoulders? She's falling asleep, and if we don't do it this way, I can't carry her and the rabbits at the same time. Okay, is everybody ready? Off we go, then. Good night and thanks."

"Bye, Jan. Bye, Melody. I'm glad we found your rabbits. See ya later. Hope you have a nice trip."

"Yeah, thanks, Karen. See ya in a couple of weeks. I'll send you a postcard." She blew her friend a kiss, clutched her newly found rabbit tighter against her, and with a big yawn and a wave, she followed her father out the door.

Epilogue

"Well, we were quite a group, wouldn't you say? If nothing else, we had a great time; believe me, we were even wilder than you could ever imagine. As I said before, we were wild, but not bad. So, Melody was up bright and early the next morning, and by the time everyone had gotten up—including the Chateaus—the entire salon had been completely cleaned up. Of course, the chair's interior was completely empty, too; they finally discovered everything in the rabbit's hutch later that day, when Honey went out to see the newborns for the first time. Oh, well, the damage had already been done; it was a good thing that the chair's frame was strong enough to withstand the lack of stuffing inside. Of course, it wasn't as soft as it had once been, but, as Pierre had said, it was old, anyway.

"Oh, yeah, she left for her trip, as scheduled, although she almost didn't. Two elements almost impeded her departure. The first included ten little newborn bunnies; she had just found them, and you heard what her reaction was when they were supposed to go camping and the missing rabbits hadn't been found yet. Honey and Ross were able to talk her into going by telling her that they would be much cuter when she got home and that until then she wouldn't have been able to play with them, anyway. The clincher was the new book, *Bambi's Children*, that they bought her so that she would have something to read during the six-hour flight. They were pretty sure she would probably fall asleep way before she finished reading the book, but with Melody, you never knew.

"The second impediment was provided by Ross and Honey, themselves. Fortunately, Melody was already safely seated between two elderly people and the plane was heading down the runway when they decided that they would really rather not send Melody to New York alone. They weren't really sure that the world was ready for Hurricane Mickey. Anyway, at that point, there was really nothing else they could do. Melody was on her way to new, unforgettable adventures."